you don't know about me

Also by Brian Meehl

Out of Patience
Suck It Up
Suck It Up and Die

you don't know about me

BRIAN MEEHL

EMBER

Text copyright © 2011 by Brian Meehl
Cover photographs copyright © 2011 by Carlos Caetano/Shutterstock (road);
Fuse (mirror); Pixland (boy)

Ember and the colophon are trademarks of Random House, Inc.

Visit us on the Web! randomhouse.com/teens

Educators and librarians, for a variety of teaching tools, visit us at randomhouse.com/teachers

The Library of Congress has cataloged the hardcover edition of this work as follows:
Meehl, Brian.
You don't know about me / Brian Meehl. — 1st ed.
p. cm.
Summary: Billy has spent his almost-sixteen years with four cardinal points—Mother, Christ, Bible, and home-school—but when he sets off on a wild road trip to find the father he thought was dead, he learns much about himself and life.
ISBN 978-0-385-73909-2 (alk. paper) — ISBN 978-0-385-90771-2 (glb : alk. paper) — ISBN 978-0-375-89715-3 (ebook) [1. Christian life—Fiction. 2. Self-actualization (Psychology)—Fiction. 3. Mothers and sons—Fiction. 4. Fathers and sons—Fiction. 5. Automobile travel—Fiction. 6. Gays—Fiction.] I. Title.
II. Title: You do not know about me.
PZ7.M512817You 2011
[Fic]—dc22
2010017101

ISBN 978-0-385-73910-8 (trade pbk.)

RL: 5.5

Printed in the United States of America

10 9 8 7 6 5 4 3 2 1

First Ember Edition 2012

Random House Children's Books
supports the First Amendment and celebrates the right to read.

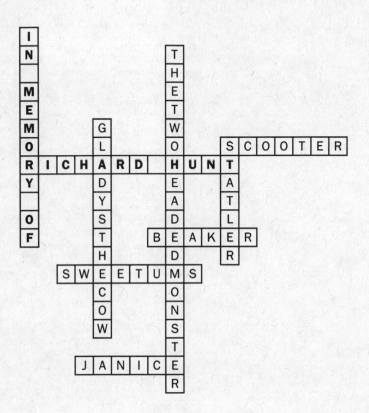

IN MEMORY OF RICHARD HUNT

THE TWO HEADED MONSTER
GLADYS THE COW
SCOOTER
STATLER
BEAKER
SWEETUMS
JANICE

To the Reader

There is a book that has been closed to the world since 1884. In the margins of the book, Mark Twain mapped out the sequel to his masterpiece, *Adventures of Huckleberry Finn*. It was a story he could not tell in his lifetime. The following story was inspired by that long-lost book, and Twain's incredible notes.

I

The Good Book

Note to the Lord

T.L.,

You're totally-knowing; got it. You know what I'm going to write before my pen hits paper. You know what rattles in my head and stirs in my heart before I have a clue. No surprise there, I'm the last to know what I think or feel. So why send You a note when it's a copy of a t-mail (thought-mail) You already got? Because, on the wonky chance You've gone less *knowing these days—and who could blame You?—or that You now use angels to screen Your t-mail, I wanted to be sure You got this.*

Here's the must-know. I'm not writing my sketchy, blasphemous story to piss You off so You can tap the smite stick and slap me with boils, leprosy, head-to-toe pimples, or whatever You're smiting people with these days. I'm telling the story of what happened last summer for two reasons:

3

1. *I promised someone I would (You know who).*
2. *And I want to see if I can write (You know why):*

Wow, soon as I wrote that—bam!—whacked with brain lock. Maybe it was You crashing my cranium for having vainglorious thoughts like I can write. Whatever, while I was staring at the cement birdbath in the backyard, hearing nada because it's so hot the birds are in the trees taking shade baths, the silence of Your creation made me remember the other thing I wanted You to know.

As this pen lays down the trail of my adventure, I don't expect Your help or blessing. I mean, it's not Your kind of story. There's no prophets or heroes in it like in the Bible. There's no one You can be proud of. Actually, there's people in it that make me think Your smite stick has been jammed lately. It's about regular people. Your people. And me. Whether I'm "regular" I don't have a clue. Still sorting that one out.

I want to finish with a prayer.
- *T.L., any time you want to God-up and hit me with some of Your zigzag loving-kindness, feel free. I always appreciate it.*
- *And please let Your only begotten Son help me Son-up and walk in His Way.*
- *Amen.*

Your big fan, then-now-forevermore,
Billy

1

The Facts of Me

At the beginning of last summer I had a grip on the facts of me.

- Born Charles William Allbright
- August 29, 1994
- Little Rock, Arkansas
- Dream: to be a champion mountain biker

I didn't stay in Little Rock long. I didn't stay anywhere long. In my almost sixteen years of life, me and Mom had moved sixteen times. Some kids get their height penciled on doorframes as they get taller. My height got marked on the old U-Haul trailer that followed us everywhere. On my eleventh birthday I shrank an inch. Then we figured out that the U-Haul tires had been pumped up. Had a laugh over that one.

I never liked moving. I was always the NIT: the Newbie In Town. Whenever I made a friend, I knew he'd never be a best buddy. Best buds are for life. We moved too much to have anything for life. Except the F-word: "faith."

Mom gave me the same pep talk whenever we moved. "Billy, God blessed you with more than the cornerstones of a house. He's given you a compass with four cardinal points." My cardinal points weren't north, south, east, west. They were Mother, Christ, Bible, homeschool. Mom said as long as I followed those points I'd never be lost. I'd walk in His Way. I'd Son-up.

When we hit a new town, the first thing we did was church-shop. It was Mom's version of "Goldilocks and the Three Bears." This church was too sinful. This church wasn't Spirit-filled enough. This church was juuust righteous. So we'd join it. We'd be dialed into it for a while, but sooner or later she'd find something wonky and wicked about our church. One time she stood up during Sunday service and shouted scripture: *"I have hated the congregation of evildoers and will not sit with the wicked!"* As she pulled me out of there I asked her what made them "evildoers." She told me I was too young to understand.

Last July, a month before turning sixteen, I totally got why we left the Assembly of Assemblies Church in Tulsa, Oklahoma. After we joined Assembly of Assemblies, the pastor let a company put a cell tower in the steeple. Mom had no problem with the company paying the church big bucks to have a comm tower in their steeple. But hellfire hit the fan when she found out that some of the stuff zapping through the tower was pornography. I couldn't fault her on that one. When you're in church launching prayers to heaven, you don't want them scummed by a layer of triple-X fornication. Mom calls it the "pornosphere." That's one of the cool things about being homeschooled. You learn things go-to-school kids don't. I learned about the stratosphere, the troposphere, and the pornosphere.

And that's just what happens when you start thinking about the pornosphere. It's like trail biking behind a bike bunny on a bumpy track. Her jiggly parts make you dizzy and you go blind to the *real* bumps. It's one of the rigid rules of mountain biking: Beware of male blindness; it leads to the kiss of dirt.

Okay, I'm jumping ahead. Back to the facts of me, and the how and why of me bombing into the world.

In the summer of 1993, when Mom was single, and still Tilda *Hayes,* she belonged to a fundamentalist group called the Jesus Brigade. One weekend, the J-Brigade got on one of those riverboats that go up and down the Mississippi. The boat was filled with sinful gamblers. The J-Brigade was there to witness for Christ, especially to gamblers with empty pockets and empty hearts.

While Mom was witnessing to this one gambler, his heart swung wide open. By the time she turned him from his evil ways he was not only slain by the Lord, he was slain by Tilda Hayes. After that, he joined the J-Brigade and joined Tilda at the altar. His name was Richard Allbright. He was so in love with her, and Jesus, that he quickly became a reverend. Not the kind who goes to school and gets a degree. The kind who gets a tricked-out piece of paper in the mail and starts circuit preaching in one-room churches in Arkansas, Louisiana, and Mississippi.

After they got married Tilda got pregnant. As she was belly-packing me around she said she had a real good feeling and a real bad feeling. The good feeling came from me pedaling around inside her. The bad feeling came from watching her husband's preaching star rise too fast. One day, when her bad feeling was super bad, she did one of her providence checks. She was going to find out what the Lord had in store. She shut her eyes and prayed till she felt the Spirit. She opened her Bible, finger-planted on a verse, and looked to see what God had to tell her. *For everyone who exalts himself shall be humbled, and he who humbles himself shall be exalted.* Mom's heart trembled.

The next day, my father was driving home after a week on the circuit. He got caught in a hailstorm but kept hammering for Little Rock. Taking a corner, his car left the road and plunged into the Arkansas River. He tried to get out. He didn't. His spirit went to heaven. According to Mom, so much of his body went to the catfish that when they found his car there wasn't enough left of Richard Allbright to bury. He never got a grave we could visit.

I didn't even know what my father looked like. All his pictures were torched in a trailer fire when I was a baby. The fire incinerated the paper that made him a reverend too, and the family Bible recording their marriage and my birth.

But my father wasn't like one of those metal bits that chips off inside your bike frame and you can't get to; my father wasn't unobtanium. The stories Mom told me about meeting him on the riverboat and watching him preach in tiny churches put a movie in my head. She said I even looked like him. Especially my nose, a big beak of a thing. To see him all I had to do was stand in front of the mirror and age-up. I'd slick down my stick-up hair. I'd use a piece of charcoal to smear on a five o'clock shadow. I'd squint till things got blurry. And there he'd be: Reverend Richard

Allbright, behind his pulpit. I'd push my voice down and preach a sermon on anything in the Bible. If there was one thing Reverend Allbright and his son knew, it was the Good Book. It was *our* cardinal point.

And that's how my compass of Mother-Christ-Bible-homeschool, with my dad's face shimmering in the glass, kept me carving a line in the trail of the Lord. Those were the facts of me. From *The Book of Tilda,* anyway.

Then, at fifteen years and eleven months old, my compass got smashed. I went ripping off trail. Gonzo off trail.

2

The Facts of Mom

Halfway through last summer we moved. We drove up from Tulsa in a heat wave that made me sticky as a glazed doughnut. The temperature didn't slip below a hundred till after sunset.

I was asleep in the front seat, in the zonk-bag, as we drove through Kansas City and into town #17, Independence, Missouri. I woke up with my neck sweat-stuck to the back of the seat. It made a twacky sound in my ear as it unstuck.

Mom held the MapQuest directions she'd printed up at the Tulsa library in one hand, the wheel in the other. "Rise and navigate," she said. "We're here."

I checked out the new "here." The street was lined with stores and a couple food places, all closed. The place was bizarro-empty for a Saturday night. That was probably why Mom picked it. Independence was independent of sinners.

The real reason we were moving to town #17 was because we had to blow out of town #16. Mom had done more than give the Assembly of Assemblies a scripture-spanking for having a steeple stuck in the pornosphere. She'd climbed into the steeple with cable cutters and severed the "tentacles of Satan."

The facts of Mom went like this:

- Forty-two
- Tall, thin
- Straight brown hair cut halfway down her neck
  Sometimes a gray hair sprang from the brown
- A face that was still pretty but could pinch tight and show lines
- Gray eyes that got super intense, especially when they were juiced with the Spirit
- Leader of the New J-Brigade

The New J-Brigade was an army of two: her and me. We didn't just show up for the big battles at abortion clinics and courthouses that married homosexuals. We specialized in the little scraps with Satan. We were ninja warriors for the Lord, playing Whac-a-Mole with demons wherever they popped up.

In Memphis we took on Satan at Piggly Wiggly. We armed ourselves with black markers, went into the supermarket, and blotted out the word "devil" wherever we found it. We eliminated the devil from devil's food cake, Devil Dogs, and Devil's Duel Sauce. We were annihilating the devil pictures on bottles of Mean Devil Woman Cajun Hot Sauce when the cops stopped us from completely casting Satan out of Piggly Wiggly. The store's security cameras caught us on tape and we made the local news. When everyone knows you and your mom are crazy criminals for Christ, and she gets hit with a fine she can't pay, it's time to disappear. That's when we left town #7 for town #8.

But the Piggly Wiggly Incursion was a picnic compared with the time we took on a motorcycle gang. In Topeka, Kansas, Mom had a job as a motel clerk. A biker gang roared up and checked in for the night. The trouble began when Mom spotted the slogan on their New Hampshire license plates. LIVE FREE OR DIE, it said in raised green letters.

Later that night, we drove to the motel with ball-peen hammers. Mom told me the slogan was a blasphemy to the Lord. "Live Free or Die" denied God's control over our lives and encouraged people to be libertines and hedonists.

We were halfway through hammering the LIVE FREE OR DIE slogans to flat-out oblivion when the biker gang poured out of a bar across the street. I did my own take on Live Free or Die and ran. A biker grabbed me. I didn't know what was more pucker-up petrifying, the mega-hairy guy holding me, or Mom whaling on a license plate and shouting, "We are sheep in the midst of wolves doing His work!" Another guy grabbed her as she yelled, "If we perish, we perish!"

I screamed, "I don't wanna perish!"

God must've heard me. A cop car shot into the parking lot just before the bikers pulped us with their mondo boots. After we were taken away, the cops said they would've put

Mom in jail for the night if it weren't for me. She must've known she was going to get fined again, or worse. That night we packed the U-Haul and left the state in our righteous dust.

As we drove to town #10—Des Moines, Iowa—Mom informed me that we were "antinomians." I'd never heard the word and thought maybe an antinomian was someone who hated gnomes, like those plastic ones in people's yards. Mom had taught me that gnomes and leprechauns were antiangels who worked for the devil. So I thought maybe our next mission was going to be kidnapping lawn gnomes and stoning them to death.

I was wrong. She told me an antinomian is someone who knows there's two kinds of law: the law of the land and the law of God. When an antinomian has to choose between following one or the other, he always chooses God's law. That's another thing about Mom's brand of homeschooling. When you're on the run, some of it's car-schooling.

But Mom was good at more than whaling holy on Satan. She could always find a job. Being a super-fast typist, she got a lot of work doing data entry. She'd usually go to work after dinner. That way she could homeschool me during the day. Sometimes it freaked me out to be alone at night. But it wasn't like I was *alone* alone. "Don't ever be scared," she'd say. "Your Heavenly Father is in the house looking after you." If I ever really got scared I'd lock myself in the bathroom, stand in front of the mirror, and become Reverend Allbright. When my father preached a mirror sermon, I wasn't afraid of anything.

Her biggest talent was field trips. My favorite was

Orni-theology Day. Ornithology is the study of birds. Orni-theology is the witness of God's awesome feathered creatures. She loved bird-watching. I did too, especially the outdoors part. We'd go to bird sanctuaries or flyways where birds flocked over by the thousands.

One fall day when I was twelve, we were at a flyway outside Omaha. I had my fingers wrapped around a cup of hot chocolate. We were watching zillions of starlings flying south. They were an endless black sheet, wafting up and down in slow motion. Mom told me we were like migrating birds.

"How?" I asked.

"Because we rise on the wings of faith and soar in the flyway of God's work."

We watched the starlings washboarding overhead until my neck ached. I took a sip of cocoa and looked at her. Mom's face was calm and peaceful. I'd never seen her look so pretty. I got why Richard Allbright had fallen in love with her.

She caught me looking. "Why are you smiling?" she asked.

"It's not fair," I said.

"What's that?"

I touched my nose. "I'm the one with a beak, but you're the one who wants to be up there with the birds."

She laughed and hugged me so tight I spilled hot chocolate on her coat. She didn't care. "Okay, we're birds. But we need a bird name. What should we be?"

A name popped into my head. "How 'bout Whac-a-Moles?"

She didn't get it, so I explained how sometimes it felt like we were playing Whac-a-Mole with the devil.

"That's it," she announced. "We're Jesus-throated Whac-a-Moles."

On that first night, driving into town #17, those were the facts of Mom. So I thought.

3

Independence, MO

As we drove down the main street, I groped on the floor for the flashlight so I could read the MapQuest directions. I found the flashlight and looked up. What I saw jolted me fully awake. A white coffin gleamed in a store window. We cruised past it. THE CASKET OUTLET, the store sign said.

What kind of town has a coffin store on its main street? I wondered if the place was filled with vampires who liked to go coffin shopping. Then I had one of my gonzo thoughts. Maybe this town is perfect for me. First, I'll cruise into the Casket Outlet and slip inside the white one in the window. I'll go Rip van Winkle and sleep for two years and one month. Then, the day I turn eighteen, I'll rocket out of the coffin and start living the life I want to live.

The U-Haul banged on the hitch, yanking me back to Planet Reality. We were stopped at the end of the street.

"Which way, Magellan," Mom said, "left or right?"

We drove down a hill into a ramshackle neighborhood. After a few turns we pulled in front of a tiny house with a yellow porch light. It was barely a house, something between a shack and a doghouse. Its little front porch, which once had two columns, was down to one. The porch roof was so small one column was plenty. I'd seen things go missing from houses, like the time the landlord took away our toilet when we were late paying rent. But I'd never seen a one-pillar porch. "Mom," I said, "the last trailer we lived in was bigger."

"It's roomier than it looks."

"How do you know?"

"I saw pictures on a computer." She forced a smile. "And there's a pretty birdbath in the backyard."

Another fact about Mom. When it comes to things, like a house, one perfect detail can blind her to all its flaws. When it comes to people, one imperfection can blind her to all that's good.

She patted my arm. "I promise, things will be different here."

"That's what you say every time," I mumbled.

She shot me a look but didn't say anything. It wasn't like she could. I was right. She had said it before.

I got out, stretched my crampy legs, and looked around. Moving was a hassle, but there was one thing about it that was cool. New neighbors. House #17 had a full set: on each side, across the street, and behind. Whenever Mom reminded me that all our migrating was part of God's plan, I wondered if His plan included me seeing neighbor women half-dressed or naked. When it happened, I got confused about the message the Almighty was sending. I mean, when He let me see a half-dressed girl or a naked lady, He was

15

obviously leading me into temptation and warning me not to covet my neighbor's windows. But when He filled windows with a saggy old woman or a naked man, what was He telling me then? The world needed more curtain makers?

Before going to bed we said a prayer and thanked God for delivering us to Independence. I added a couple silent bits: (1) I thanked Him for getting me out of summer Bible camp, which I would not be mentioning to Mom in case she had plain forgotten about it. And (2) I reminded Him that when it came to neighbors, He'd been hitting me with the curtain-maker message a lot lately. If He wanted to be sure my heart was fortified against lust, I was overdue for some carnal temptation.

I checked out the two windows in the tiny bedroom in the back corner of the house. The neighbors' houses were dark shapes. I saw something in the backyard that looked like a big black mushroom. I figured it was the birdbath Mom liked.

I wasn't totally bummed. Even if it was too late for the neighbors' windows to be showing awesome mounds and curves, I'd seen enough of Independence to know it had some sweet-looking hills. And good hills meant gnarly bike trails.

4

Taffy Town

We woke early Sunday morning. Picking the first church to scope out in a new town always depended on what growled louder, our stomachs or our souls. This time, the road food in the cooler had spoiled, so our stomachs won the growling contest. That meant that we were headed to a megachurch. Megachurches had the best doughnut spreads.

Mom consulted her *U-S-Pray Directory* and found a megachurch. The name was perfect: Feast of Faith Church. I was looking forward to the doughnut spread and was relieved that Mom would be dialing her righteous rage to mellow. She had a rule: If a church wanted to stray from His Way, that was its business; but after she joined, it was also hers.

The doughnut spread at Feast of Faith was mega-praiseworthy. But it was going to be a one-time feast. Strike one against Feast of Faith was a worship band playing CCM. Mom said they could call it contemporary Christian music till Judgment Day, but any band with guitars and drums, no matter how loud they praised Jesus, was a stepping-stone to the concert of sex, drugs, and rocky souls. Strike two: the cameras and the huge screen above the stage showing a jumbo version of the service. Putting your service on cable TV was a sure sign it was a "dead church." Any church that encouraged people to worship from a Barcalounger instead of a pew was promoting the sin of sloth.

But the Feast of Faith's big whiff was Communion. The deacons passed around trays of tiny containers, like those half-and-half things in a diner. Under a plastic top was a dime-sized wafer. Then under a foil top was a swallow of grape juice. Me and Mom skipped Communion. I was with her on that. The body and blood of Christ should never be served as a Lunchable.

The pastor preached about how Christ told his disciples not to hide a candle under a bushel but to let their lights shine so everyone could see their good works. He said God has a higher purpose for all of us, and that everyone needs to find their calling so they can shine their light on the world.

I listened close. In Tulsa I'd started doing some mega-cranial time on God's plan for me. When I was little it was a done deal. I would be a Jesus-throated Whac-a-Mole and Mom's wingman in the New J-Brigade forever. But I'd been wondering about what would happen if Mom went to jail, or worse. I wasn't sure I had the strength of faith to be a one-man J-Brigade. Christ says it only takes a mustard seed of faith to make you a believer. What He didn't say was the opposite. It only takes a mustard seed of doubt to make you a doubter.

After the service, I snagged a couple more doughnuts. When I got the stink eye from a group of guys, I scooted outside.

Driving back to the house, we passed one of the things watering my seed of doubt. At the end of a football field, a

18

big scoreboard announced, WILLIAM CHRISMAN HIGH SCHOOL—HOME OF THE BEARS. Maybe wanting to go to high school wasn't exactly a calling, but it felt like mine. And wanting to go on the pro mountain biking tour, of course. But the pro tour was the Big Jump. The ramp to the Big Jump was going to high school and being a normal kid. Whenever I brought it up Mom said no way. She claimed high school was "high" school because it was where kids got high on drugs. That didn't worry me. I'd snuck off and ridden enough trail with heathens and other freaky kids to know my soul could survive the devil's tribe of high schoolers. The fact was, the last thing I wanted was to start tenth grade at One-Pillar High—Home of the Jesus-throated Whac-a-Moles.

After we unpacked the U-Haul I finally got to go for a spin. I wanted to do two things: check to see if the coffin store was real, and scope out Independence for off-road trails. If I got lucky, I might even find a pack of bikers my age.

Downtown was a bunch of brick buildings sticking up two or three stories. I bunny-hopped the curb in front of the Casket Outlet. The coffin in the window was hot white in the sunlight and tricked out with gold handles. I wondered how many other kids in Independence had the same itch I'd had the night before: to jump in the coffin and Rip-van-Winkle till they were eighteen. The chance that someone had beat me to it got me thinking; the coffin store needed a neon sign like a motel: VACANCY or NO VACANCY.

On the next street I spotted a candy store called Sweet Sam's. I stopped in front of the big window and balanced a

19

track stand for a few secs before parking my sneakers. Inside, a man was making candy. Maybe he was Sweet Sam, maybe not. I'd seen taffy made before. I watched him pull and stretch and fold the taffy like a giant blob of bubble gum.

It didn't cause any cranial disharmony at the time, but looking back on what happened in the next two weeks my ride into town was like one of Mom's providence checks. Instead of opening the Bible and letting a finger fall on a verse to reveal God's will, I'd opened the Book of Independence, my sneaks had dropped in front of Sweet Sam's, and the taffy man was a sticky sign from God: *The truth is like taffy, Billy; you can pull it and stretch it and fold it till it's just how you want it.*

After spinning away from Sweet Sam's, I spotted something jutting over the treetops. It looked like the biggest witch's hat in the world, a silvery-blue cone swirling up into the hot blue sky. A few blocks closer, I saw the "hat" rising from a round building with a huge silver cross. It was the most humondo church I'd ever seen. It was a *giga*church. But what church had a spire corkscrewing hundreds of feet toward heaven?

Riding toward it, my insides went shaky with excitement. It was how people must've felt when they spotted the Tower of Babel in the distance. Huge gardens and parking lots surrounded the gigachurch. Then I saw the sign. I slammed on the brakes so hard I almost did an endo faceplant. CHURCH OF CHRIST. It was Mormon.

I'd been so stoked about church-shopping the place. But no way would Mom step inside it. She said the Mormons were blind sheep led by false prophets.

20

I popped a wheelie, spun, and rode off. I'd seen enough stupid buildings. The heat coming off the pavement made me want to find some woods and trail. But I couldn't get the twisting witch's hat out of my helmet. Dark thoughts skittered in my brain like spiders. Mom had to know about the huge Mormon temple. So why would she move us to a place full of Mormons? The answer hit me like a sprung branch. She was planning an attack on the temple. The New J-Brigade was going to David-up on the Mormon Goliath!

The vision was so terrifying I tried to race away from it. I went into full hammer-spin. It was no use. I was so racked on what might happen—we assault the temple; Mom screams "If we perish, we perish!"; she gets her wish—everything shot by in a blur. I didn't look up till I'd power-slid in front of William Chrisman High. Going to high school wasn't just my calling anymore. It was the only way I'd be saved from a suicide mission, from Mom turning us into martyrs. I didn't want to be a martyr! *I wasn't even sixteen!*

I dropped my bike and ran to the row of glass doors. I grabbed a handle, pulled. The door clunked, not budging. I tried others. All locked. I cupped a hand to the glass. No one in sight. I saw a sheet of paper taped inside. It said homeroom assignments and schedules would be mailed by August 2. The first day of school was August 16.

Then I did what I did best. I dropped to my knees. I prayed for God to intercede, to send a letter to my new house telling me my homeroom. I prayed for the glass wall to tumble down like the walls of Jericho. I promised God that if He let me walk into high school on August 16 I'd gear-up in body-'n'-soul armor and ride a clean line through temptation and evil. If I listened to music it'd be CCM minus guitars and drums. If they had computers I'd only visit Christian websites. If they tried to teach me evolution I'd wear earplugs. I'd witness for Christ. I'd be a Jesus-throated Whac-a-Mole, taking the fight behind enemy lines!

When I was bursting with the Spirit, feeling like this was the best covenant God had been offered in some time, I asked for a sign that He'd heard me. Then I said, "Amen," stood up, and added a PS: *Thanks for not letting anyone see me praying in front of school.*

God has funny ways of letting you know when you've asked for one thing too much, when you've toed over the greedy-line. I turned around and jumped.

Four guys with skateboards stared at me from the curb. I recognized them even though they'd changed into shorts and T-shirts. They were the guys who'd given me the stink eye at Feast of Faith. My stomach chunged tight. It looked like a taste of high school was coming my way sooner than later.

5

Corndog

The biggest guy had a mullet haircut, and a sneering grin. "Guess you didn't get enough knee time at church."

"I wasn't praying," I said, hoping one little lie wouldn't make God rip my covenant into a million pieces.

22

Mullet-guy dropped his skateboard with a loud *clack*. "So what were ya doin'?"

"I was seeing if I could pick the lock."

The other guys snickered. A short guy with a ripped body like a wrestler turned to Mullet. "Maybe he got the miracle this morning. Maybe the light under his bushel is bein' a burglar." They all laughed.

It was a good sign one of them had listened to the sermon. Maybe they weren't as tough as they looked. "I wasn't gonna steal anything," I said. "I just wanted to check out my new school."

"What grade?" Wrestler-guy asked.

"Tenth."

"Us too."

Mullet socked Wrestler in the arm, then glared at me. "You can't wait to scope a new school? What kinda fred are you?"

I shrugged. "Dunno. I'm still waiting for God to tell me."

Everyone but Mullet huffed a chuckle.

"Tube it," he snapped.

They shut up, so I figured that's what "tube it" meant. I'd never heard that one before. That's another thing about living in a lot of places: you're always picking up new lingo.

He gestured at my bike. "Whacha ridin', roadie?"

"I'm not a roadie," I said. "I do trail."

His face hardened. "That's not what I asked."

"It's a Cannondale. You got trails around here, right?"

"Plenty." Mullet's face twisted in its sneer-grin. "And I got just the one for ya. C'mon." He pushed off on his board and two of the guys followed.

23

Wrestler-guy hung back. He could see I was hesitating. "You better come, or the next trail Case shows you will be a death march."

Him saying "death march" gave me hope. It was biker talk. Maybe he was a biker too. As the others skateboarded ahead of us, I rode beside Wrestler and we traded names. He was Ben. The other two, besides Case, were Roger and Randy.

"Were you really trying to pick the lock?" he asked.

I'd lied too much already, so I went with half a lie. "With my mind, yeah." Ben laughed. I changed the subject. "So where we going?"

He shrugged. "Beats me. When Case gets a session in his head he just goes for it."

"And you guys follow?"

"Pretty much." Ben grinned. "Don't worry, dude, if Case is gonna mess with you, it won't be 'cause you're some lock-pickin' Jesus junkie."

"Why would he wanna mess with me?"

"Kinda obvious." He pointed at my Cannondale. "You're a gear queer."

I came right back. "We got names for boarders, too."

"Yeah, like"—he pushed off hard and shot his arms in the air—"the superheroes of cement!"

I caught up with him and hit him with some trash talk I'd heard back in Tulsa. "No, gays on trays."

He laughed. "Never heard that one. Don't say it around Case. He'll taco your bike and stuff you inside it."

We bombed a hill and came to a big park scattered with

trees and lots of burnt-out grass. In the middle was a kid-die water park with fountains and metal trees that filled buckets with water, then dumped them on whoever was underneath. Little kids played in the water.

At the bottom of a long drop of cement steps, Case and the R-boys were doing stunts on benches. I figured they were waiting for us to catch up and we'd keep going. I rode down the grassy hill while Ben jumped on the cement ramp bordering the stairs and screamed down it. He jumped off just before his board hit bottom and flew toward Case. Case caught the board with his foot. I popped a nose wheelie next to them.

"What do ya think?" Case asked.

"Of what?" I asked.

He gestured all around. "Our track."

"It's not exactly a trail."

"Are you kiddin'?" He pointed at the stairs. "It's got steep and everything." He poked me in the chest. "You sayin' our track isn't good enough for a pro like you? C'mon, hotshot"—he waved at the stairs—"let's see you nail the grade."

I looked at the stairs and the two cement ramp-skinnies on each side. I'd cleaned stuff like it hundreds of times. "Local or express?"

"Express!" the R-boys shouted.

I ground up the hill, bunny-hopped onto the top of the ramp Ben had taken, and held a track stand for a sec while I checked the line. It was twenty feet of rail a foot and a half wide. The only brutal part was the bottom. It wasn't like I was on a board and could bail like Ben had done. I had to time the impact of the flat just right and ride it out. I pushed my butt behind the cockpit and ripped down.

While the guys whooped, I heard a loud *clack*. I couldn't take my eyes off the ramp to see what made the noise. Flying toward the bottom, I pushed forward so my butt would catch impact on the seat and not the back tire. There was nothing nastier than a rhoid buffing. Of course, moving forward added speed.

I suddenly saw what had made the noise. A skateboard shot to the bottom of the ramp. My front tire caught it square, popped the board into my frame, and locked my back wheel like I'd hit a brick wall. I endoed over the handlebars. Luckily, I catapulted over the cement and ragdollied on the grass. I totally pranged, but nothing was broken.

Case and the R-boys went hysterical. Ben's face appeared over me. "You alright, dude?"

"Yeah." He helped me up. "Who's the asshole?"

Case hurried over trying not to laugh through his bolted-on look of shock. "Sorry, man, it was the weirdest thing. My board just shot away from me."

I brushed past him. "Yeah, right." I checked my bike. The front rings were totally potato-chipped.

Case sounded behind me. "Of course, it could've been an act of God. I mean, maybe He was punishing you for lying."

I turned and faced him. He was taller than me and had me by thirty pounds. I didn't care. "What's your problem?"

"You bullshitting us. So I'm gonna ask you again. Were you trying to break into school, or were you praying like Mother Teresa on steroids?" The R-boys snickered. "C'mon, gear queer, admit it. You were prayin'."

I wanted to flatten his face. I'd dealt with enough bullies to know how this would end. "Okay, I was praying."

"There!" he shouted, socking me on the arm. "That wasn't so hard."

I didn't flinch. "I was praying for you gays on trays to go fuck yourselves."

His face froze for a second, then he staggered away, clutching his chest. "Oh, man! Why'd ya havta do that? Now we're gonna havta wash your mouth out."

The R-boys grabbed me and pulled me across the grass. Ben tried to stop them. "C'mon, guys. Give 'im a break."

Case snapped at him. "We're not done with this skinny fuck till I say so."

They dragged me to the fountains and held me under one of the bucket trees. Little kids scattered as the bucket overhead filled with water. Case raised his arms and shouted, "In the name of the Fart, the Toot, and the Holy Gas, we christen you . . . Corndog!" He grabbed my hair and jerked my head back. The bucket dumped its load, drenching me and splashing them. They didn't care. They were having too much fun.

They hauled me to a patch of dust, held me down, and threw dirt on me till I was covered from head to foot. Case grinned down at me. "See you around, Corndog."

After they left I lay there all hot and shaky, like a volcano

27

wanting to blow. When I sat up they were gone. Except for Ben. He watched from the top of the ridge. As soon as he saw that I'd seen him, he turned and boarded away.

I pushed my bike out of the park. My brain boiled with revenge fantasies. But a thought kept interrupting. I'd asked God for a sign that He'd heard my prayer. Instead, He'd given me a test. *You really wanna go to high school? Prepare yourself. It's a death march.*

6

The Prayer Rug

Before I went into the house, I took a sec to get ready for the grilling Mom was going to give me. I could see her through a front window, arranging things how she liked them. She was banging a nail into the wall. It was for one of our pictures. Most of them were of me, from little-kid ones to the one she took last spring when I graduated from ninth-grade homeschool. She calls it my "class photo," though I don't get how one person can be a "class." A couple of pictures were from the few trips we'd taken that weren't forced relocations, but real vacations.

One was taken in San Antonio when we visited the Alamo and the hotel bar that Carry Nation smashed up during her fight against alcohol in 1900. The gouge where she buried her hatchet in the bar was still there. That was cool. We got our picture taken wearing period costumes. Mom dressed like Carry Nation holding a hatchet. I

28

dressed like a newspaper boy in short pants. After the picture taking, we bought a Carry Nation hatchet for twenty bucks. It cost so much because it had TEMPERANCE carved in the handle and was a real hatchet. When we got home, Mom wired it to a board with our picture stuck under it. She always said that if the New J-Brigade ever needed an ax, we would use Carry Nation's.

I stepped onto the porch. I hoped she didn't have plans to use the hatchet on the Mormon temple. But using it on Case and the R-boys would've been okay. I opened the screen door and went inside. Mom rushed over and asked if I was okay. I said I was fine.

"Who did this?" she demanded.

"I dunno, I didn't get their names," I told her.

She went to the kitchen sink and yanked the faucet on. "We'll find out who they are."

"They jumped me from behind; I didn't get a good look at 'em." I was surprised how easily the lie popped out. She came over with a wet dishcloth. I tried to move away. "Mom, I don't wanna be wet anymore." There was no stopping her.

After giving my face a mud-ectomy, she told me to take my clothes off so she could soak them. I was way too old to strip down in front of her. Besides, I'd chalked up so many lies I wanted to give her a chance to even the score. "I'll take 'em off in a sec. First I wanna know why we moved here."

Mom pushed her hair back and stared at me. "We need to pray." She grabbed my hand and tried to pull me down to the throw rug that always marked where our living room was.

29

I pulled away. "I'll pray after you tell me why we're here and how things are gonna be different."

She flashed me a look Carry Nation probably had sported before she'd swung her hatchet. "I told you yesterday, it's a shining city on a hill with fine churches and God-fearing Christians."

"I've seen the place, Mom. The shiniest thing in town is a huge Mormon temple. Did you know about that?"

"Yes, and I made sure it was on the other side of town."

"Are you planning to take on the Mormons?"

"We do what the Lord tells us to do."

"Okay, I'll tell you what He's telling me to do." I swallowed and went on. "He wants me to go to high school."

She took a step back like she'd been pushed by an invisible force. "That's not God talking, that's Satan." She came at me, wagging a finger. "He won't fasten his grip on you."

I darted away and gave her the speech I'd patched together on the way home. "Most kids stop homeschooling after junior high, and go to high school so they can witness and bring others to Christ. I checked out the school; it looks nice. I prayed in front of it. I asked God to send me there and make me like my father. You know, like you said he always preached. 'Be a fisher of men: you catch 'em, let Jesus clean 'em.'"

She pitched the dishrag in the sink. "You've had your say, now listen up. You will not go to a school filled with the wicked. *Be ye not unequally yoked together with unbelievers.*"

"How do you know they're unbelievers?"

"Look what a bunch of them did to you!" she shouted.

30

"They're not unbelievers. They were in church this morning!"

Her eyes narrowed to slits. "You said you didn't recognize them."

I flushed red—totally busted.

She stepped close. Her voice went low and scolding. "You lie to me. You covet a school filled with sinners. You dishonor your mother and you dishonor God. Now I know why the Lord intervened and guided me to a decision."

I swallowed the dryness in my throat. "What decision?"

"I picked up a brochure at church this morning, and while you were off getting in trouble I found a pay phone and made some calls. Before you resume your education in *this* house, you're going to Bible camp."

"Bible camp!" I yelled so loudly spit flew out of me. "It's almost August. It's too late for that!"

"It's never too late," she said with iron in her voice. "You've fallen away, Billy. Your heart needs to be put right in the eyes of God."

"My heart is right," I pleaded. Then I told her how I'd do extra Bible study and go to church every day if she wanted.

She wasn't listening. Her eyes were all shiny with Spirit juice. When she gets that way a verse is bound to drop from heaven and land on her lips. Sure enough, one did. *"The heart is deceitful above all things, and desperately wicked,"* she recited. *"Who can know it?"*

The answer is that only God can know what's in your heart. I fought the urge to tell her she wasn't the lord of my heart.

She moved to the rug and knelt. "If you can't see how defiant you're being, I'll pray for you alone."

When we argued like this it always felt like she was giving me two choices: get down and pray, or run away. When it happened—and it had been happening a lot more—the same two questions popped up. Where would I go? Who would I run to? The fact was, there was no one else.

So I did what I always did. I invented a reason to obey. On that day, it was easy. Bending my knee and joining her was punishment for the lies I'd been heaping up all day.

She clutched my hands and prayed for God to rescue our eyes from tears, our feet from stumbling. She prayed for me to get back to growing in Christ. She prayed for God to show us a sign that coming to Independence was His plan. And, when she felt that my prayer wasn't as Spirit-filled as hers, she prayed for God to show me that kneeling to Jesus never works if you're still standing up inside.

That's the thing about Mom. Sometimes she's so right. My insides weren't kneeling. They were back on my bike, wanting to race back to town and leap in that coffin, vacancy or not.

7

Stupid Neighbors

Accepting Bible camp was easier after I got a look at the new neighbors. The house behind us had some ancient couple with closed curtains in all their windows. I sure hoped they'd stay closed. The house out my other window was full of good news–bad news. Good news: not a curtain in the place. Bad news: a few windows were broken. Good news: everyone who lived there was naked. Bad news: they were all bats.

After a dinner of chicken-fried steak, macaroni 'n' cheese, and peas, I took my chair out on the porch and put my feet up where the missing pillar should've been. I was armed with a plastic straw and the two paper napkins from dinner. At dusk, the bats started coming out of the house next door. They dove around the streetlight catching moths, mosquitoes, whatever flew. I tore off little pieces of napkin, balled them up, and shot them from the straw high in the air. A bat would dive for it thinking it was a juicy moth, then shoot upward when it realized it had been fooled. I shot dozens of paper bullets in the air. The bats fell for it every time.

Stupid neighbors.

When I ran out of paper, I watched the flicker of TVs in the other houses on the street. We didn't have a TV. Having a TV and watching fun shows was one of the things I wanted to do in the future. Mom believed TV was a box filled with profane babblers eclipsing the light of Christ. She also said that when the Antichrist came during the End Times, TV was going to be his favorite tool to infiltrate the minds of the unsuspecting. When I thought about it her way, the TVs up and down the street looked less like flickering portals of fun and more like the glowing eyes of the Beast.

Stupid neighbors.

My mother brought her chair outside. I asked her something that had been bugging me. "Why did you unpack my suitcase when you knew I'd be going to Bible camp in a couple days?"

"I didn't want you thinking of this place as a motel," she said. "I want you to remember it as home."

It was weird. She never called any place "home" until we'd been there a few weeks. I didn't tell her I wouldn't be spending any time at camp being homesick for the one-pillar doghouse. Especially with no neighbors with curves to covet.

When I asked her about the Mormon temple again, things got wonkier. She quoted a verse I hadn't heard before. *"Never take your own revenge, but leave room for the wrath of God, for it is written,* Vengeance is mine, I will repay, *says the Lord."*

I asked her if that meant we were going to stop Whac-a-Moling and let God do the whacking from now on.

"It's not so black and white," she answered. "There are followers of false prophets whose armies are so vast that God will deal with them Himself. But He still needs us to perform small missions. We're His guerilla warriors."

I wasn't convinced she'd taken the Mormons off her target list. But it was good to know she wasn't planning some insane mission like scaling the Mormon's hat-shaped steeple and sticking a couple of horns on it.

Then she told me something that really tweaked my brain. "There are countless ways to reveal God's glory," she said. "But the most important is to raise you up as a child of promise, a man of the Good Book. You're the brightest candle God gave me. It's my duty to let it shine."

She'd never talked like this before. It made my insides feel sketchy. I didn't want to be anyone's candle. I just wanted to be Billy Allbright, champion mountain biker.

She looked out into the darkness, staring at nothing, or a million things I couldn't see. It was so still and quiet that when she stood up the scrape of her chair made me jump. She walked stiffly to the screen door, opened it, and turned back. "When I said things would be different here, Billy, I meant it."

"Does that mean I still have to go to Bible camp?"

"Yes." She nodded. "But next summer, it's your decision."

Later, I lay in bed and watched the bats under the streetlight. Remembering how they dove for the spitballs filled me with a weird wonderment. I was awed by their beautiful, darting flight, and by how dumb some of God's creatures could be. Diving for spitballs, realizing they were nothing, swooping back up, then falling for it again and again. I wondered if the pleasure I got from watching such beauty and stupidity was the same pleasure God got from watching His human creations. Swooping and diving for worthless things, then soaring back up, only to fall for the same trick over and over.

Stupid neighbors.

8

Everyday Miracle

The sunlight filling the room surprised me. Mom usually got me up early for Bible meditation. I threw on some clothes. In the main room, there was a box of cereal on the table, along with a note saying milk was in the fridge and that she'd be back soon. I took a bowl of cereal out on the porch.

I was on my third bowl when Mom pulled up in front of the house. She jumped out of the car and slid something out. She came around the car carrying a cardboard box. She practically skipped onto the porch. The box was filled with junk mail and magazines.

She was good about having our mail forwarded to us when we moved. The only time she didn't have it forwarded was if we left a town where we'd broken a law they might chase us for. So far, nobody had sent a posse to hunt us down.

The only mail for me was usually from homeschool supply places or some ministry. One time, I got a Victoria's Secret catalog by mistake. Talk about make-you-dizzy "neighbors." The underwear bunnies kept me entertained for weeks. Whenever I felt like they were luring me to hell, I told myself I was doing a Bible experiment to see what it had been like to be King Solomon with his thousand wives and concubines. The experiment ended when Mom found the catalog under my bed and took her wrath out on me and the mailman.

Mom held the cardboard box like it was a Christmas present. "There's something for you." I peered into the box. "Dig down."

I fished around till my hand hit something big. I pulled a package out. It was heavy, wrapped in brown paper, and addressed to Charles William Allbright in squiggly writing. Whoever wrote it had a real wonky hand. "There's no return address," I said.

Mom beamed. "There doesn't have to be."

"What do you mean?"

"Just open it."

I noticed a corner of the brown paper had been torn away. Something gold flickered inside. I had a hunch what it was; I suspected Mom knew for sure. I tore off the wrapping. It was a fancy Bible, bound in black leather, with gilt edges on the pages.

Mom scooted into the chair next to me as I opened the cover. There was no note, no inscription, nothing showing who it was from. Fifty-dollar Bibles don't show up in the mail every day. "I wonder who sent it."

"Who do you think? It's from God, Billy. It's a miracle." She was almost laughing with joy. "It's the sign we prayed for last night. The Lord's telling us He wants us in Independence."

"Mom, if it's from God, why'd He send it to Tulsa first?"

"Doesn't matter. The Book found us here. It's where the water springs up that makes a well, not where you dig a dry hole. Our new home is going to be a wellspring of hope and joy."

I didn't buy it. I mean, I believe in everyday miracles, like biking through a jungle tunnel, catching a black widow in your helmet, and not getting bitten. Or the miracle of making a friend who's got a TV and an Xbox. Or the miracle of going rafting at Bible camp, getting pitched out of the boys' boat, and being rescued by the girls' boat. But I didn't believe God had his miracles forwarded by the post office.

I was looking for an earthly sign of who had sent it when I noticed a ribbon bookmarker. I opened the Bible to the marked page. It was the book of Joel. There was a verse highlighted in yellow.

Mom sucked in a gasp. "Two, twenty-eight," she whispered. "Praise Jesus."

I got a weird feeling. It was like someone knew about her finger-pointing providence checks and had done one for me.

"Go ahead." She nodded at the yellowed verse. "Read it."

". . . *and your sons and your daughters shall prophesy, your old men shall dream dreams, your young men shall see visions.*"

"It's more than a sign, it's a prophecy!" she exclaimed. She was so exalted I thought she was going to bust out in tongues. She went on about how the passage was an Old Testament prediction about the coming of Christ. But now, God had dropped a Bible in my lap marked with that verse, and that confirmed what she'd said the night before about her purpose: to raise me up as a child of promise and a man of the Book.

Until I figured out who had sent the Bible I didn't want to rain on her exaltation parade. She was so juiced she began to overheat. She fanned her face with a hand, then went inside to fetch two glasses of ice water.

I stared at the "miracle." I lifted it by the spine and flapped it. Nothing fell out. Except a feeling. Not a gut feeling, a finger feeling. The back cover was stiff, like something was inside the leather. I spread the back cover open. Near the binding, the leather was slit. Something was tucked inside.

I dug my fingers in and pulled the thing out. I stared at a silver disc in a paper sleeve. A DVD. I turned it over. Staring up at me, in the same shaky handwriting as on the brown wrapper, was:

To CWA,
For your eyes only.
From your father,
RA

My heart stopped; my breath stopped; the world stopped.

The clink of ice came from inside the house.

I jammed the DVD back inside the cover a second before Mom opened the screen door.

Resurrection

Mom handed me a glass of cold water. I bit my lip to stop myself from asking if my father could still be alive. If I did, she might make a connection to the fifty-dollar Bible.

I listened to her go on about how God had spoken, and how things were going to be so different in Independence that we might never move again. I thought I was going to explode from not being able to jump up, go find a DVD player, and see what was on the disc making my head spin with questions. Was it a fake? Some kind of joke? Was it him? If it was, what did he really look like?

After what felt like hours, Mom calmed down enough for me to say I wanted to go to the library to check out some books for camp. I went inside, grabbed my sneaks, slipped the DVD from its hiding place, and shoved it in my cargo-shorts pocket. As soon as I got out of sight, I started running. I didn't stop till I reached the library I'd spotted earlier.

The man at the information desk told me I had to do two things before I could use a computer: get a library card and stop sweating. I spent another five minutes of torture filling out a form.

I got my card and convinced the info man I was done sweating. He took me to a computer. He handed me a box of tissues and told me to clean the headphones when I was done. I threw on the headphones and tried to feed the DVD into the slot. My hand shook so much it took several tries before the slot grabbed the disc and gorped it.

The screen started all black, then words came up: FOR CHARLES WILLIAM ALLBRIGHT. A picture blipped up. An old man stared out at me. He was in a bed, propped up on pillows. One hand, wrapped in tape, dropped to his lap. At first the hand looked bandaged, but it was a remote control taped to his palm. There was no guessing his age because he looked so sick. His gray skin hung on his head like a wrinkled sock. His longish white hair fanned back against a pillow. This can't be my father, I thought, it's Methuselah. I'd seen my dad countless times in the mirror, but the mirror door had swung open and a ghost was staring out at me. I wanted to shut that door, pretend it was a dream. I couldn't. The ghost had me hypnotized.

He blinked, real slow. His dark blue eyes disappeared, then reappeared. His mouth cracked open. "Hello, Billy. I know I'm not much to look at." His voice was stronger than he looked. And it sounded like his tongue was shoveling sand along with his words. He sucked in a raspy breath. "Nevertheless, to quote Darth Vader, 'I am your father.'"

The last word shot a bolt of pain through my chest, like there was an invisible arrow sticking in my heart that he'd reached out and batted. Part of me wanted him to bat it again. He was my father, back from the dead!

His wrinkled face bunched into a smile or a grimace, I couldn't tell which. "I suppose it's rude and presumptuous quoting Darth Vader when your mother has probably shielded you from the corruption of popular culture. But that's me, rude and presumptuous Richard Allbright." The more he spoke, the more the life in his eyes spread into his face.

"Maybe you're wondering how I ascertained that you're called Billy, and that you've been raised as a God-fearing, Bible-thumping, Christo-terrorist. Well, I've been keeping my eye on you and Tilda for some time."

His head slowly turned. His hand, the one with the remote, lifted and reached offscreen. I stared at his profile. Under the wrinkled curtain of skin, his nose was just like mine: a big beak. My stomach ballooned like I'd whoop-de-dooed over a hill. Before I could find the next piece of him that was me, he pulled something across the screen.

It took me a second to recognize what it was: a white board with a map of America's middle. Pushpins poked from the map in all the places me and Mom had lived. Colored string zigzagged between the pins. It was the zigzag path of my life with Mom. "I've kept track of you by Googling Tilda's name," he said. He sounded so close in my headphones. "I've read the entertaining accounts of your exploits in police blotters and local newspapers."

He pulled the board away and stared at me again. "Your mother's Christian zeal is why I've come to you tucked inside the Good Book. The Bible is my Trojan horse."

He swallowed as slow as he blinked. "But why, you may be wondering, has your ancient, deadbeat father suddenly materialized? First the bad news. By the time you see this I will have *un*materialized. I will be dead."

"No!" For a second I couldn't understand why he didn't hear me.

He kept going. "I may sound like I've got some time, but I assure you my hour upon the stage is up. If it wasn't, I'd—" His hand waved the thought away. "Enough of that. To the news that isn't bad. I'll let you decide how *good* it is. It comes in two parts. The unvarnished truth about the past. And a possible truth about your future."

He took another raspy breath. "I don't know what Tilda has told you about your birth. Here's what I know. We met on a Mississippi riverboat. She was there to get gamblers to bet on Christ. I was there taking part in a conference on Mark Twain and giving a talk on one of his books. That's who I was, and still am: an expert on Twain, and a professional collector and trader of all things Twain. I've sold everything from first editions of his books to a strand of his hair I found in his dictionary. I call myself a Twainiac."

I was in a trance, hanging on his every word.

"Your mother, the beautiful Tilda Hayes, wandered into my talk. We spoke afterward and fell in love. I don't know why a Twainiac and a Bible-thumper fell for each other, but we did. Maybe it was Twain playing a joke on me from the grave, or God playing a joke on both of us. In any case, our undying love lived long enough for me to come to Jesus and for you to be conceived in a reckless moment of passion. Then the trouble began. As you grew inside Tilda, the life-in-Christ growing in me miscarried. The unbeliever I'd been before meeting your mother was born again. I kept offering to marry her, but she refused to wed a man who hopscotched from sin to salvation and back to sin again. For her, there was only one explanation for her dire circumstance. I had been sent by Satan to tempt her and she had failed God. When she was four months pregnant she disappeared without a trace. The only thing she took was my name."

The throbbing pain in my chest was back again, worse. Now he was grabbing the arrow and twisting it. He was calling me a bastard. I wanted to rip the pain from my chest and plunge it into him. But I couldn't even talk back to him.

He sucked in another breath. "For years I didn't know what had happened to Tilda, or to my child. After I found you on the Internet, I wrote letters to you. I suspect she intercepted them, because I've never heard back. Perhaps she has intercepted this. I even showed up at some of the places you lived, hoping to see you. But you had always moved on by the time I got there."

I wondered if he was telling the truth. I wondered how hard he'd really looked for me. The answer I got was a twisted smile. He went on. "I don't have the strength to dwell on past failures. I want to talk about your future. I have something for you. Your inheritance. Like me, it doesn't look like much. It's only a book." His white eyebrows lifted. "I call it the 'bad book.' Of all the things I've held in my hands that Mark Twain once held in his, the bad book is the most valuable of all."

I had no clue what he was talking about, but as he spoke his craggy face filled with life. His gray skin shaded pink. His cheeks seemed less sunken. He began to look like the Reverend Richard Allbright I'd always seen in the mirror.

He pushed his head off the pillow. A strand of white hair slipped to his shoulder. "The world has never seen the brilliant story Twain feverishly scribbled in the bad book. It's the sequel to his masterpiece, *Adventures of Huckleberry Finn*. For scholars, the story is priceless. For collectors, it's worth hundreds of thousands of dollars. For me, it's the only thing I'll ever give to my son"—his eyes shut, he leaned back into the pillow—"Charles William Allbright."

I didn't care about some book. I didn't care about the money. I only heard the echo of his words—"my son." I wanted to hate him for never finding me, for never being my father. I couldn't. How could I hate a man who'd pushed open the mirror, like a lid on a coffin, and uttered my name? He was my Rip van Winkle sleeping all this time. He was my father.

His eyes opened again. "Here's the problem. I can't send you the bad book. If your mother saw it, she'd say it was written by the devil and destroy it. If I could, I'd bring it to you myself. I can't. You have to fetch it, by yourself. And because I fear Tilda might be watching this, finding the book won't be easy. It will be a treasure hunt." He swallowed and went on. "Your first clue is a riddle. Here it is: Where do you find the book of Genesis and human conception?"

I listened to a breath rattle through him.

"If and when you begin your hunt, here's my advice. Be like Huck Finn. Huck said, 'I don't take no stock in dead people.' In other words, Billy, don't take no stock in invisible fathers. Only take stock in what fathers leave behind."

He blinked in slow motion. His eyes were wet and shiny. "Before I fade to black—I have no right to say this, but I will because I never had the chance. I love you. Then, now, forevermore."

45

He lifted his other arm from under the covers. There was a tube sticking out of it, snaking offscreen. His hand with the remote reached for a knob on the tube. I suddenly realized what he was about to do.

"Don't!" I heard my voice shout outside the headphones.

His quavering fingers turned the knob. He looked at me; his voice scratched in my ears. "I pray to all the gods, let his adventure begin with my end." His finger moved onto the remote. The picture went black.

What I remember after that was like a foggy dream. The info man was at my side, acting like something was wrong. He pushed the box of tissues toward me. I knocked it out of his hand, or maybe he dropped it. I shouted that I wanted my DVD back. He must've given it to me. Running out of the library, I felt it burning in my hand.

10

Wicked Hearts

As I ran I couldn't tell where my tears left off and my sweat began. All I felt was rage. I hated my father for dying, hated my mother for living, and hated God for letting me be born. How could they all be so cruel? How could my father rise from the river Mom drowned him in, wave a map in my face, and end his life a few minutes after his resurrection? Why didn't he try harder to find us? Why didn't he try harder to find me? Was I that worthless? The answers were now entombed in silence. My rage kept punching the tears out of me: a total tear-ectomy. And there was no taking it out on "invisible fathers," my earthly one or heavenly one. The only one I could rage against was Mom.

I burst into the house, grabbed the leather Bible from my room, and shoved it in her face. I shouted that the book was no sign from God. It was no miracle. I screamed it was from Richard Allbright and threw it on the floor.

She stood there, dead still. Dust swirled up from the floor, darting in the sunlight like angry gnats. She reached down. I beat her to it, snatching the book up. "It's mine! It's the only thing I'll ever have that he touched!" I wanted to keep yelling but a sob grabbed my throat.

"That's not true," she said, moving toward me. "He touched me. You have me."

I stepped back. "I don't want *you!*"

The words struck us both. They hit her harder than hearing his name. And they knocked out whatever tears I had left. I was done crying over a man who'd always been alive, hiding behind the mirror. A man who was now dead and gone before anyone gave me the chance to know him. To weep over him was as dumb as crying over a great-great-grandfather you'd never met. Whoever said "I don't take no stock in dead people" was right.

I asked her if it was true about them never marrying and her ditching him before I was born. When she asked me how I'd heard such things, I slammed her with the best scripture on lying she'd taught me. *"Liars shall have their part in the lake which burns with fire and brimstone."* There's nothing like a little Revelation to put the fear of damnation in Mom.

47

She sank into a chair and hid her face. I waited for her to spill.

Between sobs, she confessed how the devil had tricked her into falling in love with Richard Allbright. At first, everything had been good, with him coming to Christ and all, but then Satan attacked them with his carnal weapons and tempted them in the way of the flesh. They succumbed, and "plowed wickedness" is how she put it. After that, God punished them by making my father stray from his walk with Christ. She said he went back to his old ways of worshipping idols. When I asked her what that meant, she said he backslid to worshipping Mark Twain: instead of seeking God's approval he was seeking Twain's approval from the grave.

"But that was his job," I said.

Her head jerked up; she wiped a hand across her cheek. "How do you know that?"

"Never mind how I know. You haven't finished."

She went on. "It wasn't only a job for him; it was idolatry. He whored after graven images, from Twain's anti-Christian books to worthless souvenirs."

She told me that after Richard refused to turn back to Christ, she prayed day and night. She asked God if she should marry a false believer, an idol worshipper, and the father of her child. God didn't answer. Then, a few months before I was born, she did a providence check. Her finger fell on the parable of the talents. The message from God was clear. Just as the nobleman gave each of his servants a coin to invest while he was away, God had given her a seed to grow and prosper. And because Richard was more like the servant who took his coin and hid it in a napkin, and did nothing with it, the Lord was going to take my father's coin away from him and give it to her alone. The coin was me.

She gazed up at me, her eyes swimming with tears and the Spirit. "My child already had a father, the Heavenly Father."

"I wanted a real father!" I yelled. "And all this time I had one! Who gave you the right to kill him when he wasn't dead?"

Her eyes went blank, cold. Her voice dropped to a whisper. "Because I know when no father is better than a bad one."

I was too locked on rage to imagine what she meant. She told me we needed to pray. Praying was the last thing I wanted to do, especially to a God who resurrected my father only to kill him. I finally threw it in her face. "He's dead!"

She fixed on me for a moment. The hum of the fridge sounded loud as a train. "How do you know that?"

I yanked the DVD from my pocket. "'Cause he let me watch!"

Something flashed in her eyes that shivered through me. I swear I saw relief. It made my insides boil. I had to get out of there before I did something I'd regret forever.

When I got to the door I was even dead to anger. I felt as cold and dead as Richard Allbright. I turned and raised his Bible. "You and God got it right. *The heart is deceitful above all things, and desperately wicked: who can know it?* I can," I said, "I've seen it."

49

* * *

I went to the only place I could think of. The high school.

I sat in the top row of bleachers and watched the football team practice. There were some other kids in the bleachers. None of them bothered me, even though I'm sure I looked Jesus-junkie weird sitting there with a big black Bible. They probably didn't mess with me because I must've looked like a mass murderer the moment before he yanks out a semi-automatic and opens fire.

After I got back to thinking halfway straight, I tried to figure out my next move. By the time the football team left the field and the sun dropped over downtown, I had a plan.

- I'd go to Bible camp so I didn't kill my mother.
- I'd try to solve the first riddle in my father's treasure hunt.
- After that, there was no plan.

At dinner we ate leftovers in silence. Mom had sunk into one of her depressions. Sometimes it took a couple days for her to pray her way out of it. Another not-so-bad thing about being homeschooled: go-to-school kids had snow days, sure, but I had end-of-the-world days.

I packed some clothes for camp. I got into bed and shoved the leather Bible, with the DVD back in it, under my pillow. It wasn't to soak up verses in my sleep or anything like that. I was worried Mom might steal it.

The amazing thing about the Bible is that it's no regular book; it's God's Word. So when you stick it under your pillow, the Word is going to invade your brain whether you like it or not. The part that crept into mine was from Job, where Job plops down on a dung heap and wishes he hadn't been born. God hadn't exactly stripped me of everything and covered my body with boils, but I knew how Job felt. I wished I'd never been born.

To stop feeling sorry for myself I asked WWJD? What would Jesus do? A handful of answers wormed out of the Bible and into my mind. The juiciest one was when Jesus is setting the Pharisees straight. *If anyone comes to me, and does not hate his own father and mother and wife and children and brothers and sisters, yes, and even his own life, he cannot be my disciple.*

If Christ's gospel of love starts with hating your family and your life, then Jesus was truly my savior. I was ready to Son-up and walk in His Way.

II

Adventures
of Billy Allbright

Note to the Lord #2

T.L.,

You made me a bastard. When I opened my Bible to find what You say about bastards, here's what I found.

- A bastard shall not enter into the congregation of the Lord; even to his tenth generation shall he not enter into the congregation of the Lord (*Deuteronomy 23:2*).

Let me see if I got that. My children, my grandchildren, all the way to nine generations, won't be going to heaven. Right?

- *But the Bible also says that children can't be punished for their parents' sins, and that only the wicked will suffer for the sins they* alone *commit (Ezekiel 18:20).*

Now I'm confused. So I can't be punished for my parents' sins, but because my parents never got married, it still means that me, the bastard, *plus my offspring for nine generations will be shut out of heaven. If both these things are true, then the only way all this can stack up and not topple over is in a riddle.*

THE RIDDLE
- *If a kid can't be punished for his parents' sins, then why is the kid whose parents birthed him a bastard punished by being shut out of heaven?*

THE ANSWER *(as far as I can figure)*
- *My parents weren't the only ones who sinned. I did too. If human life, which is sinful, starts at the moment of conception, then so does sin. So sometime between the moment I was conceived and the moment I was born, I sinned in my mother's womb, and my punishment was being born a bastard.*

Makes sense to me. Did I nail it?

There's just one thing I'm still wrestling with. What about the nine generations after me? I mean, You're saying that, for whatever reason, they're still going to be so sinful (in the womb or after) that they'll be denied entrance to heaven too? So if I'm going to be the father of nine generations of sinners all going to hell, shouldn't I do You and the world a mega-merciful favor and not have kids?

As You can see, my prayer rug's in a twist over this. I hope You can help me untangle it.

Looking forward to Your answers, thoughts, Word slams, lightning bolts, or whatever zigzag loving-kindness You can spare.

> Your confused fan, then-now-forevermore,
> Billy

1

Between the Covers

I woke before dawn and checked under the pillow. The Bible was still there. Questions and worries zipped through my brain like bats. Morning takes forever when you've got brain bats.

After breakfast I tossed my backpack and suitcase in the back of the car. I vowed to be sullen and silent during the ride to the bus taking me to Bible camp. But, as Mom had proved with my father, the flesh is weak. One of my nagging questions jumped out. "If you weren't married, and he was such a sinner, why did you take his name?"

She sighed. She looked like she'd had a rough night too. "If I didn't take his name, no one, including you, would have believed I was a widow, now, would they?"

She had a point. "What's it say on my birth certificate?"

"Hayes."

"So when I get my driver's license and have to show my birth certificate, I'll be Billy Hayes?"

"I don't know." A muscle in her jaw bunched up and relaxed like a frog's throat.

We drove the rest of the way in silence. Obviously, a

59

name wasn't any more solid than taffy. It could be stretched into whatever lie you wanted it to be.

We stopped in a church parking lot near a big coach bus. When she hugged me goodbye it was weird; she felt like someone else. She *was* someone else. It was the first time I'd hugged Tilda *Hayes*.

I got on the bus and passed the little kids in the front. I recognized older kids from Feast of Faith. They were wearing a variety of stuff, from hippie tie-dye to black goth. I wondered how much Mom had looked into this Bible camp.

I found two empty seats, dropped my backpack by the window, and sat in the aisle seat. Then I saw a guy get on the bus; my stomach flopped. It was Ben. My gut coiled tighter as other guys came up behind him. Luckily, Case and the R-boys didn't show.

Ben said "Hey." I said "Hey" back. He jammed his skateboard in the overhead, dropped his backpack on the floor, and plopped down in the seat across the aisle. I wasn't going to bring up the other day if he wasn't.

As Ben fished an iPod out of his backpack, I asked, "Are all these kids going to the same camp?"

"Yeah," he said. "We've got preppies, geeks, hipsters, goths, emos, granolas"—he pinched his thumb and finger together and sucked air—"even some stoners."

A red-faced man stood up at the front of the bus. He said he was Brother Jeremy. After he led a prayer for a safe trip the bus rolled out of the parking lot. I saw Mom standing on the sidewalk. She couldn't see me through the tinted windows. It didn't stop her from waving goodbye. I didn't wave back.

60

I looked over at Ben. An iPod earbud was jammed in his ear, and he jerked to music. The little kids in the front started singing a song about going to Bible camp. They sang it so many times, Brother Jeremy got up and fed a DVD into a player. The TVs hanging from the overheads started playing one of the Chronicles of Narnia movies. There was only one DVD I wanted to see: my father's. I needed to hear the exact words of his riddle again.

There are times in life, and not nearly enough, when God actually hears your thoughts and says, *You know, I haven't answered any of that kid's prayers lately. Maybe I'll toss him a kindness.* And that's what He did. As Ben reached into his backpack, I spotted something silver about the size of a book. "Is that a portable DVD player?" I asked.

"Yeah."

"Can I borrow it for a minute?"

He shot me a sketchy look, pulled the player out and handed it over. "I guess I owe you something after the other day."

I said, "Thanks," hoping he was done talking about my little baptism. I pulled the leather Bible from my pack and slid the DVD from the slot in the back cover.

"Weird place for a DVD," he said.

"You think?" I stood up.

"Where are you going?"

"To the bathroom."

"Dude, is that porn?" He reached for his player. "No way you're gonna use it to jerk off."

I pulled it away. "It's not porn, trust me. You said you owe me, right?"

"Alright," he grumbled. "But if I find out that's porn"—
he broke into a grin—"you are so loaning it to me."

I stepped into the bathroom at the back. Between being
unsure how to work Ben's player and the buzz of seeing
my father again, it took a while to get the thing to work. I
fast-forwarded to the part at the end where my dad gave
me the riddle. "Where do you find the book of Genesis and
human conception?" I hit the stop button. I didn't want to
hear the rest. The last thing I needed was to come out of the
bathroom doing another tear-ectomy.

When I handed the DVD player back to Ben he took it
like it had some flesh-eating disease. He told me if I'd
slimed it with impure thoughts or anything else, he'd have
everyone calling me Corndog by the end of the day. I
thanked him, then shut my eyes like I was going to catch
a nap.

As I tried to answer the riddle, Ben having his head in
the pornosphere helped me solve it. Of course, it also
could've been God who made me think of fornication.
Genesis is found in the Bible. Human conception usually
happens in a bed. So the answer to the riddle was "Between
the covers." Since my father had hidden the DVD in the
back cover of the Bible, I figured the next between-the-
covers was in the front.

I pulled the Bible out. My heart was banging so hard I
thought someone might hear it. Luckily, *Narnia* was in the
middle of a loud battle. I put the Bible on the window seat,
turned my back so Ben couldn't see, and opened the book.
Inside the front cover was another slit in the leather. I

poked a finger inside. I felt paper. Trying to pull the paper out, it started to rip. I opened the slit wider. I could see a narrow stack of pages. I carefully pulled them out. They were from a small book. The top page read *Adventures of Huckleberry Finn*.

I slid the page aside. It only got weirder.

Above "Chapter 1" there was a note scrawled in my father's shaky writing.

> You don't know about me without you
> have heard stories from your mother.
> Read these pages, follow the clues,
> and you will know me better.

My eyes shot over the first sentence of Chapter 1.

> You don't know about me without you have read a book
> by the name of *The Adventures of Tom Sawyer*; but that
> ain't no matter.

2

Geocaching

On the bottom of the first page of *Huckleberry Finn* was the first clue. The "hunt" in "hunted" was highlighted yellow. I flipped the page. On the next page, "er" in "Huckleberry" was highlighted. Put them together and they made

63

"hunter." Maybe that was me, the treasure hunter. Whatever, it didn't mean much. I went back to the start of Chapter 1 and started reading.

I didn't get far before I realized I didn't like the story. The language was kind of hillbilly, and the kid telling the story, Huck Finn, seemed like a loser, starting on page one. I mean, he believes everyone lies, and he doesn't even think it's bad. Okay, I wasn't one to talk about lying, but at least I knew it was bad. Huck also smoked, wanted to go to "the bad place" (to hell instead of heaven), and said the N-word like some people say "like." On page six he says the N-word seven times. And Huck wasn't just a bad character; he was so fickle his nickname could've been Switchback. I mean, one minute he believes every stupid idea Tom Sawyer puts in his head, like why they need to form a gang of murdering outlaws, and the next minute Huck's having deep thoughts about prayer and saying "there ain't nothing in it."

All this happened in the first eleven pages. If you ask me, Huck was a total fred and a jerk. I got why *Huckleberry Finn* was a banned book. Mark Twain was a crappy writer and the story sucked. There's no way I would've kept reading if it weren't for my father and the clues I was supposed to find. And yeah, I was wondering if my father was a few links short of a full chain.

I kept reading. On page fourteen, I found the next clue. It was big. There was a highlighted part at the end of the chapter. It's after Tom Sawyer tells Huck about rubbing genies out of magic lamps, and how they make your wishes come true. Huck does an experiment to see if there's any truth to it. The highlighted part was when Huck says:

> I got an old tin lamp and an iron ring, and went out in the woods and rubbed and rubbed till I sweat like an Injun, calculating to build a palace and sell it: but it warn't no use, none of the genies come. So then I judged that all that stuff was just one of Tom Sawyer's lies.

Why were those words highlighted? The answer was on the next page. In the space above Chapter 4 my father had written a poem in his barely readable scrawl.

Huck might judge that Tom S. lies,
But "genies" do live in da skies.
They fly in "lamps"—more or less—
Satellites with GPS.
Get a device, your "iron ring,"
Then geocache, that's the thing.
Read Huck Finn to map and measure,
And Genie-PS to find your treasure.

I knew a lot of lingo from moving around, but I'd never heard "geocache." I knew about GPS; it was the navigation system we didn't have in our car, and never would because Mom said we already had GPS. Our "God Positioning System" she called it.

I was going to need some help. I tucked the *Huck Finn* pages in the Bible and turned to Ben. He was watching

Narnia while bobbing his head to the music from his iPod. I tapped him on the arm.

He pulled out his earbud. "Wha'?"

"Do you know what geocache is?"

"Huh?"

"Geocache."

"Geocaching, sure, dude. It's how you get techies who are paler than vampires to go outside and catch some rays."

"Seriously, what is it?"

"Why do you wanna know?"

"I just read about it."

He glanced at the Bible on the seat. "Geocaching in the Bible. Never knew."

I laughed. "No, no, in another book."

"Geocaching is treasure hunting for science geeks," he said. "But they don't find treasure, they find worthless stuff, like key chains and other junk."

"How does it work?"

"They go to a website, get the longitude and latitude co-ordinates of"—he air-quoted—"a 'geocache' that someone has hidden, and they use a GPS device to wander around till they find the coordinates and the cache. It's usually a can with some trinket in it. Then they scurry back to their computers, go online, and brag about their find."

"Sounds totally lame," I said, trying to seem disappointed.

"Totally. Any more questions? Secret of the universe? Why God hates us?"

"No, that's it. Thanks."

He jammed his earbud back in.

I figured he might watch me after that. I didn't want him seeing the *Huck Finn* pages and asking questions. I waited until he was back into the movie and his music, and re-opened the Bible to the *Huck* pages.

I reread my father's poem and it made more sense. He was telling me to get a GPS device and use it to look for a geocache. That was how he'd hidden the bad book. But if GPS was going to be my "genie" and lead me to the treasure, there had to be more clues. One of the poem's last lines said, "Read *Huck Finn* to map and measure."

I flipped through the rest of the pages. I found another highlighted word: "can." A few pages later, the "sus" in "missus" was highlighted. "Can" and "sus" didn't make any sense. Then I remembered how I'd put "hunt" and "er" together. "Can" and "sus" together made "cansus." Kansas. It only took a second to switch gears. My father wasn't calling me a hunter. He was pointing me to a town: Hunter, Kansas. The treasure he wanted to give me, the bad book, was there.

Just one problem: the bus was headed east on I-70, across Missouri, away from Kansas. And another: Hunter could be a big town; a book could be anywhere. If geo-caching was like Ben said, with longitude and latitude, there had to be more clues.

I kept flipping pages. I found highlighted letters, num-bers, syllables, and punctuation. I wrote each one down in the Bible. They added up to *N 39 14.011 lat, W 098*

23.679 long. "Lat" and "long" had to be short for "latitude" and "longitude." They were the exact coordinates in Hunter, Kansas, of where my father had hidden the book!

Back to mondo problem #1: I was getting farther away from Kansas. And new, mondo problem #2: I didn't have a GPS device, much less know where to get one or how to use it.

I was at a fork in the trail and had to choose a track. Take the safe one: go to Bible camp, go home, save up till I could fix my bike, buy a GPS device, jump on my steed, and ride to Hunter, Kansas? Or take the gonzo track: leap off the bus, buy a GPS device with my camp money—if I had enough—and hitchhike to Hunter? I liked the gonzo track except for the hitchhiking. I'd heard so many horror stories from Mom, I thought hitchhiking was another word for suicide. And what good was treasure if I ended up being an organ donor in some pervert's trunk?

Then it hit me. Maybe God had something to say about it. I went for one of Mom's providence checks. I shut my eyes and prayed till I felt the Spirit. I opened the Bible, finger-planted on a page, and looked. I choked back a laugh. My finger touched a verse in Mark. *Honor your father and your mother; and Whoever curses father or mother shall be put to death.* Talk about a weird sign. If I honored my father and ran away to Hunter, I'd dishonor my mom. If I honored my mom by going to Bible camp, and ignored my father and the inheritance he left me, I'd dishonor my father. If God was telling me anything it was *I'm on the fence, kid. Your call.*

68

I knew the track I had to take. It was just a matter of waiting for the right moment to make my move.

As I waited, I started reading *Huck Finn,* picking up where I'd stopped in Chapter 4. It was kind of freaky. Huck's father shows up out of nowhere, like my father had. But the similarity ended there. Huck's dad, Pap, is a drunken bum who beats his son. He kidnaps Huck and holds him prisoner in a log cabin until Huck escapes, and then Huck fakes his own death so nobody will come after him. I wasn't going to fake my death, but I was going to make sure nobody came after me.

3

My Getaway

After *Narnia* ended, Brother Jeremy announced that we were stopping at a truck stop. He told us to buddy up with someone and stretch our legs. We were to stick with our buddy and return to the bus in ten minutes. Ben and I buddied up. When I grabbed my backpack, he asked me why I needed it. I told him I was carrying so much money I took it everywhere.

"You didn't take it to the bathroom," he said.

"That's 'cause I knew you'd watch it for me," I said. We got off the bus.

Inside the truck stop, I steered Ben to the DVD racks and told him I wanted to buy him a DVD for lending me his player. I gave him fifteen bucks and said I was going to the restroom. When he brought up the buddy system I told him it was for little kids. He gave me a "whatever" shrug and went back to the DVDs.

I found a side door and slipped outside. In the parking lot there was an SUV with a tangle of bikes on a rear rack. I undid two straps and pulled down a Diamondback. The seat was too low; it didn't matter. As I ripped across the lot I was out of the cockpit and pumping hard.

My plan was simple. Find a small highway heading west and ride until I could do two things: (1) Buy a map and a GPS device, and (2) When I was far enough away, start hitchhiking.

I felt bad about nabbing someone's steed. I told myself there were so many bikes, and the car was so big and chichi, buying another Diamondback wasn't going to kill them. But it didn't make me feel better, or make me forget that I was busting another commandment: Thou shall not steal.

The thing about trail rides, even a roadie-run on stolen treads, is that the track is always going to throw you a few death cookies you don't expect. The first one hit me as I climbed the overpass above the interstate and looked back at the truck stop. A man in a Hawaiian shirt was running across the parking lot. He wasn't jogging like he'd forgotten his wallet. He was running like he'd seen a punk steal a bike off his SUV. He jumped in the SUV; it jackrabbited forward.

I topped the overpass and bombed the hill on the other side. There was no way I was going to outrun an SUV. I had to disappear before he hit the top of the overpass and

70

got me in his sights. I screamed toward a big service center at the bottom of the hill. The huge neon sign on the roof flashed 1-7-OASIS—FEED UP FUEL UP.

I carved around the back, power-slid to a big Dumpster, and popped off. I lifted the bike and pushed it over the rim of the Dumpster. The bike disappeared and crashed on the bottom.

I looked around. No one had heard it. My first instinct was to climb up and jump in after the bike, but it seemed too obvious. Hawaiian-shirt might find his bike, but he couldn't find me.

I spotted metal rungs running up the back of the service center. They led to the flat roof. I ran over and climbed so fast my backpack trampolined on my back. Halfway up, I saw the SUV tear past the service center. The driver hadn't seen me turn off behind it.

I swung onto the roof and scooted through the poles under the 1-7-Oasis sign. I hunkered down behind the low wall and looked across the highway. I could see the truck stop on the other side and the bus. Kids were gathered around it. Brother Jeremy was pacing; once in a while he'd throw an arm at Ben. Ben just stood there, his head hanging. He might've been crying, because he kept wiping his face.

I suddenly felt meaner than Case and the R-boys put together. They'd only tacoed my front rings and given me a crappy name. Poor Ben was thinking that because he'd let me out of his sight, I'd been pervert-snatched and stuffed in a car and would soon be maggot meat.

A girl ran off the bus with a piece of paper. It was the

71

note I'd tucked in my seatback for someone to find. It was to Mom, telling her I'd run away to visit my father's grave in New Orleans, and to find out what I could about his life. I picked New Orleans because it would steer them away from Kansas. New Orleans was also a sinful place, the kind of place a Mark Twain idol worshipper like my father might've lived. Mom would buy it.

When Brother Jeremy finished reading the note, he put a hand to his face. I imagined it was getting redder by the minute. Then he looked in my direction.

I was so jittery I ducked behind the wall, like he could actually spot my cranium poking over it. I kicked myself for being so paranoid and looked over the edge. He was holding a hand to his ear, like he was on a cell phone. I hoped he wasn't calling my mom so soon.

I hadn't thought that part through. I'd been so mad at her I hadn't pictured her hearing that I'd run away. It made me feel like the meanest kid in the world. A couple nights earlier she'd told me I was the candle she wanted to shine on the world. And here I was, about to run away on a trip that might snuff her candle out. Even if I made it back to Independence, her worrying and fearing would carve her up big-time. With all that guilt carving *me* up part of me wanted to jump up, wave my arms, and scream, *Here I am! Ha-ha! Big joke! Fooled ya!*

But I didn't, for another reason: the Golden Rule. Do unto others as you would have them do unto you. Mom followed the rule; so did I. And if she could rob me of a dad for sixteen years, I could rob her of her little shining candle for a couple days.

72

A car gunned up to the gas pumps in front of the Oasis. It was the SUV. I watched the man get out and talk to a service guy: probably asking if anyone had seen a kid on a bike. He didn't look like he was getting the answers he wanted. He threw up his hands, got back in his SUV, and slammed the door.

As he drove back up the overpass, I noticed a group of people, a mom and three kids, standing in the parking lot. When the SUV reached the group the man gestured at them. They all got in and the SUV headed back toward the interstate.

I was right about one thing: they had enough money to lose a bike, and vacation on. It didn't make me feel less rotten about stealing some kid's steed. But it was too late to do anything about it. I was a liar, a runaway, and a thief. I'd sunk as low as Huck Finn.

The wail of sirens froze me. That's who Brother Jeremy had called: the cops. The sirens came from all directions. One cruiser came down the interstate and zoomed off the exit toward the truck stop. Another came up from behind the truck stop and was the first to get to the bus and Brother Jeremy. Then a third squad car came flying down I-70 from the other direction, took the exit under my nose, and shot across the overpass.

The first cop started talking to Brother Jeremy. When the other two got there, one spoke to Ben, and the other talked to the kids. They were probably getting a description. Ben might remember what I was wearing. Even though my clothes were in my suitcase, I'd stuffed a last-minute T-shirt in my backpack. I dug it out, stripped off my blue

73

button-down, and put on the T-shirt. With cops all over, grabbing the bike out of the Dumpster and riding west would have to wait.

It took an hour before Brother Jeremy stopped talking to the police, making phone calls, and filling out paperwork. The cops covered both sides of the interstate, looking around, talking to people and probably giving them my description. But they never checked the Dumpster, and they never came up on the roof. The bus finally took off for Bible camp. Now they had something else to pray about when they got there: the kid who ran away to sin camp in New Orleans.

I didn't take any chances. I stayed on the hot roof all day. Whenever I moved to stay in the shade of the sign, my sneaks would stick to the tar seams like gum. I didn't have any water, so I ended up with wicked cotton mouth. I fell asleep and woke up to the sound of a fly. It buzzed out of my gaping mouth. If I'd come to any faster I might've gorped it.

Whenever I needed to distract myself from being hungry and thirsty, I read more *Huck Finn* pages. But reading about Huck and the runaway slave, Jim, hanging out together on Jackson's Island only reminded me how much better they had it than being stuck on a tar roof in the middle of a Midwestern heat wave. They were on an island in the Mississippi River, and had all sorts of berries, food, and plenty of water. But then Jim did get bitten by a rattlesnake and got drunk as part of his cure. My hideout only had tar snakes that smacked at my sneakers. The Diamondback I wanted to get to was down in the Dumpster.

Every once in a while, I checked to make sure the bike

was still there. It was, and getting covered in layers of trash. My new plan was simple. In the morning, I'd wait until there was traffic, dig the bike out from the garbage bags and old auto parts, and start riding west on small highways. After I'd bought a map and a GPS device and gotten far enough away from the exit where I'd disappeared, I'd dump the bike and start hitchhiking.

That night, by the glow of neon, I started the last *Huck Finn* chapter I had. In Chapter 11, Huck goes sketchy. He disguises himself as a girl to try to find out what's going on in his hometown.

I got sleepy before I finished the chapter, but it made me say a little prayer before hitting the z-bag under the neon and the stars. *Lord, in my adventure over the next couple days, if I turn into a total weenie and put on a dress, have no mercy. Zap me with one of Your supernova-hot, jagged-judgment bolts.* I mean, I'd robe-up and become a Muslim before I'd put on a dress.

4

My Raft

Clanging metal jolted me awake. Hearing the grinding whine of hydraulics I jumped up and ran to the back of the roof. The sky was graying up. The neon sign threw light on what was making the racket. The Dumpster was getting pulled onto a truck's skid-bed. It was stealing my bike! Okay, not *my* bike.

I grabbed my backpack and started down the ladder. Whoever was working the winch loading the Dumpster onto the skid-bed was on the other side of the truck. I jumped from the last two rungs, ran to the rising Dumpster, and threw my backpack over the side. I clambered after it and into the Dumpster. When the tilting Dumpster banged down on the skid, I dropped between a wedge of garbage bags. Something hard jabbed me in the back. I rolled and felt it: a bike pedal.

The winch went silent; so did I. The last thing I needed was the driver thinking I was a raccoon or a big rat in his Dumpster. Then it hit me there might be *real* rats in there with me. It smelled like rat heaven: a swirling cloud of french fries, fried chicken, and sour milk. Under the low idle of the diesel, I heard the driver walk around the truck, get in the cab, and shut the door. So far, no stowaway coons or rats, just me. The truck ground into gear and jerked forward. I wasn't hitchhiking, and it was no raft, but it would do.

I lay on my garbage-bag mattress and watched street-lights flicker off as the sky brightened. Whenever we stopped at a light, the smell of old food swirled into my nostrils. With each stop it smelled less old. Me and mom had never been so poor or so hungry as to go Dumpster dining, but I hadn't eaten in almost twenty-four hours, and my throat was so smack-cotton dry, I was ready to stick a straw in a mud puddle.

I tore open garbage bags and looked for food scraps. I found a take-out box of uneaten ribs someone had forgotten to take out, half a baked potato still in tinfoil—but no

76

sour cream—and a big Slurpee cup two-thirds full of soda. It wasn't the Feast of Faith doughnut spread, but it tasted like a feast. Besides, Dumpster dining was in the Bible. They didn't call it that—no Dumpsters back then—but they always left the fallen bits of the harvest in the fields for the poor people to "glean." I told myself I wasn't Dumpster dining, I was doing some latter-day gleaning.

After we turned onto a highway, I cleared trash off the bike and pulled it to the top. I found my backpack; it had a black stain where it had come to rest against a box of discarded oil filters. I checked inside, and some of the waste oil had spread onto the leather Bible. The pages were now a mix of gilt-edged and oil-edged. I grabbed a rag and wiped off as much as I could. I'd broken enough commandments without turning the Good Book into the Gunk Book.

We turned off the highway and headed for a big landfill. I two-shouldered my backpack and got the bike into position. The truck backed up to the dumping area and stopped. I waited for the driver to get out and gave him a few seconds to walk around to the controls on the other side.

I must've waited too long, because the hydraulics suddenly kicked in. I lifted the bike and dropped it over the side. The Dumpster started to tilt. I hoisted myself over the edge and jumped backward, making sure to clear the bike.

"Jesus!" someone shouted in a high voice.

Between the voice scaring me and the weight of my pack, I landed off balance and back-stacked. More surprising was the driver on my side of the truck working controls. *Most* surprising was the driver being a she: a short woman with tattoos covering her thick arms.

"How long you been in there?" she asked, her eyes bulging.

I jumped up. "Just for breakfast." I snatched the bike off the ground and popped on. "Thanks for the ride!" I hammered away. If she said anything it was drowned out by the sound of the garbage sliding out of the Dumpster.

I hit a highway called WW and headed away from the sunrise. I had to go west and needed a map of Kansas. I had no idea how far Hunter was. The first gas station I passed was closed. The sun was still shining up the rolling farmland.

After an hour, I rode into Columbia, Missouri. I stopped at a 24-Hour Petro Mart and bought a Kansas map. I took it outside and looked in the index for Hunter. It was a tiny town in the center of the state. I figured it was about four hundred miles away. It was a long day of hitchhiking or I could bike there in three to four days. As long as I didn't have to ride through Independence and get nailed by Mom, or picked up by the cops.

I went back inside the Petro Mart and asked the whiskery old man at the counter, "Do you have GPS things?"

"No," he said, giving me a cockeyed look. "You'll have to go to Bass Pro on the north side of Seventy."

As I was leaving he pointed outside at my bike. "You gonna ride that all the way to Kansas?"

My stomach wonked. What if the old guy had seen my picture on the news? Now he knew I was headed west and he might tell the police. "Nah," I told him, "I'm just on a scavenger hunt with some buddies. I gotta find a Kansas map and borrow a GPS thing." It was a lie I thought Huck Finn might be proud of.

I crossed the interstate. The Bass Pro Shop was a giant wooden building the size of an airplane hangar. I rode past a parking lot filled with fishing boats and hid the bike behind the building. I didn't have a lock; the last thing I needed was someone stealing my stolen steed.

I found the electronics department and got a guy to show me their cheapest GPS device. I barely had enough money; it cleaned me out. I wasn't worried. No matter how long it took to get to Hunter, I wouldn't starve. Once you've eaten at McDumpster's, you know where to find a Crappy Meal.

Outside, the lot was filling up. Going back around the building, I did a panic skid in my sneaks. There was a police car cruising the lot like the cop was looking for something, or someone. I put it together in a flash. The old guy at the Petro Mart *had* seen my picture, called the cops, and told them I might be at Bass Pro.

I did a one-eighty and started the other way. I glanced back and saw the cop car doing its own one-eighty. Luckily, he hadn't checked behind the building and found my bike. But he was coming my way again. I had to hide. There were no ladder rungs leading up the side of Bass Pro. The only way to get on the roof was to go back inside and buy climbing equipment.

Then I spotted a second cop car coming from the other end of the lot. They were closing on me like a vise. I slid back into the store and looked for another exit. It was just a matter of time before the cops came inside. I slipped out a side entrance into another lot. It was for campers and big RVs.

I ran between RVs, using them for cover till I could get to the woods and hide. Reaching the end of the RV alley, I peeked around a camper. One of the cop cars was cruising toward me. He didn't see me, but I had to disappear, quick.

I backtracked and checked the doors on RVs. All locked. I came to a small camper that looked like a puffy white mail truck. I tried the side door. It opened. I slipped inside and shut the door. It was empty. I had no idea when the owners would be back: minutes or hours.

My heart almost locked up as the front of the cop car nosed into view through the windshield. I scrunched down in the narrow aisle. There was a door next to me. I waited a few seconds for the car to pass, then opened the door. Inside was a tiny bathroom. I scooted in, shut the door, and sat on the toilet.

5

Behind the Wheel

Sitting in the closet-bathroom, it felt like time had stopped, like I was holding my breath. I tried to look at the upside. If I had to hide there all morning at least I had a pot to piss in.

Just when I was thinking it might be safe to slip out and sneak a look through the camper windows, an explosion made me jump. The driver's side door had opened. I listened for the other door, or kids coming in the rear side door. Nothing. The door thudded shut. The engine revved to life, the transmission clunked into gear. The room lurched forward.

The bathroom had transformed into my second "raft" of the day. But I had no clue where it was going. I felt the camper drop down a hill. A few seconds later the room jerked to a stop. I grabbed the sink so I didn't slide off the toilet. Fear shot through me, like a wave of heat between my scalp and my skull. What if the driver had figured out that I was in the bathroom? The room jumped forward again. I looked through the only window: a small skylight over the tiny shower. A stoplight arced through it. I had to hold on again as we took a couple corners. It felt like we were driving in circles. Then we shot down a hill, up another, and started picking up speed. I heard a semi roar by. It seemed like the camper had gotten on I-70. But which direction: east or west? As the tiny room bounced along, sunlight beamed through the skylight. It hit the mirror at the front of the room. The sun, still climbing in the east, was behind us. I was heading west!

As the camper reached cruising speed, my escape pod settled into a vibrating drone. The sunlight also lit up a little shelf above the sink. Behind a rail keeping things from falling was a row of stuff: toothpaste, mouthwash, deodorant, hand cream, aftershave—okay, my driver was a guy. But the last items on the shelf, three cans of shaving cream, got me thinking. Great, I thought, the guy with his hairy knuckles on the wheel is a Neanderthal. Or someone trying to shave away the fact that he's a werewolf.

I was tempted to open the door, sneak a peek, and see if God was punishing me by putting me in a camper with a werewolf who cruises around looking for boys to fatten up and scarf down when they're plump and juicy. I didn't touch the door. If he saw me and kicked me out, I'd be a sitting duck for the cops. I had to stick with hairy whoever for as long as I could, even if he was Bigfoot.

I pulled the GPS device out of my backpack and unwrapped it. I put the batteries in, fired it up, and held it in my armpit in case it beeped. It didn't. While it searched for satellites, I read the manual and learned about entering a destination, or waypoint. I pulled out my Bible, opened it to the page I'd written the coordinates on, and entered the latitude and longitude into the GPS: N 39° 14.011, W 098° 23.679. I hit Goto. A screen flashed up telling me I was 312 miles from the spot as the crow flies. The electronic compass arrow pointed almost due west. The miles number clicked down. I was definitely going in the right direction and getting closer to where my father had stashed my inheritance.

As I watched the miles tick down, the vibrating drone and heat in the tiny room made me drowsy. I fought off sleep. My head bumped against the wall. In the end, I leaned into the black pillow of the z-bag.

My eyes twitched open. After a nanosecond of confusion, came recognition: the bathroom, my skin clammy with sweat. But the vibration and drone were gone. It was still and quiet. I heard footsteps. They came closer. There was no time to throw open the door and dive out the camper's side door. I could only pray that the footsteps would stop,

the side door would open, and the driver would step outside. But God had answered too many of my prayers for
one day.

The handle turned. The door swung open. I stared up at
a towering, twentysomething black guy. I screamed.

He screamed.

I jumped up. The door slammed shut.

"Shit!" he yelled.

The door opened again.

The door opening-shutting-opening had been like a fan
hitting my sticky skin with cool air. But why did my lap
feel like it was on fire? I looked down. My blue jeans dark-
ened with a growing stain.

I looked up at the man's shaved head, his stubble of a
beard. His face was widening, flashing big white teeth. He
burst out laughing. Between eruptions he shouted, "I'm glad
to see—ha-ha!—that you're more scared—ha-ha-ha!—than
me!" In the middle of another booming laugh, he suddenly
stopped and threw up a giant hand. With his fingers
stretched wide, his hand almost spanned the width of the
narrow doorway. "Don't move!" he ordered. "Better to
piss in one spot than spray the field."

I didn't budge. Not because he said so. The sight of his
open hand pinned me there, same as if he'd slammed me
against the wall. It wasn't because it was big as a dinner
plate; it was the calluses. I'd seen calluses before but they
were mosquito bites compared to his. He had a mountain
range of calluses.

He glanced down at the puddle around my sneaks.
"Looks like you're done. Go ahead, step outside." He

opened the side door, dipped his bald head, and jumped to the ground like a big cat. I realized why all the shaving cream: he was a head shaver.

I grabbed my backpack and jumped out. I hit the ground and didn't look back. I moved down a gravel road in the middle of wide-open nowhere. I heard an eighteen-wheeler's diesel stacks in the distance. Beyond a green corn-field, cars zipped along the interstate.

"Where you going?" the man called after me. "You can't just piss in my RV and walk away." I kept moving. "I'm not asking you to clean it up. I'm asking for an explanation."

I turned, walking backward. "I needed a ride. Thanks."

"Do you know where you are?"

He had a point. I stopped. I didn't know how long I'd been asleep. I looked around. Except for some trees in a creek bed, there was nothing but fields of soybeans and corn, and low hills in the distance. "Where am I?"

"Kansas. Just past Topeka."

"Really?" I couldn't believe it. I'd been asleep for almost two hundred miles. Maybe there was a little Rip van Winkle in me after all.

"Where you trying to get to?"

I glanced toward the distant highway. "To my next ride."

He took a step toward me.

I backed up, ready to run.

He stopped, holding up his hands again. "Look, you're not gettin' a ride with piss-stained jeans and smelling like a bum. Why don't we clean up your mess, rinse out your clothes, and you can ride with me a ways? You can even sit in a seat instead of on the can."

I stared at him. I was thinking that anyone who acted so nice after someone pissed in his camper must have something up his sleeve.

"Besides," he added, "if you try to hitch on the interstate the state troopers will grab you."

He kept making sense, but I still didn't trust him.

He looked up and down the deserted road. A gust of wind rattled the corn. "And I don't see a lot of prospects here."

I didn't move.

His long arms flapped at his sides. "Alright, here's the thing. I pulled off the highway to take a piss, and I almost did before you beat me to it."

I held back a smile.

"Now I can't use my own bathroom." He flapped his arms again. "So what I'm gonna do is step into the woods, then get back in my ride and keep heading west. If you want a lift, you're more than welcome. If you don't, then hit the interstate and see if you can do better than a brother in a wide ride." He started toward the creek bed, then turned back. "Oh, and it was nice screaming with you."

I couldn't fight off smiling at that. Luckily, he'd turned and disappeared into the trees.

If it weren't for reading the beginning of *Huck Finn*, I probably never would've gotten back in that camper. But standing there at another fork in my trail, I figured it wasn't a coincidence. It was either the spirit of my father having a little fun with me, or it was God working in His weird way. Mark Twain had put Huck on a raft with a runaway slave; and God, for whatever reason, had put me in a camper with a black dude.

6

Cat and Mouse

As he mopped the bathroom, I got a better look at his "wide ride." It was a little apartment on wheels. Opposite the bathroom was a closet, the rear side door, a kitchen with a mini-fridge, a stove, and a patch of countertop. In front of that was a booth like in a diner, with windows. Across the narrow aisle was a couch. Above the driver and passenger seats was a sleeping loft. Mom should've gotten one of these. It could've been the New J-Brigade's home and getaway vehicle all in one.

The man gave me a pair of his long cargo shorts and left me inside to wash up and change. The shorts were too big, but I rolled them up till they fit. I used the chance to pull out my GPS device, and check how far I was from Hunter: 133 miles.

I bungee-corded my rinsed-out jeans to the bike on the back of the camper to dry. The license plate was a Pennsylvania one, but the real jaw-dropper was the bike. It was a roadie, a super-pricey Trek. He was either some rich poser, or he really spoiled himself when it came to his steed.

After getting back on the interstate, we kept it to small

talk. Then he asked the question I knew he was going to pop sooner or later. "How old are you?"

"Eighteen," I answered.

He chuckled. "If you're eighteen, I'm thirty-five."

He didn't look thirty-five. More like *twenty*-five. He glanced over. His eyes were hidden behind wraparound sunglasses. I could see myself in the mirrored lenses. I was all distorted from the fish-eye effect. My head was so huge and my body so tiny, I looked like a baby.

He turned back front. "What's your name?"

"Billy."

"I'm Sloan." He extended his hand.

I stared at his calluses for a sec, then shook his hand. He had the grip of a boa constrictor, or one of those animals like a hippo or a croc that grabs their prey and holds them underwater till they drown.

"Where you headed?" he asked.

"Hunter. It's a little town in the middle of the state."

"What's there?"

"My father."

He nodded. "So whenever you wanna visit him you get there by stowing away in somebody's RV."

I swallowed. "I usually take the bus."

"Why didn't you take it this time?"

I didn't have an answer. "I'd rather not talk about it."

He threw me a look. "Fair enough. Life would be a bust without secrets." He dug in the pocket of his shorts. "If you wanna ride with me for a bit there's one thing you gotta do."

"What?"

He pulled out a cell phone and put it on the console between the seats. "Call your mother, or whoever you live with, and tell 'em you're safe."

"My mom doesn't have a phone." Even though I was finally telling the truth it sounded like a lie. "We just moved to In . . . into Columbia and we don't have one yet."

He studied me from behind his shades. "Right. There's a town coming up at the next exit. If you don't make the call I'm pulling off and taking you to the police station."

I zipped open my backpack, pried out the Bible, and slapped my hand on it. "I swear to God she doesn't have a phone yet."

He gave me a weird smile.

My stomach gripped up as the exit approached. He sailed past it. "Thanks." I felt like I owed him an explanation. "My mom hates my dad and hates me visiting him. I heard from my uncle that my dad's dying." The words were still riding the air as I flashed on my father turning the knob on the tube, ending his life. Feelings chunged up inside me, but I smooshed them down and went on. "Even with him dying, my mom wouldn't buy me a ticket. That's why I'm hitching."

His eyebrows popped up. "Stowing away in an RV isn't hitching."

"I know, but I wasn't getting a ride. I remembered how hobos used to ride freight trains. I figured I'd try it with a camper."

"Okay, I'm buying," he said. "But how'd you know I was headed west?"

"I didn't. But when I saw your Pennsylvania plates, and that the bike on the back was a way expensive Trek, I figured whoever was driving it had to be rich people traveling west." I was stunned how my lies kept flowing. I figured it was because I'd been reading *Huck Finn*, which is pretty much a how-to book on lying.

"But I could've just as easily been headed back east," he said.

"If you were, then you never rode the bike once. It's a total cleanie."

He laughed. "Pretty good detective work."

"Thanks."

We drove without talking for a bit. A sign said we were in the Flint Hills. The highway rose and fell like a black inchworm crawling across Kansas. Tractors moved across dusty gold fields harvesting wheat. The silence felt weirder than not talking. "Can I ask you a question?"

He shrugged. "Long as I have the same right not to talk about some things."

"Sure." I pointed at his hands. "Why are your hands like that?"

He lifted one off the wheel and opened his plate-sized hand. "Melanin."

I squinted with confusion. "Melanin?"

"It's what makes me black and you white." He said it as casual as saying what he'd had for breakfast. "My skin's packed with melanin to stop the African sun from burning it up and giving me skin cancer. Yours is white so the weak northern sun can get to your skin and supply you with vitamin D and a bunch of other good stuff. The only reason my palms and the bottom of my feet aren't black is because the sun doesn't hit me there."

I half smiled. "That's not what I was asking about. I was asking about your calluses. I've never seen so many."

"Oh, these," he said, flexing his fingers. "I get 'em in my line of work."

"What's that?"

"I'm an entertainer. Mostly in casinos and on cruise ships. I'm a juggler."

"What do you juggle to get calluses like that?"

"Big stuff. From baseball bats to chain saws. Sometimes I even juggle chairs."

I looked back into the little apartment behind us. It was kind of messy, with some clothes thrown around, but I didn't see anything you might juggle. "Where's your juggling stuff?"

"I'm on vacation. Jugglers need vacations too."

"Where are you going?"

"For now, as you deduced, detective, west." He patted the dashboard. "That's the great thing about an RV. You can just hop in and blow with the wind."

For a while the only sound was the drone of the engine and wind-rush through the open windows. Purple clover spilled over stone outcropping on each side of the road. The hills were sparse and green, and the only trees had slid into the creek bottoms. We passed a barn with big white letters proclaiming NO GOD, NO PEACE. KNOW GOD, KNOW PEACE.

He chuckled. "I was wondering if we were in God's country. Now it's a fact."

He said it kind of sarcastic, like he was a nonbeliever. He'd seen my Bible; he knew I was a Christian. If he wanted to start some religious debate, I wasn't taking the bait.

"So, where is Hunter exactly?" he asked.

I was glad I'd studied my map earlier. If I didn't know where Hunter was my story about my dad would've been a bust. "West of Salina," I said. "Exit two-oh-nine."

"On the interstate?"

"No, Hunter's about twenty-five miles north."

"Tell you what," he said. "I'll take you to your exit on one condition."

I shrugged, trying not to look too excited about getting another hundred miles out of the ride. "What's that?"

"When we get there you call four-one-one and see if your mom has a phone yet. If you've disappeared I'm sure she's trying to get a phone."

"Okay."

We dropped into another silence.

Even though I'd lived in a lot of places, I was looking at new country. I'd never been this far west, or seen such open land. It wasn't flat exactly. Pale green hills rolled to the horizon, like an endless ruffle of green quilt on a giant bed someone had forgotten to make. It took God six days to make the world. Maybe on one of those nights He had slept here.

7

Hunter

Sloan took Exit 209, turned at the bottom of the ramp, and pulled off the road near a historical marker. I tried to look cool, like I'd seen the road dozens of times. But the road to Hunter was nothing but a rail of blacktop cutting through a patchwork of green corn and tan wheat stubble. The only traffic was a turtle crossing the asphalt.

Sloan got out and unhooked my dried jeans from the bike. He left me inside to change and told me to use his cell phone to call 411. Luckily, there was still no listing for Tilda Allbright. I wasn't ready to talk to her. I wanted to get to Hunter and find the bad book first. Calling her would be a lot easier if I were heading home.

When I got out, Sloan walked back from the historical marker and pointed northwest. "Twenty-seven miles that way is the geodetic center of North America."

"What's that?"

"It's the starting point, the dead center of all the lines and boundaries in the U.S."

"Right." Shouldering my backpack I realized I probably should've known about something so close to Hunter. "I forgot the weird name for it."

"I could run you up to Hunter and then go see it."

I didn't get why he was being so super nice. It made me

92

suspicious. "You don't have to. Some cars will come along soon."

He looked at the turtle, now taking a break in the middle of the road. "That turtle doesn't think so."

I chuckled. "I know it doesn't look it, but people do live around here."

"I'm sure they do, but I came out here to see the country. And you can't say you've seen Middle America until you've seen the true *middle* of America. C'mon, I'll drop you in Hunter on the way."

I looked at the turtle. It was back to inching across the blacktop. And not because a car was coming. "Alright."

The road north was like a roller coaster for eighty-year-olds. We did whoop-de-doos over the rises. Coming up over some of them you felt like you were on top of the world. You could see fields and rangeland for miles and miles. And there was another sign that the road was always empty. The mourning doves and other birds on the blacktop were so unused to traffic they waited till the last second to spring into flight.

Sloan asked me questions about my dad. I made up a story about how he used to have a farm, but lost it, then drove harvesting equipment for other farmers until he retired. I was totally Hucking-up.

As we got close to Hunter it was way past lunch and my stomach started growling. Stomach growling is like the yawning thing: you can pass it on. I heard Sloan's stomach too.

"Is there any place to eat in Hunter?" he asked.

"Ah"—I fumbled for an answer—"I don't think so."

"What do you mean you don't think so?"

"Last time I was there, there was a diner, but I think it was about to close."

"Well, if you're starved you can hop in the back and make a peanut butter and jelly."

Even though my stomach sounded like the cat house at the zoo, I didn't go for his offer. It didn't fit my story. "Nah, I'll wait and get something at my dad's."

We crossed railroad tracks and drove into Hunter. It looked like a ghost town. Main Street was a short stretch of run-down, empty buildings. My fib about the diner was almost true. The Hunter Café had an old sign saying it was moving across the street, but it hadn't survived there, either. The only building with a car in front was a post office not much bigger than the stamps it sold. And there was a tiny museum called Yesterday House.

"Huh," Sloan grunted, "looks like they should rename Hunter 'Yesterday Town.'"

"Yeah," I said, "it's not much, but my dad has always liked it here." It was hard acting sad about seeing my dying dad when all I wanted to do was snatch the GPS out of my backpack and follow its compass arrow to the treasure. I pointed to a street with run-down houses and trailers. "That's his street."

As Sloan turned onto it, I looked for a house with no vehicles in front and that wasn't boarded up. I pointed to a paint-chipped house near the end of the street. "That's it."

We stopped in front of a rusty mailbox. The door was flapped open and the box was jammed with uncollected mail. I got out and shouldered my backpack. "Thanks a ton for the ride. I really appreciate you going so far out of your way."

He broke into a friendly smile. "Right now nothing's out of my way. Sometimes you just go where the road leads."

"Yeah," I said, smiling back. "I know what you mean."

He nodded toward the house. "I hope your dad catches a miracle." Then he glanced at the mailbox. "And gets the chance to catch up on his mail." He extended his hand. "Good luck, Billy." I shook it. "Enjoyed your company."

"Me too." My cheeks went hot. It was one of those totally bozo things that had a way of jumping out of my mouth. Did "me too" mean I enjoyed my own company or his?

As Sloan turned the camper around at the end of the street I made a big deal of pulling all the mail out of the mailbox. I waved as he went by. The second the camper disappeared around the corner, I stuffed the mail back in the box.

I pulled out my GPS, turned it on, got satellite, and thumbed to the distance and compass screen. I was four-tenths of a mile from the cache. I knew from the manual that the electronic compass was only good if you were moving. I started walking, and the arrow swung to the right. I walked back to Main Street and followed the compass north. The distance clicked down to 0.2. I thought I was going to walk right out of town, but the arrow started moving right again.

The blast of a horn made my heart almost rocket out of my chest and explode over Hunter in gooey fireworks. My eyes shot up; I dodged a huge harvesting machine hogging the road. It was my first lesson in geocaching: eyes-on-screen-not-on-trail gets you buried but no treasure.

I kept walking till the compass arrow pointed dead right, to a patch of green with a carved stone sign: HUNTER CITY PARK. The GPS distance number was down to several hundred feet. Walking into the park, the feet clicked down like crazy.

I knew from the manual that the GPS was only accurate to about thirty feet; inside that the satellite pinpointing could get blurry. The other problem was the tree cover in the park. It could mess with the satellite reception. I kept losing the signal and having to walk around till I picked it up again. The closest I got to the waypoint, where the cache was supposed to be, was in the middle of a grassy area. I couldn't believe my father would have actually buried the bad book. It would've been way too hard to find, and books don't do well underground.

I went over to an old wooden merry-go-round, sat down, and got out my *Huck Finn* pages. I wanted to double-check to make sure I'd entered the exact coordinates that had been highlighted in the pages. As I flipped through the pages, I accidentally dropped the last one. The wind started blowing it across the grass. I chased it down and stepped on it.

Lifting it up, I thought it was the first page because my father's scrawly handwriting was on it. But it wasn't his first poem. It was a *second* one, written on a page I hadn't read: the last page of Chapter 11. I read the poem.

When Huck slips into girls' attire,
Things really begin to misfire.
He's such a mess as a miss,
You can't trust 'im to take a piss.
He would forget to take a seat,
But stand and shoot like Piss Pot Pete.
So look where genders do part ways,
To find out where your treasure stays.

I didn't have to finish the part where Huck dresses up as a girl to know my father was giving me a major clue. *So look where genders do part ways/To find out where your treasure stays.*

I looked up and saw a small white building across the park. I ran over to it. There were two doors, marked MEN and LADIES. Padlocks were on both doors. I circled around the building. There was nothing that would hide a book. I checked the GPS. I was twenty feet from the geocache. It had to be here somewhere. I looked up. The building's roof was flat. Of course, it was on the roof!

I found the nearest tree and monkey-climbed the trunk. The roof was covered in crappy old leaves, nothing else. I jumped down. The bad book had to be inside one of the restrooms. I had two options: (1) Go find whoever had the keys and explain why I needed to get inside, or (2) beg, borrow, or steal a bolt cutter.

I banged my back against one of the doors, slumped to the ground, and cursed. Why would my father hide it in a place that might be locked up? Why would he force me to bring someone else in on the treasure hunt or break the law? It didn't make sense.

As I sat there fuming, something in a nearby wall of trees and brush caught my eye. A patch of gray. I stood up and walked toward it. I pulled back a branch. There was more gray. It was some kind of wooden shed. The door was gone. I pulled back another low branch and spotted two strange shapes: whitish ovals, like horseshoes. Then I realized they were old toilet seats on open boxes.

I'd seen them in farmyards before but never up close. It was an outhouse, a two-seater. It was the park's men's and women's restroom from another era. It was where "genders part ways" and "treasure stays."

I didn't waste a second wondering about the rules and regs of using a two-seater in another century. I grabbed a stick, cleared the spiderwebs curtaining the door, and stepped inside. Deep shadows filled the corners but I could see shapes. There was a thick beam above the toilet bench. Nothing on it but dust. I spun around. Nothing in the lower walls. I looked up at the support beam above the doorway. An odd-shaped box sat on the beam. I pulled it down, feeling its cool metal. I shook it. Something rattled inside. It felt surprisingly light. Maybe the bad book wasn't as thick as I'd imagined it.

I took the box outside, into a splash of sunlight. It was an old ammo can from the army. I unclipped the lid. Inside were three plastic ziplock bags. I knelt on the grass and pulled them out. Inside one were some twenty-dollar bills. Another held a small plastic toy: a raft with Jim steering and Huck fishing from it. The last bag held a small bundle of pages, beginning with Chapter 12.

My insides ricocheted off one another. I was thrilled I'd found the cache my father had planted; I was crushed that the only book was more *Huck Finn*. It was like Christmas when you open a present and it's not what you'd wanted. I'd expected my treasure, my inheritance. But I'd gotten some pages from an old book, some money, and a kid's toy instead. At least the money would buy the lunch I'd totally forgotten about.

I took the bags to a picnic table and opened the one with the pages. I turned the first one over. On the flip side was a new poem my father had scribbled.

> Wondering why such a place
> Is waypoint one in your chase?
> It's just because, from where I stand,
> I do not know where you began.
> So I did choose the Midwest middle
> In which to plant your next riddle.
> From our nation's belly button,
> You pick more <u>Huck</u>, no homebound
>   glutton.

That was why he'd picked Hunter, Kansas. It was at the center of the huge circle where he thought I might live. He'd only been off by one state and a few hundred miles.

I started flipping through the new *Huck Finn* pages. The first highlighted words were "St. Petersburg." After that came four highlighted words and syllables: "call," "oar," "add," and "o." I put them together. "Call-oar-add-o." Colorado. Maybe that's where my father had lived, and where my treasure was. St. Petersburg, Colorado.

I had to keep going west. But how far? I went through more pages and noted all the highlighted letters and numbers. They added up to N *40° 33.183 lat,* W *102° 49.146 long.* I held down the GPS's thumb stick to set a new waypoint. I entered the coordinates and clicked on Goto. The distance to St. Petersburg, Colorado, flashed up: 241 MILES.

8
Packin'

I walked back through town. I figured I'd hitch back to the interstate, get something to eat, and then hitch as far as I could that day. I also decided to spend some of the five twenties I'd found in the ziplock bag on supplies, starting with a sleeping bag.

I walked out of Hunter and tried to thumb a ride. After a half hour, in which two vehicles blew by me, I spotted a white puffy thing in the distance. It was either a camper exactly like Sloan's or the same one.

One of the cool things about wide-open spaces is that when you see someone you know coming your way, you have plenty of time to make up a story about why you are where you are and not where you said you'd be.

Sloan pulled to a stop and stared at me with a curious expression. "What are you doing here?"

"What are *you* doing here?" I asked back.

"Alright, I'll go first," he said. "When I was looking for the geodetic center of the U.S.—"

"Did you find it?"

"No, it's on someone's ranch, and you can't go there unless you do a song and dance to get permission. Anyway, something kept bugging me. The magazine on the top of the mail in your dad's mailbox was *Glamour*. I didn't picture your dad as a *Glamour* man, so I thought maybe he wasn't there anymore and that was someone else's mail piling up."

"You're right," I said. "He wasn't there anymore."

"Did he go to the hospital?"

"No. I asked one of his neighbors and they said my uncle came and got him. He took my dad to his house in Colorado."

"Really?"

"Really."

After a pause, he asked, "Are you going to Colorado or back to Columbia?"

"I'm not sure. First I wanna get back to the interstate and get something to eat."

He offered me a lift and I gladly took it. As we drove south he must've caught me sucking up the peanut butter smell coming from the back of the camper because he suggested I make a sandwich. I didn't hesitate. It was fun trying to keep the peanut butter and jam jars from sliding off the counter as we drove. I took my sandwich up front; it was the best PB&J I'd ever eaten.

101

When I was done, I told him I'd made up my mind. I was going to Colorado.

He glanced at his cell phone on the console. "If you're going that far, don't you think you should let your mom know?"

"Last time I tried she still hadn't gotten a phone."

"That was a few hours ago." He pushed the phone toward me. "I'm sure she wants to know you're safe."

"What makes you sure I'm safe?" I asked, trying to change the subject. "Colorado's a long ways. Anything could happen."

"True," he said. "But you're safe for now, 'cause I'm packin'."

The hairs on my neck prickled. "You have a gun?"

"Of course." He slipped off his shades and gave me a sketchy look. "Doesn't every black dude? Wanna see it?"

I shook my head. "Not really."

He waved a hand at the glove compartment. "Go ahead. It's in there."

My fingers were sweaty as I pulled the compartment handle and it dropped open. There was no flash of silver or black steel. There was just a worn book. "It's a Bible."

He laughed at his twisted joke. "That's right. You're packin' and I'm packin'. It's the only weapon I'll ever need."

I shut the glove compartment harder than I meant to. "Why'd you do that?"

"You mean freak you out?"

"Yeah."

He slid his sunglasses back on. "I was checkin' you for coolant."

"Coolant?"

"Yeah. You gotta check a radiator to make sure it's got enough coolant. You gotta check a person to see if he's got cool." He smiled. "You got it."

"Thanks. But why do you care if I'm cool?"

"'Cause if I'm gonna drive someone west the rest of the day, they gotta be cool."

"You'd do that?"

"Like I said before, right now I'm just going where the road leads."

I didn't exactly know *who* I was riding with, but the way I looked at it, it didn't matter. If there was one thing I'd learned in those past few days it was this: you can ride with someone all your life and not really know who they are.

9

Busted

I borrowed the road atlas Sloan had in his door pocket and looked in the index for St. Petersburg, Colorado. It wasn't listed. St. Petersburg had to be so tiny, it wasn't on the map. I noticed the latitude and longitude on the edge of the Colorado map and matched them up with what I could remember of the numbers I'd found in the new set of *Huck Finn* chapters. St. Petersburg was somewhere in the northeast corner of the state.

After we got back on I-70, the rumpled quilt of field and rangeland began to smooth out. We were almost to the town of Hays when we stopped for gas. Pulling into a big truck stop, Sloan stopped at the pump farthest from the mini-mart and restaurant. He handed me some cash and asked me to go pay for the gas. I wondered why he didn't use a credit card, and why he wanted me to go inside, but I didn't ask. I had other things to worry about.

I looked up through the windshield. A security camera pointed down at the camper. I didn't know how hard the police and Mom might be looking for me. I pulled my baseball cap out of my backpack and slipped it on. Heading for the mini-mart, I walked toward a woman gassing up her pickup. She stared at the camper. I looked back. Sloan had put on a cowboy hat.

When I passed her, she checked me out, too. For a second I worried she might've seen my picture on the news. But I was three hundred miles west of Independence. TV stations wouldn't be showing my picture that far away. Then I realized she was checking us out because we made a weird pair. In western Kansas, a black dude and a white kid traveling together probably wasn't an everyday event.

I gave the cashier the money. When I got back outside, I was glad to see that the lady was gone. But her pickup still stood at the pumps.

While the camper guzzled octane, Sloan gave me a handful of change. "My cell's not getting a signal. Go find a pay phone and see if you can get through to your mother." I didn't want to call her, but it seemed like he wasn't giving up till I did. "Don't forget my change on the gas," he shouted as I went back inside.

I found a pay phone and dialed 411. Luckily, there was still no listing for Mom. But it was beginning to seem weird. I mean, Sloan had a point. If she was worried about me, why didn't she have a phone yet? I'd been a runaway for over a day.

I heard a TV in the walkway to the restaurant. I went over to make sure they weren't showing me on it.

The TV was turned to a sports report. It showed baseball highlights as a sportscaster rattled off scores. Then a picture of a ballplayer flashed up on the screen. The sportscaster called him "Ruah Branch" and said that he'd been put on the "fifteen-day DL," whatever that was. The player's weird name caught my attention, but it was his picture that froze my blood. It wasn't the red cap with a big C on his head. It wasn't the long dreadlocks spilling out from under the cap. It was the smile splitting his face. I'd been seeing that smile all day.

The TV cut to a commercial.

I jumped as a hand hit my shoulder. It belonged to the woman with the pickup. Her leathery skin was bunched up around a tight smile. "Havin' a nice vacation, sonny?"

"Yes, ma'am." I stepped back, pulling away from her hand. I figured she'd scoped the Pennsylvania plate on the camper.

"That's a smart RV you boys got." She hitched a thumb behind her. "Is that your big brother drivin' it?"

"No, ma'am," I answered with a half laugh. She wasn't

going to catch me on that one. "We're not exactly the same color."

Her smile bent tighter. "You don't say. If he's not kin"—her head cocked—"who is he?"

It was creepy how she kept asking questions. I swallowed to buy time. "He's my coach, my baseball coach," I tried to keep my voice calm and cool. "He's taking me to Bible baseball camp."

Her eyes ratcheted open. "Bible baseball camp? What'll they think of next?"

"I dunno, ma'am. I gotta go."

Her hand shot forward onto my shoulder again. Her grip was as tight as her smile. "What position do you play?"

I was no baseball expert, so I didn't take her bait. "A little of everything."

"You pitch, too?"

"A little of everything," I repeated, wiggling out of her grip.

She eyeballed my long arms. "With those arms, I bet your fastball hits forty miles an hour."

I forced a smile. "On my best days, yeah."

Her look told me I'd fallen for the bait anyway. Her eyes gleamed with excitement. "You're no ballplayer, and he's no coach. I *know* who he is."

I was done being nice. I dodged around her, pushed open the door, and jogged to the camper. "Sloan" was behind the wheel with the motor running. I jumped in. "I know who you are," I blurted, "and so does someone else!"

His reaction blew away any chance he really was Sloan. He threw the RV in gear and took off.

I looked back and saw the lady come outside. She was dialing a cell phone. I didn't know if she was calling the police about me, or some friend to say she'd just gassed up next to a star baseball player.

"Jump in the back," he ordered. "See if anyone follows."

Watching out the back window, no pickup or flashing police car came after us. The camper swerved, and the interstate slid away as we took an exit.

I went back up front. "Where are you going?"

"A little evasive action," he said. "Neither of us wants to get caught, right?"

"Who wants to catch you?"

"Fans. They can be brutal."

"You really are Ruah Branch?"

"Unfortunately, yeah."

At the top of the exit ramp he took a left, heading south. It wasn't the direction I wanted to go, but I wasn't about to argue. When your getaway driver goes off trail, you go with him till you're in the clear.

He must've sensed what I was thinking. "Don't worry," he said, "I'll take the first decent road going west we come to."

I got out the road atlas and checked the map. In a few miles we'd come to a road that would get us to Route 4, which headed straight west, toward Colorado.

I looked at Ruah and decided I'd been cool long enough. "So who are you?"

10

Speaking in Tongues

Ruah chuckled. "You're not a baseball fan, are you?"

"Not really," I said. "I just know you play for a team that's C-something. I don't even know what the C stands for."

"Good."

"I thought famous people wanted all the fans they could get."

"Not me. I don't want people thinking I hung the moon 'cause I can hit a baseball a long way. And it's nice hangin' with someone who isn't pushing stuff at me to sign. To you, I'm just a weird brother in an RV, and I wanna keep it that way. So what happened back there?"

I told him about the sports report on the TV and how it said he was on the DL. He told me "DL" was short for "disabled list." I told him about the woman who grilled me about traveling with him and how I blew my story about being a pitcher going to Bible baseball camp.

"Helluvan effort," he chuckled.

I wanted to change the subject. "Are you really injured?"

"Yeah." He tapped his forehead. "Up here."

"Did you get hit with a baseball?"

He laughed. "*That* I could deal with. Let's just say I've got some screws loose." He must've sensed how that might sound scary to a runaway in his camper because he added,

"Don't worry, kid. My screws are loose in a good way, not a bad way."

"Did the loose screws make you shave your head?" I asked.

"The dreadlocks go with my image. I'm taking a break from my baseball card."

"So you didn't lie."

"What do you mean?"

"You *are* on vacation. And you *do* juggle bats."

He laughed. "Sure, I juggle bats, and your fastball rips along at a wicked forty miles per."

"Hey," I protested, "it sounded fast to me."

"In case you try that one again, at your age you should be throwing it seventy to eighty. Most big leaguers hurl it over ninety."

"Really?"

"Some rip it a hundred."

We reached our turnoff and headed west on the county road that would get us to Route 4.

"Here's what I'd like to know," he said. "What kind of smoke would Christ hurl if He came back and took the mound?"

I grabbed the chance to let Ruah know I wasn't an idiot about everything. "When Christ returns He's not gonna play baseball."

"Don't be so sure. His father pitched. It says it in the Bible: the Lord likes to pitch."

"No, it doesn't."

"I'm not kidding. Hebrews eight, two. *The Lord pitched.* Look it up if you don't believe me."

I started pulling out my Bible.

"Okay-okay." He raised a hand in surrender. "He pitched a *tent,* not a baseball. But I still say T.L. and his son could be the aces on my team."

"Who's T.L.?"

"Short for 'The Lord.'" He frowned. "You see, that's what Christianity needs these days: funking up. Brand Jesus needs a makeover, don't you think?"

I laughed. I'd never heard anyone talk about the Savior that way.

"Here's another example," he said. "Jesus freaks love to talk about how powerful their faith is, but wouldn't it be full-on cool if we talked about how powerful *doubts* are?"

"What do you mean?"

"Faith is a two-sided coin, and we always tend to look at it believer-side up. But you can't hold the faith coin without touching both sides, and the other side—the side we don't like to look at—is doubt. I'm just saying if we spent more time turning the coin and studying the doubt side, and not just by ourselves, but with others, our faith might get stronger. Questions don't disappear if they're ignored; they disappear if they're answered."

"That's a weird kind of fellowship."

"Yeah, I call it witnessing for doubt. Wanna try it?"

"I'm not sure. It sounds . . ." I wanted to say *against God,* but he was right. I'd been taking peeks at the doubt side of faith for some time. I'd just never talked about it to anyone.

"Okay," he said, "maybe 'witness' is too heavy. How 'bout we call it doubt-swapping."

"Doubt-swapping?"

"Yeah. We trade stories about a time we had a major doubt about T.L., C.J., whatever."

He'd lost me again. "C.J.?"

"Christ Jesus. I mean, 'J.C.' is so formal and stuffy. 'C.J.' sounds more like someone you can really hang with. And isn't that the point: *relationship* to Christ, not religion?"

Even though I felt like I was watching someone speaking in tongues, I got what he was saying. "Okay," I said, then let out a breath. "Let's doubt-swap."

11

Doubt-swapping

Ruah nodded. "I'll go first. The first time I had major doubts about my faith was when I joined the show."

"What show?" I asked.

"Sorry. The show's the major leagues. My walk on the doubt side began the night before my first game. I was called up from the minors and drove to Cincinnati. That's what the C on the hat stands for, the Cincinnati Reds. I went to bed early. I'm lying there praying to T.L. to let my first day in the bigs not be my last, when someone starts banging on the door. I get up, open it, and there's the manager of the Reds. He looks like he's had a few drinks. He says, 'Are you Ruhah Braahanch?'"

I laughed at his imitation of a drunk.

"He's had more than a few," Ruah said. "'Yes, sir,' I tell

'im. Then he says to me, 'If you do-oo three things tamara, you'll be fi-hine. Whone'—he holds up a finger and looks at it cross-eyed—'eat Whea-ties fer breafest. Twho, befhore tha game, stuff a sock in yer jockstrhap. An tha-ree, when ya go-da bhat, if tha pisscher tries ta hitcha, led 'im hitcha.'"

Ruah waited for me to stop laughing. "Okay, my manager's really drunk, and now I'm thinking he's crazy, too. But he *is* my manager, and I'm only nineteen years old, so maybe he knows some things I don't. 'Sir,' I say, 'is there a reason I should eat Wheaties for breakfast, stuff a sock in my jockstrap, and try to get hit by a pitch?' His face flushes redder than it already is and he screams, 'Do whhhat I say, rhook, an' dohne assk qwheshuns!' Then he staggers down the hall and disappears.

"I didn't think much about it until the next morning when I'm praying and asking T.L. to protect and guide me through my first shot at the show. I get the answer I usually get when I pray to God about baseball. *Play your game, Ruah, play your game.* But when I go to breakfast, I can't get the manager's advice outta my head. I think, why take any chances? Why not take God's advice and the manager's, too? So, what do you think I have for breakfast?"

"Wheaties?"

He nodded. "And when I'm suiting up for the game, what do you think I stuff in my jockstrap?"

"A sock?"

"Yep. Then, when the team gathers around the manager for a talk before the game, I have such butterflies I can't even wait till he's done before I run into the bathroom and hurl breakfast. When I come out, and the team's headed for the field, I see the manager grinning at me. 'Wheaties,' he says, 'the breakfast of champions. 'Cause they go down easy, and come up easy.'

"A little later I step out of the dugout for my first introduction in a major league stadium. After they announce my name, the crowd's so big and the cheers are so loud, I wet my pants."

I snorted with laughter. "No way!"

"See," he said, "you're not the only one who's had bladder freak-out. But technically, I didn't wet my pants, I wet my *sock*. So I go back in the dugout and start for the locker room. The manager stops me and asks where I'm going. I say, 'To change my sock.' He busts a gut laughing. By now I'm thinking his advice is pretty good, so when I step up for my first at bat, I lean into an inside pitch and get hit."

"Was it a hundred miles an hour?"

"I don't know, but it felt like it as I jogged down the line. After the game, the manager calls me into his office. I went two for four at the plate, so I think he's gonna pat me on the back for batting five hundred my first day in the bigs. He looks up at me from his desk. 'Branch,' he says, 'you're gonna do fine.' Then I say, 'Sir, I get the Wheaties thing and the sock-in-the-jock, but why look to get hit in your first AB?' He fixes on me and says, 'It shows 'em you're here to play the game, and playing the game is doing *anything* to get on base.' I nod, thank him, and start out. 'Branch!' he yells. When I turn back he's around his desk and coming at me. He gets in my face. 'I hear you're a Jesus freak,' he snarls. 'Yes, sir,' I answer, and then he gives me a look I'll never forget. 'Here's how it's gonna work,' he says. 'You can have your god in heaven but I'm your god on earth. And don't forget it.' After that, when it came to baseball, I only listened to my 'god on earth.'"

It was a funny story, but I didn't get the ending. "How did all that make you doubt God, or your faith?"

"Good question," Ruah said. "The more that manager molded me into a good player, the more I tried to convince myself that this drunken, blasphemous man was an angel sent by God. But in my heart I didn't see how it could be. T.L. didn't send angels from heaven in the form of drunken, blasphemous heathens. It really began to eat at me."

"Why?"

"Because I'd always believed my talent for playing ball was God-given, that baseball was my calling. But why, I kept trying to figure out, would T.L. use a sinner to help me achieve my higher purpose? I prayed until I got the answer. T.L. doesn't care about baseball. It's only a game. He made me good at it, but that didn't make it my *calling*. Using a blasphemous, drunken heathen to make me a better ballplayer was God's incredibly sly way of saying, 'Dude, baseball's *not* your higher purpose.'"

"So what is?"

He pulled in a breath and let it out. "Don't know." He tapped his head. "That's why the screws are loose. I'm more than on the Reds' DL"—he chuckled—"I'm on the DL of T.L."

114

12

I Witness

The county road fed us onto Route 4, and we kept driving west through monster sky country. As the land flattened, the sky just reached down farther. The clouds towering in the west reminded me of what Mom always said: "Clouds are the dust kicked up by God's feet."

Ruah took a slug from a water bottle. "Your turn."

I'd forgotten we were doubt-swapping. "I'm never gonna top your story."

"It's no contest. We're just sharing a walk on the doubt side. All you gotta do is think of a time when you looked up and shouted, 'T.L., I know You da Man, but if You want me to figure out the latest mystery bomb You dropped on me, I'm gonna need another clue!'"

"I've never done that."

He laughed. "Of course not, you're a better Christian than me. Okay, lemme put it this way. Did you ever find yourself in a place where you were thinking, 'God must be on vacation, 'cause there's no way He would've put me in the spot I'm in now.'"

I laughed.

"What's funny?"

"Have you ever heard of Jesus-throated Whac-a-Moles?"

"I have now. What are they?"

I told him about the New J-Brigade and how me and Mom went around whacking evil in the name of God. And how when people asked me what kind of work my mom did, I told them she drove a wrecking ball.

"Sounds like you've got some doubts about being a Jesus-throated Whac-a-Mole," he said. "So were you ever on a mission when you wanted to grab your mom and say, 'Mom, we can stop now. Satan has left the building.'"

"No, but there was a mission where I thought *God* had left the building."

"Okay, that's taking a lead to the doubt side. Lemme hear it."

I took a drink of water and thought where to begin. "Have you ever seen *Sesame Street*?"

"When I was a kid, sure."

"I only saw it when I visited friends' houses, 'cause my mom's anti-TV. A couple of times I saw *Elmo's World*. I thought Elmo was really funny and cool. I wanted an Elmo toy, but my mom said toys were bad. She called Toys 'R' Us 'Satan's workshop.'"

"You're kidding."

"Wish I was. According to her, Toys 'R' Us sold board games with dice that turned kids into gamblers. But the aisles of dolls and actions figures were the worst."

"What did they do?"

"Their naughty parts were so real, if you played with them you'd end up a pregnant teenager, get an abortion, and be a baby killer."

"Man, that's harsh."

"Yeah. Anyway, a few years after I liked Elmo they came out with Tickle Me Elmos."

"You wanted a Tickle Me Elmo?"

"Nah, I was over Elmo by then. But Tickle Me Elmos really bugged my mom. She said they were made of lint from the devil's cape, and Satan put them on earth for one reason."

"What?"

"To introduce kids to the sin of 'unrestrained pleasure.' "

"Unrestrained pleasure?"

"That's how she put it." I drained my water bottle. "Anyway, one day before Christmas, my mom told me the New J-Brigade was gonna take on an army of Tickle Me Elmos. As we drive to Toys 'R' Us, I'm terrified. I keep seeing a nightmare. I mean, what if one of the Elmos comes to life, points at me, and rats me out. 'Elmo got new friend! Elmo want Billy! Billy want Elmo!'"

Ruah laughed during my Elmo falsetto.

"When we get to Toys 'R' Us, we park, and Mom reaches into the backseat. She holds up a claw-bladed knife and clippers like she uses to cut my hair. But these clippers run on batteries. 'Here's the plan,' she says. 'When we get to the Elmo aisle, you cut the tape on top of the box, open it, and hand him to me. Then I'll'—she flicks on the clippers, which buzz to life—'lop the hair off his head. That's why we're calling it Operation Samson. It's gonna rob Elmo of his powers. No one's gonna buy a bald-headed Elmo.'

"When we walk into Toys 'R' Us, the place is packed with Christmas shoppers. The most crowded aisle is the one with Tickle Me Elmos. There're hundreds of 'em standing in their clear plastic boxes. Under each lid is a red furry Elmo, staring at me with his oogly white eyes. Mom grabs one, hands me the box, and shouts scripture. *'My sword shall be bathed in heaven. We shall hew down the graven images of their gods!'* I cut the tape on the top of the box, pop it open, and give it to her. She jams in the clippers, and the inside of the box sprays with red fur.

"In a minute we're standing among boxes of scalped Tickle Me Elmos. Mom's hands are coated in red fur, and we're surrounded by screaming moms and bawling kids. As Mom takes another box and gives Elmo a buzz cut, I see how miserable everyone is. Mom's yelling at me to feed her another box, but I'm frozen. Part of me says, *You're doing what Mom and the Heavenly Father want you to do.* But another part of me sees all the screaming, crying people and wonders why God wants to make everyone, except my mom, so miserable.

"Later, after the police showed up and the real mess began, I asked God why He let the whole thing happen. I mean, why did He want us to ruin Christmas for all those kids?"

"Did you come up with an answer?" Ruah asked.

"Yeah, a bunch. My first answer was that God wasn't there."

"T.L. had left the building."

"Yeah. I even tried to tell myself that He wasn't there 'cause He was busy decorating Heaven for Christmas. But it didn't take away my doubts. I knew better. God *never* leaves the building. Then I got another answer. Everyone was crying and miserable because it was part of God's punishment."

"Punishment for what?"

"For me craving an Elmo toy. For idol worship. For putting another god before the One True God. Which made me think of another question. When you sin, why doesn't God punish you in private? Why does He make other people suffer too?"

"Did you get an answer?"

"Yep. The best punishment for your sins is making you watch innocent people suffer for your sins too."

"Tough answer. Did you believe it?"

"Not really. I guess that's when I took my first walk on the doubt side. I mean, why does God have to be so cruel? Why does the wrathful Old Testament God keep showing up after He sent Jesus with the new covenant? Maybe that's how God planned it all along. I mean, maybe it's like a good cop, bad cop thing. The Heavenly Father plays bad cop, His Son plays good cop."

Ruah lifted his sunglasses and looked at me. He stared long enough to make me think that he was going to run off the road. He finally looked away. "Anyone ever say you're wise beyond your years?"

I laughed. "Maybe I know the Bible, and a bunch about mountain biking, but that's about it."

"Hey, having Bible cred and biking cred could be a great combo," he said. "You could ride around the world and become famous as the Mountain Biking Missionary."

I knew he was kidding, but I liked the picture it put in my head. I could be the first to ride to the top of Mount Everest and convert all the Sherpas on the way.

13

Phone Call

I watched the heat mirages shimmering on the road ahead. The pavement kept rising from the silver, like God was rolling out a carpet to Colorado for me. I wanted to look at my GPS and see the miles tick down, or at least pull out the new *Huck Finn* chapters and find out what happened to Huck and Jim after they jumped on the raft and headed down the Mississippi. But Ruah would've started asking questions I didn't want to answer. To stick to my story about seeing my sick dad, I had to keep my GPS and the *Huck* pages out of sight.

How far he was driving west, I didn't know. But I did ask if he planned to cut back north to the interstate. He said we were making good time on Route 4, and there were no speed traps because all the troopers were up on I-70, where the traffic was.

When we were west of Scott City, Ruah pulled out his cell phone. "I've got bars. Your mom's gotta have a phone by now."

I dialed 411. This time, there was a listing in Independence. As it dialed through I reminded myself of what I'd put in my note to her. I was going to New Orleans.

"Hello," she answered.

I could hear the strain in her voice. "Hi, Mom."

"Praise God! Are you alright?"

I was glad she didn't start crying right off. "I'm fine, Mom. Did you get my note?"

"Why are you doing this?"

I guess that meant she got the note, or someone had read it to her. "Did the police come to see you?"

"Yes," she said sternly. "I told them you got off the bus to come home." I could see her, ramrod straight, telling the world how things should be. "I told them you're not a runaway."

"You're right, Mom, I'm not."

"So you're coming home?" Her voice got billowy with hope.

I felt bad that I'd misled her. "No—I mean, yes, after I see where my father lived. I'm gonna find out about Richard Allbright." As soon as I said it I realized that the truth didn't fit the story I'd been giving Ruah. I glanced over. He was still staring straight ahead.

Mom's voice, with the iron back in it, jumped in my ear. "I can tell you everything you need to know about him."

"You had your chance, Mom. You gave me a bunch of lies."

She fired scripture. *"You are of your father the devil, and you want to do the desires of your father. There is no truth in him."*

It pissed me off that she, the lying sinner, was throwing scripture at me. "There was enough truth in him to let *your* desires out," I shot back. "That's why I'm here!"

121

She went silent. I thought she'd hung up. I snuck another look at Ruah. He kept staring at the road. He was either trying to give me privacy or not wanting to listen. I couldn't blame him. I didn't want to hear any of it either.

The sound of a muffled sob came through the phone. "God is punishing me."

"I don't wanna fight, Mom."

"Neither do I. Please, come home, Billy."

"I can't." I quickly added, "I mean, I can, but I'm not coming back yet."

She sucked in another sob. "What if you don't come back?"

"You've always trusted God to protect us. You gotta trust Him now."

That broke the lock on her tears. Between sobs, I told her I loved her, said goodbye, and closed the phone.

We rode in silence until Ruah said, "So your father's already dead."

"Yeah."

"You wanna talk about it?"

"Not really."

We didn't say anything after that. It was fine by me. I had thinking to do. Something Mom said kept bugging me. I couldn't figure why she hadn't told the police that I was a runaway. Maybe she'd really believed I'd gotten off the bus to come home. But now that she knew I wasn't coming home, she would call the police and tell them I was headed to New Orleans. That was fine. They could look for me in New Orleans all they wanted.

To keep from worrying about stuff I counted cars on a

coal train heading east. But it's hard not to worry when the sun begins to set, you're riding in a stranger's camper, and you're wondering where you're going to spend the night.

When we got to the main intersection in Scott City, Ruah turned north. "There's a campground up ahead in a state park," he said. "I'm stopping there for the night. You're welcome to camp with me if you want. My PB&J is decent, but my real specialty is barista burgers."

I wasn't sure what to say. I felt like I was wearing out my welcome. Especially after he had to listen to me and Mom fight. "What's a barista burger?"

He shrugged. "You'll have to go camping to find out."

"Alright," I said. "A barista burger sounds good. Thank you."

He chuckled. "Don't thank me till you've tasted it."

"I mean thanks for giving me a ride almost all the way across Kansas."

He shot me a quick smile. "Just helpin' a mountain biking missionary who's lost his bike."

Lake Scott State Park was filled with RVs and tents. We found a spot in a cottonwood grove. Ruah made dinner in the camper while I collected kindling for a fire. He gave me money to buy firewood at the park store. I used the money from the geocache to buy a sleeping bag and some cargo shorts. It also gave me the chance to check my GPS device. I was 171 miles from St. Petersburg, and the compass arrow was pointing northwest.

We ate inside the camper at the dinerlike table. Ruah's barista burger wasn't like any cheeseburger I'd ever had. It was spiced up with garlic, onion, soy sauce, ginger, and even honey. It was really good, especially dipped in ketchup.

During dinner, I asked him about one of my worries. "Is there any way my mom could find out where I called her from? Or that it was your phone?"

He wiped mustard off his mouth. "It's not my phone. I borrowed it from a friend in Cincinnati. And it's not easy tracing a mobile call to where it was made from, even for the police."

I relaxed. Even if they traced the call to the phone number in Cincinnati, it was the wrong direction. "Why are you using a friend's phone?"

"If I were to use my own cell, there'd be people with access to my call history. I'm trying to cover my tracks, just like you. I don't want the Cincinnati Reds coming after me, and you don't want your mom and the cops coming after you, right?"

I nodded. "Yeah, but I'm not sure she told anyone I ran away." I explained how she'd told the police I was coming home and insisted I wasn't a runaway.

He took a bite of salad. "From what I've heard about your mother, she might not want the cops digging into her past. It sounds like she might have unfinished business with a few judges. Has she ever decided not to show up in court?"

I chuckled around a bite of burger. "Oh, yeah."

"Having outstanding warrants would make it risky filling out a missing person's report. Which means you're probably not officially missing."

"So I won't be showing up on any milk cartons."

"Right."

As I helped clean up, I thanked Ruah for the great burger and told him I'd start hitching for Colorado in the morning.

"You headed northwest or southwest?" he asked.

"Northwest."

He didn't say which way he would be going; I didn't ask. He'd taken me halfway across Missouri and almost across Kansas. If God kept tossing me such good luck, I'd get to St. Petersburg the next day.

14

Giff

After dark, we hung out and watched the campfire shoot spark fireworks. A man strolled toward us. I didn't know if there were rules about walking into people's campsites. It was my first time camping.

The man was black, looked about sixty, and had a friendly face. He stopped near the fire. "Evening."

Ruah nodded. "Yes, it is."

I wasn't sure if he was making a joke, or trying to be rude so the man would leave. As they talked about the weather, the man studied Ruah. Ruah wore his cowboy hat, but the fire lit up his face. I knew what was coming.

"You look familiar," the man said. "I know you from somewhere. Or I've seen you on TV."

"TV," I said, speaking for the first time.

"Say what?" he said.

"You've seen him on TV." Ruah shot me a dirty look.

"He's an assistant pastor at the Feast of Faith Church in Missouri. Our services are on TV and people see 'em all over the Midwest."

"Is that right?" The man seemed to buy it.

"Yes, sir." Ruah nodded in my direction. "He's exaggerating, but folks recognize me now and then."

The man jabbed a thumb back toward the camper. "I see your plates are from Pennsylvania. That's a long way from Missouri."

"It's a rental," Ruah said. "I didn't check the plates when I drove it off the lot. But thanks for letting me know."

If he was hinting that the conversation was over, the man wasn't taking it. "What brings you out this way?" he asked.

I jumped in again. "We're going to Denver for a Bible bee. I made the nationals, and Pastor Sloan is taking me there." Out of the corner of my eye, I saw Ruah purse his lips. I didn't know if he was going to spit or start laughing.

"What's a Bible bee?" the man asked.

Him not knowing about Bible bees was good. Maybe I could scripture him to death till he left. "It's like a spelling bee, but all the questions are based on one book in the Bible."

"So you're a Bible whiz kid?"

I gave him a big stupid grin. "If I win, yeah."

"And he will," Ruah added, getting in on the story. "I'm coaching him all the way to Denver. We even gave the RV a biblical name to let the Lord know we mean business."

I had no clue where he was going.

"Really?" the man said. "What'd you name it?"

"Giff."

I knew he'd gone too far. There's no *Giff* in the Bible.

"Gift? I've never heard of Gift," said the man. "Unless you mean the gift of the Magi."

"No, that's 'gift.'" Ruah pointed at his camper. "This is *Giff*. It's short for G.F."

"What's G.F.?"

"Even shorter for"—he raised his hands and air-quoted—"the great fish."

I finally got where he was going. "You know," I said, jumping in, "the great fish from the book of Jonah."

The man rocked back with a laugh of recognition. "You mean the whale that swallowed Jonah."

"Actually, there's no whale in the Bible," Ruah said with a sour face that even had me believing he was a pastor. "A whale swallowed *Pinocchio*. The Good Book never says anything about a whale. Jonah was swallowed by a great fish."

The man raised a hand. "Alright, I 'preciate the catechism. But why name your RV after the fish that swallowed Jonah?"

Ruah flashed a quick smile. "Because we're sailing along in its belly just like Jonah."

"We even think it looks like a fish," I added. And we could have. I mean, the camper kind of looked like a big albino catfish with one whisker, the antenna.

The man squinted at the RV. "If that's the great fish"—he looked back at the two of us—"which one of you is Jonah?"

Ruah jabbed a finger at me. "God called him, just like God called Jonah to preach to the city of Nineveh. But this young man is gonna deliver the Word to the National Bible Bee in Denver."

Firelight flickered on the man's dissatisfied expression. "I'm no Bible expert, but wasn't the great fish taking Jonah *away* from Nineveh, and *away* from his calling. Your great fish, Giff, is taking you *to* Denver, *to* your calling."

"You're right," I told him. "At first the fish was taking Jonah away. But Jonah repents, gets right with God, and then the Bible says, *And Lord spake unto the fish, and it vomited out Jonah upon the dry land*. For all we know the fish hurled Jonah right next to Nineveh." I got out of my camp chair. "I can get my King James and check it if you want."

The man waved his hands. "No, I believe you." His face eased into a smile as he turned to Ruah. "Reverend, looks like you got yourself a champ. Good luck, and good evening."

"Evening," Ruah said with a friendly nod.

As the man walked away, I sat down and stared at the fire. I didn't dare look at Ruah. I would've cracked up.

When I did look up, he grinned, shaking his head in disbelief. "How in the hell did you know that verse?"

I shrugged. "When I was little I thought Jonah was the coolest book in the Bible. I memorized all four chapters."

"What was so cool about it?"

"The fish. I had a pet goldfish, and I thought the great fish in Jonah was God's pet. But God's fish wasn't any fish; it knew *tricks*. God had taught him 'swallow the man' and 'hurl the man.' For months I tried to train my fish to swallow things and boot 'em back up, but it never listened. It made me realize how powerful God was. When He talked, fish listened."

Ruah laughed. "Man, you put the freak in Jesus freak."

I slept on the couch. Ruah slept up in the loft.

Sometime in the night a sound woke me. It was the bathroom door shutting. I stared through the windows over the couch. At first I thought I was seeing a swarm of fireflies. But they were stars, thick as a bug cloud: the Milky Way. Mom once told me the Milky Way was a giant nest in heaven where the angels folded their wings and spent the night. Each morning the sun woke them up and they flew down to earth in a flock of blessings.

The toilet flushed, the bathroom door opened, and Ruah made his way down the aisle past me. His body caught the starlight. In nothing but his white boxers, he looked like a pillar of glistening coal. He climbed back into the sleeping loft.

I wondered if I'd ever have muscles like that, or if I'd be stuck with a corn-dog body all my life. I stared at the Milky Way. Maybe one day an angel would dive down and turn me from corn dog to beefcake. You know, give me a total hunk-over.

I was dreaming of high-pitched birds, like canaries, when I woke up. I thought I was hearing morning birdsong, but when I popped out of the z-bag, it was pitch black. The Milky Way was gone. The chirping was coming from the oven racks as the camper got buffeted by gusts of wind. A flash of lightning lit up the windows, followed by a rattling *boom*.

"Shut the windows!" Ruah yelled as he cranked a sky-light shut. I slid the side windows shut. The rain slammed into us.

Maybe it was God letting us know He didn't appreciate how we'd used His Word to fool the visitor at our campfire. Or maybe T.L. was joining the fun of turning the camper into a great fish. Whatever, there's something about rain on a metal roof that tucks you in a drum of sound and comfort. I dove back into the z-bag deeper than ever.

15

The N-Word

In the morning it was still raining buckets. Water ran down the windows like liquid cellophane. I got up before Ruah and waited for it to let up. I would've walked to the highway and started hitching but I didn't have rain gear. Everything would've gotten soaked, including my GPS and the *Huck Finn* pages.

I got out the new *Huck* chapters and started reading. Huck and Jim were floating down the river on the raft at night and hiding during the day so they wouldn't be caught. They were a mini version of the Jonah story too. They had their great fish, the raft.

Ruah woke up and peered over the edge of the loft. "What are you reading?"

"An old book."

He stroked his chin, in deep-thinker pose. "Hmm, I hear there's a lot of those."

"*Adventures of Huckleberry Finn,*" I told him.

He climbed down the ladder. In the daylight, his back muscles bunched and rippled like a bag of black snakes.

He pulled on a shirt. "What's a nice Christian boy like you reading a book like that?"

"I found it," I said, stuffing the pages back in the big pocket on my shorts. No way was I going to let him see the highlighted words and numbers. "I wanted to know why so many people hate it."

"Have you found out yet?"

"I get why some people might not like it, but I haven't gotten to the hate-it part. I mean, it's not as bad as I thought it would be."

He moved to the kitchen area and started pulling out breakfast stuff. "How often does it say 'nigger'?"

"A lot."

He flipped a box of cereal in the air and it stuck a perfect landing on the table. "Where I went to school, that was the hate-it part. And how the black dude, Jim, is a step-'n'-fetch-it, bow-to-the-man, stupid nigger out of a minstrel show." He put two bowls on the table. "Now, just 'cause I'm serving you breakfast, Masser Billy, don't get any ideas."

"Sorry," I muttered, and started to get up to help.

He chuckled and pushed me back down. "That was a joke. One breakfast ain't gonna make me your nigger."

I felt my face go hot. I'd heard black people call themselves the N-word, but not while they were fixing me breakfast. "Jim's not exactly stupid," I said.

"How so?

"In the chapter I just read, Jim makes wise King Solomon look like an idiot for wanting to cut a kid in half."

"Really?"

"Really."

Ruah slid into the opposite bench with a carton of milk. He filled his bowl with cereal and looked out at the pouring rain.

"Not exactly hitchhiking weather, is it?"

"It'll let up," I said. "If it doesn't, I'll go to the camp store, buy a garbage bag, and make a poncho."

Ruah leaned back and looked at me like I had a morning booger the size of a walnut. "First you wanna hitch after you piss your pants, now you wanna hitch in a garbage bag. Are you sure you've earned your hitchhiking merit badge, scout?"

I started to feel hot again. "I know what I'm doing," I muttered.

"Sure you do." He took a spoonful of cereal, crunched, and swallowed. "Got a proposition for you, Billy."

I shrugged. "What?"

"I'll keep driving you west."

"Really?"

He nodded. "On one condition."

"If it's calling my mom every ten minutes—"

He waved his spoon, cutting me off. "No, it's not that. You ride with me, you read to me." He flashed a smile and shoveled another bite of cereal. "*Huckleberry Finn.* I wanna know if it's as badass ugly as everyone says."

I thought it was a great deal. I just had to make sure as I read the loose pages I didn't let him see the yellow high-lights or my father's clue poems. After the fun we'd had last night, I trusted Ruah. He was a nice guy, but I had to remind myself: yesterday he'd turned out to be someone else; there was no telling who he might turn out to be today.

As we drove through the downpour toward I-70, the lash-ing rain smacked the windshield, and the wipers flung the water off Giff's giant eye. I watched water stream off the outside mirror and jump onto the side window. Then it wound in a swirl, like a churning whirlpool trying to bore through the glass. Giff would have none of it. We were high and dry inside the great fish.

Ruah wouldn't let me summarize the first eleven chapters of *Huck* that I'd already read. He wanted me to read it out loud from the beginning. I gave in when I realized I only had seven new *Huck* chapters from the geocache in Hunter. I didn't want to run out of chapters to read. Then I'd have to explain why I didn't have the whole book. So I started from page one.

I got as far as the middle of page three when I stopped midsentence. *"By and by they fetched the—"*

"What?" Ruah asked. "Fetched the what?"

"I can't say it."

"Can't say what?"

"The N-word."

He laughed. "It's not like you're *using* it, you're just reading it."

"I can't read it."

He gave me a cockeyed look. "C'mon. In your whole life, you've never said 'nigger'?"

"No, I mean, yeah, I mean"—just talking about it had me all flustered—"I've never said it." And I hadn't.

He chuckled. "That's a *biiig* problem if you're reading *Huck Finn*. So lemme set you straight, dude. It's not the words you speak, it's how you speak 'em." He gestured at the pages in my lap. "Now, go on. If we gotta stop every time we hit the N-word and give you nigger therapy, we'll never get past chapter one."

I found my place on page three. *"By and by they fetched the niggers in and had prayers . . ."*

Saying it wasn't as bad as I'd thought it would be. Which wasn't necessarily a good thing.

16

Colorado

I read as we plowed through the rain. It was still coming down hard when we hit I-70. I read the eleven chapters and started on the new ones from Hunter. The only time Ruah interrupted was when we got to the part where Huck stops two slave hunters from finding Jim on the raft. Huck fools them into thinking the raft is infected with smallpox and they won't go near it.

"How bogus is that?" Ruah exclaimed.

I looked up from the page. "I dunno, I thought it was a pretty good trick."

"Not the story." He pointed up ahead. "The sign."

I read the Colorado welcome sign as it shot by. WELCOME TO COLORFUL COLORADO.

"I mean, what are they saying? Colorado's filled with people of color?"

I'd never been to Colorado. "Is it?"

Ruah looked at me like I had another walnut-sized nosepickium. "That was a joke."

The sign reminded me of a game I played with all the welcome signs I'd seen moving from state to state. I'd rewrite them. I also needed a reading break. I only had a chapter and a half left before I ran out of pages, and then I'd have to make up something about not having the rest of *Huck Finn*. "Maybe the sign would be better if it was 'Discover the Color in Colorado.'"

He nodded. "Cool, or how 'bout, 'Colorado—You're Not in Kansas Anymore.'"

I didn't get it. "Is that a joke too?"

He slid me a look. "You're kidding, right?"

I shook my head.

"'We're not in Kansas anymore.'"

"I know," I said. "We just crossed the line."

He pulled his head back like a turtle. "Are you telling me you've never seen *The Wizard of Oz*?"

"I've heard of it but never seen it. My mother says it's part of the toxic culture."

"What's toxic about *The Wizard of Oz*?"

"There're witches in it, right?"

"Oh, right, forgot about the witches. You folks don't like witches and Wiccans, black magic and all that satanic stuff."

"Exactly."

"So, according to your mom," he said, waving to the pages I was holding, "what's toxic about *Huckleberry Finn*?"

I scoffed. "That's a no-brainer. Huck lies, steals, smokes, and makes fun of Christianity."

"Even worse, he saves Jim from slave hunters."

I ignored his sarcasm. "Yeah, well, maybe that's not so bad."

"But he's breaking the law."

When he said that, it suddenly hit me. "He's an antinomian."

"A what?"

I explained how that's what mom and I were, and how we answered to a higher law than the law of the land. We answered to the law of God. Huck, in his own way, was an antinomian too.

When I finished I realized the rain had stopped. Also, I'd forgotten how far St. Petersburg was into Colorado. I told Ruah I had to take a piss. I had put the GPS device in my cargo-shorts pocket so I could check it now and again.

In the bathroom, the GPS had St. Petersburg 93 miles away. The compass was pointing to about eleven o'clock, north-northwest. Pretty soon I needed to stop going west and head north.

When I got back to the front, we were on dry interstate in bright sunshine.

"You gotta keep reading *Huck*," Ruah said, putting on his sunglasses. "I'm totally into it, and besides, you've learned to say 'nigger' with the best of 'em."

I laughed at his joke this time. He was right. Saying "nigger" in front of him—reading it, anyway—had become just saying another word. I pulled out the chapter I'd been reading.

"By the way," he said, "what's with all the loose pages? Didn't your *Huck* come with a cover?"

"Yeah, but I bought it used and it was falling apart." I held up the pages, making sure the top one didn't show any highlighting, and tried to make a joke of it. "You can't judge a book by its cover when it doesn't have one."

He chuffed a laugh. Even better, he stopped asking questions. I read out loud for another five minutes till his cell phone rang. He picked it up and checked the caller ID. He dropped the phone on the console.

"It wasn't my mom, was it?" I asked.

"No."

He didn't say anything else. He seemed lost in thought.

After a while, he said, "Oh man, sorry. I totally forgot about *Huck*."

"That's okay."

"Do you wanna take a break or keep reading?"

"My voice is getting kind of scratchy."

"Yeah, let's take a break."

It was weird that he suddenly wanted to stop. I mean, part of me wanted to stop because I was almost out of pages. But part of me wanted to keep reading, because we'd reached a part where Huck's caught in a longtime feud between two families, the Grangerfords and the Shepherdsons, and a new shoot-out was about to begin. I figured whoever had called Ruah must've upset him.

When we got to the Colorado Welcome Center, Ruah took the exit and pulled into a parking spot. "I gotta make a phone call," he said. He got out and walked onto a grassy strip.

I checked my GPS. We were 91 miles from St. Pete. The compass was pointing almost straight north. I checked the map in Ruah's atlas. All the roads up to northeastern Colorado were north-south. I could either cut north from the welcome center, or go another twenty to thirty miles west and then go dead north.

I watched Ruah pacing out on the grass. He was on his cell and slicing the air with his hand. Then he shouted at whoever was on the other end. "I'll pull the trigger when I pull the trigger, okay? Until then, fuck off!" He hung up, turned his back, and stared at the sky.

I didn't know if "trigger" was just a figure of speech or the real thing. Whatever, it creeped me out. I figured it was time to find another ride.

I eased the door open and grabbed my backpack. As I slid out, Ruah was headed back to the camper.

"Billy," he called, the anger totally gone from his voice, "you taking off?"

I shouldered my backpack. "Yeah." He wrapped a hand

around the outside mirror. "It sounds like you've got some stuff to deal with, and I can probably get another ride at the welcome center."

He shot me his friendly smile. "I'm sure you can, but what about the rest of *Huck Finn*? I'm hooked on the story of a black dude trying to free himself from the chains of his time. You can't leave me wondering what happens to Huck when the feud between the Grangerfords and the Shepherdsons is about to detonate."

"Maybe they have a copy in the welcome center—one with a cover."

He laughed. "I doubt that. Tell you what, if this is about what I think it's about, and you're freaked about my phone call, I'll make you a new deal. I'll tell you the twisted story of my call if you'll ride a little farther and finish the chapter you were reading so I know what happens to Huck. After that, we'll go our separate ways, and I'll find my own copy of *Huck*."

I still needed to go a few more exits west before heading north. I also figured the ride you know is better than the ride you don't. Not that I completely knew who Ruah was, or what he was dealing with.

I was about to find out—most of it, anyway.

17

Trading Secrets

Back on the road, he told me about the phone call. "It was my agent, Joe Douglas. Remember how I said there are certain people I don't want tracking me down? He's top man on the list."

"What does he want?"

"First, he wants me back in uniform and on the ball field. Every day I don't play he loses ten percent of my take. He loses seven grand a game."

I did the quick math. No wonder Ruah could afford a Trek. He could afford a truckload of Treks. "You make seventy thousand dollars a game?"

"Yeah. Next year, after filing for free agency, I could make a lot more. Which is the second thing Joe wants: to negotiate my new contract so he can keep raking it in. But I'm done with him. I wanna fire him."

"Why?"

"That's another story. The problem is I can't fire him."

"Why not?"

"He's got something on me."

"What?"

Ruah laughed. "If I told you, you'd have it on me too. The thing is, if I fire him he's gonna go public on me."

"And if you don't fire him he'll shut up."

"Now you're getting the picture."

"That's blackmail."

"Pretty much." He thought for a moment. "It's a little like the feud in *Huck Finn* between the Grangerfords and the Shepherdsons."

"How so?"

"Baseball has its own little feud. The two sides seem to be the nicest, most civilized people in the world when they're with their own. But put them together, and they wanna kill each other because that's how it's always been with the feud, no questions asked."

"What feud are you talking about?"

He shrugged. "It's a baseball thing. The point is, I'm tempted to ditch it altogether."

"Ditch what?"

"Baseball. I'm thinking about retiring."

I stared for a sec, not getting it. "Aren't you too young to retire?"

"Yeah, but when you make seventy grand a game, you can retire anytime you want."

We rode in silence. I could tell he didn't want to say any more about what Joe Douglas had on him and why he was AWOL from baseball. But there was one thing that kept bugging me. "If you borrowed your friend's phone so no one could track you down, how did Joe Douglas get your friend's phone number and call you?"

He stared ahead. "The best I can figure is that Joe went online, pulled up the call record on my cell phone, which I left back in Cincinnati, and called every frequently dialed number till he reached me on my friend's phone."

"But if you had just let him call, and didn't call him back, he never would've gotten to you."

He shot me a look. "True."

"So if you didn't want him tracking you down, why did you call him back?"

He chuckled. "You're getting too good at this, detective. Like I said yesterday, life would be a bust without secrets." He nodded toward the pages sticking out of my cargo pocket. "Now how 'bout finishing the chapter so we can find out what happens to Huck in the feud."

I read the last few pages, about a bloodbath between the Grangerfords and the Shepherdsons. Huck feels terrible because it began after he delivered a note hidden in a Bible. A bunch of people get killed, Huck escapes and reunites with Jim, and they head back down the river on the raft. At the very end, Huck says:

> I was powerful glad to get away from the feuds, and so was Jim to get away from the swamp. We said there warn't no home like a raft, after all. Other places do seem so cramped up and smothery, but a raft don't. You feel mighty free and easy and comfortable on a raft.

There was another clue poem from my father scrawled at the bottom of the page, but I didn't risk reading it. Ruah might've seen me.

Ruah didn't say anything for a long time. The weird thing was how he didn't ask me to keep reading. It's almost like he knew I was out of pages, that there were no more in my pocket.

Finally, he said, "Alright, I coughed up a secret and told you why I'm on the run. Now I'd like to ask you something."

I tensed up. But what he said was true. He'd told me about his agent and being blackmailed, even though he wouldn't tell me what his agent had on him, or what the feud in baseball was about. I figured I'd do the same: tell him something but not everything. "Okay," I said, "ask away. But I may not be able to answer."

He pointed at the pages I'd read. "What's with the yellow highlights?"

I pulled the pages closer, but it was too late. His eyes had been better than my lame attempts at hiding the highlights.

"You told me you bought it used. So someone must've read it and marked it up," he said. "What do you think all the highlighting's about?"

I thought on it, just like Huck was always doing. Since Ruah was a multimillionaire, it didn't seem likely he would muscle in on my treasure hunt and try to steal the bad book. I mean, in four or five baseball games he made what my father said the book was worth.

So I told him how the pages were from my father, and he was the one who had marked them up. I told him the highlights were clues to towns and coordinates. I showed him my GPS, told him about how I was using it to geocache, and that it was going to lead me to a rare book my dad had left me. And that's what I was hoping to find in St. Petersburg.

He was fascinated by all of it. At one point he said, "Man, I thought I had secrets!"

Then he asked a bunch of questions that made me tell him about getting the Bible with the DVD in it from my father. I told him how I'd never really met my father, but now it was too late because he was dead.

But I didn't tell him about being a bastard, and I didn't tell him about the bad book being some sequel to *Huck Finn*. I trusted Ruah, but not that much. And besides, if he wasn't going to tell all neither was I.

When he was done asking questions, he said, "If you want a ride to St. Petersburg, I'm good for it."

I looked north. There was nothing but wheat and rangeland, not a farm, a house, or a vehicle in sight. Looking at the vast emptiness between me and St. Petersburg I did a little rewrite. The ride you have sure beats the one you may never get. "That would be great," I said, grinning. "Thanks."

"There's just one problem."

"What?"

"You haven't told me where it is."

I pulled out my GPS and turned it on. The compass arrow was now pointing north-north*east*. "We just passed the turn north."

Ruah took the next exit and we backtracked.

18

Bad Samaritans

As we drove north on Route 59, the road was more deserted than western Kansas. A sign said COPE 27 MILES.

I checked my GPS. "After Cope it's another sixty miles, and St. Petersburg isn't on the map."

Ruah gazed at the empty road. We hadn't passed a vehicle yet. "Hitchhiking this might've been tough."

"I could've found a bike and ridden to St. Petersburg in a day."

"Yeah, you could've." Ruah patted the dashboard. "But then Giff would've never swum across the Sea of Nothing."

After Cope, we kept heading north, through rangeland scattered with islands of pale green grass. It was so wide open and treeless it actually began to look like a rolling sea.

When my GPS ticked down to 40 miles, a plume of black smoke rose on the horizon. We figured it was a brush fire or someone burning a field. As we came over a rise, about a mile away, we saw the flames. They were licking up from something on the road. It was a burning car.

Ruah slowed down. The car was engulfed in flames and just off the road. There were two men near it. As we got closer, they waved for us to stop. One of them moved to the middle of the road. Ruah slowed and started to pull onto the shoulder. When the man in the road came toward us,

145

Ruah suddenly swerved back on the road and gunned it. Shooting past them, they yelled at us. The closest man hardly had any teeth. He punched the end of the camper as it sped by.

I whipped around to Ruah. "What'd you do that for?"

His eyes darted between mirrors. "It didn't look right."

"Their car was on fire! They needed help." I gestured to the back. "And we have a fire extinguisher."

"No fire extinguisher was gonna put that out. I didn't like the look of 'em. It could've been a setup for a robbery."

I started to say something and stopped. I mean, it was his camper.

He looked over. "Besides, with all that smoke, the police and fire trucks will be coming. The last thing we need is the cops asking you or me for ID."

He was right about the ID but I was still feeling guilty and annoyed. "We're in the middle of nowhere. The nearest cop or fire truck could be fifty miles away."

He handed me his cell phone. "Okay, be a Good Samaritan; call nine-one-one."

I called 911 and told the operator about the burning car and the two men stranded on Route 59. I gave her the milepost number we'd just passed. When she asked me if I was at the scene I said, "No," and hung up.

"Feel better?" Ruah asked.

"A little, but I still feel like a bad Samaritan."

"Neither of those guys looked hurt. Part of being a jock is going with your gut, and something told me not to stop.

If it was wrong, I'm sure God will find a way to punish me. He usually does."

It was a weird thing to say for someone who was blessed with being a millionaire baseball player. If T.L. punished me like that, in a few years I'd have money and bulging muscles and be a champion biker. It made me wonder if Ruah was on the run from more than his agent blackmailing him over a dark secret. Maybe the reason he didn't want to talk to the cops was because he was a fugitive. I mean, what did he see that made him think the two men were bad guys? It takes one to know one, right?

Before I went off the paranoid deep end, I reminded myself that even if he *was* a fugitive it wouldn't be the first time I'd traveled with one. Mom was a double fugitive: from the law and my father.

When we got to a town called Yuma we started following county roads north. The miles on my GPS clicked under 30. Whenever we came to an intersection we took whatever turn kept the compass pointing due north. At about 14 miles from St. Petersburg we headed up a road called RD XX. It was perfect. X marks the spot. When the GPS showed less than 10 miles the readout went to tenths of a mile and clicked down even faster. My heart was banging away at the same pace.

The compass arrow began swinging east. We were about there but it was off to the right. When the needle hit three o'clock we came to an intersection. A big sign pointed east: ST. PETER'S CHURCH 1 MILE. I could see a few buildings down the road. I asked Ruah to stop. I pulled out my last

147

pages of *Huck Finn* and read out loud the clue poem my
father had written.

> Just as Huck took Bible in hand,
> Causing dead boys to fill the land,
> Take up your quest to Holy St. Pete,
> Then find letter boxes trim and
>   neat.
> Look for a family, the house of Huss,
> Whose four little angels never fuss.
> "Cramped up and smothery" they may
>   seem,
> Their feuds of life are but a dream.
> Walk amidst their peace of mind,
> And what you seek you will find.

19

St. Petersburg

We got out in front of St. Peter's Church. There were only
three houses in the place, so there weren't a lot of "letter
boxes," or mailboxes, to check. The weird part was that
my GPS was pointing out of town, and saying we were
0.22 miles from the geocache.

The first house, all closed up, had a mailbox pole but no
box. The second house had a mailbox but no name on it.
The third house, a farmhouse to the southwest, was where
the compass pointed.

As we started walking toward the farmhouse a pickup pulled up. A farmer leaned out the window. "Can I help ya?"

"We're looking for a family named Huss," I said, and pointed to the farmhouse. "Do they live over there?"

He shook his head. "No, that's my house."

"Does anyone named Huss live around here?"

He shook his head again. "Not anymore."

"Where did they go?" I asked.

"They moved."

"Where?"

"Over yonder." He jogged his head in the direction of his house.

I couldn't see any other houses. "But you said they didn't live here now."

He stared at me as his tongue worked inside his craggy cheek. "I didn't say anything about 'live.' They moved to where we all move one day."

Ruah chuckled. "Are you saying that's a graveyard up there?"

The farmer nodded. "Yep. And full of Husses."

After he drove off, we walked to the graveyard. There were about ten rows of gravestones. Ruah started walking through them, looking for Husses. I checked my GPS. We were 60 feet from the geocache; the compass pointed toward the back of the graveyard.

"When your father was talking about 'letter boxes trim and neat,'" Ruah said, "he must've meant gravestones, huh?"

"Yeah." I followed the arrow and walked down the grass

149

path that ran through the graveyard. The feet kept ticking down. A cell-phone ring made me jump. I turned as Ruah pulled out his phone and checked the caller ID. He didn't answer it.

I went back to my GPS. I was 20 feet from the cache. I had to be on top of it. I looked around. A few feet away was a big reddish gravestone with HUSS carved on it. "I got it!" I looked around the gravestone for a geocache. "This can't be right. There's no cache, unless it's underground."

Ruah joined me. "You think your dad wanted you to become a gravedigger?"

I shook my head in frustration.

"What did the poem say at the end?" he asked.

I pulled out the page and reread it.

Look for a family, the house of Huss,
whose four little angels never fuss.
"Cramped up and smothery" they may
    seem,
Their feuds of life are but a dream.

I felt a tap on my shoulder. Ruah pointed toward the back of the graveyard. There was a metal sculpture with a welded sign: GOD'S LITTLE ANGELS. Beside it were seven small crosses.

We moved closer. The silver-painted crosses displayed little nameplates. Each nameplate had a family name and BABY. The four crosses in the middle all had the same name: HUSS. I read the poem's last lines again.

walk amidst their peace of mind,
And what you seek you will find.

I looked at Ruah.

"You first," he said.

I walked between the four crosses, toward the wire fence at the back of the graveyard. On the other side was over-grown grass. I leaned over the barbed wire at the top of the fence. Deep in the grass was a patch of metal. I reached down and pulled up a camouflage-painted ammo can.

Ruah watched from the other side of the crosses. "It looks like he didn't wanna hide something in the graveyard and disturb the dead."

We sat on a bench in the graveyard and unclipped the lid on the can. The geocache was like the one in Hunter. One plastic ziplock bag had some money, another had some more *Huck Finn* chapters, and the third had a trinket—actually, two trinkets: a plastic crown and a little net bag filled with plastic gold coins.

"What's with the crown and the bag of gold?" Ruah asked.

"The last cache had a toy raft in it," I explained, "and the chapters were all about Huck and Jim rafting down the river. Maybe in the new chapters, one of them gets crowned king and becomes filthy rich."

I flipped through the chapters to find the next highlighted words. The first one was "Providence."

Ruah stared down at it. "What's that?"

"Probably a town." I kept flipping until I found two

151

highlighted syllables: "ut" and "aw." They added up to "utaw." I picked up my GPS, went to Find, Cities, and entered Providence, Utah. After hitting Goto, a number flashed on the screen. I wanted to throw the GPS over the fence. "Four-hundred-seventy-five miles? That's on the other side of the Rockies!"

Ruah picked up the ziplock bag with the new *Huck Finn* chapters. "Looks like your old man wanted you to do some serious traveling, and some serious reading."

"Yeah, but for all I know, *Huck Finn* is a thousand pages long and I'm gonna end up geocaching all the way to China."

"Treasure hunting's not supposed to be easy."

I stared at the plains rolling west. The Rockies weren't even in sight. I couldn't believe my father was sending me on such a wild-goose chase. I had no idea where it would end, or even if there would be some "bad book" waiting for me. For the first time I wondered if Mom was right. Richard Allbright was a crazy-ass sinner who would've made a crappy father.

Ruah broke the silence. "If you want, I'll take you there."

I stared at him, trying to figure out what was going on behind his dark glasses. "Why would you wanna do that?"

"You mean besides wanting to know if Jim or Huck becomes a king and strikes it rich?"

"Yeah, besides that."

"Because you're good company, and I need a front man."

"A front man?"

"Until yesterday, no one recognized me with my

dreadlocks shaved off. But the lady at the gas station pegged me, and last night the man at the campfire almost did too. As long as I keep driving and trying to sort things out, I need to stay out of sight. I could use someone to go into gas stations and grocery stores. If you'll be my front man, I'll drive you to Providence."

I didn't know what rule or law Ruah had broken for his agent to be blackmailing him. It didn't matter. Mom had raised me as an antinomian, and right then whatever law of the land Ruah had broken was less important than one of God's laws: *Billy Allbright, honor your father.*

"It's a deal," I said, reaching out to shake on it.

He held up his hand. "There's one more thing."

"There's a catch?"

He nodded.

"What?"

He pulled out his cell phone, flipped it open, and punched three numbers. "Denver, Colorado," he said into the phone, grinning at me. "Ever been to a major league baseball game?"

"No. What's that got to do with—"

He cut me off as he got an operator who dialed him through to the Colorado Rockies box office. As he listened to recorded messages, he punched more numbers on the phone, then hung up. "We won't be able to make tonight's game, but there's a day game tomorrow. Next stop, Coors Field." He stood up and started out of the graveyard.

I threw the stuff back in the ammo can and started after him. "I thought you wanted to stay out of sight. A baseball game is hardly out of sight."

"True, but I haven't seen one from the stands in years. I'd like to see the game from where I first fell in love with it. Maybe it'll help me decide between quitting or playing."

"What if someone recognizes you?"

Ruah pulled his cowboy hat low over his face. "Hat." He tapped his sunglasses. "Sunglasses." He pulled a long face. "Frown. When Tiger Woods smiles—bing—everybody knows it's Tiger. When Tom Cruise smiles—bing—everyone knows it's Cruise. But if Ruah Branch never smiles"—he pulled his face even longer—"no one knows it's him."

I stared at his long, sad face. He really did look different.

"Do we have a deal?" He reached out a hand. "*Huck,* baseball, and the road to Providence."

"Yeah." I grinned. "We have a deal." We shook on it and my insides jumped. It wasn't from his boa-constrictor grip this time. I had a ride over the Rocky Mountains and to the next geocache.

20

Reset Buttons

After we found I-76 and headed for Denver, I started reading the new chapters of *Huck Finn*. Neither Huck or Jim becomes a king or gets rich. Instead, a couple of con artists, who say they're a king and a duke, join them on the raft and do all sort of scams on the local yokels as they travel down the river. By the time we pulled into Chatfield State

Park outside Denver, I'd read almost half of the twelve new chapters. I could've finished them, but I kept taking breaks to stare at the Rockies rising in the distance. They looked like a jagged saw blade running the length of the horizon. And the saw was flecked with white where patches of snow were stuck in its teeth.

After dinner we sat by the campfire and Ruah read a chapter of *Huck* out loud. As it got dark we decided not to read any more and save the rest for the long drive to Utah.

We talked about how the two frauds, the king and the duke, kept becoming different people. One minute one of them was a born-again pirate, the next they were Romeo and Juliet. In the chapter Ruah read they'd just become Englishmen and "long-lost relations," as they tried to cheat a family out of its inheritance.

"It's like they walk around with reset buttons," I said. "And when they wanna become someone else they just hit their buttons."

"Not a bad thing to have," Ruah said.

"Especially if you're using it to rob and cheat people."

He stared at the fire. "What if you had a reset button to undo things—you know, reverse the clock?"

I wondered if he was talking about what his agent, Joe Douglas, had on him. But I didn't ask because I wasn't sure I wanted to know whatever secret Ruah was hiding. "Yeah, that'd be cool," I said. "Whenever I said something dumb to a girl"—I poked myself in the forehead—"beep, I'd hit it. And once I knew it worked, I'd probably just hold it down—beep-beep-beep-beep-beep—until I'd rewound my entire life."

"Until you were *really* born again?"

"Yeah."

"Who would you wanna be reborn as?"

I started to say *Billy Allbright for real,* but I stopped. I didn't want to get into my real name being Billy Hayes, being a bastard, and all that.

It's almost like Ruah read my mind, because he said, "You don't have to answer that."

And I didn't.

We watched the fire for a while. Then he said, "According to some Jewish people, humans really do have reset buttons."

"Really?" My mom had told me that Jews believed a lot of strange things—not eating bacon, not driving on Saturday, ruining every boy's first birthday by giving him a puppy cut—but I'd never heard of Jews and reset buttons. "Maybe they believe in a reset button 'cause they wish Christ never happened."

Ruah laughed. "No, that's not quite it, and their reset button's not on their forehead."

"Where is it?"

"The story, the way the rabbis tell it, is that before a Jewish kid is born, he knows the Torah by heart. But right before he's born, an angel touches the baby here." He poked his finger between his upper lip and his nose. "The angel's touch leaves the little groove above your lip, and it makes the baby forget all his knowledge of the Torah. After that, the kid spends his lifetime relearning what he knew before he was born."

"Yeah, but what about the groove above a Christian's lip? How did *it* get there?"

"Maybe an angel does the same thing to Christians: they forget the Bible and have to relearn it."

I scoffed. "Whatever, it's a sketchy story."

"What's sketchy about it?"

"It says that first God makes you smart, then he makes you dumb."

He shrugged. "That's Old Testy for ya."

"Old Testy?"

"God of the Old and New Testaments: Old Testy and New Testy. But the thing about going from smart to dumb isn't just Old Testy; it's New Testy, too. Paul says, *If any man among you seemeth to be wise in this world, let him become a fool, that he may be wise.*"

I didn't say anything. I was too weirded out. I mean, I'd run away from a scripture-spouting mom, and who does God throw me into an RV with? A scripture-spouting dude. Whoever thinks God doesn't do humor should be sent to hell for not having faith in the Hilarious Father. "How do you know all this stuff?" I asked.

"Before I signed to play in the majors I almost went to Princeton. I wanted to go into seminary."

"Why did you pick baseball?"

"I can always go back to school." He threw a log on the fire. "The story about the Jewish baby unlearning everything is how I feel about baseball right now. An angel hit me right here"—he poked his lip groove—"and took away my knowledge of the game. Now I have to relearn the game

157

from scratch, starting tomorrow, with sitting in the stands and just watching."

It felt like he wasn't talking to me; he was talking to himself, and whatever demons were carving trails in his head.

A cell-phone ring made us both jump. Ruah dug out his phone and checked it. Flipping it open, he got up and walked away from the fire, out of earshot. After a while he hung up, came back, and slumped in his chair. He looked like he was practicing his long face for the next day, or someone had died.

Someone had.

He told me the call was from his friend in Cincinnati, the one who'd loaned him the phone. The Cincinnati police had come to see his friend. They'd been contacted by the Colorado Highway Patrol because my 911 call about the burning car had been traced to his cell phone. "The Highway Patrol wanted to know who made the nine-one-one call," Ruah said, "about a murder scene."

I wasn't sure I'd heard right. "What?"

"The two guys trying to flag us down had killed a man in the car, and set it on fire to make it look like an accident. After the nine-one-one call the cops showed up and caught 'em."

"So if we had stopped—"

"Who knows. Fact is, we didn't."

His phone rang again.

"Who's that?"

He checked it. "It's the same number that tried calling

in the graveyard this afternoon. Probably the Colorado cops. I didn't answer then, and I'm not answering now."

"We gotta tell them what we saw."

"Sure, in time. But I'm not walking into a police station and making a statement now. They caught the bad guys. They can wait to hear from us." The phone stopped ringing. A second later it beeped with a message.

He stared at the phone in his hand. "Right now the call log on this, past and future, is in the cops' hands." He looked up at me. "You know in *Huck,* when they touch a rattlesnake skin and it brings 'em bad luck?" He held up the phone. "This is our rattlesnake skin."

He tossed the phone across the fire. I caught it before it hit me in the chest. "Take it down to the lake and throw it in," Ruah ordered.

"Aren't you gonna listen to the message?"

"I'll call the Highway Patrol when I get back to Cincinnati." He waved his hand. "Get rid of it."

I looked down toward the lake. It was a long ways off and the trail was pitch black. "Now?"

"Now!"

I shot to my feet.

I headed down the trail in the darkness. Besides the flat black lake, barely visible on the moonless night, the thing I saw the clearest was a vision: getting back to the campsite and finding it empty. I'd never seen Ruah angry. As I stumbled along, I listened for the sound of the camper starting up. The sound of him ditching me.

Reaching the lake, I started to throw the phone. Thoughts

159

grabbed my arm. What if he does ditch me? I'll need the phone in an emergency. He doesn't want it anymore. And even if he doesn't ditch me it's stupid to throw it away. If I keep it and don't tell him, maybe I can send it back to him in Cincinnati after I get home. And he can give it back to his friend.

I stuck the phone in the deep pocket of my cargo shorts and hurried back up the dark trail. He hadn't ditched me. The only light in the camper was a glow from above the stove. He'd gone to bed.

I stood by the dying fire, catching my breath, letting the fear drain out of me. I crept inside the camper and lay on the couch.

His voice drifted down from the loft. "Is it swimming with the fishes?"

"Yeah," I lied.

There was a pause. "Thanks for doing what I asked."

The kindness in his voice made me feel guilty, made me want to run back to the lake and throw the phone in for real. Of course, I didn't. Then he would've known and ditched me for sure. I vowed to toss it in the lake the next morning.

I didn't go to sleep for a long time. The day had been a total roller coaster. It had started in a deluge, which turned into a fire, which turned into a murder.

I thought about what Ruah had said earlier about re-learning things, about becoming a fool before you become wise. I realized he and I were in the same boat. And I don't mean the same *raft* or great fish. We had more in common than that. We had both been poked by that Jewish angel.

160

We both had to relearn something from scratch. For Ruah, it was relearning something about baseball. For me, it was relearning everything: who Mom was, who my father was, who I was.

21

Out at First

The wocking of magpies woke us up. They were like an alarm clock with no snooze button. Ruah was all pumped up. He couldn't wait to take me to the Rockies game and show me his "crib."

We had time to kill before going into Denver, and I needed an excuse to go to the lake to throw the phone in. I was about to ask Ruah if I could borrow his Trek, take a ride, and get rid of the phone, but he beat me to it. He said we should stretch our legs and take a hike around the lake before going to the game.

I never got a chance to dump the phone. I figured I'd drop it in a garbage can at the game.

Coors Field looked like a spaceship made of bricks. We parked in a lot for buses and RVs. Ruah pulled a hand over his face and said, "Long face, good to go." With his cowboy hat, dark expression, beard stubble, and sunglasses, no one in the parking lot recognized him. The fans were too busy with their tailgate parties. It reminded me of lots outside big revival meetings. The only difference was what everyone drank. Rockies fans drank Coors; believers drank the Holy Spirit. When we reached the stadium, Ruah added one more thing to his disguise. He bought two Rockies jerseys, and we put them on.

I figured if I was going to my first major league game with a baseball star I wanted the full ride. "So," I asked, "who's your favorite player?"

"Of all time?"

"All time."

"Warren Sandel."

I'd never heard of him. But I was no baseball fan. For all I knew Warren Sandel was as famous as Babe Ruth. "Who does he play for?"

"Nobody anymore. He's long gone—played back in the forties. But he still holds the record for having fun."

"There's such a thing?"

"There should be. Sandel would do things like go up to bat without a bat."

"You're kidding."

"Nope. In one game he'd been up against the same pitcher three times and struck out every time. His fourth time up against the guy, Sandel figured he couldn't hit off him, so he goes to the plate without a bat. The catcher protests and tries to make Sandel go back and get a bat. But the ump says there's nuthin in the rule book about having a bat, and tells 'em to play ball. It made the pitcher so mad he tried to hit Sandel with a pitch. He missed four times and Sandel got a walk."

I laughed as we stopped at a ticket window, where Ruah bought two bleacher tickets with cash. We followed a river of people onto a mezzanine overlooking the huge green field. The smell of hot dogs made my mouth water. We made our way to a railing above the seats behind home plate. While Ruah checked a scoreboard showing the standings of major league teams, I watched fans. A few wore purple wigs. A half-dozen guys with no shirts had purple letters painted on their chests.

"Good news," Ruah said, "the Reds have climbed into second place. Bad news, they got there without me."

The stadium announcer told everyone to rise for the national anthem. An American Indian played the song on a native flute. When he finished, the crowd erupted in a cheer.

"Let's go," Ruah said, pointing across the field to the bleachers beyond left field. "Our seats are out there."

We moved along the mezzanine, which arcs around the field. Fans carried small boxes of food and drinks. My stomach growled. The hike around the lake had totally bonked breakfast. "Are we gonna get something to eat?"

"When we're closer," he said.

To get my mind off stomach thunder, I asked, "So what else did this Sandel guy do?"

"One time he got two low pitches that the ump called strikes. When Sandel complained, the ump told him they were in the strike zone. So Sandel got down on his knees, and the next pitch he blooped outta the infield for a single."

A cheer went up from the crowd as the first batter was announced.

"C'mon, game's starting." Ruah picked up the pace.

"My favorite was when Sandel was pitching in a night game and the stadium lights were so bad he couldn't see his catcher's signs. He asked the ump to call the game but the ump refused. The next inning Sandel took a book of matches to the mound and started lighting 'em so he could see better. The ump threw him out of the game." Ruah lowered his head and chuckled. "They don't make players like that anymore."

He veered toward a food stand. We loaded up with bison burgers, fries, and drinks, and headed for our bleacher seats. The walkway was filled with latecomers getting snacks. I heard the *crack* of a ball on a bat followed by the crowd's roar.

"Oh, man," Ruah said, "we're missing the—" He stopped so fast his beer sloshed on the cement. He spun around. "Follow me," he muttered, walking back toward the food stand.

I caught up with him. "What's up?"

"Follow, or walk away," he whispered harshly.

Moving past the stand, he dropped his box of food on a condiment cart. Then he ducked in a doorway-sized recess between steel uprights. I kept my food and followed him into the shadowy gap. He slid down the steel column to a crouching position. He yanked off his hat and sunglasses. "Get down," he rasped.

I slid down the column behind me and banged my knees into his. He reached out of the recess and pulled a garbage can in front of the gap. Seeing that it didn't cover me on the other side, he crooked a finger. "Over here."

I pivoted and jammed into the corner between the brick wall and his shoulder. Sweat trickled down his temple. His jaw muscles worked overtime. "What's going on?" I asked.

"I saw my agent."

"Joe Douglas?"

"Yeah, he's here with some goon."

"Why?"

"He's looking for me."

"How'd he know you'd be here?"

"The cell phone," he said, keeping his voice down. "Joe's phone number was on it; when the Colorado cops got the call record it led to Joe. They had the Cincinnati cops visit him, too. If Joe figured they had a call record, he probably bribed 'em for a copy. He saw that I called the Rockies box office; that's why he's here."

I felt the phone still hidden in my pocket. It was like Ruah had said: the phone was like the unlucky rattlesnake skin from *Huck Finn*. And I'd been the one who turned it into bad luck, by calling 911. "I'm sorry."

"Don't be. I should've been more careful."

"What does he want?"

"What all agents want: more money." He wiped his sweating face.

We heard a voice. Ruah's finger raised, shushing me. My mouth was so dry I wanted a drink of soda, but I was scared of rattling the ice. Sweat dripped under my shirt.

A sharp voice sounded. "See what I mean? People are flaky. They buy shit and waste it." The voice got closer. "Why? 'Cause they think they can always buy another."

Something exploded in the garbage can. I jumped and almost shouted. The man with the sharp voice had thrown something in, maybe Ruah's burger and drink.

The voice continued. "They think whenever they reach in their fuckin' pocket there's gonna be another ten bucks. Gimme some ketchup."

"Yeah," another man answered.

They were at the condiment cart. I stole a glance at Ruah. He mouthed, *It's him,* then shook his head in disbelief.

The voice started again. "That's what I'm talking about with fuckin' Branch. He thinks he can walk away from a deal and pick up another like it's paper on the street. Well, I'm gonna teach him a lesson. He's not wastin' nuthin. Not his free agency, not his career, and 'specially not me."

The other guy talked through a bite of food. "You really think he's here?"

"Yeah," Joe Douglas said through his own mouthful.

"If I had his money I would've rented a skybox."

"He's smarter than that. He's not gonna use his credit cards, 'cause he knows I'd be all over it. He won't even use his nonny card."

"Nonny card?" the other man echoed. "What's that?"

"When players order shit on the phone, or want a hooker, you think they use plastic with their name on it? No way. Every marquee player's got side plastic. The wives don't know it, nobody knows it except their agent and business manager. And if anybody needs cover it's Ruah Branch."

"I didn't think he was that famous."

Joe let a out a yip of a laugh. "He would be if everyone knew what he did at night."

"What's the harm? It's not like he's married."

"It's not like he'll *ever* be married."

There was a pause and the goon asked another question. "What are you saying?"

"I wish I could say he's a monk"—Douglas slurped his drink—"or he wears a triple-A cup. But if Branch had his way, he'd rename the team the Cincinnati Lavenders."

There was another pause. I wasn't sure what they were talking about. I looked at Ruah. His eyes were clamped shut. He looked like he was praying.

"Jesus," the goon exhaled. "Branch is a fag?"

The word knifed into our clammy hiding place. I felt Ruah's shoulder squashed into mine. I pushed away, spun, and landed against the opposite column. I saw his hand reach out, then fall, as he stopped himself from grabbing me. I couldn't look at him. I stared at the bison burger and fries spilled in my lap. The sight of them made me gag. Bile burned my throat; I swallowed it back.

I heard Joe's tight laugh, then another loud slurp. "No big deal," he said. "Me and half the team have known for years. But it's a major deal if he wants to out himself and fag up baseball. If he does, his next contract goes to twenty cents on the dollar, his endorsement deal with Pneuma Sports goes poof with the poof, and I'm out a fuckin' fortune."

"Not good," the goon said.

"Break's over," Joe snapped. "You check the Rockpile, I'll do the right-field bleachers." His voice got closer. "No wonder they left their shit. This bison burger's a buffalo pie."

The garbage can exploded again. I held in a scream. Then everything slowed down. Like when you're in a fight and every second stretches long, things around you get bigger, brighter, right in your face. Everything suddenly made sense. It's why he'd been so nice. It's why he'd given me a ride all this time. He was queer!

I looked up.

Ruah was staring at me, stone-still. Streaks of sweat crawled down his face.

My voice came out dry and scratchy. "Are you?"

Sweat tumbled over one-eye. "They say I am."

I shot up like I'd been trapped underwater. The lid flew off the soda in my hand, spilling all over him. I didn't care. He could've drowned in it for all I cared.

22

Escape

I ripped down the stairs and out of the stadium. Some people were still in the parking lot. If he came after me, I'd scream. Reaching the camper, I found a rock by the fence. I broke the side window and yanked open the door. The alarm blared. I ripped off the Rockies jersey, threw it down. I grabbed my backpack and ran across the lot toward the elevated highway.

As I looked back to see if anyone was chasing me, I

thought my eyes were playing tricks. The stadium looked gigantic. Then I realized, behind it, spreading like huge wings, was a wall of clouds. A storm. But something about it looked wrong. It didn't look like rain. It looked like brown cotton candy.

I slid down an embankment. At the bottom was a small river. I picked my way along the brushy bank, looking for a shallow crossing point, or enough rocks to stepping-stone across. Up the long steep on the other side was the highway.

I sloshed across the river and started grinding up the steep. My legs went rubbery. Halfway up, they blew out. My knees dug into the sandy dirt. I bailed on my butt before the weight of my pack and gravity sent me backpack-sledding. I looked back at the ballpark. The storm had pushed closer. Bigger and darker, the clouds bulged over the stadium. Cars were leaving the parking lot.

I finally grabbed a moment to think. I wished every lightning bolt in the black clouds would hit Ruah Branch. He had a dark secret alright; it wasn't doing steroids or going criminal. He was a fag, a queer, an abomination to the Lord. I wanted to throw thunderbolts at him myself. I wanted to see him writhe and twist and suffer. He'd lied to me. He'd tricked me into riding with him, into becoming his friend. And all that time, his mind had been crawling with faggot thoughts.

When God doesn't want you to imagine certain things, sometimes He steps in; He stops you. The moment I started seeing things Ruah liked to do, God twisted my insides into a fist and punched. My stomach leapt out of my throat. I hurled. Nothing came up but air. I heaved again. More air.

With no trail mix to spew, a stomach gets confused. It keeps twisting up, heaving, trying to boot whatever is down there, even if it's nothing but bile and hate. I honked so many times it felt like I was throwing up barbed wire. All I could do was lie in the dirt and gasp for air between throat-tearing heaves.

It finally stopped.

I dropped my head in the dirt and cried. I thanked God for making it stop, for not letting my body turn inside out. And I prayed. I asked God if I should use the money I had left for a bus ticket back to Missouri. Or if I should climb up to the highway and keep going. I pulled out my GPS and turned it on. I was still 385 miles from Providence.

As usual, God didn't answer my prayer directly. He had this way of answering me with whatever I gave Him. If I gave Him confusion, He'd answer with His own version of confusion. And confusion on God's megascale is more like chaos. I looked up and saw His answer. The ballpark was gone, swallowed by the storm of dirty cotton candy. The stadium lights were on. They glowed inside the giant cloud like the eyes of a beast. The beast wasn't a thunderstorm. It was a monster dust storm, devouring everything in its path. His answer wasn't *Go east* or *Go west*. It was *Billy, right now you're not going anywhere.*

I scramble-crawled the rest of the steep to where the highway made an overhang. The wedge of space under the road looked like a good shelter from the storm. I crawled into the cave of steel girders and loose dirt. I watched the mondo storm eat the river. I listened to it moan. Then, in a mad dash, a wall of dust swallowed the collapsing light.

Dust and biting sand slammed into me. My eyes stung, my throat clogged, my nostrils plugged. The air was filled with flying needles, and I was the dartboard.

I dug a shirt from my backpack and wrapped it around my head. It helped a little. Then my mouth got so dry and clogged I couldn't spit. It felt like swallowing sandpaper. I began to feel dizzy. I had to move. If I didn't, I'd keep sucking dust. I'd be buried alive from the inside out.

I grabbed my backpack, slid down the embankment, and found the river. I could just make out the water in the boiling dust. It had been clear before; now it was muddy brown. I washed out my mouth and nose, jammed with so much nosepickium it was nose*pack*ium. I dunked the shirt and held it over my face. Each time it got hard to breathe I rinsed out the shirt and plastered it back on my face.

I kept waiting for the dust to stop. I had no idea how long a dust storm lasted. It was my first. I wondered if it was going to be my last.

Then I remembered something I'd learned about buffalo and cattle in a storm. Buffalo are smart when it comes to surviving. Buffalo put their heads toward the storm, walk into it, and move *through* it. Cattle put their butts to a storm, move *with* it, and sometimes never escape. If I was going to suck dust till I died of an air-ectomy, I was going to die like a buffalo, not a stupid cow. I stumbled down the river, into the storm, back toward the ballpark.

Between not being able to see an arm's length and

squinting against the dust, I didn't see the fence. I face-planted into it. The fence stretched across the river and up both banks. I followed the chain link up the closest embankment.

At the top, my sneaks hit asphalt. I kept walking into the blowing dust. Soon I could see ten feet, twenty. The storm was letting up, or I was getting to the back of it. If I weren't hacking, and my mouth, nose, and lungs weren't stuffed with powdered doughnuts, I would've run.

I saw some cars. I figured I was back in one of the big parking lots. I'd come full circle. It was strange how few cars there were. Rockies fans must've known about dust-nadoes, or whatever they called them, and knew how to escape them.

A shape loomed in the distance: a cone of light, plowing through the haze. As it got closer, I saw they were headlights. Behind the headlights was something squarish and brown. It looked like a UPS truck. It didn't make sense. What would a UPS truck be doing in a stadium parking lot?

A tear of light opened in the dust. I saw part of the ball-park. I looked back at the truck. Its lights had turned toward me. It was the camper, corn dogged in dust. I could see Ruah behind the wheel. I never wanted to lay eyes on him again.

23

The Faggot Bomb

I hurried toward the growing split of light. The passenger side of the camper drew alongside me. I glanced through the broken window. The cab had a matching dust interior. I didn't look at him. I kept walking. The camper kept rolling next to me.

"I don't care about the window," he said. "I would've done the same."

I stayed fixed on the widening light and the safety of the ballpark.

"Are you gonna stop and let me talk to you?" he asked.

"No." My voice wheezed like an old man's. I hacked and spat.

"Will you at least tell me where you're going?"

I figured if I answered maybe he'd stop following me. "I'm gonna wash up and hitchhike."

He waited for me to finish blowing bran-flake boogers out my nose. "The first part's a good idea," he said, " 'cause right now, you're almost as black as me."

I really wanted him to go away. I shot him an ugly look. "At least my dirt comes off."

His head jerked. "What's that supposed to mean?"

"Nuthin." I walked around a parked car to get some distance.

The RV swerved around the car and pulled back close. "Okay, lemme guess," he said with an edge. "I don't think by 'dirt' you're referring to my skin color. It must mean you think I'm dirty on the inside. That I'm a faggot, a fairy, a fruit, pansy, queer, homo, poofta, cocksucker . . ."

I stopped. His voice trailed off as the camper kept going. He must have been looking ahead and not at me.

The camper rocked to a stop.

I braced myself. If I saw the door open, I was going to run. It was less than a hundred yards to the ballpark; I could see people moving around.

Something flapped out of the camper's broken window. A white towel. He was dusting off the outside mirror. The towel sucked back inside; the camper backed up. It drew alongside me.

"Did I leave any out?" he asked. "Any other names you wanna call me?"

I glared at him. My throat clenched. If I was going to hurl again, there was finally something in my stomach to boot: dirt. "Abomination," I said.

"Right," he said. "Forgot that one. When you drop the faggot bomb you never wanna forget 'abomination to the Lord.'"

It pissed me off that he wasn't getting mad. He was just taking it. But what else was he going to do? He knew what he was.

He rubbed his hand over his head. "Okay, here's the deal."

"There is no deal," I snapped.

He lifted his hands. "Okay, no deals. How 'bout I just

tell you what I'd *like* to do? I'd like to drive you to the bus station and buy you a ticket to Providence, Utah, home, or wherever you wanna go. Can you trust me enough to do that?"

I stared at him for a sec, then looked away. "Why would you wanna do that?"

"Number one, the ticket's not gonna bust my bank, and two, it seems like the Christian thing to do."

He had no reason to be generous. Unless there was something behind it. Unless he'd say *anything* to get me back in his RV.

"While you're making up your mind," he said, "if you're asking yourself, *What would Jesus do?* I've got the answer."

"Oh yeah, what's that?"

"Christ liked to chill with the scum of the earth, but there's nothing in the Bible about Him chillin' with a homo. So whether you decide to let me drive you to the bus station or not has absolutely nuthin to do with 'What would Jesus do?' It's about what *you* would do."

I wasn't sure of my next move. Climbing back into the camper scared me. But I felt he owed me. He owed me for being a liar. He owed me for being so nice and acting like a friend, when, all that time, there was something else behind it.

He leaned toward the open window. "Billy, I'm not asking you to come over to the dark side. I'm only offering you a ride and a bus ticket."

24

Thinking Twice

I opened the camper door and dropped my backpack. It kicked up a cloud of dust. You don't think twice about sitting in dust when you're already dusted. You do think twice about climbing in a camper with a homosexual.

As we drove out of the lot, I tried to ignore the fear and disgust coiling inside me. I focused on the expanding light and sky. The sun punched through the haze. The backside of the dust storm blew to the north. But it had left a mini version in the camper. The wind coming through the broken window stirred up a dust devil. Ruah rolled down his window to clear it out. He made a stab at conversation. "I've never seen a ball game called because of dust."

I thought about saying *I've still never seen a ball game,* but I didn't. I didn't want to make small talk, or any talk. I just wanted to get to the bus station.

He tried again. "Your head's probably full of worries and fears and questions, right?"

I stared ahead. "Pretty much," I mumbled.

"So hit me with one of 'em."

No way was I going to tell him about my worries and fears. But I did have a question. "Why would you wanna tell the world you're gay?"

"I don't."

I wondered if he was lying. "Joe Douglas said—"

He cut me off. "I heard what he said, that I wanna turn the Cincinnati Reds into the Lavenders. It's not true. I'd rather stay in the closet forever. But when I told Joe I was gonna switch agents he went berserk. He threatened to out me if I fired him."

"And that's why you're thinking about quitting baseball?"

He nodded. "Pretty much."

I could've left it at that, not asked another question, just got to the station and gone my way. But I fell for the temptation of curiosity. "What are you gonna do?"

He let out a breath. "Don't know. All I know for sure is that I've reached a crossroads, and I can't stand there the rest of my life. I gotta go one way or the other."

I stole a look at his face; his eyes were fixed on the road. His tense expression made me wonder why they were called "gay." "Queer," yeah, but not "gay." I shut my eyes.

After a few seconds he asked, "What are you doing?"

I kept my eyes shut. "Praying."

"For what? Me to be straight?"

I kept praying. "Partly."

"You're that sure being gay is a sin."

I finished and looked up. "It's in the Bible. *Thou shall not lie with mankind as with womankind: it is abomination.*"

A laugh jumped out of him. "Yeah, good ol' Moses in Leviticus, I know it well. And a couple of chapters later Moses lays down the punishment for men lying with men."

The answer popped out of me like I was in a Bible bee. "*They shall surely be put to death.*"

He shot me a look, then scowled. "Mr. Bible Cred knows his homophobic scripture. So you're saying what was true back then should be true today, right?"

"The Bible's truth is forever."

"Amen to that, brother!" He raised his hands in mock praise. "How 'bout we make *all* the abominations that Moses said deserved the death penalty true today. Anyone who commits adultery: death. Anybody who's a medium or a wizard: death. Anybody who curses or blasphemes the name of God: death. Anybody who works on the Sabbath: death. A child who curses his father or mother: wash his mouth out with death! I say bring on *all* the death penalties. It'll rid the world of politicians, porn stars, astrologers, Harry Potter, foulmouthed comedians, atheists, Walmart workers who show up on Sunday, and every snot-nosed kid who ever gave his mom or dad any crap. We'll never worry about population control again. We'll all be dead!"

He tossed his sunglasses onto the dash. "It's what drives me crazy about fundies like you, and everyone else from the First Church of Cherry-picking. You pick verses that support your narrow view and ignore the big picture. You cut and paste the Bible till it's as shallow as a rack of greeting cards. I mean, I keep waiting for the ultimate cherry-pickers' Bible: *The Good Book for Dummies*!"

He pumped several breaths in and out, letting the last one out slow. "Okay, you got me going. Now it's my turn to ask you a question, Billy Allbright. When you do the Galatians thing and try to get Christ to live in you, what does that mean?"

I wanted to not talk anymore, but I couldn't. In the time

178

it took to get to the station I had a chance to witness. "It means I walk in the way of Christ. I try to be as Christlike as I can."

"So you're wearing the T-shirt?"

"What T-shirt?"

"WWJD. What Would Jesus Do?"

"Yeah, what's wrong with that?"

"Did Jesus walk around in a WWMD T-shirt?" He answered my puzzled look. "WWMD: What Would *Moses* Do? Jesus wasn't a lockstep Jew trying to be Moses; he was a rebel. So if you really wanna be Christlike, you can't be a lockstep Christian marching around in a WWJD T-shirt. You gotta be a rebel too."

"I am a rebel. That's what me and my mom do. When we take on evil we break the law all the time."

"That's not being a rebel," Ruah scoffed. "That's being an enforcer, a terrorist, a jihadist who does nothing but tear down in T.L.'s name. You said it yourself; your mother drives a wrecking ball. I'm talking about the kind of rebel who believes Christ delivered us to a new law: *faith*. And that faith is in a God so loving He'll stand by me even if I stand against Him. Even if I shout 'God is dead!' my faith tells me God'll laugh and shout back, *The report of My death is greatly exaggerated!* God knows better than to let me kill 'im. You can't *shock* T.L. God is greater than any sin I can commit, even if it's being gay. T.L. isn't gonna judge me by my lifestyle. He's gonna judge me by my faith-style."

He was speaking in tongues again. His words sounded like gibberish. But I had this feeling, the strange feeling I got when I heard someone speaking in tongues. Envy. I

179

envied his lack of fear. His God didn't have a grip on the smite stick.

Ruah started laughing like his little sermon had been a joke. He finally got a talking-breath. "Do you have any idea how freaky it is to be a ballplayer and have this kind of chatter in your head?"

"Maybe you should have been a preacher instead."

"That's the beauty of baseball. You can leave young, when there's plenty of life down the road."

He pulled the camper over. Across the street was a big building with a metal arch on top that said UNION STATION.

Ruah grabbed his shades and jumped out. "While I'm getting your bus ticket you can take a shower and change clothes if you want. Or you can clean up in the station. Your call." He put on his cowboy hat. "Where's it gonna be, Billy Allbright? Providence, back home, or someplace you haven't told me about?"

I stared at my dusty, oil-stained backpack. I had survived a ride in a Dumpster, a brush with roadside killers, a dust storm, and driving a thousand miles with a homo. I sure wasn't going home. But the idea of taking a bus to Utah didn't feel right either. Something was bugging me, and I couldn't nail it. I looked at Ruah standing outside, waiting for an answer. "Besides it being the Christian thing to do," I asked, "why do you wanna buy me a bus ticket?"

He stared for a second. "You really wanna know?"

I nodded.

"Because you're a stupid kid who doesn't know shit about the world, and since I drove you this far I figure it's my duty to get you a ticket. Does that answer your question?"

"Pretty much."

"Got any others?"

I did. "If you buy the ticket with your nonny card will Joe find out, and think you're going from Denver to Utah?"

He shrugged. "Maybe. What's it to you?"

"I already messed you up with the cell phone. I don't want him finding you 'cause of me."

"Don't worry, he'll only find me when I want him to."

I swallowed. My throat was still coated with dust scum. "What if I said I wanted to stick to our deal?"

He froze for a sec, then slowly took off his glasses. "Which deal is that?"

"You drive me to Providence and I keep fronting for you."

His eyes widened in surprise. "If you mean it, you have to tell me why the hell you'd wanna do that."

I took a breath. "'Cause I'm a stupid kid who doesn't know shit about the world, and I've learned more in the past few days than I've learned in years."

A smile tweaked his mouth.

"Also," I added, "we didn't finish the *Huck Finn* chapters I got in St. Pete."

"No, we didn't." His smile disappeared. "But here's the biggie. Are you sure you can stand driving with a fag?"

I shrugged. "As long as all the fag does is drive."

He laughed hard, then pulled open the door and slid in. "Believe me, kid, you're not my type. But if you wanna stick to our contract, I do too." He started the engine. "Just don't do like Huck and call me your nigger. Deal?"

I nodded. "Deal."

I thought we might shake hands again, but he didn't offer. It was fine with me. Like I said before, when you climb in a camper with a homo you're always thinking twice about stuff.

25

Continental Divides

Back on I-70 Ruah said I needed to get cleaned up before we stopped for food or gas. "If someone sees you like that," he said, "they're gonna think you're some kinda zombie fresh from the grave."

I looked at my shorts and legs caked with dirt. I'm sure my face was just as bad. But given what I knew, I didn't feel like going in the back and taking a shower. "I'd rather do it later."

"Okay," he said, "but in a few miles we're heading into the mountains and the roads are gonna get windy. If you wait till then, you'll get tossed around the bathroom like shoes in a dryer. Or you can wait till the next campsite. But if I were you, I'd take it when we've got a smooth ride."

I realized he was dropping a hint. He knew I was paranoid about traveling with him and that I'd be more comfortable taking a shower when he was driving. "Okay," I said, "I'll get it over with."

182

I took a quick shower. I couldn't believe how much dirt washed off me and came out of my T-shirt and sneakers. After drying off, I shook out my cargo shorts. I had forgotten about the cell phone, and it flopped out. I made sure it was still off, then stuffed it back in the pocket. I wrung out my T-shirt and pulled it back on.

When I came out of the bathroom, Ruah asked if I was hungry. I hadn't eaten anything since breakfast, except dirt. While making myself a PB&J, I made a vow. If he talked about homosexuality and the Bible again, I wasn't going to say a word. On that subject I was taking a vow of silence. Huck Finn says what to do in situations like I was in. It's when Huck's trying to get along with the con artists, the king and the duke. *But I never said nothing, never let on; kept it to myself; it's the best way; then you don't have no quarrels, and don't get into no trouble.* Reading more *Huck Finn* out loud was the perfect way to keep Ruah and me away from any more homo-Bible talk. And there was plenty more to read.

As we drove out of Denver, I read about the king and the duke's latest con. They were pretending to be Englishmen who'd come to see their dying brother, but the brother had died before they got there, and they were trying to cheat the brother's family out of its inheritance.

I stopped reading so I could check out the Rocky Mountains. We were driving up steeps so awesome it felt like we were climbing into the sky. The patches of snow in the highest peaks kept getting bigger and bigger. Looking at the amazing mountains, I kept thinking what a total fred I was for calling all the off-road biking I'd done "mountain

183

biking." It had been more like "anthill biking" compared to the grinders, jumps, and trail plunges I saw everywhere I looked. Part of me wanted to crawl out the window, camper-climb to the back, unstrap Ruah's Trek, and take it for a high-octane, totally gonzo ride in the Rockies.

We passed a sign saying the next exit went up to the Continental Divide. I had a vague memory of Mom teaching me about it. "What's the Continental Divide?"

Ruah scratched his head. "If I remember from school, it's a line that was drawn to answer an age-old question."

"What question?"

"If a tree falls in the mountains and no one's around to hear it, does it make a sound?"

"That's not what it is."

"Really," he insisted. "Everyone on the east side of the line believes a tree falling with no one around makes a sound, and everyone on the west side of the line says a tree falling with no one around doesn't make a sound."

"Yeah, right," I scoffed.

He pulled a confused face. "Or is it the line dividing people on opposite sides of the chicken-or-egg question?"

"Very funny," I said. "You've forgotten what it is too."

He grinned. "Okay, you're right. Wanna go relearn it?"

Part of me wanted to keep going straight to Providence. And part of me wanted to go up to where the snow was. "Will it get us closer to the snow?"

"There's only one way to find out."

We took the exit and climbed a two-laner with severe switchbacks. At the top, we got out at the scenic lookout. A sign said LOVELAND PASS—ELEVATION 11,990 FT.—

184

CONTINENTAL DIVIDE. A marker explained how the rivers on one side of the Divide flowed east toward the Atlantic Ocean, and the rivers on the other side flowed west toward the Pacific.

On each side of the turnoff were walking trails leading up to bowls of snow. There's no way I was going to go to the top of the Rockies without making a snowball in the middle of summer. We hiked up to the nearest bowl of snow. We both made snowballs. I threw mine as hard as I could down the mountainside. It flew for a while, then exploded on some rocks.

"C'mon," I said, "you're the baseball player. Let's see it."

Ruah wound up and gave his snowball a heave. It rocketed so fast it made a sound as it ripped the air. It flew so far it disappeared down the mountain and I never heard it hit. It was pretty cool, but I didn't say so.

On the way down, Ruah stopped and pointed off the trail. Standing on a rock was an animal with thick reddish-brown fur and a black face. It was smaller than a groundhog but fatter. We had a staring contest, which the animal won when we kept going.

Back at the turnoff, Ruah found an information board and looked to see if it said what the animal was. I went back to the camper and turned on my GPS; we were still 342 miles from Providence. It was already midafternoon. Seeing the top of the Rockies and the Divide was worth it, but I made another vow: no more side trips.

Ruah got back in the camper. "It was a yellow-bellied marmot." He chortled and started the engine. "That's the tough thing about being an animal. People give you a crappy name and there's nothing you can do about it."

As we took off, I wondered if he was talking about more than animals. I wondered if he was talking about him and his kind and the names they get called. But I kept quiet; I had my vow of silence. I was doing a Huck: keeping it to myself. And the best way to keep it to myself was to read his story.

That was my plan, anyway.

26

Word Shrapnel

I read up to where Huck meets a girl who's part of the family that's getting cheated out of their inheritance by the king and the duke. Huck thinks Mary Jane is awesome. I didn't like Huck getting unglued over some girl; he was smarter than that. But he's so rag-dolly in love with Mary Jane that he says to her, *I don't want no better book than what your face is.* Words to boot by. That wasn't his only spew.

> You may say what you want to, but in my opinion she had more sand in her than any girl I ever see; in my opinion she was just full of sand. It sounds like flattery, but it ain't no flattery. And when it comes to beauty—and goodness, too—she lays over them all. I hain't ever seen her since that time that I see her go out of that door; no, I hain't ever seen her since, but I reckon I've thought of her a many and a many million times.

186

When I finished the chapter, I took a break because my voice was getting scratchy. I also wanted to check out more of the Rocky Mountain grades I couldn't ride. Not yet, anyway. After I collected *my* inheritance and made it on the pro mountain biking circuit, I was definitely coming back to scream the Rockies.

Ruah still had his head in the story. "Too bad Huck never saw Mary Jane again," he said. "Sounds like he lost his forever love."

"Yeah, but if he fell for her and stayed there in Arkansas, his adventure down the river would've been over."

Ruah nodded. "True, the *Adventures of Huckleberry Finn* would've turned into a *miss* adventure." He cracked up at his joke. Then he asked, "What about you? Ever had a miss adventure?"

"What do you mean?"

"You know, a girlfriend?"

I wanted to say yes, but it would've been a lie. Girlfriends don't come easy when you're a jump-around Jesus freak. "Not really," I said, then something popped out of my mouth before I could stop it. "That doesn't make me gay."

He burst out laughing. "That's not why I asked, but don't worry, I'm *sure* you're straight. You see, we have this thing called 'gaydar.' We can pick up the vibes of whether a person is gay or not. And when it comes to you, the gaydar screen is as blank as blank gets."

I stuck with my vow of silence. Okay, I was the one who'd said "gay" first, but it was an accident, like when you're talking to someone and food shrapnel flies out of your mouth. There was no hitting a reset button, but there *was* changing the subject. My throat suddenly felt better; I began reading the last two chapters we had. Of course, just when you think you're doing the right thing to steer clear of "queer," you run smack into it, not once, but *twice*.

At the end of Chapter 29 I had to read about Huck being "fagged," even though I'm pretty sure it meant he was totally spent as he ran for his life. Of all the words the writer could've used—zonked, bonked, cashed—he had to go and use the F-word. I gave Mark Twain the benefit of the doubt on that one because it probably didn't have the same meaning back then as it does today. But then what he wrote at the end of Chapter 30 was unforgivable.

It's after the king and the duke's plan to swindle Mary Jane is discovered and they're busted. Huck and Jim have escaped and think they're finally rid of the crooks. But the king and the duke escape too and jump back on the raft. The swindlers fight over how they almost got hanged, till they get drunk, hug, and make up. Then, on the last page, things get mega-creepy. The king and duke crawl into the lean-to on the raft, get "lovinger," and "went off a-snoring in each other's arms."

It's gnarly enough riding shotgun with a homo; it gets skin-crawl creepy when what you're reading goes from a pretty decent story to one about two old queers sleeping together.

Ruah must've heard something in my voice as I read the last part. He said, "You're not thinking what I'm thinking, are you?"

I played dumb. "I'm not thinking anything."

He didn't take the hint. "I mean, if we had the next chapter, would we find out the king and duke are *gay*?"

I caught his sarcasm, but I wasn't falling for it. I lied again. "No way. They're just a couple of old drunks who passed out."

"Yeah, I think you're right."

He tried to ask me a bunch of school questions, like what I thought was going to happen next and stuff like that, but I kept my answers snap-short. He finally got that I didn't want to talk and just wanted to watch the scenery.

The highway cut through a canyon with towering rock walls and the Colorado River tumbling along below the road. As I watched white-water rafters riding the rapids, I started thinking how differently things happen in life compared to in a book. I mean, on the white-water rafts there probably wasn't one person even close to being as bad as the crooks Huck and Jim had on their raft. The white-water rafters were just normal people looking for a thrill. But in a book it's all fireworks and drama. Like the king and the duke screaming at each other, beating each other up, then getting drunk before they hugged and made up. Real life was so different. Ruah and I weren't going to scream at each other, beat each other up, and get drunk. No, we were just going to ride along in silence, agreeing on one thing: we were done talking for a while.

The canyon widened, opening on the beginning of sunset. As the sun hit the rock walls, it lit up all the tiny layers in the cliffs. They looked like giant stacks of stone tablets. Like the place was God's Staples, and this was where He kept all the blank tablets He had yet to write on. Or maybe they'd been written on already, and these were the stacks of stone journals God had kept ever since creation. Written on the tablets were all the things God had heard people *think* but never say. Things like the words I wanted to shout at my mom but didn't dare. Things Ruah wanted to say to me but stopped himself before he did. Things I imagined saying to my father, or he had imagined saying to me, but neither of us would ever get to say because he was dead. I liked thinking that all the unspoken things God had heard were buried in those cliffs. They were stone chapters in His Book of Life.

As we headed toward Grand Junction, Colorado, the sunset pushed the hills even wider. Everything was stubbled with sagebrush. It looked like land in need of a shave.

We hadn't said anything for so long it got weird. I told myself Ruah probably had plenty to think about. And even if he had the urge to share some of it, or if I had the urge to share my thoughts, it was like we were both taking Huck's advice: . . . *kept it to myself; it's the best way; then you don't have no quarrels, and don't get into no trouble.*

Just before the Utah border, we passed a big wood sign: LEAVING COLORFUL COLORADO. As the Utah sign shot toward us, Ruah started laughing. He swerved onto the shoulder and slammed on the brakes. The camper almost did a nose wheelie in front of the billboard. It just said WELCOME TO UTAH. Below it was a picture of a ski jumper in midflight.

Ruah kept laughing and pounding the steering wheel. "That's the best one yet!"

I didn't get it. "What's so funny?"

190

"Look at it!" He swept a hand at the horizon. "We've gone from colorful Colorado to a frying pan of scorched desert, and what do they put on their welcome sign?" He cracked up before he could say it. "A ski jumper looking for a place to land!"

"Yeah," I muttered, "it's kinda random."

"Random? No way. It's totally a sign from God!" He broke up again.

I'd heard of some strange signs from God but never an actual billboard.

He stopped laughing and wiped his eyes. "A ski jumper in the middle of the desert? Don't you get it?"

I shook my head.

"He's as out of place as we are. There's me, a poof in the major league closet, and you, a homophobe-in-training, and we're riding together. But it's even more bizarre than that. We're about to do the whole desert-wandering thing, and we're looking for a place called Providence." He looked up at the billboard. "Thank you, Lord, for this wonderful sign. I just wish I still had my phone."

I tensed. "Why?"

He waved at the sign. "I'd take a picture of it. And every time I thought I was some freaky fag in the majors, I'd get out my picture of my buddy, the poor desert ski jumper lookin' for a place to land, and I'd say, 'Pal, I know how you feel.'"

I came super close to digging out the phone and handing it to him. But if he got mad about it, this was no place to get dumped. Like he said, we were about to go wandering in the desert.

He sucked in a breath and exhaled. "I think I need some coffee."

We stopped to gas up, and I picked up fast food for dinner. I checked my GPS. We were 160 miles from Providence; the compass pointed north-northwest. We ate and kept driving. After it got dark, we turned north. I started nodding against the doorframe.

"You can go in the back and get some sleep," Ruah said.

"Are you gonna keep driving?"

"Yeah. Who knows, maybe I'll make it clear to Providence."

As I got in my sleeping bag a thought kept nagging at me. Why was he still driving some kid he didn't seem to like? The only answers I came up with made me nervous. Maybe he had plans I didn't know about. Maybe he'd lied when he'd said I wasn't his type, and he was waiting to make his move. Or maybe he wasn't as rich as he said, and he wasn't any different than the king and the duke. Maybe he was planning to steal my inheritance.

What finally let me relax enough to sleep was a realization: there was a huge difference between me and Ruah in a camper and Huck and Jim on a raft. Nobody had to drive the raft; it floated down the river by itself. As long as Ruah had his hands on the wheel, I was safe. My last hundred thoughts before dropping into the z-bag were a mantra: If the camper stops, wake up . . . if the camper stops, wake up . . .

27

Providence

I bolted awake to a voice. "Run!" It shouted louder. "Run, Tony! Run!" It came from outside. I realized the camper was stopped; it was early morning. I looked through the window.

A man ran toward our campsite. He wore zebra-striped pants and a bright orange shirt. He was some kind of prisoner. He turned toward the camper. I fumbled in my pocket for my knife. The man grabbed the garbage can at our site and spun back to the road. A pickup pulled up, a trash container in its bed. Behind the truck was a flatbed with a bunch of men all wearing the same zebra-striped pants and orange shirts. The prisoner emptied the garbage can in the pickup, dropped it back on the ground. "Run, Tony, run!" one of the prisoners yelled, and they all burst out laughing.

I heard the curtain slide in the sleeping loft. The shouting had woken Ruah up. He groaned. I listened as he rolled over and went back to sleep. I was wide awake.

I went outside. The rising sun painted the mountain peaks to the west with light. The other campsites were dead quiet. I pulled out my GPS and turned it on. I was stunned to see we were only 6.9 miles from Providence. Ruah had driven most of the night. I wanted to grab my pack and start walking to Providence. I could be there in two hours. But I also felt like I had to wait. I mean, he'd driven me so far.

I walked to the end of the campground, where there was a stone bench. It overlooked a sparkling lake with chalky cliffs on the far side. I sat down and tried to figure out what to do. Then it hit me. The garbagemen were actually a sign from God; they were His messengers. One was telling me, "Run!" The other, the man emptying the garbage can, was a warning. If I didn't go now, God was going to show up and dump me out of the camper like garbage. God was telling me His junior Jonah had traveled long enough in Giff. And just like Jonah, who spent three days and three nights in the belly of the Great Fish, I had spent three days and three nights in Giff. It was time for me to be spit out.

God's will had opened to me as clear and sparkling as the lake in front of me. My insides swelled with flowy giddiness. I remembered how Huck had put it when everything became crystal clear. *Here was the plain hand of Providence slapping me in the face.*

I slipped into the camper and lifted my pack. I thought about waking Ruah to thank him and say goodbye, but he was sleeping soundly. I wrote him a note.

Providence is 7 miles north. I'm going up there to find the geocache. If you want, I'll meet you at whatever diner's up there. I'll buy you breakfast, and we can say goodbye.

Billy

Whether he came to Providence or not was up to him. I was giving him an out. If he'd finally gotten tired of riding with a "homophobe-in-training" and wanted to ditch me, he was getting his chance.

The campground was on the edge of a town called Hyrum. Following the compass arrow on the GPS, I walked up the main street to the highway. I put out my thumb and got a ride from a guy going to work in Logan. He dropped me on the commercial strip outside of Providence. As I walked into town, the GPS ticked down to 1.5 miles from the cache.

Providence was mainly nice houses on tree-lined streets. I walked up Center Street, following the compass toward a big hill rising behind the town. The cache site was looking very different from the first two. It wasn't in a dying little town, or the graveyard of a dead one. Of course, with a name like Providence, you'd expect something nicer.

But for all the nice houses, the town didn't seem to have a diner or any breakfast place. If Ruah was going to meet me for breakfast it would have to be back down on the strip.

At the top of Center Street was a lush green park called Vons Park. A mountain stream ran through it; the compass pointed up a trail next to the stream. My GPS ticked down to 0.35 miles.

Remembering how tree cover can mess with GPS reception and accuracy, I pulled out the last *Huck Finn* chapter—where the drunken king and duke fell asleep together on the raft—and read the clue poem my father had scrawled at the end.

195

Upon the raft four sinners dwell,
But only one is bound for hell.
To find out which will take some
  tricks,
Although your crick's no River Styx.
You'll find no crossing on Charon's
  boat,
Not a single troll or billy goat.
At trail's end is nature's span,
Across the way, hell in a can.
As you seek, don't be daft,
Remember Huck is on a raft.

I got that the "four sinners" were the king, the duke, Huck, and Jim. But why only one of them was going to burn in hell I didn't know. From what I'd read of *Huck Finn*, I would've guessed they were all going to hell, except maybe Jim. His only sin was running away from being a slave. He was pretty much an antinomian: breaking land law to obey God law. God doesn't believe in slavery.

I started up the trail along the stream. The path climbed through woods, opened onto a little meadow, then rose through thick woods like a tunnel. My eyes darted between my GPS and the shadowy ground; I didn't want to step on any snakes. At 0.1 mile it switched to 525 feet; the numbers ticked down super fast. My heart raced along with it.

I had no idea what my father meant by "River Styx" or "Charon's boat," so I focused on "At trail's end is nature's span." I figured I could decipher that one.

The trail got tighter and creepier as I got under a

hundred feet. I used a stick to do some cobweb clearing. I half expected to trip over a dead body.

Then I saw it. "Nature's span": a tree trunk fallen across the creek. I tightroped over the trunk and almost fell in the water when my foot slipped. I looked in the undergrowth for "hell in a can," whatever that meant. I thought maybe it would be a red gas can, you know, like fire in a can. I looked all around for twenty to thirty feet, but found nothing.

I checked the GPS. I was still 70 feet from the cache. With the heavy tree cover I could've been off by fifty or a hundred feet. I reread the poem's last line. "As you seek, don't be daft/Remember Huck is on a raft." It made no sense. There was nothing like a raft, low, high, or anywhere.

I started back across the creek to see if the GPS's distance reading would get better in a tree-cover hole above the trail. As I crossed I glanced down at the GPS. The compass needle swung back upstream. I lost my balance. I threw the GPS toward the trail as I fell off the skinny. I could get wet, but my GPS couldn't. I landed on my ass in the stream. The water was really cold.

I clambered out and pulled the GPS out of a bush. It still worked. Then I saw the overgrown path, barely visible as it continued up the creek. I yanked out the pages in my wet pocket and hoped my father hadn't written the clue poem in bleeder ink. Luckily, he hadn't. When I saw the line, I slapped myself on the forehead. "You big dope. 'At trail's end is nature's span.'" I wasn't at trail's end.

I ran up the trail. There it was: another fallen tree

197

spanning the creek. My GPS was showing less than 30 feet. Since I was already half soaked I didn't bother with the tree crossing. I splashed through the water. On the other side there was more dense undergrowth, but this time there was something else. A bunch of old limbs lay side by side on the ground. "As you seek, don't be daft/Remember Huck is on a raft."

I yanked up dead limbs, keeping an eye out for snakes. Something yellow flashed. I jumped up, banging my head on a branch. The yellow didn't move. It was the plastic lid of a coffee can half buried in rotting leaves. I pulled the can out and peeled off the top.

I wasn't surprised by what was inside. Ziplock bags with some money, a thin stack of book pages, and a little plastic toy: a devil with a pitchfork. Okay, someone in *Huck Finn was* going to hell. And I wasn't surprised that "hell in a can" hadn't turned out to be the bad book. It was getting pretty obvious my father didn't want me finding it till I'd read *all* of *Huck Finn*. I just hoped *Huck* wasn't as brick thick as the Bible. If it was, my treasure trail was going to be a death march to Mongolia.

On the second page of the new chapter I found a highlighted word: "not." In the next few pages, four more highlights followed: "us," "I," "da," "ho." Notus, Idaho? What kind of name was that?

28

A New Plan

Heading back down the trail, I entered Notus, Idaho, into the GPS. It was a real town, and not too far: 290 miles. With some luck, I could hitchhike there in a day.

I left Vons Park, walked down Center Street, and started reading the new *Huck* pages. Chapter 31 was a shocker.

- The king and the duke give up Jim to slave hunters for a reward.
- When Huck finds out Jim's going to be sold to a bad plantation down south, he thinks Jim would be better off back upriver with his owner, Miss Watson. He thinks about writing her a letter telling her to come fetch her slave.
- Unsure what to do, Huck prays over his decision. He realizes his mind is telling him to do the right thing, to write Miss Watson, but his heart is telling him to do something else. As he prays, he realizes you can't fool God. He says, "You can't pray a lie."
- He writes the letter as a test. He thinks it's a fine and righteous letter. But then he starts remembering his adventures with Jim and the great times they've had.
- He picks up the letter and knows he's got to decide between two things: to do the good thing and send the letter to Miss Watson, or to do the bad thing and

not. He has to decide between being good or being a sinner, forever.

- He rips up the letter and says, "Alright, then, I'll *go* to hell."

When I read that I heel-planted. It was so lame. I mean, the world's full of choices, but I'd never heard of anyone who *wanted* to go to hell. That's *never* the best choice. It got me thinking. What if all the notes Mark Twain scribbled in the bad book about the sequel to *Huck Finn* were about just that? Huck going to hell. For all I knew, it might even be called *Huck Finn in Hell*. No wonder my father called it the "bad book."

I stood on the sidewalk, dumbstruck. Did I keep going another 290 miles for a book that might be that stupid? Was my treasure hunt for a total piece of crap?

I flipped to the last page of the two new chapters to see if my father had left another clue poem. He had.

Now that Huck has set his waypoint,
And goes on down to Satan's joint,
Do consider what he might drive,
If he wishes to survive.
Look for fuel to throw on fire,
There you'll find your heart's
    desire.

I stared at the last three words: "your heart's desire." What did he mean by that? What was my heart's desire? More chapters of *Huck Finn*? Didn't think so. Was it the bad book itself? And then it hit me like a ton of bricks. My heart's desire wasn't more chapters of some old story about a boy and a runaway slave on a raft. And it wasn't some "bad book" with a bunch of Mark Twain scribbles in it. My heart's desire was to get the damn book and sell it. My heart's desire was the freedom it was going to buy me!

I started striding down the sidewalk. The plan was simple: go to the highway, start hitching.

I didn't get a block before a white shape appeared at the bottom of the street. A small camper started up the long hill. I stopped. It was Giff. I'd totally forgotten about the note I'd left Ruah.

Coming up the street, the camper flashed through patches of bright sun and shade. In an intersection, it flashed bright white, like it was on fire. It sparked something in my brain, a question: What if I'd gotten the sign God sent me that morning all wrong? The searing doubt ignited more questions. What if God's garbageman messenger wasn't telling me to run *from* something? What if he was telling me to run *toward* something? What if the messenger emptying the white trash can wasn't tossing *me* from the camper? What if God had been showing me that what He wanted tossed from the camper was the trash of *sin*?

As the camper drew closer, and I saw Ruah through the windshield, the answers rained down like the sunlight piercing the trees. Just as Huck turned on a dime to try and save Jim from slavery, I had to turn on a dime too. God wanted me to save Ruah from another kind of slavery: the slavery of sin.

The camper pulled to the curb. I couldn't hold back a

grin as I stepped over to the window. "I found it." I pulled the ziplock bags from my pocket. "It's the next two chapters, some more money, and a toy devil."

His head pulled back. "What's the devil about?"

"You'll get it when I read you Chapter Thirty-one."

His face pinched as he grunted. "Hmm, I thought you were done reading to me. Your note said you wanted to say goodbye."

"Yeah, but something came up."

He stared at me. "What's that?"

I shouldered my backpack. "I'll tell you later. Right now I wanna buy you breakfast."

He smiled for the first time. "Sounds good. Let's do it."

I got in and we drove down the street.

Ruah looked at the new chapters still clutched in my hand. "So, where's your next geocache?"

"Notus, Idaho."

"Where's that?"

"Two hundred and ninety miles northwest."

"As long as there's more *Huck* to read"—he smiled and patted the dashboard—"me and Giff are good for it."

29

Saving Ruah Branch

We took the road atlas into breakfast, found Notus in southwest Idaho, and plotted a course.

After we drove through Logan and headed west, I pulled

out my Bible. I turned to Genesis and went right to the Word Ruah needed to hear. *"So God created man in his own image, in the image of God created he him; male and female created he them. And God said unto them, Be fruitful and multiply."*

As I turned to another verse Ruah snickered. "What are you doing?"

I let the Word answer. *"Therefore shall a man leave his father and his mother, and shall cleave unto his wife, and they shall be one flesh."*

"Excuse me," he said. "What happened to reading the new chapters of *Huck Finn*?"

"I'll get to 'em." I flipped to Leviticus.

"So this is what changed your mind about saying goodbye? You wanted to save my perverted soul first."

"It's God's will that everyone should be straight."

The camper swerved; my eyes shot up from Leviticus. We bounced along the shoulder and lurched to a stop. A car flew around us, its horn blaring.

Ruah yanked off his sunglasses and fixed me with hard eyes. "Maybe goodbye should be sooner than later. I don't need to be saved, by you or anyone else."

"Everyone needs to be saved."

He flicked a hand at the door. "Ride's over."

I opened the door, jumped out, and grabbed my pack. I shut the door, making sure to slam it.

As I hiked on my pack he said, "Look, Billy, it wasn't always the case, but I'm perfectly happy being gay."

"If you're so happy what are you doing in the closet, or locker room, or whatever you call it?"

"It's 'closet.'"

"You didn't answer my question."

He took a deep breath. "Alright, Billy Allbright, you need a ride to Notus, Idaho, right?"

"Yeah, and I also wanna help you."

He frowned. "I'm sure you do. You're such a Good Samaritan, you'd give a drink of water to a drowning man."

"What's that mean?"

"Never mind," he said, slipping his shades back on. "Here's the way it's gonna be if you want a ride. For every antigay, homophobic piece of scripture you throw at me, you read me a chapter of *Huck Finn*."

"But I've only got two new chapters."

He shrugged. "Then you've only got two shots at saving my ass. I wanna hear *Huck,* and you wanna hear me cry 'straight.' I think it's a fair deal. You gonna take it or leave it?"

I climbed back in. I felt so juiced with the Holy Spirit, I figured I only needed one shot. Because if there was one thing I'd learned about as a Jesus-throated Whac-a-Mole protesting at homosexual weddings, was the best scripture bombs to throw to smoke the devil out.

We got back on the road. I opened the Bible to Leviticus.

"Whoa," Ruah said. "What happened to Genesis, and all that cleaving, one-fleshing, and fruity multiplying?"

"It was *'Be fruitful and multiply.'*"

"Right, but here's my question. Is Old Testy's order to cleave and multiply an all-or-nothing deal? I mean, if you just cleave, but don't multiply, does that mean you're defying God?"

"Yeah," I said. "God wants everyone to have children."

"So if a couple can't make babies they shouldn't be cleaving?"

"That's not what I said."

He shouted out his window. "Hear that, peeps? And I'm talkin' to all you non–baby makers: the infertile, the sterile, the old, the homos. Stop cleaving this instant! Stop getting married! And for God's sake, stop becoming one flesh! There's nuthin nastier than doin' the one-flesh with no new flesh to show for it!"

I didn't laugh. I told him he could make fun all he wanted, but it didn't change scripture. I told him he was turning God's Word into Play-Doh so he could mold it into whatever he wanted.

"Great minds think alike," he said, pointing at my head. "Martin Luther said scripture was like a wax nose; you can twist it any way you like."

"You're doing all the twisting."

He nodded. "Maybe so. But now that we've heard from Genesis, it's time to hear from Huck." He grinned. "Chapter Thirty-one, please."

I didn't want to, but I had to keep my side of the bargain. I pulled out Chapter 31. It was much tougher to read out loud. Especially to a black guy. Huck says "nigger" and refers to Jim as "my nigger" so often I began rushing over the word.

Ruah interrupted me. "Just go with it and stop

mumbling 'my nigger.' I'd rather hear that flying out of your mouth than 'faggot' and 'abomination to the Lord.' "

When I got to the end, I asked him about what had bugged me the first time I read the chapter in Providence. "If there was a sequel to *Huck Finn*, do you think it would be *Huck Finn in Hell*?"

He laughed. "Once a literalist, always a literalist."

"What do you mean?"

"If Huck's literally going to hell, then so are you and your mother."

"No way."

"You said it before; you're both antinomians. You break the law of the land and answer to a higher law. Huck's no different. He refuses to turn in a runaway slave 'cause he's obeying a higher law: the law of the heart."

Ruah drummed on the wheel. "Okay, I'm dying to hear the next chapter, but we got a deal. Billy Bible Cred gets another chance to save me from the abyss of swish."

As I turned to the slam dunk of Bible stories against homosexuality we crossed the border into Idaho. The big blue sign said WELCOME TO IDAHO, and then a little sign added IDAHO IS TOO GREAT TO LITTER.

Ruah laughed and shook a finger at me. "And they're not just talking trash-trash. They're talking trashy *ideas*. So don't be littering the beautiful Idaho countryside with crappy ideas, 'cause the Idaho thought police will fine your ass for sure. And they don't care if your trashy idea comes from the Bible or not. If it's trash, it's trash."

I gave him a half laugh, shut my Bible, and tucked it in the door pocket. I could wait on my slam-dunk scripture until two things happened. (1) I got some food in my stomach and some juice on my dry throat. And (2) he wasn't so full of himself that he wore attitude earplugs to God's Word.

30

Into the Desert

After stopping for body fuel, we followed the Snake River, a shiny ribbon winding through southern Idaho. The river was the blue stripe in the middle of a fatter "snake" of checkered green pastures and milk-shake-brown fields. On both sides of the valley were dry hills covered in sagebrush and scrub cedar.

When we passed a sign for an old hotel, THE SAGE STEPPE INN, I asked about the weird spelling. Ruah told me that sage steppe was one of the names for the high desert that stretched beyond the river valley. It was a wonky name. I mean, it looked to me like the kind of desert where no one had ever *stepped,* and if they had, they might've never stepped out of it again.

As we got off the interstate and followed the Snake River up to Notus, the sage steppe to the south got drier and wilder-looking. We even passed some giant sand dunes, like they'd been airlifted from the Sahara Desert.

The steppe looked so unstepped on by humans or animals, it got me thinking. In the Midwest, it looks like every square inch of land has been trod on by a person or an animal at sometime or other. And if footprints never went away—like dinosaur tracks in rocks—the Midwest would be a huge carpet of footprints. But out west, in the high desert, there would be places that no human or animal had ever tread. Sure, there'd be trails and tracks from the past, but there'd also be islands of ground where no creature had *ever* set foot or hoof. There'd be places as untouched as the moon.

It made me want to ask Ruah to stop so that I could get out and walk into the desert to one of those untouched islands. When I thought I'd found one, I'd kick off my sneaks and be the first creature to ever step on that piece of God's earth. On that one little island, I'd be Adam.

It was just one of my dopey fantasies, but it was also God reminding me of something. Most of His good earth had been corrupted by the foul footprint of sin. And God's will, before I got to Notus, was to save Ruah from his sinful path.

I opened my Bible to Genesis, where the Lord destroys Sodom and Gomorrah. I read it out loud. It's as straightforward as scripture gets.

- Two angels, in the form of men, visit the town of Sodom.
- A man who lives there, Lot, invites the two strangers into his house. He feeds them and offers them shelter for the night.
- A mob of Sodomites shows up and orders Lot to give them the two men so they can "know them," meaning have sex with them.

- Lot begs the mob to take his daughters instead. They refuse. They want the two men.
- The two men pull Lot back into the house and, being angels, blind all the Sodomites outside. The angels tell Lot to take his family and leave Sodom because it's going to be destroyed for its wickedness.
- And that's what the Lord does: He rains fire and brimstone on Sodom, killing everyone and everything.

I shut the Bible. Ruah didn't say anything. I looked over. He'd taken off his sunglasses. His face looked puzzled, but his mouth was set in a smirk. "That story always struck me as this really sick tale about what some fathers think of their daughters."

"That's not what it's about," I said.

"Really? What's it about?"

"God destroyed Sodom because it was filled with homo-sexuals. And that's why 'sodomy' is still the word for what you people do, and a 'sodomite' is someone who does it."

He slowly nodded. "Very good on the etymology, kid. Does it also follow that if anyone should know about the story of Sodom, it would be a sodomite?"

"I don't know about that."

"Well," he said, with his smirk back, "as a latter-day sodomite, I'd like to throw out another reason why T.L. destroyed Sodom."

I couldn't wait to see him try and wiggle out of this one.

He raised a hand. "Okay, I'll admit, even though there's

no actual man-on-man sex in the story, there is the *threat* of it. But what the story's really about is two opposites: brotherly love and male rape."

"What does brotherly love have to do with it?"

"It's another term for doing someone a kindness, for hospitality, don't you think?"

I gave him the benefit of the doubt. "I guess so."

"In the Holy Land, and in desert culture, when the nights get so cool, one of the worst things you can do is leave someone out in the cold. So, all through the Bible there are stories, and laws, about how strangers should be given shelter for the night, and food. But there was another good reason to be kind to strangers. You never knew when the stranger wandering into your camp or village might be a god or an angel. And that's exactly who Lot ended up taking in, two angels disguised as men, right?"

"What does any of that have to do with homosexuality?"

"I'm getting to it. You see, if the mob of Sodomites that showed up at Lot's door were really homosexuals, and if they were anything like gays today, they would've simply knocked on the door, asked if the two strangers wanted to go out for a beer, maybe hit a club, and take it from there. But no, the mob that tried to break down Lot's door wanted to 'know' the two strangers. They wanted to rape them."

"Exactly," I said, "which makes them homos."

"No," he said, stretching out the word. "They weren't homos any more than cops using toilet-plunger handles to violate suspects are homos. It's not about sex. It's about domination and the humiliation of male rape. And believe me, back in the good ol' holy days, male rape happened all the time."

"No way."

"I wish you were right, but ancient cultures had their gnarly ways. Aztecs ate the hearts and drank the blood of their conquered foes. The Holy Landers had a different way of sticking it to their beaten enemies: they raped them. But they didn't do it because they were gay. They did it to strip them of their manhood, to turn them into women. If you turned your enemy into a lowly woman, then you'd shamed him, broken his spirit. He was as good as dead. I mean, look at what Lot thought of his daughters. He offered them up as rape substitutes."

Ruah shrugged. "Hey, if you don't believe me, think about how men still run around busting other guys' balls. You hear it in every locker room and on every playing field where guys insult each other with names like pussy, faggot, and cocksucker. Of course, we don't call it rape. We have a nicer name for it: trash talk. I hear it every day. And it goes all the way back to that mob in front of Lot's door.

"The Sodomites weren't a bunch of gays looking for a quickie. They were a lynch mob, or, in their case, a rape mob. They weren't blinded by the angels and destroyed 'cause they wanted to stick it where the sun don't shine. They were destroyed for violating the sacred law of hospitality. Their sin was a complete lack of what God sent Christ down to make clear to the world: 'Love your neighbor as yourself.'"

I'd followed his crazy, zigzag trail from the destruction of Sodom to Christ's teaching, but it was like following a blown-up balloon that's let go and whirligigs around the room. I didn't know what to say.

The only thought I had that made sense was that it wasn't Ruah who was messing with what I knew in my heart. It was God. And His message went like this: *Billy, you're gonna have to do better than that if you wanna argue sodomy with a sodomite.* But I didn't have another chance, not until I'd read another chapter of *Huck Finn.*

31

Shaken Out

I pulled out Chapter 32.

Ruah waved a hand. "Wait a minute. You didn't finish the chapter."

I held up the *Huck Finn* pages. "I haven't even started it."

"No, I mean chapter nineteen in Genesis."

"What?"

"If you're gonna convince me that the destruction of Sodom and Gomorrah is about homosexuality, the least you could do is read the whole chapter."

I didn't know what he was up to, but I opened the Bible and read the last eight verses of the chapter. I'd forgotten about them. Talk about a shocker.

- Lot and his two daughters escape to a cave in the mountains.

- Lot has no sons and no chance of having any because his wife looked back at the destruction of Sodom and Gomorrah and was turned into a pillar of salt.
- The daughters decide their father has to have sons.
- The first night in the cave, the daughters get Lot drunk and the older daughter has sex with him, but Lot doesn't know it because he's so drunk.
- The second night they get Lot drunk again, and the younger daughter has sex with him, but he doesn't know it.
- The daughters give birth to boys, giving Lot sons. Of course, to the daughters, they're sons and *brothers*.

After I finished, Ruah stroked his beard stubble. "Hmm, now that we've heard the *whole* story of Lot, what the heck is *that* all about? I don't know about you, but for me the way it depicts bad sex and good sex is really confusing. I mean, let's say you're right, and that man-on-man sex is nasty and bad no matter where, when, or why. But when Lot offers his daughters to be raped by the mob we don't hear a peep from God. And when the daughters date-rape their dad, not once but twice, Old Testy doesn't lift a finger. Call me crazy, but the only sensible one in the whole wacko crew is Lot's wife."

"What's she got to do with anything?"

"If I was married to a man who would throw my daughters to a rape mob, and I had daughters who had it in 'em to date-rape their own dad, I'd turn into a pillar of salt too."

I just shook my head in disgust. "Can I read Chapter Thirty-two now?"

Ruah shot me a huge smile. "I thought you'd never ask."

I read the chapter from start to finish. It was about Huck going to the Phelpses' farm to free Jim from slavery. But things get complicated when the Phelpses think Huck is Tom Sawyer and Huck goes along with it, pretending to be Tom.

When I was done, Ruah said, "Now we know why your father picked Notus, Idaho, for the next cache."

"Why?"

"'Cause Huck is *not* himself, he's Tom."

"Maybe so." He might've been right about that but I knew he was wrong about his way of life, because the Bible said so. But I wasn't bringing it up again until the right moment. I was going to do like Huck says before he gets to the Phelpses' farm. I was going to go . . . *right along, not fixing up any particular plan, but just trusting to Providence to put the right words in my mouth when the time come; for I'd noticed that Providence always did put the right words in my mouth if I left it alone.*

As the sun dropped toward the horizon I checked my GPS. We were 44 miles from Notus. Then the most incredible smell rolled through the cab. "What's that?"

Ruah inhaled a deep breath. "Mint?"

We stared at the field of dark plants. "I've never seen a mint field before."

"Me neither."

We rode for a couple miles just sucking up the smell. It felt like my nostrils and lungs were being scrubbed out. The sun began to set as the mint field changed back to sage steppe.

Ruah broke the silence. "We might never see eye to eye

214

on the whole gay thing, but as you were reading *Huck* it gave me an idea that might help you get it."

I didn't say anything. I just stared at the wall of clouds on the horizon swirling with yellow and orange.

He went on. "When Huck pretends to be Tom it doesn't change who Huck is. He's still Huck. He can make people think he's Tom, but it doesn't change who he is. It's the same for a lot of gays. We can pretend to be straight, we can live in the closet, but it doesn't change who we are. We're still gay. And when you, or anyone else, try to turn a gay into a straight it's as impossible as truly turning Huck into Tom. There's a term for what I'm talking about. It's not in your Bible. It's called 'sexual orientation.'"

"Is that like gaydar?" I asked. "Do you have a sexual orienter, like a compass, and it points you in the direction of gay people?"

He laughed. "Now you're busting *my* chops. But I like that. I'll have to tell the Society of Gay Scientists to start working on a sexual orienter."

"There's really such a group?"

He laughed harder. "Billy, you gotta stop believing so much of what people—"

Something flashed in front of us, coming from my side. I saw its black curved horns, and the shock of its white flank as it tried to leap away.

Ruah swerved to the right but hit the antelope. Its hind end thudded against the camper. We flew off the road, bouncing violently through the brush. Something grabbed the front wheels, I heard Ruah swear, the camper nose-dropped. It all happened in a split second: the front of the camper plunged—we caught air for a nanosec—full-body blow from an air bag. It hurt.

Everything went still. We weren't falling down a ravine, or a canyon. We weren't plunging to our death.

I heard Ruah fighting his air bag and sucking air through his teeth. "Fuck! Fuck!"

My air bag went squishy; I pushed it away. It was strangely dark in the cab. We had stuck a nose wheelie in a dry gully. The sunset's band of orange had leapt to the top of the windshield. The headlights, augured in dirt, emitted a dusty glow.

Ruah swatted his air bag with his right hand. He hissed in a breath. "You alright?"

"Yeah."

"Turn on the light."

I turned on the overhead.

His left hand was caught in the steering wheel. There was a weird lump in his wrist. He tried to move it with his free hand. He winced in pain. "Shit." He closed his eyes, sucking in air.

"Is it broken?"

He nodded and breathed out. His eyes opened. "That's it."

"Someone will come along soon," I said.

"That's what I'm scared of."

I couldn't take my eyes off his wrist. "We gotta get you to a hospital."

He turned to me with a clenched expression. "*We* aren't doing anything. The cops show up, your trip's over, I'm busted. And I sure don't wanna be busted with a teenage kid in my RV."

"But—"

His right hand flew in front of my face, his finger nearly poking my eye. "Be quiet and listen." His hand dropped to the console as he winced. "We've had our little debates, but this isn't one. You're gonna grab your backpack, a couple water bottles, the flashlight, your sleeping bag, and the bike off the back. You're gonna walk off the road, hide the bike in the brush, then walk into the brush until you're outta sight. Someone's gonna come along, get me to the hospital, and I'll deal from there. Tomorrow you'll get on the bike and ride to Notus; it's less than twenty miles. Trip's over, Billy. It's been a great ride. Now get going." He jerked his head toward the back of the camper. "That way, it's probably safer."

I looked at his hand still caught in the steering wheel. "Are you gonna be alright?"

"Don't worry, I've had plenty of broken bones. Now get going before someone shows up."

I grabbed my pack and scrambled over the console. I didn't have to go far for the water bottles. I stepped on one. In the crash, the fridge door had flown open and bottles and jars had slid to the front of the aisle. I walked up the tilted aisle. It was weird, like walking up a slide in a playground. I pulled the flashlight from the netting over the couch and grabbed my sleeping bag. I opened the side door. It flapped open and banged against the side of the camper.

I looked back down the aisle. Ruah was watching me in the rearview.

"If you're ever in Cincinnati, look me up," he said. "I owe you a ball game."

I couldn't see anything but his eyes. "Will you be playing in it?"

"Dunno, kid. Now get going."

I dropped out the door and landed on dusty ground. I looked for the shape in the road that would be the antelope. There was nothing. The back of the camper stuck up in the air like a crash-landed spaceship. I could barely reach the Trek and undo the straps. I wanted to tell Ruah that the antelope had only been grazed and had gotten away, but headlights loomed down the road.

I pushed the bike into the brush. When I heard the car, I looked back. Ruah had turned on the flashers. The car slowed. I dropped the bike behind a bush and ducked down as the car pulled over.

I watched a man get out of the car; a woman on the passenger side stayed inside. The man talked to Ruah for a bit, and it looked like he was helping him do something. The camper's flashers turned off. The man helped Ruah out; his left arm was now in a sling made from a towel. In his right hand, he carried a book. I would've sworn it was a Bible.

As Ruah moved to the back of the car, he looked toward me, then got in. Before they drove away, I saw the glow of a cell phone in the woman's hands. I didn't know if she was calling a doctor, a hospital, or a tow truck. It made me realize I still had Ruah's cell phone.

I sat for a while, watching the stars come out. Only two

other cars drove by. I was surprised how calm I felt. The crash had gotten me all revved, but I was back to a low idle. It felt weird not to be scared. I remembered what Mom always told me when she left me alone at night. "Don't be afraid. Your Heavenly Father is here in the house, looking after you." He was in this house, too. The ceiling was just higher.

I turned the flashlight on, climbed up the slope, and looked for a flat spot to sleep. I didn't find one, but I did find a barbed-wire fence. It stopped my climb. I scooped out a level patch in the dirt and got in the sleeping bag. The stars were even thicker than at Lake Scott.

The most awesome thing was the silence. It was so still and intense it seemed to make a noise. I told myself it was the sound of God breathing. I knew He was close. How could He not be? That's the thing about God. When He sends you a sign, like He sent me that morning, and you don't read it right, He comes back to make it *real* clear. That morning, He'd sent messengers disguised as prisoners emptying garbage cans. I'd listened at first, then twisted His message into something else; I'd climbed back into Giff, the great white trash can. God doesn't like being misunderstood. It pisses Him off. So He grabbed the can and shook me out.

Before going to sleep I thanked Him for tossing me out gently. And I asked Him to do two things: (1) Heal Ruah's wrist so he could play baseball again, and (2) heal his gay heart.

32

Notus

I woke at sunrise, and jumped out of my sleeping bag. Beyond the highway, sage steppe reached to a faraway ridge of dry hills. The camper was still sticking its nose wheelie in the gully.

I ran down the hill to see if the cops had come in the night. But there was no orange sticker like the kind they leave on the window or mirror of disabled vehicles. I wondered if Ruah had even called the cops. I climbed into the camper and checked the glove compartment and the console. All the paperwork—the rental agreement, the registration—was gone. That was why Ruah had taken his Bible; he'd hidden the paperwork in it.

As I walked back up to get my stuff, I saw what was beyond the barbed-wire fence: a long slope up a high hill. The steep was spotted with thinning sagebrush till it got bald at the top. I bent through the fence and climbed. I didn't see a critter or snake all the way up.

On top, I found a big patch of dust. I took off my sneaks and walked to the middle of it. I dropped a foot in the soft dust and lifted it away. A perfect impression of my foot stared back at me. *Adam was here.*

As far as I know, that footprint, only seen by soaring hawks and eagles, is still there. And will be, then-now-forevermore.

I packed up and mounted the Trek. According to my GPS, I was 15.5 miles from Notus. I could ride it in an hour. I started fast to put distance between me and the camper before any vehicles spotted me. Luckily it was early; there was no traffic.

After a few miles, I left the highway for county roads as I followed the GPS's compass arrow north. If I'd had a mountain bike instead of a roadie, I could've gone off-road. That would've been awesome, especially since I was back in mint-farm country. Bombing through mint fields, crashing in the mint, and bringing home a mint Christmas tree would've been a first ever. But riding road wasn't bad either. When your lungs are sucking mint clouds you don't *grind* up a steep, you *fly* it.

I crossed a small river and some railroad tracks, then hit a highway that took me into Notus. It was a dusty little town, with boarded-up stores and one main intersection where a couple places still survived: a restaurant-market and an auto parts store.

The compass pointed to a square white building between the road and the railroad tracks that ran past a grain elevator. Next to the white building was an old fire truck with faded red paint. It said NOTUS VOLUNTEER FIRE DEPT. on the door.

As I rode toward the building, my GPS raced down to under 70 feet. I couldn't believe it was going to be this easy. I got off the Trek and leaned it against the fire truck. I was 30 feet from the cache. I walked around the building, which turned out to be a tiny museum all shut up. On the GPS's screen, the feet ticked higher and the arrow swung back toward my bike.

I went back to the fire truck and pulled out the last page of Chapter 32. I reread the clue poem.

> Now that Huck has set his waypoint,
> And goes on down to Satan's joint,
> Do consider what he might drive,
> Should he wish to survive.

I had to laugh. If you're going to hell, go in a fire truck. I walked around the truck. The back bed, where they used to put ladders, was empty. So was a storage box in a side panel. I tried to unscrew the caps on the hose connectors. They were rusted shut. Then I remembered the last lines. I yanked out the page.

> Look for fuel to throw on fire,
> And there you'll find your heart's desire.

I went around to the truck's gas cap, opened it, got the flashlight out of my pack, and shined it down the hole. Nothing but an old spiderweb snaring a couple dead beetles. I racked my brain for what else "fuel" might mean. I drew a blank. I rechecked my GPS. I was inside 15 feet; I was right on top of it. I looked under the truck, around the gas tank: nothing. I jumped up on the running board. The ladder beds were empty, but the two hose spools behind the cab were coiled with cracked hoses. And there, behind the spools, was what I was looking for. Two old five-gallon gas cans.

The blast of a train whistle almost knocked me off the running board. I looked down the tracks. Luckily, the train wasn't slowing down.

I moved down the running board, lifted one of the gas cans, and shook it. Even if there was something in it I wouldn't have heard it. The train began thundering by. I waved to the engineer like I was just a kid checking out a fire truck.

Turning back to the gas cans, I spotted a small, one-gallon can tucked down between the two big ones. It was the perfect size for a book. I lifted it out—it was heavy. I unscrewed the cap and shined the flashlight inside. The glimmer of ziplock plastic bounced back. I had it!

"Hello!" a voice shouted over the train.

I dropped the gas can and flashlight. My already banging heart almost blew a fresh coat of red paint on the fire engine. I spun around and tripped off the running board.

A few feet away, a man with a fancy straw hat and a white beard stood behind the open door of his car. He grinned at me as the back of the train roared past. "Sorry to scare ya!"

"It's o-okay," I stammered, checking him for a badge and a gun. Whoever he was, he didn't have either. At least, not showing. My face felt ten times whiter than his beard. He probably thought I was an albino.

"I drove by and saw you studying what looked like a GPS device," he said, still grinning. "Are you a geocacher?"

I rubbed my face to try and get some blood in it and buy time for a lie. "No, I'm doing a school project on old fire-fighting equipment."

His face fell, wiping away his smile. "So you're a muggle."

"What's a muggle?"

"Someone who doesn't know about geocaching."

"Right, that's me, a muggle."

He clucked in disappointment—"Too bad"—and slid back into his car. "You don't know what you're missing."

I wanted to say, *You don't know what* you're *missing,* but I kept my mouth shut.

He closed his door. "Well, good luck with your project."

After he left I realized how exposed the site was. There were cars and trucks passing and the auto parts store across the street had a view of the fire truck.

I jumped back on the running board, lifted the small gas can, hid it behind my body, and wedged it in the sleeping bag bungee-corded on my backpack. The whole time something kept clunking around inside the can. It *had* to be the book.

As I got on the bike a thought gave me major cranial disharmony. How does a book get inside a gas can?

33

Cache Prize

I rode toward the restaurant-market, which was called Kings. Several pickups were parked in front and on the side street. I was starving, but first I needed a place to get the cache out of the gas can without being seen. I spotted an old phone booth half hidden by an ice machine in front of Kings. I headed for it but some young guys came out of the restaurant lighting cigarettes.

I veered down the side street and swung into an empty parking lot behind Kings. I jumped off and leaned the Trek against the back corner of the building, near a Dumpster. The gas can slipped out easily from the sleeping bag. For the first time, I noticed a black line around the middle of the can. Most gas cans didn't come with black waistlines. It was plumber's tape. I peeled it off. Underneath was a thin seam. That's how you get a book inside a gas can. You cut the can in half and reseal it.

I pulled on the handle. The top half slid off. What I saw inside made my throat go tight. No book. Just ziplock bags. I dropped to the ground and lifted out the two bags with a few new pages and money. Whatever was in the third bag was much bigger than a plastic trinket. It was what had given the can weight. It looked like the heel of a shoe but was made from some kind of metal, like bronze.

When I pulled the bag out, it got weirder. The other side

of the bronze heel had small dark circles in it that made a cross. I didn't have a clue what that meant. Maybe Huck got religion, saved Jim body and soul, and didn't go to hell after all.

But I didn't care where Huck's story was going, I wanted to know where *I* was going. I pulled out the new pages: Chapter 33. That was all, one chapter, six pages, no highlights, nothing—till the last page. It was more than a highlight. Scotch-taped to the bottom of the page was a business card. The logo on the card was the same as the metal object: a boot heel with a cross in it. My hand was shaking so hard I couldn't read the card. I held the page against my thigh. The jiggling letters steadied.

BOOT HEEL COLLECTIBLES
RICHARD ALLBRIGHT
366 NEW COUCH ST.
PORTLAND, OR 97232

That's where he had lived. That's where X marked the spot. That's where I'd find *my heart's desire*!

I was so excited I almost didn't feel the hard shape under the card. I started to flip the card over but a loud *hoot* sounded around the corner of the building. Thinking it was the guys who were smoking, I jumped up and grabbed the bike. As I pushed it into a space between the building and the Dumpster, I crammed the pages and the bags into my pockets. I didn't want the guys catching me doing weird stuff behind their hangout. Good news: nobody came around the corner. Bad news: the bike got away from me and jackknifed around the back of the Dumpster.

"Ow!" a voice yelled. A freaky-looking man leapt to his feet. He wore a ragged coat. His dirt-caked face peeked through a hedge of wild hair and a bushy beard. His eyebrows looked like mini woolly mammoths stampeding across his forehead.

"Sorry," I sputtered. I picked up the bike and tried to back it out. The bike clanged against the Dumpster.

The man grabbed the handlebars and slapped a thick finger to his lips. "Keep it down, Lance flippin' Armstrong." He tried to whisper, but his voice was so gravelly it came out like a growl.

I stared at his dirty hand on the handlebars. Below it, the ground was strewn with ripped-open garbage bags.

"What's the matter," he grumbled, "never seen anyone Dumpster dining?"

For the first time I noticed his eyes peeking out from under his woolly-mammoth eyebrows. They were as blue as robin's eggs.

"I asked a question, Lance." His free hand poked me in the chest. "Did your mama forget to teach you manners?"

"No, sir," I blurted. "And, yes, sir, I've seen homeless people before."

His eyes rolled. "Oh, nice. Call me 'homeless.' Rob the penniless of the only thing we have left: dignity."

"I'm sorry."

"You keep saying that, Lance. But if you were really sorry you'd park your bike, march into Kings, order me a steak 'n' egg on a roll, with salsa, and march it back out here before I die of starvation and the buzzards eat my eyeballs for brunch."

He didn't look like he was starving. He didn't even look like he was scrounging for food. Most of the stuff spilling out of the garbage bags was paperwork and receipts.

A door slammed above us. We snapped toward the sound. A deck railing jutted above the restaurant roofline. A man in a white apron appeared at the railing lighting a cigar. The homeless man grabbed my shirt, yanking me down. It was too late.

"Son of a bitch!" the man on the deck yelled. "I told you if you came back— LouAnn, call the sheriff!" The man disappeared; the door slammed again, his voice trailing inside. "Tell 'im to come and arrest me for second-degree murder!"

The homeless man grabbed something on his coat collar. "Eighty-six, Mo. Eighty-six!" I noticed a tiny wire and a microphone in his beard.

Tires squealed in the alley behind Kings. An engine roared down the alley. A second later a van did a one-eighty in the lot behind Kings and rocked to a stop in front of the Dumpster. Its side door was open. The homeless man jumped inside and spun around. He grabbed a bundle of rags off the floor, thrust it toward the driver. When it came back into view, the rag bundle was on fire. He tossed it into the Dumpster and flames mushroomed out. I jumped away.

"Whoa, hit the grease bucket!" the man shouted. "Three choices, Lance! Eat buckshot for breakfast, get arrested"—

he yanked a fistful of receipts from under his coat—"for attempted identity theft, or take a ride with Bonnie and Clyde!"

I heard shouts. The guys who'd been smoking came around the corner. The first one had a tire iron. It was the only kick I needed. I grabbed my pack and jumped in the van. It took off like a missile. I crashed into the bench seat in the back.

As we shot down the alley, the driver, a woman in a floppy hat, jerked the wheel. We careened around several corners and I got thrown from side to side on the seat. The man, braced in a wide stance in the middle of the van, rode the corners like a surfer. It looked like he'd done it before. As the van tore down a street he stripped off his coat, beard, and wig. The coat's inside pockets overflowed with credit-card receipts. The man was dressed in black Under Armour and was trimmer than the padded coat made him look. He had a white ponytail.

He grabbed a wet towel hanging from a hook and scrubbed his face and hands. He threw open a long box behind the front seats and tossed in the towel, along with the coat, beard, and wig. Then he shut the box and locked it with a padlock. "Cat's in the bag," he told the woman.

"And the dog's aren't howling," she said, checking the rearview mirrors. "Nothing like a little fire to keep 'em minding the store." She pulled off her floppy hat. Long blond hair tumbled over the seatback.

As we shot into the countryside, I looked out the back window. Notus retreated under a rising trail of black smoke.

34

The Potlatchers

The man sat on the long box, cocked his head, and stared at me with his twinkling eyes. They were even bluer under his salt-and-pepper eyebrows. His weathered skin was deeply lined. He had a solid nose, like the kind you see in pictures of Roman emperors.

"Mo," he said to the driver, "I want you to meet Lance flippin' Armstrong."

"You mean *the* Lance flippin' Armstrong?" She looked back. Her face was leathery from too much sun, but she was still pretty.

The man leaned forward with a wink. "Do we call you Lance, Lance? Or do we go on a real-name basis?"

The woman answered for me. "I like Lance."

The man jumped over the box into the passenger seat. For a white-haired guy, he was in good shape. "Not sure it fits him anymore," he said. "He lost the bike he rode in on."

She flapped a hand. "Nico, you don't need a bike to be on the tour."

"Last time I checked you did."

"But he's not on the Tour de France. He's on the Tour de *Fleece*."

"The Tour de Fleece!" the man shouted, cracking up. "That's my Mo!" His shoulders pumped up and down as he laughed.

While they were having their fun, I slipped the *Huck* page with the business card on it from my pocket and flipped the card over. Taped to the back was a key. Below the key were some scribbled coordinates. Under the card, on the page, another poem was scrawled. I didn't get a chance to read it.

"You're not one of those kids who's always texting and Twittering behind people's backs, are you?" the man asked.

I crammed the page back in my pocket and looked up. The man squinted at me like I'd blown a gnarly fart. "No," I told him. "I've never owned a cell phone."

"Alright!" He gave me a fist pump. "My man! We used to have one, but we're always giving stuff away."

The woman looked back and flashed a smile. "It's so true, Lance. We just can't hold on to things."

"My name isn't Lance."

"Tut-tut," the man said to the woman. "Turns out he's one of those real-name-basis guys." He turned back. "So what is it?"

"Billy."

His eyebrows jumped. "What about last?"

The woman turned quickly, making her hair dance. "Don't answer that, William." She spoke rapid fire. "You have the right to remain silent—anything you say can and will be used against you in a court of law—you have the right to speak to an attorney and to have an attorney present during any questioning—if you cannot afford a lawyer one will be provided for you at government expense."

I'd heard the cops read Mom her rights before, but it was doubly weird hearing it from a crook.

The man nodded seriously. "You're right, Mo. We've sucked too much four-one-one outta him already." He extended his hand. "Pleased to meet you, Billy William Whoever-You-Are. I'm Nico Potlatcher." We shook hands.

"I'm his partner in pranksterism," the woman said. "Momi."

"What's pranksterism?"

Nico grinned. "It's a school of filmmaking."

"You make movies?"

"Yes, but we call them un-movies."

"What's an un-movie?"

Momi hit the horn. "Time's up! Our turn. We've never seen you in Notus, William. Did you just move there or were you passing through?"

"Passing through," I said.

"To where?"

"Portland, Oregon."

Nico did a double take. "You're kidding."

Momi looked back with bugged-out eyes. "This is *so* freaky."

"What's so freaky about going to Portland?" I asked.

Nico turned to Momi. "Didn't I tell you the planets were aligning?"

She nodded. "You did."

"Didn't I say something wonderful was going to happen to us?"

She lifted a finger. "But, Nikki, it's happening to *him*, not us."

"C'mon, Mo," he said, raising his hands. "How many times have I told you? We're all part of the same cosmic

232

body." He threw his hands at me—"He is us"—then slapped his chest—"we is him!"

She sighed and looked at me in the rearview mirror. "Please excuse my dear mentally departed husband, William. Sometimes he gets so far ahead of himself his head runs right up his ass. What he's trying to say is that *we're* going to Portland too."

Nico bounced in his seat. "That's right! We're taking our new film to the film festival there."

Momi turned with a friendly smile. "And it would be totally cool if you went along for the ride."

I didn't know whether to be thrilled or terrified. I had a ride to Portland, with *crooks*. "Okay," I said, returning her smile. "Thank you." When it's not clear who's throwing you the good luck, God or Satan, it's good to do a little investigating. "If you guys are moviemakers—"

"*Un*-moviemakers," Nico corrected.

"Right. Why were you acting like a homeless man and going through people's garbage?"

"It's called fund-raising."

"I thought you called it 'identity theft.'"

"That's what the pigs call it," Momi said. "We think of it as robbing from the rich and giving to the poor in imagination."

"Right. We're not really Bonnie and Clyde." Nico's eyes twinkled. "We're Robin Hood and Maid Marian with a thirty-five millimeter."

I should've been scared driving up into barren hills with a couple of criminal nutcases. Surprisingly, I felt weirdly calm. Maybe it was because they were a little like Mom.

233

They ran around breaking the law for a cause. They were antinomians from a different church: the Church of Moviemaking, or Un-Moviemaking, whatever that was. And there was another thing that made me feel okay. They were married. They were straight. There was one thing that worried me, though. Except for the long box behind the front seats, the van was empty. There were no suitcases or anything else that people would take on a long trip.

"Are you going to Portland right now?" I asked.

Nico grinned. "We've got a stop to make: Earth Wars Productions."

"Also known as our house and hideout," Momi added.

"And then you're driving to Portland?" I pressed.

"Absolutely. But not in this junker." Nico beamed. "When we do a film festival, we go styling!"

"What's styling?"

"You'll see."

35
Detours

We drove higher into a range of sunbaked hills. Gulches turned into small canyons, and every road we turned on got smaller and dustier. I tried to memorize the turns in case "You'll see" was something I didn't want to see.

The dirt track we were on became wheel ruts. The van bounced along for another mile, passing canyon openings.

We turned into the mouth of a tight canyon blocked by a wall of brush, and stopped in front of the brush.

Nico jumped out. "C'mon, Billy. Help me with the gate."

"The gate?"

"Yeah, it's our brush picket fence."

I got out. "You live here?"

He waved at the brush. "No, rabbits and rattlesnakes live in the fence."

I stopped and saw a rusty box half hidden in the brush. "Is that a mailbox?"

He laughed. "They don't deliver mail up here."

"Then why do you have a mailbox?"

"It's a FedEx box. He's the only deliveryman we need." Nico stuck his hand in the brush. I heard the beeps of a keypad. He grabbed something and pulled. The brush started to swing out. "Are you gonna help or not? Don't worry, the rattlers are cooling their heads under rocks this time of day."

I helped open the gate. Momi drove the van through. Beyond it there were tire tracks curving around a bend in the canyon. I started forward.

Nico held up a hand. "You need to wait here."

Momi jumped out of the van, carrying my backpack. "It's a little trust exercise, William." She handed me the pack. "We don't take your personal stuff, and you wait for us here. I mean, for all we know you might be some teenage serial killer who has a thing for murdering people in their home canyon."

Nico's wild eyebrows slammed together. "Or worse, you

235

could be a spy from Hollywood sent to destroy our un-movie before we get it to the festival."

I understood why they might think I was some serial killer: I had the same thought about them. "Why would anyone wanna destroy your un-movie?"

"Because when it hits the theaters it's going to turn Hollywood into a ghost town. No one will ever want to see another blockbuster again. *Batman*, *Spiderman*, *Iron Man*, they'll all be vaporized from the collective consciousness."

"It's going to undo the old and bring in the new!" Momi added.

"Popular culture will be replaced with a new paradigm," Nico declared. "Unpopular culture!"

I didn't have a clue what they were talking about. "Okay, I probably don't wanna see your canyon. I'll wait here."

Nico slapped me on the back. "Knew you'd see it our way. We'll be back in a jiff with the styling-mobile."

"And we'll bring you a sandwich," Momi yelled as she climbed back in the van.

I stepped back as they disappeared behind the swinging brush gate. It closed with a dry *shush* and a metallic *click*.

Standing there in the hot sun, I felt pretty dumb. For all I knew there was no canyon. It was really a road and this whacked-out couple really were killers. They had a thing for abandoning kids in the desert, watching them die of heatstroke and get pecked to the bone by buzzards.

I pulled out my GPS and turned it on. I got out the last *Huck* page with the business card taped to it, entered the coordinates written on the back, and went to Goto. I figured I was southwest of Notus, in the ridge of hills I'd seen earlier that morning. I might have even crossed into Oregon. The GPS showed 315 miles to Portland. The compass pointed west-northwest.

I read the clue poem hidden under the card that I'd seen earlier.

> With Huck and Tom found in Notus,
> You're oh so close, almost got us.
> Card and key are your invite,
> To the cache of Huck's last write.
> My verses will now fade from sight,
> Giving rise to things Allbright.

I wasn't sure what he meant by "last write," but I had a hunch. I undid a shoelace from my sneaker, got out my Leatherman, and cut off a long piece. I put the key on it and hung it around my neck. I memorized the address on the business card, then put the card in the Bible.

The metal boot heel was weighing heavy in my pocket, so I decided to put it in the pack. As I slid it out of the plastic bag, I dropped it. It hit the dust with a thud. When I picked it up it left a print in the dust. I stared at the print. Inside it was the cross pattern of little circles. It hit me where I'd seen the pattern. Okay, not *seen* it, *read* it.

I dug out the first chapters of *Huck Finn* from my cargo pocket and started flipping through them. On page sixteen, right after Huck finds some tracks in new snow, he says, *There was a cross in the left boot-heel made with big nails, to keep off the devil.* Huck knew it was his drunken father's boot print. He knew Pap was back in town and looking for him.

My father had named his store after that boot heel. And he'd put it in the last cache to tell me something. Huck saw the print and knew Pap was coming for him. My father left the boot heel to tell me *I* was coming for *him*.

The screech of a bird jerked me back to reality. A buzzard soared overhead. Finding my father's treasure wasn't going to happen if I became buzzard chow. On the chance that actually happened, I figured I'd better call Mom. If it meant that Ruah's friend in Cincinnati found out I still had his phone and told Ruah, so what. I wouldn't be seeing Ruah again.

I dug out the cell and turned it on. It was a good time to call Mom for a couple of reasons. (1) It was Sunday morning, so she'd be in church and I could just leave a message. (2) If I was about to become desert kill, I wanted her to know I loved her. I pressed buttons till I found her number in the call record. I got her voice mail and left a message about how I was fine and that I loved her. I didn't pour it on too thick. If I did she would've known I was in trouble. The only lie I told her was that I was almost to New Orleans.

After I hung up, I started thinking maybe I wasn't the only liar in the middle of nowhere. Nico and Momi had had plenty of time to swap vehicles and come back.

Another buzzard showed up. That did it. I started walking toward the last dirt road we'd been on. The soaring buzzards suddenly veered away. I heard what spooked them: a vehicle on the other side of the brush fence.

I saw Momi, ran back, and helped her open the gate. The

"styling-mobile" pulled through. It was a bigger, newer van, with one of those expandable roofs. But no one was going to raise it soon. Something big, lumpy, and longer than the van was wrapped in a tarp and tied to the roof.

I opened the side door and expected to see a mini version of Ruah's camper. The inside was more like an office, with a desk, computer, printer, and what looked like movie-making equipment. The back was jammed with boxes and hanging clothes. Some looked like costumes. Momi reached back from the passenger seat and swiveled the plastic desk seat to face forward.

For the next hour we headed west, into Oregon. Whenever I snuck a peek at my GPS, the miles were ticking down steadily. Then we turned south onto a county road. There was a big wooden sign with an arrow: TO BURNING MAN. "Where are we going?" I asked.

Momi answered with a question. "You've never heard of Burning Man?"

"No."

"It's not the mother of all Burning Man festivals in Nevada," she added, "but it'll still blow your mind."

I didn't want to blow my mind, I wanted to keep blowing west. "You said you were driving to Portland today."

"We'll have you there by sunset tomorrow, promise," Nico said. "But if you haven't seen Burning Man, you can't miss it."

I leaned back in the hard seat. "What is it?"

"Mo, how would you describe it?"

She shrugged. "How do you describe the color purple to a blind man?"

"You don't," Nico answered. "You heal him and let him see for himself."

"Does the thing on the roof have to do with Burning Man?" I asked.

Momi gave me a solemn look. "That isn't a 'thing.' That's the Tree of Life."

"And, yes," Nico added, "it has everything to do with Burning Man."

She let out a gleeful shout. "Where you're gonna see Wachpanne Papa do his thing!"

It seemed like the more questions I asked the less I found out. "Who's Wachpanne Papa?"

Nico shot me a grin. "Billy boy, you're lookin' at 'im." His shoulders did more laugh gymnastics.

36

Burning Man

We drove into a widening basin. The sagebrush carpet began to show worn spots of putty white dust. As the bare spots grew bigger, the Potlatchers told me we were headed into a dead lake bed that hadn't held water for thousands of years. "Alkali flats" they called them. It was as if God had ironed the land like a white shirt. And the heat made it feel like His iron had just lifted. In the distance, the wind blew up a smoky curtain of dust.

Behind the white curtain a city began to take shape. It was made of giant tents, strange towers, and a mega-sprawl of RVs, tents, and small domes. Nico said it was Burning Man, Oregon. The tallest tower looked like a giant stick man, with arms spread like Christ. Nico said when the tower got torched, Burning Man would be over, and the city would disappear overnight.

As we drove closer to a plastic fence, Momi told me how the "MOOP fence" surrounding Burning Man caught windblown litter. MOOP was short for Matter Out Of Place. Burning Man was big on leaving nothing behind. "The only thing it leaves," she said, "are memories of radical self-expression smoldering in every burner's brain."

We stopped at an entrance manned by a hippie-looking guy with long hair and a beard. He was naked except for a carpenter's apron. I felt like a COOP: a Christian Out Of Place. I wondered if "radical self-expression" meant "hippie-heathen, drugged-out orgy fest." If it did, I didn't want to be there. But it wasn't like I had a choice. Everyone was going into Burning Man, not out. And walking out of the alkali flats in the blistering heat would've been a suicide march.

Nico handed hippie-guy a ticket. It confirmed what I'd begun to suspect. They'd never planned on going straight to Portland.

Hippie-guy put his palms together and bowed. "Welcome, Wachpanne Papa. Awesome that you've come with your bodacious squaw, Yellow-haired Woman, and"—he looked back at me—"who's this? Glorious spawn of Yellow-haired Woman and Wachpanne Papa?"

Nico laughed. "Not quite. This is our new assistant, Billy Lost His Bike."

Hippie-guy gave me a little bow. "Welcome, Billy Lost His Bike. May you leave here as Billy Lost His Virginity."

Nico and Momi cracked up. I turned red and leaned back in the shadows of the van. I was sure there were heat waves coming off my face, like the ones shimmering above the baked ground.

Taking a road into the sea of tents and RVs, we got stuck behind a water truck sprinkling the dusty road. A dozen naked men and women danced behind the truck playing in the spray of water. And that was only the beginning of naked people. Every other person was naked or topless. Some people I thought were dressed weren't dressed at all. They were wearing nothing but paint and glitter.

"Better get used to it," Momi said, turning to me with a giggle. "This place is clothing-optional."

The weirdest part was how most of the naked people were doing normal things, like barbecuing and playing Frisbee. I mean, nobody was acting like they were in a drugged-out orgy-fest. Sure, there were people drinking beer and stuff, but I didn't see any falling-down drunks, or drug-crazed hippies climbing towers and jumping off because they thought they could fly. I reminded myself it was still day. Maybe at night, all the nakeds dropped their burger-flippers and Frisbees and went drunken, drugged-out orgy-fest.

As the Potlatchers looked for their campsite I wondered if God was playing a joke on me. I mean, back at the one-pillar doghouse I *had* prayed for some pretty neighbors and a lusting-in-my-heart test. So what does God do? He tosses me into a nudist colony. And all the naked and top-less women I was seeing hadn't exactly rolled out of a

Victoria's Secret catalog. Some of them were as old as my mom. The worst was a fat woman so covered in dust she looked like one of those fertility goddesses you see in a museum. God had answered my prayer alright. *So, Billy, you want naked women? You got naked women. But you're gonna see so many in so many different shapes and sizes you're gonna wanna put on a blindfold. And, since you're such a wicked, sinning Peeping Tom, I'm also gonna show you naked men!*

When we drove by two naked guys walking along, holding hands, that did it. I forced myself to look at things that didn't jiggle, swing, or bounce. Luckily, there was plenty of distracting stuff. Most of the campers, tents, and domes were covered with wild decorations. Everything from fake palm trees around an Arab-looking tent with a herd of plastic camels to an RV that looked like a birthday cake with huge candles on top and naked-girl blow-up dolls leaping out of the cake. There was no getting away from naked.

Momi turned with a big grin. "Talk about an escape from the ordinary, huh? Wall-to-wall extraordinary!"

I wanted to tell her I'd been on the run from the ordinary for a week and wasn't sure how much more extraordinary I could take. I just asked, "So what's Wachpanne Papa gonna do with the Tree of Life?"

"It's no big deal," Nico said with a shrug. "The great Sioux medicine man, Wachpanne Papa, will perform the sacred Sun Dance and heal our sickly Earth Mother."

Momi beamed. "And this year we rented a show tent twice the size."

We drove past a huge tent with a big sign on top: CAMP

243

RENEWAL. We followed a dusty track down the side of the tent, and pulled into an empty campsite. My butt was sore from sitting on the hard seat, and I had to take a leak. I spotted a row of port-a-sans at the end of the road. Momi had to go too, so we walked there together.

There was a line at the port-a-sans. Luckily, there were distractions from all the body parts flapping in the breeze. The port-a-sans were decorated too. There was one made to look like a big green pea called the Pee-Pod. Another was covered with Dr. Seuss characters. On the door were the two little creatures from *The Cat in the Hat,* but their names had been changed from Thing 1 and Thing 2 to Fling 1 and Fling 2. And there was one my mom would've attacked with her Carry Nation hatchet. It also happened to be the one that opened up when it was my turn. The outside was covered with scripture and copies of the Left Behind series, the famous books about the End Times. Above the door, the port-a-san's name was stuck on two rubber butt cheeks: THE RIGHT & LEFT BEHIND SERIES. The best part was the sign on the door that let you know if the port-a-san was vacant or not. Instead of OCCUPIED it said RAPTURED.

37

Across the Playa

When we got back to the campsite, Nico was pulling a large banner out of the van. I helped him and Momi hang it over the entrance to the Camp Renewal tent. The banner announced, WACHPANNE PAPA—SUN DANCE #2. They told me how the Sun Dance had to be performed four years in a row, with the four corners of the world—north, south, east, west—each being danced to before the entire Sun Dance would heal the earth.

I had more questions, but people started coming around. Some had seen Sun Dance #1 and were excited about the next one. Momi passed out flyers saying that Yellow-haired Woman would be "bartering for witness cards in Camp Meccumenical at sundown." Nico pounded a stake in the ground with an arrowhead-shaped sign attached. The sign announced:

1
TIME!
TONIGHT!
MEDICINE MAN
WACHPANNE PAPA
OF GREAT SIOUX NATION
PERFORMS THE BLOODY
SUN DANCE!
ONCE OUTLAWED!
NOW SACRED PATH
TO SAVE MOTHER EARTH!

I wanted to know what was so bloody about it, but they said it was "bad medicine" to talk about the dance right before performing it.

Some Burning Man volunteers helped get the Tree of Life off the top of the van and into the big tent. They helped

Nico and me dig a hole in the middle of the "new-life lodge" and "plant" the Tree of Life. It's not like the Tree of Life was going to grow. It was just a trunk, about fifteen feet high, with a thick fork at the top. It was barkless and polished white from wind and sun. I told Nico it looked more like a giant hunk of driftwood than a Tree of Life. He said, "Before night is done it will grow a bounty of fruit." He was beginning to talk funny, like Wachpanne Papa, I guess.

When I asked him if he was really an Indian, he told me he was a "raging confluence" of Indian and white blood. "My forefathers include the fierce warrior Crazy Horse," he said, "and General Custer. Sometimes my red and white blood gets into such a riptide I want to scalp myself." He put his hands on my shoulders and stared at me with his blue eyes, probably from the Custer side of the family. "You see, I dance the Sun Dance to heal not only the earth. I dance to heal myself."

We finished planting the tree and Momi came into the tent. She wore a long Indian dress covered with bright beads and trinkets. Her hair was braided and woven with beads and feathers. She carried a buckskin shoulder bag stuffed with something. She was now Yellow-haired Woman. She asked me to come with her so Wachpanne Papa could begin his "sweat-lodge purification." I'd been sweating all day, so I was fine about missing the sweat-lodge thing.

The sun was dropping behind the giant Burning Man statue. We crossed a big open area Momi called the playa.

It was dotted with wild towers and statues. People drove around the playa in "art cars." One art car looked like the Fountain of Youth rolling on paddle wheels. From the top, a Spanish conquistador threw water bottles to people. Then I saw a huge boat-car filled with giant stuffed animals. As it drove by, I read the name on its side: NOAH'S CAR'K. It got me wondering, so I asked Momi, "Are there any Christians here?"

"Absolutely," she said. "And Jews and Muslims and Hindus, and Buddhists and Sufis, you name it. That's where we're going now." She pointed across the playa. "Camp Meccumenical is the ultimate in religious tolerance."

Before I asked about it, I saw a guy riding a bike toward us. He was fat, naked, and painted green. You haven't seen *gross* until you've seen a naked fat guy riding a bike. I had to find something else to look at. I spotted a girl walking our way. She was dressed in green leafy branches and flowers.

"Why are so many people green?" I asked Momi, as the girl's green bits zapped the memory of the fat guy's green bits.

"Every year Burning Man has a color and a theme," she said. "This year it's green and renewal."

The girl waved. "Hello, Yellow-haired Woman." She had an English accent.

As the girl reached us Momi said, "You must be Spring."

"Spot on!" The girl spread her branchy arms. Even though her face was green and she was dressed like a shrub, I could see how pretty she was. She looked about twenty. "And who are you?" she asked me.

247

"We're still looking for his burner name," Momi answered.

The girl grinned. "Let's call him Gob-smack."

"Why Gob-smack?" Momi asked.

"'Cause he keeps looking around"—she flapped her mouth open—"with his gob wide open."

Momi laughed. "Gob-smack it is."

The girl jabbed me in the shoulder with one of her stick fingers and winked. "Pleased to meet you, Gob-smack."

I was glad we were facing the sunset. Maybe the orangey light covered my blush.

Before I could remember how to say hi, the girl turned to Momi. "So, got tickets to the Sun Dance?"

Momi crossed her arms. "I don't have 'tickets.' I have witness cards."

"Right, witness cards. Gotta have one." She started to dig in a pouch attached to her waist. "How much?"

"Two leaves from the Tree of Founding Fathers," Momi answered.

The girl giggled. "Last year it was frog skins, this year it's the Tree of Founding Fathers. I love it. Which leaves?"

"One Andrew Jackson, one Alexander Hamilton."

She pulled out a twenty and a ten. "One Jackson, one Hamilton."

Momi took the money and handed her a witness card. It looked like a ticket to me.

"See you tonight." Rustling away, the girl looked back. "Hey, Gob-smack. When the dust blows be sure to shut that mouth of yours."

I caught up with Momi. "What was that about?"

"She was flirting with you."

"I mean about the money."

She shot up a finger. "Ah-ah, that's one of the few rules here: no money. There's only bartering, goods for goods."

"But you bartered for cash."

"No, I traded a witness card for Founding Father leaves. And if you won't play along, I'll send you back to the van."

I didn't get a chance to say any more. Just when I thought I'd seen the grossest thing in the world, I saw the grossest thing in the universe. A group of naked men on bicycles, with shaved heads, rode toward us. "I wish there was a rule against naked guys on bikes."

"Those aren't *guys*." Momi put her palms together and bowed as they passed. "They're the most famous biker gang here: the Nudist Buddhist Nut Peddlers."

I pretended to boot. "Gross!"

"You wouldn't say the same about their rival gang, the Critical Tits Dyke Bikers." She took my arm and pulled me toward some big tents. "C'mon, I have leaves to gather."

Camp Meccumenical wasn't like any revival meeting or Bible camp jamboree I'd ever seen. There was every creed on earth, from Amish farmers to Zen monks. Some looked real and some didn't. Most of the Amish guys were wearing fake beards. And then there was the guy dressed like a Plymouth Rock Puritan. He carried a gun with a funnel-shaped barrel that was actually a Super Soaker. He kept shooting people with "holy water."

After sunset, Momi traded her last witness card. Her buckskin bag was stuffed with leaves. The air cooled as we walked back across the playa.

At Camp Renewal the tent was closed. Momi said Wach-panne Papa was inside "preparing the new-life lodge." She and I ate salami and cheese sandwiches from a cooler in the van. I thought the bread was homemade because it was dusted with sweet flour. Then I realized it was alkali dust. Momi explained that dust was the official condiment at Burning Man. After we finished the sandwiches, she asked me to take a walk and come back in a half hour to help collect witness cards at the door.

"Can't I just take a nap in the van?" I said.

She shook her head. "Yellow-haired Woman has rituals to prepare herself for the Sun Dance."

Walking out on the playa was like being on another planet. In the darkness, the statues and art cars glowed with bright neon colors. The best was a phoenix rising from a real ring of fire. The people walking around had glow sticks looped around their arms and legs. Some looked like they were wearing neon pajamas. Some looked like walking skeletons.

I went over to the phoenix fire, got out my GPS, and checked the distance to Portland: 221 miles. I'd be there the next day. Then I pulled out the new chapter of *Huck* that I hadn't had a chance to read. There was a funny part about Tom Sawyer kissing his aunt on the mouth. It made me think of the girl I'd met earlier, Spring. When she came to the Sun Dance I wondered if she'd still be green and covered in foliage. I wanted to see her real skin and what was under her leaves. But I also hoped she was still green and leafy. Otherwise, I wouldn't recognize her.

At the end of the chapter, I stared at the last two lines of my father's poem. "My verses will now fade from sight/ Giving rise to things Allbright." Walking back to Camp Renewal, I kept wondering: the bad book was *one* thing, but "things" is more than one. What did he mean by "Giving rise to *things* Allbright"?

38

The Sun Dance

As we let people into the tent, Momi and I collected over two hundred witness cards. I did the math; it added up to more than six thousand dollars. Whether you called them frog skins or Founding Father leaves, it was major bucks.

Spring was one of the last ones there. She was green and leafy but had changed her foliage for a dress made of cattails. Her head was covered with a wild wig of green glow sticks. She looked like a woodland fairy after a nuclear accident.

"I'll save a seat for you," she said as she went inside, throwing me a wink. Something flashed on her eyelid but I couldn't see what it was.

As Momi closed the tent I went inside and walked behind the low circle of bleachers. It was dark except for the hazy light of glow sticks. Spring was easy to find with her green fountain of glowing hair. I climbed up the back of the bleachers and sat next to her in the top row.

Her glow-stick wig lit up her face. "Aren't you going to ask me why I changed into cattails?"

"Why did you change into cattails?"

"They're the traditional gift you bring to a Sun Dance."

I wanted to ask if that meant she was going to give her dress to someone, but every way I tried to put it in my head it sounded crude. I just said, "Oh."

She stared at me and pointed at her eyes. "Just so you know, I can see you with these." She closed her eyes. I jumped. Her eyelids were painted with green eyes. "But I can read your *mind* with these."

I tried to sound like I'd seen plenty of girls with a double set of eyes. "So what am I thinking?"

Her fake eyes kept staring. "You're wondering who's the freaky girl with four eyes."

I chuckled. "The four-eyes part is right. How did you get them on there?"

"Tattoos."

"They're permanent?"

She opened her eyes, closing her green ones. "Don't be silly. They're stick-ons. But I had to have them for tonight."

"Why?"

" 'Cause even when I blink"—she flashed her green eyes—"I won't miss a nanosecond of the Sun Dance. And, I can keep my eyes on *you*." She shut her eyes and pushed her fake eyes closer. "Just remember, I *know* what you're thinking."

I laughed nervously and tried to think of something to hide the sinful thoughts wallpapering my mind. I was saved by a rapid-fire drumming.

"Here we go," Spring whispered, squeezing my knee.

The drum settled to a slow beat. Between each thump I

252

felt a silent thump in my knee where her hand had squeezed. The drumbeat moved into the dark space the bleachers circled. The Tree of Life was a black silhouette. Yellow-haired Woman beat the drum and spoke in a low flat voice. "The beating heart of Mother Earth we do not always hear. We hear it now."

Across the space a ball of fire ignited. It was Wachpanne Papa with a torch. "The fiery eye of Father Sky we do not always see. We see it now." He wore a full eagle headdress. His upper body was bare and covered in white dust. I was surprised by his big barrel chest. His lower body was wrapped in Indian-looking material, like a long tight dress.

Yellow-haired Woman kept beating her drum slowly. "As we hear the heartbeat of Mother Earth, so she hears us."

Wachpanne Papa lifted his torch. "As we see the fiery eye of Father Sky, so he sees us. So he sees me, Wachpanne Papa, who the Great Creator took to the center of the earth. There, he showed me the heart and soul of Mother Earth. It was a breaking heart. It is breaking still." The drumbeat changed to a thudding groan. "It was a weeping soul, weeping still." The drum growled and moaned. "Then, Great Spirit, you gave me a vision of how to mend the breaking heart of Mother Earth. Of how to return her weeping soul to song." He raised the torch and shouted, *"Hetchetu aloh!"*

The audience shouted back. *"Hetchetu aloh!"*

"What's that mean?" I whispered to Spring.

"'It is so indeed.'"

Wachpanne Papa lowered his torch and walked around the circle of bleachers. His voice changed to one that was casual and friendly. "Welcome two-leggeds, and any four-leggeds or six-leggeds or eight-leggeds that may be crawling on you." The audience laughed. "Yes, we can joke as long as we stand outside the hoop of the world, but all is sacred once we step inside." He stopped at two torches set in the ground like a gateway. He lit the torches. "Welcome, East, which brings us light and understanding." He kept circling around and looked up. "Welcome, wings of the air." He lit two more torches on poles. "Welcome, South, which brings us warmth and growing." As he walked he looked at Spring and smiled. "Welcome, roots of the ground." Her cattails rustled as she giggled.

He lit two more torches. "Welcome, West, which brings us rain." Walking, he spread his arms. "Welcome, Great Creator. Thank you for stepping outside your tepee of clouds sewn together by lightning, and leaning close to hear our song." He lit the last two torches. "Welcome, North, which brings the cold, cleansing wind."

The lit torches made four gates in a circle carved in the dirt. The drumming quickened as he moved back around it, waving his whooshing torch and pointing at the crowd. "You, the people. You are the outer hoop of the world that runs around it like ants, doing what ants do: digging holes, building mountains, and copulating so your holes and mountains are filled with the peoples of the earth. *Hetchetu aloh!*"

"*Hetchetu aloh!*" everyone echoed.

He stopped by the torches of the east. The drumming went back to slow. His voice grew soft. "But tonight, you are here not to dig, or to mound, or to copulate."

The crowd laughed. Spring giggled.

Wachpanne went on. "You are here to give your hearts, beating with the heart of Mother Earth, and your eyes, seeing with the light of Father Sky, to the Sun Dance. *Hetchetu aloh!*"

"*Hetchetu aloh!*" everyone shouted.

He stepped through the torch gate into the circle, sweeping a hand around it. "This, the inner hoop, is the world, our only world." He pointed to thick lines on the ground running from the rim of the circle to the Tree of Life in the center. They were dark and made of brush. "These lines of sweet sage and the wisdom of all medicine fathers are the beliefs of the world." He walked, stepping over the lines. "Some beliefs are held by so many, they are called religions. These beliefs are as bright as the twelve moons. Some beliefs are held by so few, they are only pinpoints of light. Whether big or small, all these faiths, and beliefs, like the spokes of a great wheel, lead to the same center of the world." He moved to the Tree of Life. Three unlit torches stuck out from it. He lit one of them. "They all lead to the same Maker of All Things." He lit another torch. "To the Tree of Life." He lit the last one. "This is where Father Sky and Mother Earth came together and brought forth the world." He stuck the torch he was holding into the bare side of the tree, and whispered, "*Hetchetu aloh.*"

"*Hetchetu aloh,*" the crowd whispered.

He looked up at a buffalo skull hanging below the fork in the top of the tree. The huge skull faced the torches in the east. Its nostril holes and eye sockets were stuffed with pale green sage. "This is our brother, Buffalo. Every people

255

has a brother like the buffalo. Without him, the people will go naked, and hungry, and die."

He pulled two big white feathers off the tree. "These are the feathers of our sister, Eagle. Every people has a sister like the eagle. Without her, the people cannot see from great heights, can have no knowledge or good medicine. Without her, the people would go stupid, and sicken, and die."

He took a bead necklace off the tree. A thin bone hung from it, and from that dangled a fluffy white eagle plume. "And this is the eagle-bone whistle that carries the cries of our prayer to the Maker of All Things." He put the necklace around his neck. The drumming got frantic and scary. In the torchlight, I could see two dark streaks on his chest. They were scars.

He lifted two long leather cords secured to the tree up by the buffalo head. He walked them back to the torches in the outer circle. "And these are the branches of the Tree of Life. They are branches bearing no fruit." He stretched the cords tight. Each end had a short wooden peg. "Here is the prayer of Wachpanne Papa." He faced the Tree of Life with the buffalo skull. "If the Tree of Life is to keep bearing fruit . . . if our Earth Mother's breaking heart is to be mended . . ." The drumming stopped and Yellow-haired Woman moved toward the circle. "If we are to hear her soul sing again, we must make offerings to the Great Spirit." Yellow-haired Woman stepped into the circle. Wachpanne Papa raised the two leather cords high. "We must bring our *own* fruit to the tree."

Yellow-haired Woman stepped in front of him. I saw a

256

flash as she lifted a knife. She grabbed the scarred skin on his chest, pinched it, and ran the knife through the bunched skin. People gasped, but most of the audience stared, hypnotized. I stole a look at Spring. Her eyes were as bright and fiery as the torches. When I looked back a streak of blood ran down Wachpanne Papa's chest.

He lowered one of the pegs attached to a cord. She threaded the peg through the wound. He sucked in air and shouted, "In this way we renew the balance of the world." Using a short loop of rawhide she turned the peg into a stirrup running though his flesh. He chanted, *"Hetchetu aloh."*

The audience echoed, *"Hetchetu aloh."*

I couldn't believe what I was seeing. It was more than being on another planet. I was in another century.

She made the same cut at the top of his other pec. He grimaced, shouting, "In this way we heal the wounds of the world." Blood ran down his torso. He lowered the second peg. As she secured it he shouted, *"Hetchetu aloh!"*

"Hetchetu aloh!"

With the two cords stretching from his chest to the tree, he was tied to the buffalo skull. Yellow-haired Woman went out of the circle, and began drumming a steady beat, faster and louder than before.

Wachpanne Papa dance-shuffled from the east gate of torches toward the Tree of Life, letting the cords go slack. "East, hear me," he chanted. "You are where the morning star rises to give men hope and wisdom. Now your star rises with hopelessness and fear. You are where the sun rises with light and knowledge. But now your sun rises behind clouds of terror and hate."

When he reached the tree, he raised the eagle feathers toward the buffalo. Then he danced back, straightening the cords. "O East, hear me. I offer the only thing that belongs to me, my flesh, to make the Great East whole again." He stuck the eagle-bone whistle in his mouth and jerked back on the cords. The whistle screamed as his flesh stretched out from his chest. The drum pounded. Streaks of blood streamed from the wounds.

I wanted to not look, and I wanted to keep watching the most pagan thing I'd ever seen. I looked at Spring. Her face was locked in a faint smile. A tear rolled down her cheek, turning green as it gathered paint.

The screaming whistle stopped and dropped from Wach-panne Papa's mouth. Keeping the cords straight, but not pulling, he shuffle-danced to his left, chanting. "I send a prayer as I dance." The buffalo skull turned with him. It was rigged to pivot around the tree. It was only a skull stuffed with sage, but when it moved it looked totally alive.

He stopped at the south gate of torches and danced toward the tree. "South, hear me. Remember when you gave us nothing but warmth, the power of growing. You brought us the life of things. Now you deliver the death of things. You bring the flooding hurricanes, the poisoning oil, and the power of destruction."

He raised his eagle feathers and danced backward. "O South, hear me. I offer the only thing that belongs to me, my flesh, to make the world whole again." Whistle in mouth, he jerked back, pulling hard on the skewers in his chest.

I felt like I was watching a crucifixion. The only thing that didn't fit was the way his chest flesh stretched out. It

258

looked like two small breasts popping out of him. If it weren't so bloody and awful, it might've been funny.

He danced to the west gate, chanting and performing the same ritual. The buffalo skull followed, like it held Wachpanne Papa's reins. He moved to the tree. "West, remember when you sent us the thunder beings. When they came I knew the rain, my friend, was coming to visit. Now you send the choking clouds of the foul-air beings, and I know my enemy is here." He danced back and jerked his reins tight. A peg almost ripped free.

I glanced at Spring. Her face was a weird mirror of Wachpanne Papa's. Blood ran down his chest, turning it crimson; tears streamed down her face, washing away her green paint.

As he danced toward the buffalo skull he staggered a little, but his words were clear. "Hear me, North, where the white giants live. Remember when you blew your cold white wind. You rubbed us with icy fingers until we were strong and robust. But now your white giants are old and shrunken. Every day they lose their great white teeth. Their icy fingers no longer reach us. The white giants are bleeding out."

Under the buffalo skull, he raised his eagle feathers high. "To you, Great North, I dance this dance. To you, I make my offering this night." He began to dance slowly back. "Hear me, pray with the broken heart of Mother Earth." Reaching the north gate, stretching the cords tight, he stuck the eagle-bone whistle between his teeth. "Hear Mother Earth scream with me." He yanked back, hard. The whistle screamed, the drum roared.

He pressed forward. It looked like he was sucking the stretches of bloody skin back into his chest. He shouted, "Hear us, pray for your great white giants to return—with their icy fingers—with their great white teeth." He pulled back, yanking on the straining flesh. The whistle and drum screamed. He tilted forward, shouting over the frenzied drumming. "Hear us, pluck the fruit from the tree!" He pulled, the whistle screamed.

Then, with the reins still taut, the drumming grew quieter. His voice went low, cracking from pain. "Hear us make the world whole again." The drumming boomed, the whistle screeched, he tugged from side to side. The pegs ripped free. The cords snapped toward the Tree of Life.

Everything went silent. It sounded like the silence I'd heard in the desert. The sound of God breathing.

Wachpanne Papa stood, knees bent, blood oozing from his open wounds. His arms hung, fingers still holding the eagle feathers. Staring up at the buffalo, he rasped, "See us, touch Mother Earth with healing feathers." The feathers dropped from his hands, fluttered down, and landed inside the hoop of the world. He wavered and fell to his knees.

I sucked in a breath, like I hadn't breathed for a lifetime.

Yellow-haired Woman appeared with an Indian blanket covered in sage and cattails. She wrapped it around him. He slumped onto his shins. "Wachpanne Papa has gone to his vision," she said quietly. "It is time for everyone to go to theirs." She gave the crowd a nodding smile. *"Hetchetu aloh."*

"Hetchetu aloh," the crowd rumbled back.

260

39

Nontraditional Gift

I felt something on my knee. Spring was gripping it. For how long, I didn't know.

She stared through watery eyes. Her cheeks were a wild striping of green and white. She leaned in and kissed me on the mouth, hard. I kissed her back.

She was the first girl I'd ever kissed. I mean, *really* kissed. I don't count when I was ten and me and Suzie Werfleman traded ABC gum under the church steps. This kiss was something else. I never imagined lust could feel so clean. I wanted all my kisses to be like that: like I was flying.

As Spring pulled away I opened my eyes in time to catch her green eyes close and her real ones open. "We need space," she whispered. She took my hand and led me out of the tent.

A breeze blew across the playa. The neon statues blurred in the dusty haze. We didn't speak. We were in a trance. We probably looked like some of the people I've seen after they were healed at a revival meeting. Zombies for the Lord.

No way had my insides gone zombie. My brain was shouting that I'd just witnessed idol worship and my next vision might be God's wrath. My heart was screaming that I'd just tumbled into lust, and God was reaching for his smite stick. But none of these fears could stop the biggest feeling surging through me. The kiss had been like a chocolate that starts in your mouth and rolls through your body. When you get a kiss like that, you don't want just one, you want the whole box.

Out at the edge of the playa it was empty, quiet. There were so many stars it looked like Heaven had blown up.

"Wanna play high-low?" Spring asked.

"What's that?"

She pulled my hand and we sat in the soft dust. "We tell the best moment and the worst moment of the dance. You first."

"The low was all the blood. The high was—does the kiss count?"

She laughed. "No."

I thought about it. "My high was the buffalo head turning with him. It was freaky and cool, like it was alive. Your turn."

She shifted onto her shins. "Low: that I have to wait an entire year before Wachpanne Papa comes back and offers his flesh to the East. High—besides the fact that we just took a giant step toward healing the planet—is when he showed how all religions and beliefs are spokes leading to the same center. I love that."

"Do you believe it?"

"Yes, but I have a different way of looking at it."

"What do you mean?"

"You know when you lie in bed at night and watch a lightning storm out your window?"

"Yeah."

262

"When there's a lightning flash, the outdoors lights up and you see everything clearly for a second, right?"

"Right."

"Well, for me, every religion is like a lightning flash that illuminates everything for a moment. But the flash is in slow motion and burns longer than a lightning bolt. It can illuminate as long as a Sun Dance, or blaze for a lifetime, like it does for Christians, Muslims, Jews, whoever. But then there's me. I don't see God's divine flash once, from a house. My window on the divine is moving, like in a car. I'm driving through God's lightning storm of truth, and every time He reveals the divine I see a different landscape, a different divine-scape. That's what I love about the Sun Dance. It accepts every religion that ever was, and says"— she raised her hands to the sky—" 'Let's all gather at the Tree of Life and heal the world!' "

She stayed there for a moment, then dropped her hands on her cattail-covered thighs. She looked at me and shut her eyes. Her mouth twisted with a smile as her green tattoo eyes stared. "You don't want to talk about this anymore, do you? You want another kiss, don't you?"

I waited for her real eyes to open. I nodded.

She leaned forward. The kiss was just as fantastic as the first . . . until I felt something. A new taste. It was sweet, and slick. At first I thought she was sucking on some kind of candy. Then I realized what it was. Saliva + dust = clay. Huck had fallen for a girl "full of sand." I was kissing a girl full of dust.

She pulled back, wiping her lip with a finger. "I just remembered something."

"What?"

"I forgot to give Wachpanne Papa the traditional gift."

"What gift?"

"My cattails." She pulled at her dress. "If I give them to you, will you make sure he gets them?"

"Okay." I wasn't exactly sure what she meant. It didn't stop my heart from beating like the Sun Dance drum.

She started pulling at ties on the front of her dress. When she undid the last one, she looked at me. "Okay, Gob-smack. Don't be surprised."

I swallowed. "Why should I be surprised? I've been looking at naked boobs all day."

She laughed. "I'm sure you have. But none like these." She lowered the cattails.

I think I gasped, I don't remember. She was right. They were the most awesome breasts I'd ever seen. But that wasn't all. They were glow-in-the-dark, electric green.

She rose to her knees, bringing her breasts closer. She giggled. "Spring awaits you."

I felt strange. My hand wanted to touch, but my eyes said *Don't move*. Something wasn't right. It was like when I saw Wachpanne Papa's chest skin stretch out like cartoon boobs. He wasn't supposed to have boobs. Spring was supposed to have breasts, but not glowing green ones.

The sound of a gunning engine pulled me away. Headlights flickered across the dusty playa. They were coming fast, right at us. We jumped up.

Spring didn't bother covering up. "Who's that?"

"I dunno."

I squinted into the headlights as they slowed and

swerved. A van skidded to a stop beside us, throwing up dust.

Momi leaned out the driver's window. The passenger seat was empty. She gave us a quick look. "Sorry to interrupt, but we gotta go. Wachpanne Papa's not looking good."

"Is he alright?" Spring asked.

"He'll be fine, but he needs stitches sooner than later. Billy, if you wanna stay, grab your backpack from the front. If you wanna go, jump in. Just make up your mind."

I looked at Spring. She was beautiful, but I couldn't stop thinking she really was a woodland fairy after a nuclear accident. "I gotta go." I jumped in the van's front seat.

Spring handed her square of cattails to Momi. "Take these. They'll bring Wachpanne Papa luck."

Momi took them with a nod of thanks. *"Hetchetu aloh."* She hit the accelerator and whipped the van into a U-turn back across the playa.

Looking back, I saw Spring wave and shout, *"Hetchetu aloh!"* Her green, glow-stick hair and her green chest faded into the dusty haze.

Hetchetu aloh. It was so indeed.

40

One More Boob

The van sped between the port-a-sans and the MOOP fence. I heard Nico groan in the back. I looked for him but it was too dark. "Aren't there EMS people here?" I asked.

265

"He needs a hospital," Momi said.

"Is there one around here?"

"Don't worry. We'll find one."

We raced through a gate and sped away from Burning Man. I remembered something, and yanked the cell phone out of my pack.

"What are you doing?" she asked.

"Calling Info to find the nearest hospital. No, I'll call nine-one-one." I started to dial. A hand snatched the phone away. I whipped around and jumped.

Nico shut the phone. "No need for that." He spread his hands and waggled them. "I've been *healed*!"

Momi turned on the overhead light. I stared at his chest. There was no blood, no wounds, not even scars.

"Say hello to Wachpanne Papa All Patched Up." He grinned. "And what about you? Do we call you Billy Lost His Virginity?"

I kept staring at his chest.

Momi snickered. "If you ask me, he's still Gob-smack."

"You're probably looking for this." Nico reached behind him and pulled up a floppy rubber vest. The front was streaked with blood from two bacon-strip gashes in the upper chest.

I couldn't believe it. "It was fake?"

Nico looked hurt. "Absolutely not. We played our parts; the audience played theirs."

"The unities were preserved," Momi said, "as we say in the biz."

"What biz?"

Nico leaned forward with a smile. "We told you, Billy, we're filmmakers."

"And before that we were moment makers," Momi added.

He laughed at my baffled look. "We're actors, Billy. That's what actors manufacture: moments. Hollywood never liked us as moment makers, but we were very good, and still are"—he shook the rubber vest—"at special effects."

I turned front and crossed my arms.

The cell phone pushed past my shoulder. "Nice phone," he said. "But didn't you say you didn't own one?"

I snatched it away. "It's not mine, I borrowed it."

After a short silence, he asked, "So what pisses you off more? That I didn't really bleed while healing the world, or that you didn't get laid?"

"Don't be mean, Nikki." Momi patted me on the arm. "Pardon my prick of a husband, William. When it comes to people's feelings he can be a total asshole."

"She's right. But when it comes to giving an audience what they want I'm a saint. It was a magnificent exchange. We did some fund-raising for our film, they got a spiritual experience."

"But it wasn't real," I grumbled.

"Which raises the question: is any spiritual experience *real*? In the movie biz 'real' is such a dodgy concept. I say spiritual experience is in the eye of the believer."

I wanted to hit him, make him bleed real blood. I wanted them to stop so I could get out, go back to Burning Man, and tell Spring and everyone that the Sun Dance was a fake. Then the Potlatchers couldn't come back next year and take their money. But I didn't. I shut my eyes and prayed. I prayed for God to tell me what to do.

I don't know if it was Him talking, or if it was just me writing a speech in God's name, but here's the answer I got. *Billy, tonight you sinned left and right. You put other gods before me by falling for that stuff about all religions leading to the same Tree of Life and Maker of All Things. You lusted for a girl sent to you by Satan. Who else would send a harlot with four eyes, a clay-slicked mouth, and green boobs? And now, with each mile you get farther from Burning Man, you bear false witness by not going back and exposing the frauds. But I will forgive all these sins if you don't break the fifth commandment: honor your father. Stay on the road to Portland, respect his last wishes, and retrieve the inheritance he wants you to have.*

I opened my eyes and took a breath. "Are you going to Portland now?"

"Portland or bust," Nico barked. "We have an un-movie to debut."

"We'll drive tonight as long as one of us can stay awake," Momi added.

I realized something that Nico had said didn't add up. "If your movie is finished, why did you have to go to Burning Man and do a fund-raiser?"

"Who said it was finished?" he asked.

"But you said you're taking it to a film festival."

"We are, as a work in progress."

"So it's not really done."

"How can it be done"—his hand dropped on my shoulder—"when we haven't put you in it?"

I escaped his grip. "I don't wanna be in your movie."

"Don't be silly. Everyone's in a movie. Life is a movie. You're in the movie of Billy William Whoever You Are. And now you're in the fantastic un-movie of Nico and Momi Potlatcher."

Momi shot me a smile. "What could be better than that?"

I was too tired to follow what they were saying. I had to trust that God was putting me in their hands for a reason. I didn't want to hear their crazy ideas anymore. "Sleep," I said. "Sleep could be better than anything."

Momi pulled over and Nico made some room on the floor in the back. I took my backpack with me and Nico got in front.

We started again. My body was totally bonked. It didn't stop me from thinking about stuff. And I kept feeling the key tied around my neck, resting on my skin. I tried to imagine what Boot Heel Collectibles would look like, and the cache where I'd find the bad book. My thoughts also flashed back on four boobs: the two that stretched out of Nico's chest during the dance, and Spring's green ones. Then there was the fifth boob: me, for getting totally punked by the Sun Dance.

My zigzag thoughts finally wove me into sleep.

41

Getting Glassed

When I woke it was still dark; Nico was driving. Momi and I switched places so she could sleep. Darkness swallowed both sides of the road. The headlights showed we were still in desert or sage steppe. I kicked myself for not checking my GPS in the back and seeing how close we were to Portland.

"How long was I asleep?" I asked Nico.

"Long enough," he said, then quickly added, "You'll be awake for sunrise on the Cascades." He flipped on the radio. "How 'bout we listen to some unities?" No sound came out. "Oops, forgot. Squawk box is broken."

"What are unities?" I asked.

He fluttered a hand in the air. "Just mini worlds people create for others to visit. Songs, books, movies, paintings: they're all unities. Each exists by itself and can be enjoyed or detested on its own. At first, you enjoyed our Sun Dance unity, then you discovered it had special effects, and you hated it."

"I didn't hate it. I just thought—"

"That Wachpanne Papa and Yellow-haired Woman are scamming a bunch of burners. That's okay, that's *your* take on the Sun Dance. Our take is that we won another victory in the campaign to rob from the rich and give to the poor in imagination." Nico waved a hand. "But enough of us. What do you say we talk about *your* unity, Billy?"

"What do you mean?"

"Everyone has a story: where you're from; why you're going to Portland."

"I don't wanna talk about it."

"Okay. Since you don't want to talk about the Billy unity, how 'bout we talk about some unity you experienced recently? You know, a book, a movie, even a video game?"

I thought about telling him about *Huck Finn,* but that would have led to personal questions, and there was one thing I'd learned from *Huck:* give a con man a glimpse of who you are, and he'll steal you blind. "I don't see movies," I said, "and my mom believes video games are the stained-glass windows of hell."

"Cool!" he exclaimed. "You're one of the few kids who hasn't been GLASSED."

I thought I'd heard a lot of slang, but that was a new one. "What's glassed?"

"*G-L-A-S-S-E-D*: the George Lucas Action Sequence and Special Effects Disease." He slapped a hand to his chest. "It breaks my heart to see kids sickened by it."

"A movie or video game can't make you sick."

"Ah, that's what everyone *thinks*. But if light flashing on a screen can trigger an epileptic fit, you better believe Hollywood can hit you with multiple doses of GLASSE until your imagination's poisoned and your brain's rewired."

He sounded serious. As serious as Mom was about some of her gonzo-wonky cranial harmonies.

271

"Let me unpack it for you," he said. "In 1975 a kid named George Lucas walked into a Hollywood studio and made a pitch that changed movies forever. He said, 'I'm gonna make a movie with a big action sequence every ten minutes.' When Lucas's first Star Wars movie came out, the blockbuster was born, and Hollywood was infected by the first case of the George Lucas Action Sequence and Special Effects Disease. Now people all over the world crowd into multiplexes showing blockbusters and can't wait to get GLASSED. They line up to be the first to get GLASSED. They come back and get GLASSED again. People are getting GLASSED so much they should stop calling them movie houses. They should call them GLASSE chambers." He did one of his shoulder laughs.

"What's so bad about seeing a bunch of action and special effects?" I asked.

He threw me a look, raising his bushy eyebrows.

"I mean," I said, "if you know it's just a movie and you're seeing tricks, then you're not getting fooled."

He shook his head and sighed. "If only it were that simple. I'll tell you how blockbusters rewire the human brain. Most of them flood your imagination with aliens, and mutant superheroes with supersuits and fantastic weapons. They overload your brain with worlds always being terrorized by psychotic villains who must be vanquished. And the only way to overcome these dastardly villains is always the same: *action!* This obsession with defeating evil through action breeds a contempt for its opposite: *inaction.* The *real* villains in blockbusters are the cousins of nonaction: idle activities like thought, introspection, hesitation. On the surface, Hollywood's moral in all the blockbusters is good conquers evil. But under the action-obese surface of the movie screen, the real moral is far more insidious: Action good! Inaction bad!"

I tried to follow what he was saying. It wasn't easy, but I sort of understood.

"When it was only *movies* stuffing young minds with action-happy thoughts, it wasn't so bad. But then came the next deadly dose of George Lucas Action Sequence and Special Effects Disease. Gaming! With video games, whatever *inaction* survived between action sequences in movies got chucked out the window. In gaming it's *nonstop* action. Yes, there's a shadow of thought in gaming, but the mind's ability to blaze with introspection and quiet reflection has been dimmed to one asinine thought: *Do I pull the trigger or not?*"

I hadn't played a ton of video games, but it sounded like he was exaggerating. "All video games aren't that bad."

Not seeming to hear me, he rattled on. "So after a kid spends his formative years being GLASSED in movies and gaming, he walks into the mess of real life with a brain that's been shrunk to an on/off switch. His brain has gone binary; the only thing it knows is action/inaction, on-trigger/off-trigger. And he knows from his training in GLASSE chambers that a superhero always, *always* stays on-trigger and blows away the villain!"

Trying to follow Nico's crazy thinking, I remembered how Ruah's ideas had also seemed totally whack. But Ruah had sounded like a Sunday-school teacher compared to Nico. "Does any of this have to do with the movie you're taking to Portland?"

"Bingo!" he shouted. "Our un-movie is going to save the world from a plague of GLASSE houses." His shoulders jumped up and down as he laughed at another joke I didn't get.

"How's it gonna do that?"

His face went serious. "When factories polluted the rivers, what did we do? We passed the Clean Water Act, cleaned up the rivers, and made America a better place. Well, for decades the movie factories have been polluting our imaginations and it's time we did something. We need to pass the Clean *Imagination* Act. And our antiaction un-movie is going to wake up the world and begin the process. *Uncle Tom's Cabin* triggered the Civil War. *Silent Spring* triggered the environmental movement. The first antiaction film is going to trigger the clean imagination revolution!"

"But people don't think their imaginations are polluted."

"Of course they don't. In the nineteenth century people didn't think they got sick from germs until Louis Pasteur discovered microbes, and proved what made people sick. In the twenty-first century, Nico and Momi Potlatcher are going to prove how GLASSED is turning today's youth into popcorn-brained, action-drunk punks. They're gonna be called Generation Z if we don't do something. And *Z* is for *Zero*!"

After that, I heard the rumble of his voice but not his words. Like when you zone out on a preacher. Sometimes you just have to drift away to another place for a while.

I was nodding out when we passed a route sign. I saw 20, but under it I thought I saw EAST, not WEST. I kept pretending to doze and worked the GPS out of my right pocket, turned it on, and stole a look. The arrow was pointing straight behind us, and we were 270 miles from Portland!

I bolted upright. "We're going east. You're going the wrong way!"

"No, we're not," Nico said calmly.

"Didn't you see the sign?"

Momi rose up on the seat behind us. "Calm down, William."

"No!" I yanked up my GPS and waved it. "We're fifty miles farther from Portland than we were at Burning Man!"

Nico eyeballed the GPS. "Aren't you full of surprises?"

"You're right, Billy," Momi said, trying to sound nice. "We're going back to Idaho."

"Why?"

"We have one last scene to shoot in our un-movie," Nico said. "It's the big antiaction sequence and we want you to be the star of it."

"I don't wanna be in your movie! Lemme out!"

Momi leaned in next to me. "We think you'll be happy to be in our film when we explain your contract."

"What contract?"

Nico shot me a fake smile. "It starts with three names. Tilda Allbright, Joe Douglas, and Ruah Branch, which adds up to Billy William We Know Who You Are."

42

Black Night

I sat there, stunned and furious. Then they told me how, before the Sun Dance, they'd seen the cell phone in the pocket of my backpack. My lie about not having a cell phone made them suspicious. When I was out on the playa before the dance, they downloaded the call record onto their computer and called some of the numbers. They talked to my mom and told her I was fine. They called Joe Douglas and learned he was the agent for a missing baseball player, Ruah Branch.

"Did you tell my mom where I was?" I demanded.

"No," Nico said. "She asked, but we believe that even a runaway has some rights to privacy."

Before I could scream that going through the phone had violated my privacy, Momi asked, "What do you know about Ruah Branch?"

"Nothing. I found the phone in a campground and used it to call my mom."

"Really?"

"Really."

"Then why does the call record show a call to your mother a week ago," Nico said, "followed by two calls from Ruah's agent—the second one going on for several minutes—followed by another call to your mother yesterday morning? Is Joe Douglas your agent, too, or did Mr.

Branch come back for his phone, make a few calls, then give it to you as a gift?"

"We doubt it," Momi added.

"It makes more sense that you and Mr. Branch traveled together for a while."

I was busted. "Okay, yeah. He picked me up and drove me for a couple days," I admitted, but I had other worries. "Did you make the calls on the cell phone?"

"No, its service has been suspended," Nico said. "And even if it worked, we'd never do anything as low as rack up minutes on someone else's phone."

"Yeah, right. Whose phone did you use?"

"We keep one for emergencies," Momi confessed.

In the dim glow I could see Nico's eyebrows working. "There was one call we couldn't get to the bottom of: the nine-one-one in Colorado."

Momi did some eyebrow work of her own. "Lots of mysteries, William. Do you want to tell us about it?"

"You've never told me the truth—why should I tell you anything?"

She looked at Nico. "He has a point."

"You never planned to go to Portland, did you?"

"No, that part's true," Nico answered.

Momi finished his thought. "We're going to the Portland International Film Festival, but it's not till February."

"Here's our proposal," he said. "We think you're perfect for our un-movie. If you'll go back to our canyon for just a half day of shooting, after that we'll put you on a bus to Portland. And we promise, we'll keep everything we learned about you and Ruah Branch under our hats."

"There's nothing to keep under your hats," I told him. "He gave me a ride for two days, that's all."

"Oh, c'mon—"

Momi shushed him. "Let me handle this, Nikki." She turned to me with a put-on smile. "Knowing how smooth you are with girls, William, I'm sure nothing happened. But we did check into why Mr. Branch might have gone AWOL. All we found were rumors. But eventually the story of where he's been will come out. And it would be a shame, given the rumors about Mr. Branch, if the world learned that he was gallivanting around the countryside with a cute young boy."

I wanted God to squash their van like a bug, even if I was in it.

"We know, Billy," Nico said. "We're despicable. That's what happens when you spend too many years in Hollywood. That's why we're making the film that'll destroy Hollywood as we know it."

Momi clapped her hands. "And we're thrilled you're going to be in it."

"It's going to make you a star!" he added. "An anti-action star!"

I prayed to God to stop me from taking out my Leatherman and slitting their throats right then and there. I could've done it easy. But I didn't. If I did, I would've had to spend more than another miserable day with them. I would've been stuck between them on some burning couch in hell, forever.

I didn't think that night could go on any longer, but it did. A lot longer.

After we drove back into Idaho, we went through tiny towns as we headed south to the Potlatchers' canyon. Going through a town called Homedale, I almost jumped out of my seat when I spotted something that didn't fit the empty streets and weather-beaten buildings. A white camper glowed under the sign for Combs Car Corral. I thought, no way could it be Ruah's. Then I saw the crumpled front end and realized we were less than ten miles from where Giff had crashed in a gully. My mind raced. Had the camper been towed there and left? Was it being fixed? If it was being fixed, could Ruah still be around waiting for it? If he was, where would he be? As we turned in the main intersection, I checked every direction. Up the street was a lighted sign: SUNNYDALE MOTEL. If he was in Homedale, he might be there.

As we rode out of town, I pretended to be sleepy. Between fake nod-outs, I snuck a hand in my pocket and held down the thumb stick on my GPS. My new waypoint was set. No matter how many turns we took getting to their canyon, I had a GPS trail back to Homedale.

When we got to their brush fence I helped Momi open the gate. She let me close it. I was ready. I had two pages from *Huck Finn*. There was just enough moonlight for me to see as I slipped the folded pages in the gate so it wouldn't latch shut. I could open it again later without knowing the security code.

On the way into "Dogleg Canyon" I could only see what the headlights hit. It wasn't what I expected. There were rusty railroad tracks, lots of strange shapes, and the bases of metal towers. The moonlight lit the towers' dark, creepy silhouettes. At the end of the canyon we stopped in front of two low buildings backed up against the rock cliff. In front of the bigger building, the headlights caught a frame of timbers holding up a rusty sign: EARTH WARS PRODUCTIONS.

With the headlights shining on the smaller building, we got out and walked toward it. At the end of the porch a bicycle leaned against the wall. A sign made of rusty metal hanging over the door read CAVE SWEET CAVE.

Inside, Nico lit a gas lantern and the sign's meaning became clear. The living room and kitchen were under a tin roof, but the bedroom was built into an old mine tunnel in the canyon wall. I kept up my sleepy act, which was a no-brainer since it was nearly three a.m. Yawning, I asked, "Don't you have electricity?"

"We'll have it tomorrow," Nico answered, "after we restart the generator."

Momi fixed a bed for me on a saggy couch in the living room. I set my backpack on a chair made from a wooden barrel. Nico came over and plucked it off the chair. I grabbed for the backpack but he yanked it away. "We'll hold it as bond for the night, in case you decide to run away. But I wouldn't advise it, 'cause the rattlesnakes *do* come out at night."

They disappeared into their cave bedroom and shut the door. Cave Sweet Cave was about right. They were Neanderthals.

In a few minutes they were snoring. I stuffed the couch-bed with pillows to look like I was sleeping and snuck outside. I pushed the bike toward the wheel ruts and mounted up.

At the mouth of the canyon the moonlight was less blocked by the high walls, so it was easier to see. The gate swung open no problem. Luckily, there were no rattlesnakes wanting to help. I checked my GPS. I was twelve miles from Homedale. I had to get there and back before sunrise.

43

Homedale

Except for a couple of buzzing neon signs, Homedale looked like a ghost town. I went to the Sunnydale Motel and walked the bike toward the rooms in the back. They were all dark. A few cars were parked in front of them. Ruah could've been in any of them, or none.

Remembering how he always stopped at the farthest pump from the mini-mart, I figured he might be in the room farthest back. I thought about knocking on the last door and working my way toward the office. Stupid: someone could have a gun and shoot me for waking them in the middle of the night. Calling his name would've been dumb too. Ruah wasn't an everyday name. If someone heard me and ID'd him, *Ruah* would shoot me. I got an idea, not much smarter, but it was the best my brain could do, given the hour. I did what Huck and Tom did when they called each other out of the house in the middle of the night. "Me-yow. Me-yow."

After another "me-yow" the window in the second-to-last room lit up. My foot was on the bike pedal, ready to rip if I had to.

The door cracked open, followed by a harsh whisper. "Shhh!" The door opened wider. With the light behind him, I couldn't see his face. I didn't have to. I recognized his cut silhouette; there was the bulge of a cast on his left forearm. "Enough catcalling," Ruah whispered. "Get in here."

I set the bike down and scooted into the room.

"Keep your voice down," he warned. "The walls are paper thin." He motioned me into the only chair in the cramped room. I sat down as he pulled on a big football jersey. He sat on the edge of the bed, shaking his head in disbelief. "What the hell are you doing here?"

"I saw Giff. I figured you might be around." I checked out his cast. "Is your arm okay?"

"It'll be fine."

"Did they ID you at the hospital?"

"Nope. I paid in cash and they went for my fake ID. I also paid the local tow guy enough to keep the cops out of it."

I started to ask another question but he cut me off. "Why are you still in Idaho? Was your father's place in Notus?"

"No, it's in Portland."

"Then what are you doing here?"

"I got sidetracked."

"By what?"

"Some people."

His brow knitted. "What people?"

I forced a laugh like it was no big deal. "Just a couple of nut jobs." I changed the subject. "Why are *you* still here?"

"I'm waiting on a new radiator and window for the RV. The parts get delivered in the morning, then I head for Seattle in the afternoon."

It surprised me; he'd never said anything about Seattle. "Why there?"

"Just my own 'nut jobs' I've gotta deal with."

I wanted to ask what he was talking about, but there was no time. "Would it be okay if I rode with you tomorrow?"

A smile split his face. "Did you get more *Huck* to read?"

I nodded, deciding not to tell him it was only one chapter.

"You're on," he said.

"Great." I jumped up to go. "I'll be back here tomorrow as soon as I can."

He stayed seated. "What's the rush?"

I moved to the door. "I gotta get back."

"To the nut jobs?"

"Yeah. I promised to do something with them in the morning."

"What?"

I figured there was no harm in the truth. "They wanna put me in their movie."

"What kind of movie?"

"They call it an un-movie."

"What the hell is that?"

"I'm not sure." I shrugged. "I'll find out soon."

He stood up. "Billy, forget the movie." He gestured to the second bed in the room. "You can stay here."

I shifted my weight. It felt like the room was crunching smaller. "I can't." I wanted to tell him about the Potlatchers

283

stealing my stuff and holding me hostage, but I couldn't. Then I would've had to explain how they were blackmailing me because they knew about Ruah. I reached for the doorknob. "I gotta go."

"How 'bout I pick you up tomorrow?"

"No, I'll come back here."

"I'd rather come get you. I'd like to see what kind of people make an un-movie."

I tried to act like the Potlatchers were as innocent as spring rain. "They're nuthin special. How 'bout if I'm done first I'll come into town, and if the camper's done first you come get me."

"Fair enough. Where will you be?"

As I gave him directions to Dogleg Canyon I made getting there sound super complicated. But he never threw up his hands and told me to just come into town. When I told him about the brush fence at the mouth of the canyon I didn't say it had a locked gate. If he did come for me I didn't want him getting past the gate. The last thing anybody needed was the Potlatchers laying eyes on Ruah Branch. He was already getting blackmailed by Joe Douglas. If the Potlatchers got their claws into him there'd be no telling what might happen.

When I got back to the canyon the horizon was graying up. Cave Sweet Cave was still black as night. I snuck back inside without knocking anything over and crawled into the couch bed. I fell asleep to Nico and Momi snoring away in the mine-shaft bedroom like a couple of hibernating bears.

44

Un-moviemaking 101

Waking came too soon. I squinted against the harsh light and stumbled to the closet of a bathroom. I wished I could climb back into the z-bag. The flushing toilet sucked away my wish and the tattered memory of a dream. I zipped up and told myself to do whatever the Potlatchers wanted for their weird movie, then get out of there.

On the kitchen table, there was a plate of banana muffins and a tall glass of milk. My backpack sat in a chair. I checked it. Everything was there. I wolfed down three muffins and chugged the milk.

I grabbed my pack and went outside. I saw the entire canyon for the first time. The walls were high and sheer, but that wasn't the big surprise. The railroad tracks I'd seen the night before, running along the canyon floor, didn't stop there. They crept up broken trestles along the walls. Some of them even spiderwebbed toward the middle of the canyon on spindly rusty towers.

"And, antiaction!" I heard Nico yell.

I followed his voice to the top of a tower. He and Momi were on a wooden platform. They stood behind a camera on a tripod. The camera pointed down at me.

Momi waved. "Good afternoon, William."

"It can't be that late," I blurted.

"Yes it can," she called down. "We wanted you to get your beauty sleep for the big scene."

"Are you filming now?"

Nico's head poked from behind the camera. "Nah, just a rehearsal. You're not in costume yet."

"I have to wear a costume?"

They started coming down the ladder in the middle of the tower. As they climbed down I looked around some more. Some of the elevated tracks disappeared into the black mouths of mine shafts in the canyon walls. The strange shapes I'd seen the night before were old bucket cars and miniature engines rusting on tracks or sunken in the dust. The canyon looked like it had been home to a rickety roller coaster that hadn't heard a scream for a hundred years.

The Potlatchers jumped off the ladder and came over.

"What is this place?" I asked.

Nico spread his arms. "Earth Wars Productions."

"I mean before that."

"An old copper mine," he said. "And it's filled with the ghosts of miners."

"That's the cast of our un-movie," Momi added.

I blinked in confusion. "A bunch of ghosts?"

"Absolutely," Nico said. "There's no better antiaction hero than a dead one." He held some kind of meter up to the sun.

I didn't like the sound of a movie about dead people. It reminded me of movies Mom used to tell me about. People kidnapped kids and murdered them on film; "snuff movies"

286

she called them. Maybe I'd have to make my escape sooner than later. I looked to see if the bike was still on the porch where I'd left it. It was gone. Fear knifed through me. Maybe they knew I'd snuck back to Homedale. I tried to stay cool. "So, in the movie, I'm supposed to be dead?"

"That's right," Momi said. "You're the ghost of a miner."

"What does a ghost miner do?"

Nico jumped in. "An antiaction sequence!"

"What's that?"

"The *heart* of an un-movie!"

"I still don't get it."

"It's very simple," he explained. "An un-movie is the opposite of a blockbuster. Instead of a shoot-'em-up action sequence every ten minutes jam-packed with special effects, an un-movie has an antiaction sequence every ten minutes jam-packed with special *defects*."

I couldn't tell if I was just confused, or if they'd put something in the banana muffins. "What are special defects?"

Momi turned to Nico. "I told you he'd need a quickie in un-moviemaking one-oh-one."

"Fine," he told her. "You go get started on his costume and makeup while I wipe the blank expression off his face."

She started toward the main building as Nico turned to me with gleaming eyes. "Herr Director will show you exactly what he means." He held up his hands, making a rectangle with his thumbs and forefingers. "Don't move or speak."

I didn't.

"A close-up of your face, held for several minutes. That's an antiaction sequence."

"So it's like a photograph."

His eyebrows shot up. "Ah-ah, you just broke the first rule of antiaction sequences: you opened your mouth. And no, a held shot of a face is never still. There's always something going on, something moving in the great landscape of the human facade. That's what moment-making is all about." My face must've scrunched, because he said, "See! That was a moment: confusion!" He dropped his hands. "Okay, here's a better example. At Burning Man, when you looked into Spring's eyes and kissed her—"

"You saw that?"

He two-fingered his eyes. "Wachpanne Papa sees everything. Just before you kissed her, when you faced off, did you see all sorts of fascinating stuff in her face and eyes?"

"Well, yeah."

"Bingo!" He snapped his fingers. "That's an antiaction sequence."

"Even when we kissed?"

"No, that's different. That's action. There's never any action in an antiaction sequence."

"So what is there, just a face?"

"Yep."

"Isn't that boring?"

"Not when a face is firing off tiny moments right and left. It's jam-packed with special defects."

"But if it's a happy moment, like when I kissed Spring, why call it a special *defect*?"

"Because, Billy, every moment in life, good or bad, every

288

feeling that tweaks the human visage, good or bad, takes us one step closer to the ultimate special defect: death."

I tried not to let my face give away how he was creeping me out with his talk about death and dead miners.

Nico threw an arm around my shoulder. I tensed. He led me toward the big building Momi had gone into. "Look, I don't expect you to understand. Besides, actors do their best work when they're underinformed. If their brains are stuffed with ideas it clogs the emotional plumbing from the heart to the face. So, go inside, get into costume and makeup, and I'll set up the camera for your antiaction sequence."

I pointed up to the platform. "What's that camera for?"

"For a long shot later. But first we do your close-up."

45

The Bullet Hole

I went into the building. It was a big room with worktables, rusty machines, and old mining equipment. Huge wrenches, drill bits, and saws made the place look like a torture chamber for giants.

Momi handed me a pair of ratty overalls, a grimy undershirt, and some holey boots. I took my backpack behind a screen of hanging ropes and pulleys and changed clothes. Before I stuffed my cargo shorts in my backpack, I took my Leatherman and put it in the overalls' chest pocket. If the antiaction sequence got too weird I'd be ready for some *anti*-antiaction. I also pulled out the *Huck* chapter with my father's card on it and stuffed it in the overalls. No way could I lose that.

Momi put me in a swivel chair in front of a mirror. There was a bunch of makeup on the table, and she started wiping some pale stuff on my face. "I don't get what's so awesome about a movie version of a photo album," I said.

She took a brush, dipped it in gray stuff, and painted shadows on my face. "Everyone on the set of *Pirates of the Caribbean* thought it was a piece of crap when they were making it, but it turned out to be a huge hit."

I wanted to say how it was probably filled with fighting-pirate sequences, but getting into an argument would only slow her down and raise the chance of Ruah finding Dogleg Canyon before I got back to town.

She picked a nickel-sized piece of rubber up off the makeup table. It was shaped like a crater. "What's that?" I asked.

"A bullet hole. It goes on your forehead."

"Do I have to wear it?"

"Yes, you do." She wiped glue on the back of it. "You're a ghost and we need to know what killed you." She stuck the bullet hole on my forehead. "If it's going to creep you out seeing it in the mirror I'll turn you around." She dipped a brush in red makeup.

I didn't want to watch what would probably look like Momi doing brain surgery on me. "Yeah, turn me around." She did and began working on the bullet hole. I tried to keep my mouth shut, but when there's a bullet hole in the middle of your forehead you want to know how it got there. "Who killed me?"

"We don't know yet."

"How can you not know?"

"That's the fun of an un-movie. We shoot your long close-up first, then we'll fill in the story of who you were later."

"How are you gonna do that if I never open my mouth?"

"It'll all be done in voice-over. Every little moment your face gives us on film will be our guide to who you were, how you got killed, and how you ended up at the mine."

"You mean I got killed *before* I got to the mine?"

"All the miners did."

"That makes no sense. What good are a bunch of dead miners?"

"That's the mystery each miner's antiaction sequence will reveal to the audience."

This movie was sounding like weird squared. "So what's the big mystery?"

"I don't want to ruin the ending."

"If I'm in the movie shouldn't I know it?"

"Okay, but don't you dare tell Nico I told you."

"I promise."

She kept working on my bullet hole. "The couple who runs the mine—"

"Are they dead too?"

"No, they're the only ones alive. Nico and I play them."

"Why do you get to be alive and everyone else has to be dead?"

291

"Would you let me tell the story?"

"Okay."

"The couple—Nico and me—are powerful psychics. We're really good at séances and communicating with the dead. And from the dead we learn a secret, a secret about gravity. Now, everyone knows that gravity is the invisible glue that holds the universe together. But what Nico and I learn from the dead is where gravity comes from."

"Where does it come from?"

"From dark matter. Just as the sun makes heat and light, the dark matter woven all through the universe makes gravity. Without dark matter the world would fly off in all directions. But dark matter is invisible to the living. All we can sense is what it makes: gravity."

As wacky as it sounded, and as much as I wanted to get out of there, I was into what she was saying. I mean, that's what mountain biking is all about: working out your own personal relationship with gravity. "Okay," I said, "the dead know about the thing that makes gravity, dark matter. Got it."

"Right, they can see it, touch it, and even collect it. So the psychic couple starts recruiting ghosts of the dead, and bringing them to this canyon to mine dark matter. They call it Dark Matter Mine."

"But why do they want to collect dark matter?"

"Because if you can gather dark matter, you can experiment with the thing it makes: gravity. And if you can control gravity, you can make a major weapon."

"What weapon?"

"A gravity bomb."

"What would you do with that?"

She studied my forehead, then dipped her brush in another makeup tin. "You could do wonderful things. If two countries went to war, you could drop gravity bombs on both sides. Everything would get super heavy and, under the force of greater gravity, everyone would go into slow motion. It would be the ultimate peacekeeping *force*. Or if a tsunami was about to slam into India, you could hit the tidal wave with a gravity bomb, slow it down to nothing, and sink it in the ocean before it killed millions."

I had to admit, I was getting into their movie. I mean, if you could throw gravity grenades during a bike run, you could throw everything into slow motion. It would be as good as mountain biking on the moon. "Is that how the movie ends? They turn their gravity bombs into weapons for peace and good?"

"Of course not," she said with a frown. "An un-movie has to have an antiaction ending."

"What's that?"

She gave me a hard look. Her eyes narrowed. "You absolutely swear you won't tell Nico I told you?"

I raised my right hand. "On the Bible."

She went back to my bullet hole. "In their effort to create a weapon that will do only good, the psychics realize that all they've done is create another weapon of mass disruption that tinkers with the way the universe works. They realize they're playing God. So, in the last long close-up, they drop a gravity bomb on *themselves*. They go into slow-motion antiaction. The audience can't tell if they're alive or in suspended animation."

293

"Are they? Alive, I mean?"

"That's for the audience to guess"—she gave me a sly smile—"and then find out in the sequel, *Dark Matter Mine Two*."

She swiveled my chair to face the mirror. I stared at the hole in my head. The edges were puffed up with blood and torn skin. In the middle, there were bits of broken white bone and purplish gray brain sticking out. If I hadn't known what she was doing to me, and she whipped me around without telling me I had a bullet hole in my head, I would've dropped dead from shock.

46

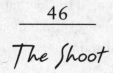

The Shoot

We went back outside. Nico made a big deal about the fantastic job Momi had done, making me look like a corpse. As long as no one tried to make me into a real one, I was cool. He led me over to a big camera on a tripod. He put me in front of it, moved me around, and adjusted the camera until the light hit me just right. He asked if I was ready for my antiaction sequence.

"I guess so," I said. "What do you want me to do?"

"Just be Billy Allbright."

"You mean with a bullet hole in my head."

"To a ghost, that hole's as trivial as a pimple. The important thing is not to speak. We'll fill in all your thoughts later."

"Depending on what my face does."

"Excellent! You're getting the hang of antiacting. Some say 'Less is more.' We say '*Nothing* is more!'" His face disappeared behind the camera. "Ready?"

"Sure."

"Camera," he said. The camera began to click and whir like it needed oil. He raised a hand—"And"—he chopped the air—"antiaction." His face reappeared. "If either of us says something or does something, don't *try* to react; trust your face. It'll give us all the special defects we need."

I felt my mouth start to smile. I clamped down on it. It wasn't right for a ghost with a bullet in his head to smile.

Nico must've seen it. "It's okay to smile," he said. "Anything goes but speech or big movement."

I tried to just listen to the camera and feel the sun on my face. Then the bullet hole began to itch. I wanted to reach up and scratch it. That almost made me laugh. I thought about wrinkling my forehead to scratch it, but then it would be really hysterical if my forehead wrinkle undid the glue and the bullet hole fell off. That did it. I had to grin.

"Excellent," Nico said, "you're doing great."

After that he totally switched gears. He started talking about when they called my mom on the phone. He told me about how upset she was. About how she threatened them if anything happened to me. And about how she ended up crying and praying for God to smite Nico dead if he lifted a finger against me.

I knew what they were doing, trying to get reactions out of me, trying to get special defects. And I'm sure they were getting plenty, including the time I glared at the camera and prayed for God to punish them for being liars, cheats, thieves, and blackmailers.

It's so weird how the Almighty answers your prayers sometimes. Most of the time it's like voice mail. You leave your message and wait for Him to get back to you. This time was a first. It was like God worked at a Chinese take-out place, picked up the phone, and said, *Hey, what's it gonna be?*

God's answer started with the faint sound of an engine behind me. It bounced off the canyon walls. The louder it got, the more alarmed Nico and Momi looked. Their faces were popping with special defects. At first I thought Ruah had busted through the gate with Giff. But then I heard more than one engine. And they were coming fast.

Nico stared past me with wild eyes. "What the hell?"

Momi's hands balled up in fists. "Shit!"

I turned to look. Around a bend in the canyon came a half-dozen pickups kicking up a cloud of dust. People stood in the beds. Some waved burning torches. When I saw a man in the lead truck—the owner of Kings restaurant—I knew who they were. The wrath of Notus was upon us.

I turned back, expecting to see the Potlatchers run, but Nico shouted orders. "Don't move!" he yelled at me. "We're still shooting! Mo, get up the tower and fire up camera two. We gotta get this!"

She ran to the tower. The roaring caravan of trucks slid to a stop in front of the two buildings. Nico swung the camera toward the action.

The restaurant owner thrust his arm at Nico. "You burned down my restaurant!"

296

Nico raised his hands. "I'm very sorry about that, King. It was never my intention."

A cloud of dust rolled over the trucks. Men jumped out and rushed into the house as King shouted, "Sorry's not good enough, Potlatcher!"

"How did you find us?"

"The FedEx guy delivered!" King jumped out of the truck, and led a gang of guys into the other building.

Nico flapped his arms. "That's it, I'm switching to UPS!"

Things smashed in the house. A barrel chair crashed through the window. A window shattered in the other building as a huge wrench flew through it.

Nico yelled up to Momi, who was just reaching the top of the platform. "Shoot first, write later, Mo! It's gonna be the new ending. The first un-movie ends by succumbing to the destruction of action! It's ironic—it's tragic—it's perfect!"

Smoke and flame mushroomed through the broken windows. I remembered my backpack. I ran toward the building.

"Don't go in there!" Nico yelled.

As I got to the open door, I ran smack into someone coming out. It was King. He grabbed my overalls, spun me around, and threw me against the wall. His eyes darted over my face. "What happened to you?"

"Nuthin," I said. "It's fake."

He squinted at the bullet hole in my forehead. "Maybe so, but what you're about to get ain't."

"I'm not with them," I pleaded. "I was biking through town and stopped behind the restaurant. You must've seen my bike."

His lips curled off his teeth. "Yeah, it's toast, just like my restaurant."

He shoved me off the porch. I stumbled back toward Nico and his camera. I couldn't believe he was still shooting, like the whole thing was a movie set. Men poured out of the house, along with clouds of smoke.

King and others came at Nico and me. Nico shouted up to Momi. "Get it all, Mo! The George Lucas Disease strikes again!" King knocked his camera away. Nico shouted "Action!" and dropped to the ground. He curled up in a ball a second before the men began kicking him with their boots.

The sickening thuds and Nico's pitiful yelps made me turn away. I saw men come out of the bigger building and head for the tower. They were going for Momi next. Then me. And it didn't look like their revenge was stopping at an eye for an eye, a fire for a fire. I remembered the knife in my overalls.

As I tried to dig it out, a flash of white came around the bend in the canyon. At first I thought it was a mirage. But it was real. Giff.

I ran toward the camper.

I heard King shout, "The woman's treed! Jimmy, Thad! Get the kid!"

I didn't look back to see who was coming after me. The camper was only thirty yards away when it turned, fishtailing into a power slide. The passenger door popped open. I jumped in.

Ruah gave me one look and took off. "Jesus! What happened to you?"

I saw he was only steering with his good arm, his right one. I gasped for breath. "Tell you later."

"Is that the real thing back there or a movie?"

"The real thing." I checked the outside mirror. A pickup was coming after us. I pushed out the window for a better look. There were two pickups. "And they're coming after us."

"I noticed, and I only got one good arm."

"I know how to drive," I said. And I did—another advantage of moving so much: Mom let me drive on back roads.

Ruah checked his mirror. "There's no time to switch."

When I spun to see how close the trucks were, I caught my reflection in the outside mirror. I still had the bullet hole. The only vigilante who knew it was fake was King. "We're not gonna outrun these guys, are we?"

"Doubt it," Ruah answered.

"I got an idea." I told Ruah what might get us out of this, just before a pickup roared past us in a cloud of dust. I jumped in the back and grabbed a blanket. A second later the camper skidded to a stop.

I was on the couch, under the blanket. I scooched up on my elbows and snuck a peek out the windshield. I could see one pickup in front of us blocking the open gate in the brush fence. The other pickup was behind us. Two doors slammed.

I pulled the blanket under my chin and pretended to shiver. The guy from the pickup behind us passed by the side windows. He was a huge guy, not much older than me, and looked like a football player.

The other one, who came to Ruah's door, I couldn't see. His voice sounded young. "You're not going anywhere, mister," he told Ruah.

"Not anymore," Ruah said. "You boys have me blocked in pretty good."

The guy at Ruah's window kept talking. "We want the kid."

"That's who I came for too," Ruah told him.

"Who are you?"

"I work for the hospital up in Boise."

"What are you doing here?"

"I got a call to pick up a patient that needed emergency treatment. Normally, I'd come in an ambulance, but when it's got a broken axle you come in what you can get."

The football player finally spoke up. "That kid's not sick. We saw him yesterday. He was fine."

"Are you gentlemen familiar with how flesh-eating disease works?" Ruah asked.

"What do you mean, 'flesh-eating disease?'" the other guy asked.

"I'm sure he looked fine yesterday," Ruah explained. "But when flesh-eating disease breaks skin, and the patient gets a fever, things get ugly fast."

"This is bull," said Football-guy.

Ruah waved a hand at me. "Go ahead, take a look."

Football-guy leaned through the passenger window and stared at me. I made sure the blanket shook along with my shivering. His eyes squinted. "What's on his head?"

"That's a flesh-eating lesion. He's got a bunch on his body."

Football-guy backed out the window. "You mean he's bleeding?"

"He's starting to. That's why I've gotta get him to the hospital, where we can deal with the threat."

"What threat?" the other guy demanded.

Ruah chuckled. "There's a reason they call it FED."

"What's FED?"

"Flesh-eating Disease, of course. And any disease that likes to feed is contagious."

Football-guy jumped in. "That's why we carry tire irons and bats."

Ruah nodded thoughtfully. "I suppose that might protect you, but anyone who gets hit with blood splatter—"

"This is total crap," the other guy interrupted. "Jimmy, grab the kid outta there and let's go."

Jimmy looked at me, then the other guy. "Why don't *you* grab him?"

"Look, fellas," Ruah said, "I'm just trying to do my job, but you guys have me outnumbered and outmaneuvered. If you want him I wish you'd take him, 'cause the longer we sit here the closer he gets to bleeding all over my camper."

There was a pause that went on forever. Then the guy I couldn't see kicked the door hard. I flinched, went into a shivering fit, and let out a little groan of pain.

"Mister," the guy said, "we're gonna cut you and that slab of plague back there a break."

"Yeah," Jimmy added, "there's no way we're gettin' FED."

"I appreciate your kindness," Ruah told them. "It's probably the best decision you'll ever make."

Jimmy squinted as his brain tried to process Ruah's meaning. He gave up and settled for kicking the door like his friend. The two of them went back to their pickups and roared away, making sure to hit Giff with rooster tails of dust.

I popped off the couch. "That was amazing!" I jumped into the passenger seat. Ruah didn't look at me. His face was tensed up.

"Yeah." He turned on the wipers to clear the dust. "Our second dust storm in a week." He looked over. His mouth did a little spasm of a smile. His eyes looked spent and sad. "Now take that damn thing off your forehead."

47

Crossing Lines

Heading to the highway that would take us north to I-84, Ruah grilled me about what was happening in the canyon. I told him about meeting the Potlatchers behind Kings, Burning Man, and going back to be in their movie until the Notus posse showed up to even the score.

As we drove through Homedale, Ruah pulled over at a pay phone. "Go call nine-one-one and tell the cops what's going on in the canyon."

"How are they gonna find it?"

"All they gotta do is follow the smoke."

I called 911, but the operator cut me off. Some hikers had already reported the fire and trucks were on the way.

When I told him it was more than a fire, he started asking questions I didn't want to answer. I hung up. Back in the camper, I vowed that when I got to Portland, I'd check and make sure King wasn't as bad as the murderers in Colorado and hadn't turned Cave Sweet Cave into Grave Sweet Grave.

The vow didn't stop me from feeling bad about what had happened. I mean, the Potlatchers weren't evil. Yeah, they were scam artists, but it's not like their sins were all about greed. They stole, lied, and cheated for a cause. They said they wanted to make an un-movie and save people from some disease they called GLASSED. They weren't the first in the world to do bad for what they considered good. The Bible's full of people like that. Jacob lies, cheats, and steals his brother Esau's birthright to the family property. Then Jacob becomes the father of Israel. And then there's Christ. Jesus wasn't exactly loving his neighbor when he grabbed a whip, lashed into the money changers, and whipped their asses out of the temple. So maybe Nico and Momi were bad, but not *all* bad. And even if they deserved a taste of God's smite stick, it still made my insides chung every time I flashed on Nico getting kicked, or imagined what the men had done to Momi.

As we drove, it wasn't just big worries scratching at my mental door. There was one rodent of a thought that kept skittering through the cranial walls. Why wasn't Ruah as pumped as I was about the awesome trick we'd played on the guys in our getaway? I was still catching air over it. So I asked him, "You know what made me think of the flesh-eating-disease thing?"

He shook his head. "Not a clue."

"Remember how Huck kept the slave hunters away from Jim by telling 'em the raft was infected with smallpox?"

"Right," he said flatly. "It was pretty smart, Billy."

"Yeah, but what if it hadn't worked? I mean, for a second there I thought you were gonna give me to 'em."

"I was playing it cool."

"But what if they still tried to take me?"

With his good hand he reached behind the seat and pulled up a sawed-off baseball bat. "Even with one hand, I still swing a mean bat."

I laughed out of relief. "Okay, but how did you know so much about flesh-eating disease?"

"I didn't," he replied. "I made it up."

"It was a great fake-out."

"It wasn't a total fake-out."

I didn't follow. Either he knew about flesh-eating disease, or he didn't.

He caught my confused look. "Hold the wheel for a sec." I did and he dug his wallet out of his pocket. He handed it to me.

"What's this for?"

"Open it, go into the deepest right pocket, and pull out what's there."

I pulled out a picture. It was of a white guy with dark wavy hair and a friendly face. What made him look extra friendly, and maybe funny, too, was a gap between his front teeth. "Who's this?"

"Jerome Silks. He was my first real boyfriend."

I stared at the picture. I had no idea what to say.

304

Ruah went on. "Jerry died from AIDS. The way he went wasn't much different than from flesh-eating disease."

Staring at the picture, I tried to come up with the right thing to say. If there was a right thing to say. I slipped the photo back in the wallet and mumbled, "I'm sorry."

Ruah chuckled. "Sorry about Jerry, or sorry you asked?"

"Him, of course."

He took his wallet and dropped it on the console. "Thanks." After a moment, he chuckled again. "I'll always remember Jerry for inventing a new Major League Baseball stat."

"What?"

"He always told me I led the league in dishonesty."

"I don't get it."

"The two of us had been together for over a year when he gave me an ultimatum. I could start being honest, come out of the closet, and we would stay together. Or I could keep lying, stay in the closet, and we'd break up. I chose the closet and the relationship ended. But we stayed friends."

Ruah stared ahead. In the late-afternoon light, his dark skin looked bronze. His face was statue-hard. It turned to molten lava as he spoke again. "A couple of seasons after we broke up Jerry got sick, real sick. I was traveling a lot, but whenever I got home I visited him in his apartment or at the hospital. Then he moved back to his apartment to die. Jerry's parents came to see him but never when I was around. I never even met them. In the last few weeks, his folks moved in. They wouldn't let me see him anymore. After he died, they even scheduled the funeral for a date I was on the road."

"Did you go back for it?"

He shook his head. "When you're in the closet, playing by 'Don't ask, don't tell,' you don't walk into your manager's office and tell him the family matter you gotta go home for is your ex-boyfriend's funeral. When they buried Jerry, I was in center field at Dodger Stadium, running down fly balls and bawling my eyes out."

I said I was sorry again, but I'm not sure he heard me.

"Sometimes," he said, "I think if I had come out, my baseball career would've been over, but Jerry Silks would still be alive."

We drove in silence after that. I started thinking about the times I'd called him an abomination. I couldn't deny it, part of me still believed it. But another part got to thinking about other abominations. Like what people do to each other. Like Jerry's parents not letting Ruah see him when he was dying. Like having the funeral on a day when they knew Ruah couldn't come.

As I sat there, something started making me feel worse. At first, I couldn't put my finger on it. Then it hit me like an antelope leaping out of nowhere. The abomination done to Ruah had been done to me. The door to his friend had been slammed in his face. The door to my father had been shut my whole life. Ruah couldn't go to his friend's funeral because he wasn't wanted. I couldn't go to my father's funeral because I never knew he was alive. Maybe those kind of things aren't abominations to the Lord; maybe you don't find them in the Bible. But they're horrible just the same. They're the abominable sin of letting a man freeze in the Desert of Cold Hearts.

We crossed into Oregon. We were on such a back highway, the welcome sign was in rough shape. It was rusty, hung at an angle, and punched with bullet holes. It still managed to say WELCOME TO OREGON—THINGS LOOK DIFFERENT HERE.

Neither of us said anything. I guess we didn't feel like making fun of it, or trying to make it better. As I look back, I know why. Sometimes the truth is too true to be made fun of.

I pulled out the last chapter of *Huck Finn* that I'd gotten in Notus and had already read on the playa at Burning Man. I read it to Ruah.

At the end, Huck says something about a person's conscience that summed up how I was feeling. Maybe it summed up Ruah's feelings, too. Huck says a conscience "takes up more than all the rest of a person's insides."

III

The Bad Book

1

S'mores

As the sun dropped lower, we stopped in a town before heading to Farewell Bend State Park. I was still wearing the ghost-miner costume, so Ruah went into a store and bought me a pair of jeans, a couple shirts, and sneakers. He joked that if people saw me in ratty overalls and holey boots, the police might arrest him for child neglect or maybe white slavery.

At Farewell Bend we found a campsite at the end of the lake. After being with the wacko Potlatchers, it felt like an old routine, getting back to how Ruah did things. As he started dinner I got a campfire going and cut marshmallow sticks.

I watched dusk slowly push the last sunlight up the bare hills that surrounded the lake. The hills were so brown and pillowy they could have been named the Breadloaf Mountains. The fishermen on the lake were bringing their boats to the boat ramp. I liked seeing how each boat trailer splashed into the water, disappeared, caught a boat, and rose out of the lake in a gush of water. Even if the fishermen hadn't caught a fish, at the end of the day they always landed "the big one," their boat.

After dinner, we got out marshmallows, graham crackers, and chocolate bars. When Ruah was s'mored out, he leaned back and checked out the stars. I made another one and gorped it down.

Staring skyward, he said, "Remember how Huck and Jim wondered if God made the stars or if they just happened?"

"Yeah."

"I got another one for you. Did T.L. carve the Grand Canyon, or did it just happen?"

I was sure God created the world, but if He'd done *everything,* right down to the Grand Canyon, I wasn't sure He would've had time for His day of rest. And I was a big believer in days of rest. "I haven't decided on that one," I told Ruah.

"Okay, you'll take a pass." He kept looking up. "Got one more. Jerry Silks—the guy whose picture I showed you—do you think he died of AIDS 'cause God was punishing him, or did it just happen?"

I tossed my s'mores stick in the fire. "Why are you asking me about what God did or didn't do?"

He shrugged like all he was doing was asking my favorite color. "Just curious. But I'll put a different spin on it. Do you think Jerry's in Heaven?"

I squinted into the fire. "I dunno."

He gazed back at the stars. "I know he's up there."

"What makes you so sure?"

"The Bible tells me so."

I almost laughed, and I would have if he'd been talking

312

about anything but his dead friend. "There's nothing in the Bible about gays going to Heaven."

"Not in those words," he said. "But when I was killing time back in the Sunnydale Motel, I opened my Bible and reread the book of Jonah. That's where I found out Jerry's in Heaven."

"There's nothing in Jonah about gays in Heaven."

"Yes there is, and no there isn't." The firelight lit up his big smile. "And I'm gonna tell you about it. You can hear it tonight, or tomorrow on the road; your call. It's part of the all-the-way-to-Portland travel package."

In the past few days I'd had my share of blackmail. At least this was more like graymail. I let out a sigh. "If I gotta listen to your crazy ideas I might as well listen to 'em on a stomach full of s'mores."

He laughed. "As long as they don't make you hurl."

"Right."

"Okay, quick review. God tells Jonah to go preach to the Ninevites—Jonah runs away—gets swallowed by mondo fish—repents inside fish—prays for God's full-on forgiveness—gets it—and goes and preaches to the Ninevites. But when the Ninevites do the *same* as Jonah—see their sinful ways, repent, and get forgiven when God pulls his wrathful punch on their city—guess who gets all pissed off?"

"Jonah," I said, trying not to sound irritated by the fact that I hardly needed the SparkNotes on Jonah.

"Right. Which makes him a hypocrite."

"I never heard anyone call Jonah a hypocrite."

"But he is. He accepts God's compassion and forgiveness

313

for *himself,* then he gets steamed when T.L. gives it to others."

"Okay, but that's got nothing to do with gays in Heaven."

"But it does. The lesson of Jonah is that life's journey, whether it takes you into a fish belly and back, to hell and back, or wherever and back, changes your view of the world, or it doesn't. Jonah's journey hardly changed him at all. At the end he's pissed 'cause T.L. didn't fire-'n'-brimstone Nineveh like He said He would. But *God* went on Jonah's trip too, 'cause God is everywhere. And Jonah's journey *did* change God."

"How?"

"When T.L. answered Jonah's prayer of repentance in the fish, it reminded God of His own capacity for compassionate forgiveness. Not just for one guy, but for a whole city. It reminded God that He doesn't always ride the hard, straight line. Sometimes He zigs, sometimes He zags. The real meaning of Jonah is obvious: if T.L. can change His mind, and let compassion overrule wrath, so can we."

I didn't know what that had to do with gays, but I didn't say a word. I just let him cruise on.

"As I was doing my Sunnydale Bible study, I realized the Jonah story was just an earlier version of the Christ story. T.L. gave His peeps the Jonah story, but a lot of 'em didn't get it. So God did a rewrite. He gave us the Christ story and people finally got it: Christ chooses compassion over wrath. God can't say it any clearer than when His Boy says, *For all the law is fulfilled in one word, even in this; you shall love your neighbor as yourself.*

"But two thousand years later there are some Christians who still don't get it. They want a hard-line, no-contradictions God. They run around screaming, 'Give 'em wrath, Lord. New York deserves nine-eleven. New Orleans deserves Katrina. Gays deserve AIDS.' They've turned *Love thy neighbor* into *Loathe thy neighbor*. You know what these latter-day Jonahs remind me of?"

I'd been quiet so long I didn't want him thinking I'd fallen into a sugar coma and he'd have to preach his sermon again in the morning. "No, what do they remind you of?"

"Hitters that can't get wood on a curveball."

It made me laugh; talk about out of left field. "What the heck do latter-day Jonahs have to do with baseball batters?"

"'Cause that's what God threw Jonah at the end of the story: the big, curving slider of merciful forgiveness. Jonah totally whiffed and went stomping back to the dugout."

I wondered if Ruah was drunk. He could've bought a bottle of something back in Homedale and drunk it while he'd made dinner. "Where do you get all this stuff?"

He flashed a smile. "From being stuck in a motel with the Book, and the fact that I know a little something about God's curveball of merciful forgiveness."

He lost me again. "What's that?"

He pointed to Heaven. "T.L. threw me one."

I didn't ask. I just watched him gather something inside himself.

"After I was with Jerry I never became HIV positive. We were careful, sure, and took precautions, but I think

315

there was something else. It's right there in Jonah, hidden in plain sight. God chooses compassion over wrath."

"Maybe He does," I said. I didn't want to say what I was thinking, but he was being honest; I had to do the same. "God didn't exactly choose compassion over wrath with Jerry."

"You could say that. But what if Jerry dying was just the AIDS virus doing what a virus does? What if God had nuthin to do with it?"

"How can God have 'nuthin to do with it?'"

"Because God tells us what He really thinks of gays in Jonah. In fact, if T.L. ever wrote the book of Gay it wouldn't be much different than the book of Jonah. It would start with Old Testy all wrathed up. He decrees homosexuality to be an abomination punishable by death. After all, back in the day, homosexuals weren't obeying His order to be fruitful and multiply. But just like in Jonah, along the way, God changes His mind. 'Cause in today's world with a surplus of baby makers and a shortage of loving couples to raise unwanted babies, maybe, just maybe, T.L. has rethought His homosexuals-as-abominations thing. And maybe T.L. is throwing peeps the same curveball of compassion He threw Jonah when it came to the Ninevites."

He stared into the fire. "But maybe that's still too much of a curveball for most people. Maybe they strike out and go stomping back to the dugout like Jonah, condemning homos, gay marriage, and Tickle Me Elmos." He smiled to himself. "Or maybe people see God's pitch coming, pick up the rotating seams on His big slider, and knock it out of the park."

316

I watched his eyes flicker with firelight. He wasn't drunk. He was just filled with his own brand of Spirit.

After that, Ruah said he was tired and went to bed.

I hung out by the fire a little longer. Listening to the curveballs flying out of Ruah's mouth, and wondering if there was any truth to his zigzag God, had burned up the last s'more in my stomach. I needed one more.

2

Wrath

The next morning we left the interstate and took a shortcut through a mountain range called the Blues. It wasn't much of a shortcut. The two-lane highway narrowed and got clogged with big RVs crawling up the steeps and spewing fumes.

On the west side of the Blues, the road didn't get wider, but some of the vehicles we got stuck behind smelled better: open-bed trucks piled with onions. Dry onion skins trailed behind the trucks; I tried to catch them as they flew by. I never snagged one, but my nose caught the cloud trailing behind: the sweet smell of onions.

I also thought about the things Ruah had said the night before. Especially about how Jonah had shown him that life's journey changes the way you see things, or it doesn't. I figured the same lesson held for any journey. I wondered if my trip, almost over, had changed the way I looked at the world.

The truth was, I felt like I'd seen more in the past week than I'd seen my whole life. And that I'd gotten more religion in a week than if I'd gone to Bible camp all summer. Of course, it would've been a tough sell telling Mom that Regular Bible Camp was nothing compared to Runaway Bible Camp.

For all my thinking, I didn't come up with a solid answer about whether my trip had changed the way I saw things. I felt more like someone who lives in a house with a couple of pictures on the wall, then I go up to the attic and discover it's filled with wild and different pictures. There's a picture of a dust storm, and one of sugary bowls of summer snow. There's pictures of more naked people than I thought I'd ever see in a lifetime. There's pictures of a Sun Dance, Spring's green breasts, a canyon with a rusty roller coaster. And there's a picture of a white camper, Giff, swimming through rain, dust, and sunlight. It felt like all those pictures were in the attic, and I couldn't decide which ones to take downstairs and hang on the wall.

I did figure out one thing. When you think you live in a house with just a couple of pictures and then discover an attic stuffed with pictures, it changes how you see the world right there. So I guess my journey *had* changed me a little.

But it wasn't over. Not by a long shot.

When we stopped at a gas station to fill up, Ruah pointed to a phone booth by the highway. He wanted me to go check in with my mom. He pulled out a phone card and told me to use it.

I didn't take it. "I just called her on Sunday . . . in Notus." Of course, I didn't say all I'd done was leave a message, or that I'd made the call on his cell phone.

"That was two days ago," he said, still holding out the phone card. "In case she got caller ID to find out the area code you're calling from, before you dial, press star-six-seven. It'll block the pay phone's number." He pressed the card in my hand. "Now go call her or I'll call her myself."

The last thing Mom needed was a call from a homosexual baseball player saying he'd been driving me around for days. I headed to the phone booth. I thought about faking the call, but Ruah kept looking my way as he pumped gas with his good hand. And the truth was I hadn't spoken to Mom directly since Kansas. Since then she'd probably prayed kneeholes into the living room rug.

I dialed star-six-seven and her number. She answered like it could've been anyone. "Hello."

"Hey, Mom."

"Billy?" Her voice sounded faint and faraway. I couldn't tell if it was the connection or it was her sounding zonked and stressed.

"Can you hear me okay?" I asked.

She stifled a sob. "Yes. Are you alright?"

"Yeah, I'm good."

"Where are you?"

When she asked that, I relaxed. The star-six-seven thing must've worked. "Almost there," I said. "Almost to New Orleans."

"It's been a week. What's taking so long?"

"I got a little off trail."

319

"What do you mean, off trail?"

I waited for a truck to rumble by. "I'll tell you about it later."

"That's how the devil works," she said. The strength was back in her voice, like the commander of the New J-Brigade had reported for duty. "He lays snares in the Way of Christ."

"I know, Mom, but you'll be happy about this. Right now I'm riding with a Christian, and we've been doing some good fellowship." I was hoping she'd be relieved, but it was like she didn't hear.

"The wicked walk on every side," she said, *"waiting to devour you like fresh bread."*

"Mom, it's not like I'm running through a forest full of witches trying to throw me in a cage, fatten me up, and eat me."

"You think it's funny?" she snapped. The iron was back in her, hard as ever. "My heart is breaking, and you think I'm making up fairy tales. Lemme tell you what I read in the paper. A boy disappeared at a mall for several hours. When they found him, he'd been castrated. It turns out there's a gang you can't join until you kidnap a boy and castrate him."

I eye-rolled. "Why do you tell me stuff like that?"

"Because it's true, and because I want you to come home."

"That's what I'm gonna do, after I find out what I can about my father, Richard Allbright."

There was a pause. When she spoke it sounded like hearing his name had done something, melted the iron in her. "That's what I fear most. That whatever's left of him will do to you what he did to me."

"What did he do that was so terrible?"

"He made me stray. Those who err from the faith are pierced by sorrow. Since you were born, Billy, I've only wanted to make sure you'd never stray. I wanted to protect you from being pierced by sorrow. I pray every hour for God to save you from that. I pray for Him to protect you from Richard Allbright." She fought back tears. "Come home now. Please, come home."

A car hauling a trailer rattled past. I waited till she could hear me clearly. "I'm almost there, Mom. I've got to finish what I started. Then I'll come home. Promise."

There was a long pause. She hadn't hung up. I felt her presence on the other end.

"It may be too late," she said. The iron was back in her, but colder, like a diamond.

"Too late for what?"

"I did a providence check. The Lord revealed a verse from Psalms. *I will set no wicked thing before mine eyes: I hate the work of them that turn aside; it shall not cleave to me.*"

I swallowed. "What does that mean?"

"Come home now, and you won't have to worry about the meaning."

It felt like I was standing outside a cave. I couldn't see the animal waiting for me in the darkness, but I knew it was there, ready to pounce. "What if I don't?"

"I'm telling you one last time, Billy. Come home now."

"You didn't answer my question. What if I don't?"

She let me hang for a moment, then her words crackled in the phone. "If we perish, we perish."

The line went dead.

I stood there, not wanting to believe it. Not wanting to believe that she was making me choose between her and my father.

I lost it. I smashed the phone in the cradle again and again, trying to keep the tightening coil in my chest from escaping. The coil won. The first sob jumped out. I cried like a windup toy with bad gears. The only thing I could control was keeping my back to Ruah. Like I could hide anything. Through my glaze of tears I saw cars shoot by. I didn't care what they thought. They were total strangers. Like my mother.

When my pathetic tear-ectomy was done, I wiped my face and turned around. Ruah was back in the camper. Maybe I caught him looking my way in the side mirror, maybe I didn't. The camper twitched as it started. He was ready to go. I thought about walking over, saying goodbye to him, and going home.

I felt something brush against my leg. The receiver was still dangling by the cord. I picked it up, put it back in the cradle. Then I echoed her words: "If we perish, we perish."

3

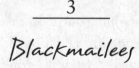

I got in the camper. Ruah had his sunglasses on and didn't say anything. A man with a Seeing Eye dog would've known I'd been crying.

After a few miles he said, "You wanna talk about it?"

I shook my head. "Mm-mmh."

"That's fine."

My insides wanted to go back to anger. But I pushed the rage down in my gut, not letting it into my head. I had to think things through. Mom was telling me to come home as the Billy Allbright she wanted, or not come home at all. But I'd made my decision. I was going to Portland. Even if it meant that when I got home she wouldn't look at me.

A bizarre thought hit me. I'd been spending a lot of time with blackmailers and people who were being blackmailed. The Potlatchers had blackmailed me, Ruah's agent was blackmailing him, and now Mom was basically black-mailing me. It was amazing how different the Potlatchers were from Mom and how much they were alike. Nico and Momi blackmailed me into the movie they wanted to make; Mom was blackmailing me into the movie she wanted to make: *Billy Allbright, Little Boy Christian*. And when it came to Ruah—even though he was gay and a big-time baseball player—we had something in common. We were blackmailees.

The way I saw it, if the two of us were going to beat all the blackmailers, we had to stick together. We were on the same team. And teammates shared secrets. The day before, he'd showed me a picture of his dead friend. Now it was my turn.

I reached under my T-shirt and pulled up the key hanging on my shoelace. "Guess what this is?"

He raised his shades. "Looks like a key."

"Yeah, a key to buried treasure."

I told him about the DVD of my dying father and how it had burned up along with the leather Bible and my GPS in Dogleg Canyon. I told him how my treasure hunt was for a "bad book" in which Mark Twain had outlined a sequel to *Huck Finn*. I told him the book was at Boot Heel Collectibles in Portland. Then I pulled out my last page of *Huck* and read him the clue poem.

When I was done, he said, "Is there a reason you're telling me all this?"

I didn't want to say how I thought we were teammates and needed to share secrets. That was too corny. I just said, "Because it's my future now." I held up the key. "It's the only place I have to go."

"Okay, say you find this 'bad book,'" he said, "then what?"

I couldn't believe he wasn't all excited about the book, and didn't want to know more about the treasure I was going to collect. "What do you mean, 'then what?'"

"What are you gonna do?"

"Not go home." I told him about the phone call and how Mom threatened to shun me if I didn't come home right away.

"Your father's gone," he said. "Your mother isn't. Do you think you're ready to go solo?"

"If I sell the bad book for half what my father said it's worth, I'll be fine. I can get a place in Portland and go to school there."

He shrugged. "Yeah, I suppose you could."

It bugged me that he was doing it again: acting so

casual, acting like starting a new life was as simple as choosing what socks to wear. "You think it's a dumb idea, don't you?"

"I didn't say that. I'm just wondering about your mom. How she'd feel about losing you."

"She pretty much told me how she feels."

"Do you think she meant it?"

"You don't know her. When she puts someone out of her life, she makes 'em dead. That's what she did to my father."

"What if she was willing to bend a little this time? What if she wanted to come live with you in Portland?"

A gonzo thought like that had never crossed my mind. "It might be okay. As long as she got it."

"Got what?"

"That my life was mine now, not hers."

"I'm glad to hear you're flexible."

"On one thing I'm not. Finding out everything I can about my father."

He chuckled. "Like mother, like son." He pulled a hard face. "You know what you want, and you're sticking to it."

I didn't like how he was twisting it on me, like I was the one being rigid. But I didn't say anything. He had no idea how unfair she could be. I figured I'd give him a taste of his own medicine. "What about you?" I asked.

"What about me?"

"Are you gonna let Joe Douglas blackmail you? Are you gonna let him keep being your agent?"

He smiled. "I'm hoping to win a doubleheader."

"What do you mean?"

"If I dump him as my agent, I win the first game. If I keep playing baseball under the 'Don't ask, don't tell' rule, I win the second."

"How can you win both?"

"I can't." He lowered his sunglasses over his eyes. "Unless T.L. performs a miracle."

"Yeah, but what if there's no miracle? What if you get rid of him and he tells the world you're gay?"

He scoffed. "You mean, what if I wake up to a sports-page headline that says 'Branch Out at Homo-Plate?'"

"Would they do that?"

"The media's the only sport with no foul lines or out-of-bounds."

"Would it end your career?"

"It sure would if one theory about baseball is true."

I wasn't sure I wanted to hear any more of his theories, but at least this one wasn't about the Bible. "What theory?"

"The Congratulations Theory."

"The what?"

"The Congratulations Theory says that baseball is getting more homophobic, not less. We see it in the way players celebrate success on the field. It used to be done with a handshake. Then the handshake evolved to the high five, eliminating the whole touchy-feely grasping part. But when everyone in the game found out that the player who first high-fived in baseball, Glenn Burke, was gay and died of AIDS, the high five was tainted. So we moved on to the even more macho more protective knuckle bump." He made a fist and faked a knuckle bump. "If the Congratulations

Theory is correct, and baseball's getting more homo-phobic, then it won't surprise me if the whole pile-on-the-pitcher mosh pit that happens at the end of play-off victories turns into a bunch of tight-assed homophobes standing around giving each other sissy knuckle taps. If that's the direction baseball's headed, then there's no room in baseball for an out-of-the-closet fag like me."

"Is that what you're going to Seattle to find out?" I asked.

"Yeah," he said, and left it at that.

We were making such slow progress on our "shortcut," Ruah decided to get off the two-laner and head up to I-84 so we could still make Portland by the end of the day. It would also be more scenic to drive through the Columbia River Valley.

It was a big mistake, or the beginning of a miracle, de-pending how you look at it.

We reached the interstate by midafternoon and only got a few miles before we ran into a huge traffic jam. On the radio we found out a tanker truck had crashed, burned, and damaged the highway. The westbound interstate was going to be closed for hours, if not longer. We eventually got to an exit, backtracked, and crossed the Colombia River into Washington State.

The sign on the other side said, WELCOME TO WASHINGTON—SAYWA! When Ruah saw the bumper-to-bumper traffic with the same idea of going west on the north side of the river, he said, "You can sayWA again. SayWA was I thinkin'?"

Short of going a hundred miles out of our way, there was

no other route to Portland. As the sun began to sink over the river valley, we decided to look for a campground and finish the trip in the morning. Every campground we got to was full. We named Washington the SayWA-Were-We-Thinkin'? state.

4

Stonehenge

The sun set as we looked for one last campground. We made a wrong turn and drove up a steep. At the top was the weirdest thing: Stonehenge. It was like the ancient one in England but not all toppled over and missing pieces. It was a full-scale replica of Stonehenge when it was new. The only difference was that this one was made of cement, not stone. It could've been called Cementhenge.

We walked through a gap in the outer circle of blocks. Inside was another circle of upright stones. Inside that were square arches horseshoeing around a flat stone that looked like a banquet table. I imagined that whenever King Arthur and his knights needed a break from eating at the Round Table, they rode over to the real Stonehenge and ate at the Square Table.

Ruah raised his arms and shouted, "Now, *this* is a campsite!"

Seeing how there was no one to tell us different, that's what we made it. We gathered wood before it got too dark and got a fire going in front of the stone table. Back in the camper, we threw together some dinner and took our chairs to the fire. As we ate, it got very dark because there was no moon. We threw more wood on the fire.

When we finished, we got distracted by a glow. It started at the bottom of one of the rectangular openings in the outer stone circle. It brightened into a sliver of moonlight. We watched the moon climb through the opening. It cast shadows inside the circle, great bars of light and dark.

I heard the crunch of gravel and saw Ruah walk toward the camper. He came back carrying his pillow, sheet, and blanket. He tossed them on the stone table. "No way I'm sleeping in the RV. Tonight I'm working on my moon tan." He sat back down in his chair.

"It's too bright for me," I said. "I'll stick with Giff."

"Probably a good idea." He lifted his arms. "I've got all this melanin protecting me. You've got nuthin. You'd wake up with a moon burn."

I laughed, said goodnight, and headed for the camper.

Inside, the moonlight was almost as bright. I shut the curtains against it. It didn't keep out the two columns of moonlight dropping from the skylights into the aisle. They made my own little moonhenge.

I lay there thinking about the day. It had gone from black to white: from blubbering in a phone booth to watching the moonrise over Stonehenge. That moonrise was the first picture in my attic I definitely wanted to take downstairs and hang on the wall. It made me think God had looked down, seen my rotten day, and decided to cheer me up.

I wondered if I was insulting His gift by sleeping in the camper. I thought about taking my sleeping bag and z-bagging on the stone table too. No sooner did I think it, then I saw a horrible picture. It was so gross I instantly pushed it out of my mind. I didn't want to think it, or see it again.

I filled my mind with other thoughts and pictures. I focused on Mom, and replayed our phone call. I thought about how she had gone latter-day Jonah on me. I mean, after a lifetime of telling me Christ had died for my sins, suddenly my sins were unforgivable. She was condemning me, telling me she wouldn't look at me or cleave to me. She'd gone total Jonah: bring on the wrath.

I watched the moon columns inch their way along the aisle. They got me thinking again about how the trip had changed the way I saw the world. I mean, even if Mom did forgive me and take me back, I didn't see myself in the New J-Brigade anymore. As much as I still thought Ruah was wrong for being gay, I didn't see myself protesting at gay weddings and shouting how queers were going to hell. Mom had her big sin—getting pregnant with me—and she lived her life saying Christ had forgiven her. Why couldn't Ruah have his big sin and live his life with Christ forgiving him? Hadn't he been punished enough by losing his friend Jerry?

Thinking about Ruah only stirred me up. It made my mind drift toward the horrible picture lurking in the shadows. I didn't want to look at it, think about it. The moon columns didn't help. They reminded me of the moon-shadow show going on in the big circle of stones. I got up and tried to block out the light. I hung clothes on the cranks that opened the skylights. It only turned the clothes into eerie ghosts. I pulled them down. I turned away and faced the back of the couch.

I shoved my thoughts back to Mom. I tried to remember the scripture she liked for praying against thoughts you didn't want, pictures you shouldn't see. I had total brain lock. I couldn't think of a verse. I wished one of the moonlight columns would ripple to life, and Mom would appear to help.

It got me wondering if I'd ever pray with her again. I mean, maybe she meant what she'd said, that she would shun me. The more that mental maggot gnawed on me the more I wanted to jump up and start walking home. It's not like she would ever know the difference of *when* I started home. I could say I had started home my first step out of that phone booth.

But it was the old me thinking. The Billy who thought he could lie and everything would be the same as before. Too much had happened. Too many ugly words had flown between us. I couldn't go home and pretend nothing had changed, that I had never run away, that I didn't have a huge new attic of pictures. I couldn't leave them up there. There were ones I wanted to bring down and make part of my life. There was no way I could go back to the old Billy. The old Billy was dead. Mom got one thing right, for sure. "If we perish, we perish," I whispered.

Hearing the words started a movie in my head.

- I'm walking down our street in Independence.
- I have a new backpack on my shoulder. The book my father left me is in it.
- I walk up to the one-pillar doghouse. There's a sign in the front window: FOR RENT.
- The place is empty. Mom has bailed, disappeared, like she did to my father.
- My insides go double-chung tight.

I shook the movie away. I told myself she'd never do that. She was my mom, she wouldn't abandon me. But I'd seen something I couldn't ignore. Another voice told me I should have seen it coming. I mean, look at her life. She zigzags all over the place being a Jesus-throated Whac-a-Mole. She condemns everyone who isn't up to her Way of the Lord. If she can't set them on her path, she takes a path away from them. She ditches them. And look at me, beginning to fight her, wanting to go to high school, running away to find a dead father I never knew.

But I'm her son, I told myself, her flesh and blood. She can't blot me out like a word on a box of devil's food cake. She can't hammer me away like a slogan on a license plate.

That's when the sickest thought slithered into my head. Maybe she truly wanted me to *perish*. Maybe she wanted to kill the baby Satan had tricked her into having. Maybe she was aborting me sixteen years later.

When thoughts overwhelm a mind, and pierce the heart with a merciless blade, a body has to stop it. A trapdoor opened inside me, dumping my gnarly thoughts into my guts, where no thoughts live, only feelings. Those feelings leapt out like a pack of wolves from a cave. They sank their teeth in me and shook.

It was the second time I cried that day. But this time, the heartache cried me to sleep.

5

Night Voices

That night, I had a dream.

- I'm driving a car in open countryside. It feels right to drive even though I don't have my license yet.
- I pull off on the shoulder. There's a crossroads up ahead. I want to walk to it. I get out of the car and walk.
- I reach the crossroads, but there's no one there. Only the wind. I start walking back to my car.
- Ruah comes along in a car. He offers me a ride. I know him, and I get in. We pass my car, but I stay silent. I just leave it there.
- The bizarre thing is that Ruah keeps changing: sometimes he's Ruah, sometimes he's my father. For some reason it doesn't bother me.
- The next thing I know we're in a motel, sharing a room. There's only one bed. Something tells me it's okay. Ruah, who's sometimes my father, talks about everyday stuff as we get ready for bed. We both get into our pajamas.

- I get into bed. Ruah—he stays Ruah now—keeps talking about stuff as he changes back into his street clothes, then back into his pajamas. He can't decide what to wear.
- He finally gets into bed in his street clothes. He snuggles up to me. I put my arm around him like it's no big deal. Then he says, "This feels nice."

I snapped awake. My heart pounded like it was a terrifying nightmare. I tried to shake away the dream. When I couldn't, I realized the dream was God telling me something. At first He'd sent me a hideous picture I wouldn't look at. Now He'd made me see it in a dream. God was leading me into temptation.

But why would He want me to become an abomination?

I thought back on everything that had happened in the past week. My dream wasn't the first sign about it. God had sent me to Case and the R-boys, and they'd called me a queer. There were all the naked women at Burning Man I didn't want to look at. I mean, what straight guy doesn't want to look at naked women till his eyeballs fall out? There was Spring. She showed me her perfect breasts and I didn't want to touch them.

But the biggest sign was right in front of me. God had given me so many chances to get away from Ruah. I never did. At Coors Field, after I knew he was gay, why did I get back in his RV? In the campground near Providence, after God sent me the messenger in zebra stripes telling me it was time to get out of Giff, why did I crawl back in? Why did I leap back in at Dogleg Canyon? The answer was the same every time. I wanted to. Why? Because the horrible picture had been traveling with me all that time, and I had refused to turn and see it.

Until now.

The last three words of the dream were loud and clear. But it wasn't Ruah speaking, it was God. "This feels nice," He said to me. By giving me the dream, He was refusing to let me drown the picture in tears, or escape it in sleep. The dream was the Lord putting it in front of me, bigger and bolder than ever. He wanted me to face it full-on. I prayed for God to tell me: *Are You telling me to do something, or just testing me?*

Of course, He didn't answer.

I lay there, shaking inside and out. I didn't know what God wanted. Except that He wanted me to choose. Get up and run away from Ruah for good. Or walk into the picture I had seen.

Then I heard a voice, as clear as if Mom *had* rippled into a moonlight column and spoken. She told me what to do. It was perfect. It gave God one last chance to show me the way.

I got out of bed, crawled over the console, and pulled Ruah's Bible out of the glove compartment. I held it between my hands, closed my eyes, and prayed until I felt His presence. His Spirit flowed through me, into my hands. I let the book fall open. My finger lifted and fell. I opened my eyes. The moonlight was bright enough to read the book— Job—but not the verse my finger touched. My free hand reached up and punched the overhead light on. I read the verse God was showing me.

335

For man is born for trouble, as sparks fly upward.

A shiver ran through me cold as a knife. *Man is born for trouble;* man is born to sin. No one was more born to sin than me. I was conceived in sin, woven in the womb of sin, and brought forth in sin. I was born a bastard in the eyes of the Father, and He wanted me to take the next step. God had put me in Ruah's camper, and returned me to it time and again for one reason. We were both sinners. We deserved each other.

I stepped out of the camper. The cool air pulled my naked skin to gooseflesh. As I walked, a furnace lit inside me. My skin ironed smooth.

I moved through an arch in the stone circle. The dirt under my feet felt soft and warm. Moving toward the square table, I caught my shadow walking with me. It made me feel less alone.

I thought I'd be more scared, the closer I got to the stone table. I felt the opposite: kind of giddy and calm at the same time. My mind, heart, and body had decided.

I'm an abomination.

I stood next to him. He lay on his back, on top of his blanket. The sheet lay over him. It glowed white in the moonlight. I stood, not moving except my breathing. I watched the sheet rise and fall at his chest. I could hear his breathing. It reminded me of the silence in the desert.

His eyes fluttered. They opened full. He stared for an unfocused moment. Like he wasn't sure if I was real or a dream.

I wanted him to know it wasn't a dream. I opened my mouth and words tumbled out. "This feels nice."

He closed his eyes, then suddenly swung up to a sitting position. It was so smooth and fast, it made me jump. He turned his head, pushing his sheet toward me. "Cover yourself."

The furnace inside me exploded. My skin felt scorched. I snatched the sheet, clutched it over me and ran. I shot through a gap in the stone circle and stumbled down the hill.

"Billy!" I heard him yell. He was coming after me.

I picked my way down the rocky hill until I found a rock big enough to hide behind. I scrunched behind it and buried my face in the sheet. I hated God with every sliver of my being. I hated Him for his cruelty. I hated Him for making the world. But I hated Him most for making me.

"Billy," Ruah called from the top of the hill.

I didn't answer.

"I won't come down. I'll let you be," he said. "Just let me know you're there, and okay."

I knew he wouldn't budge till he knew. "Go away!"

"That'll do."

6
___

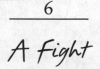

At dawn the river valley below was buried in fog. Anyone else might've thought they'd woken in Heaven and were looking down at the cloud-covered earth. Not me. It was

God's way of torturing me more. He'd put me in hell and made it look like Heaven. The Hilarious Father strikes again.

I thought about what to do. Ruah would probably still be sleeping. Maybe I could sneak back in the camper, grab my clothes, and start hitching. There's no way I could ride with him to Portland. Not unless I could hide in the bathroom and finish my trip the way I'd started it: safe in my pod, like he didn't know I was there, like he'd never opened the door, like last night had never happened, like the whole thing had been a big fat nightmare.

I wrapped the sheet around me and climbed the hill. Reaching the top, I found my clothes folded on a rock next to my sneaks. I saw a movement through the gaps in Stonehenge. Great, I thought, he's awake.

I grabbed my clothes, hooked the sheet over my head, and got dressed under it. As I yanked on my shoes, I figured I'd go back down the hill, find the road, and sneak away. Then he called from inside the stones. "I got breakfast if you want it."

He had a small fire going and had set cereal and milk on the stone table. I couldn't look at him. It was totally bizarre. He was acting like nothing had happened. Or, if I was really lucky, maybe he thought the whole thing *had* been a dream. That would've been fine with me.

I ate a second bowl of cereal. I wasn't hungry, I just had to do something with my hands.

When I finished he said, "There's something we haven't done the whole trip. We've never prayed together. Would you like to?"

I shrugged. "Whatever."

338

He stood up and stretched out his hand.

I stood. I didn't take his hand. He didn't drop it. I told myself it was just a prayer, and took his hand.

He lowered his head. "T.L., thanks for showing us another day. Thanks for showing us the night. Even last night."

I tried to pull away; he clutched my fingers.

His voice stayed steady and calm. "Thank You for sending a child of God, who reminded me of Your most important teaching: 'Above all things, put on love.' Thanks for sending me a messenger. But next time You send Billy Allbright to spread the gospel, You might want to remind him that putting on love doesn't start with taking off clothes. Love isn't always naked."

My cheeks felt on fire. I couldn't believe he was talking about it in a prayer. Like God needed to be reminded.

"If I'm not mistaken," he continued, "putting on love starts with simply being present. So I thank You for the blessing of his presence on my journey. We pray You'll help Billy find his father's book. We pray You'll help me"—he hesitated—"find the right path in Seattle. We ask You to guide us and protect us in these last miles to Portland, and on our separate roads ahead. In Christ's name we pray, Amen."

"Amen," I muttered as he let go of my hand. I glanced over.

He was smiling. "Thanks, I needed that. Now I wanna show you something."

I shrugged.

"It's waiting for us on the road. As long as you still want Giff to deliver you to Portland."

He was waiting for an answer. I didn't know what to say. "Do we have to talk?"

He shook his head. "Nope. But we need to get going. I checked out the tourist shack in the parking lot and someone's gonna be opening it up any minute. You take the breakfast stuff back to the RV. I'll douse the fire and bring the rest."

I grabbed the bowls and milk and headed for the camper. In the parking lot I noticed a bike by the tourist shack. It hadn't been there the day before.

Suddenly, a guy came around the back of the camper. He was about my age. He didn't look friendly. "Did you camp here last night?" he demanded.

"No," I answered. "We drove up this morning to have breakfast and take a look around."

"You're lying. I saw you by the fire, holding hands. This isn't a campground for faggots."

The word made my insides tighten up. "We were praying."

"Bullshit, faggot."

I lost it. I slammed my hand in his face. He came back at me. After that, all I remember were fists and milk flying. We rolled on the ground punching fast and hard. The next thing I felt was something hitting my back, lifting me in the air.

It was Ruah. "Enough!" he shouted.

The guy jumped up and started after me again. Ruah raised one of his huge hands. "No!"

The guy heel-planted. He knew he'd have to get

340

past Ruah to get at me again. He pointed. "He's fuckin' mental!"

Ruah lowered his hand without taking his eyes off the kid. "I've never seen him throw a punch. It had to come from somewhere."

The kid jerked his jaw at the folding chairs on the ground behind us. "You're not supposed to camp here!"

I noticed the sheet, now folded, on one of the chairs. Ruah must've found it where I left it on the rock.

"It's the only place we could find," Ruah said as he pulled out his wallet. He took out two twenties and handed them to the kid. "Maybe this'll make it right."

The kid wiped his bloody nose on his sleeve and grabbed the money.

"Have a blessed day," Ruah said before pushing me toward the camper.

Less than a minute later we were winding down the road below Stonehenge. "I know you don't wanna talk," he said, "but that was before you started whaling on the locals. What the hell was that about?"

"He saw us by the fire," I told him. "He didn't believe we were praying."

"He thought we were something else."

"Yeah."

"So you decided to hit him?"

"Yeah."

"Is that what Jesus would do?"

"You told me not to walk around in a WWJD shirt. You told me to be a rebel."

He laughed. "That's true. And you're a rebel, no doubt about it."

I didn't know if he was talking about more than the fight. I didn't ask. Like I said, I didn't want to talk. I didn't even want to think. I took a vow of not thinking.

7

Drugstore

We didn't get far before he messed up my vow. Crossing over the river into Oregon, he said, "Say goodbye to the SayWA State."

I looked to see if the Oregon welcome sign was the same as the old, shot-up one we'd seen the day before. At the end of the bridge the sign said WELCOME TO OREGON — WE LOVE DREAMERS. If I hadn't been so miserable I would've laughed my guts out.

Ruah passed the entrance to the interstate and drove toward a town.

"Where we going?"

"To the thing I wanna show you."

We parked in front of a drugstore. I followed him inside, and he stopped in an aisle. "See the magazines?"

At the end of the aisle was a wall of magazines. "Yeah."

"I want you to do a little experiment." He took a can of Old Spice shaving cream off the shelf. "Go find the magazine covers with half-naked people on 'em. They'll be girls

342

and guys. Open one of each, look at the pictures, and see which ones throw your switch."

I felt my cheeks turn red as the Old Spice can. "You're kidding."

"That's the deal." He kept studying the can. "You wanna ride to Portland, you gotta see what throws your switch."

I went over to the magazine rack, found a girlie magazine, and opened it. The naked woman staring back at me threw my switch right away. I turned a few more pages. The women made Victoria's Secret models look like nuns in skimpy habits. Then I took down a magazine with an oily muscleman on the cover and flipped it open. What stared back at me gave me a major case of chung. I shut the magazine and turned around. Ruah was gone.

I went outside. He was in the camper.

Driving to the interstate, he said, "Did your body tell you something?"

"Yeah."

"For sure, for sure?"

"Absolutely."

"Good."

There was a long pause. I couldn't believe he wasn't asking me what. "You don't wanna know?"

He lowered his shades over his eyes with a slight smile. "I'm all *'Don't ask, don't tell,'* remember? Besides, I thought you didn't wanna talk."

But I did. I wanted to do more than talk. I wanted to shout out the window. *Hey, everybody, I passed the crotch test! I like girls! I'm not queer!* I didn't, of course. It would've been rude, considering Ruah. I also didn't because I still didn't get why I'd trampolined off the gay cliff. I just said, "I'm straight."

He nodded. "Congratulations. That's gotta be a demon off your back."

A laugh jumped out of me.

"What's so funny?" he asked.

"Yes and no," I said.

"Yes and no what?"

"Yeah, it's a demon off my back, and no, it's not, because last night I was sure it was God's will for me to be gay. I'm a little confused about God right now."

His forehead wrinkled. "I was wondering about that. I mean, it's one thing to be horny and do something crazy. It's another thing to think T.L.'s the one pulling your strings." There was a long pause, then he asked, "Ever heard of walking back the cat?"

"No."

"It's from the spy business. When something bad goes down—like a cat killing a mouse—you walk the cat backward to figure out how it happened." He looked over. "Someday, not necessarily today, you should walk back the cat on last night."

I thought about it and realized today was as good as any. I mean, who else was I going to walk back the cat with? Mom? Case and the R-boys? Yeah, right. So I started telling him about the signs God had thrown me that made me think I was gay.

I told him about kissing Spring, and not liking her glow-in-the-dark boobs. He said anyone might be turned off by

344

that. "When you kiss a girl, wanna make love to her, and her tits turn out to be bright enough to read by, that's usually a deal breaker." After I stopped laughing, he said, "Don't tell me you thought you were gay because of one encounter with Martian boobs."

"No." I wanted to tell him about the dream, but I couldn't. I skipped that and cut to the chase. "The Bible made me do it."

"The Bible made you do it?"

I told him about my providence check, and how God guided my finger to the verse in Job about me being born to trouble.

He shook his head in disbelief. "I'm not sure poking your finger in the Bible to see if you're straight or gay is a good idea. It's the Good Book, but it's not *that* good."

I was debating whether to tell him about the dream or not, when he started chuckling. "I mean, if everyone decided sexual orientation by the finger-in-a-book test, imagine what would happen if someone didn't have a Bible around for their moment of truth. What if some kid who only had *The Polar Express,* poked his finger in it and discovered God wanted him to be a Santa-sexual? Or if someone stuck their finger in *Moby-Dick* and decided they were a whale-sexual? And what if, God forbid, someone opened their favorite cookbook? There'd be some miserable guy out there convinced he was an eggbeater-sexual."

I knew he was having fun and trying to make me laugh— and I did a little—but it made me realize that the only way he was going to understand why I did what I did was to tell

345

him about the dream. If I was going to walk back the cat, I couldn't lift the cat over that one.

After I told him, he thought about it for a while. "I'm no shrink or dreamworker," he said, "but it sounds to me like your dream confirms it."

"Confirms what?"

"That you're no different than any other teenage boy: you think everything is about sex. But maybe your dream wasn't about sex at all. Maybe you're confusing sex with intimacy."

"I don't get it."

"In your dream, you said it felt natural to put your arm around me, and I said, 'This feels nice.' Maybe that's all it was. Maybe your dream was asking, 'What do you want your relationship with Ruah Branch to be?' And the answer was simply, 'Close buddies.' "

"But we were in a motel in the same bed."

"We've been in the same camper for a week, sleeping five feet away from each other. That doesn't make anyone lovers." He shook his head. "I hate to disappoint you, Billy, but I'm ninety-nine-point-nine percent sure you're straight. If you doubt it just give yourself another test. Next time you walk down the street, ask yourself who you imagine naked, the women or the men."

"It's that simple?"

He laughed. "For guys, pretty much. We're pretty dumb that way. Of course, I'm talking about sex, not love. Love's a whole different ball game. And for God's sake, don't spend the rest of your life beating yourself up over last night. People get loopy and do crazy things. When you're young, experimentation with the big three—sex, drugs, and rock 'n' roll—sometimes just gets down to the company you keep. Hell, if you'd traveled two thousand miles with a whale-sexual, you might've gotten to Portland, forgotten your father's treasure, and headed straight to the water for some whale watching."

"You keep talking about whale-sexuals," I said with a smirk. "Are you saying you're one of those, too?"

He laughed. "No, I'm not bi. But I do believe every man and woman walking the earth has it in 'em to be a zigzag-sexual."

"A zigzag-sexual? Is that something you learn in health class?"

Ruah grinned. "You'll only hear it from me. It's one of my dumb theories."

"And I suppose it comes with the all-the-way-to-Portland travel package?"

"No, this one's an extra. You see, hard-core straights say God makes everyone straight, and that gays are sick and need to be cured. Hard-core gays say we're all hardwired to be straight or gay and being either is our 'sexual orientation.' What if they're both wrong? What if the sexual urge is like any other human appetite: it can change over a lifetime? I mean, if a little kid who despises eating his vegetables grows up to be a full-on vegan, then you have to say his 'vegetable orientation' has changed. When it comes to the appetite for sex and intimacy, I don't think it's much different. Appetites change. So if we're made in God's image, and He *is* a zigzag God, then we're capable of zigging and zagging right along with Him."

I heard what he was saying, but I had zigzagged to other things. My eyes were seeing the morning sun bouncing off the Columbia River. My head was filled with a parade of pretty dresses moving along a street. And my imagination was doing whoop-de-doos on the mounds and curves underneath them.

8

Boot Heel Collectibles

Before driving into Portland, we took an exit for gas. I did the usual and went in to pay. Next to the counter was a newspaper rack. One of the papers had a box in the corner that read CINCINNATI LAVENDER? I opened the paper to the story. It was about a rumor that Ruah Branch wasn't rehabbing with a Triple-A team in Louisville, but had "gone AWOL to the YMCA."

I bought the paper and showed it to Ruah. "What's it mean?"

"It means Joe is tired of losing seven grand a game."

"What are you gonna do?"

"Get to Seattle ASAP." He threw the paper in the garbage. "Grab our change and buy a Portland map."

We drove to the old part of downtown between the office towers up the hill and the docks by the river. The closer we got to the river, the more run-down things got. There was a big Salvation Army cross sticking out from one building. A grungy park was jammed with trailers selling

348

ethnic food. Farther down, among Chinese shops and hippie stores, we turned onto Couch Street. The camper rattled and squeaked on the potholed street.

"There it is!" I shouted. I didn't need to see the address to know it was Boot Heel Collectibles. Sticking out from the store was a boot-shaped sign. I kept thinking how my father's footsteps had sounded on this street hundreds if not thousands of times. My heart thudded against my ribs like his ghost was running down the street to meet me.

Ruah pulled past the store toward a parking space. BOOT HEEL COLLECTIBLES arched in gold letters on the plate-glass window. A Closed sign hung in the door. The lights were out. The sun lit a dusty layer of junk in the window. Beyond that was darkness.

We parked past an alley. Ruah pointed to a pay phone up the street. "I'm gonna make a call, then I'll see you at the store."

I jumped out and ran down the sidewalk, yanking the shoelace-key over my head. In the door, a handwritten sign under the Closed sign read DUE TO A DEATH IN THE FAMILY. I'd never thought of it. Maybe he had a family. A wife, kids, my half brothers and sisters.

I slid the key in the doorknob. The door swung open. A bell *dinged* over my head, making me jump. I stepped inside and hit a light switch on the wall. Nothing came on. There were light sockets hanging from the ceiling, but the lightbulbs were missing. Why would anyone take out the lightbulbs?

I waited for my eyes to adjust to the semidarkness. Some light spilled through the window. Between the narrow aisles, glass cases and counters were cluttered with stuff. A lot of it was printed with the same black silhouette and MARK TWAIN. There was everything from ash trays and dusty Mark Twain bourbon bottles to wooden swords with TOM SAWYER and HUCK FINN painted on the blades. His store was almost completely dedicated to the spirit of Mark Twain. But there was another spirit roaming there: Richard Allbright. I studied everything. Even the smallest item might give me the last clue to where my father had stashed the bad book.

When I circled back to the big window, I saw a thickset man hurry by, out on the sidewalk. There was something weird about him. His jacket collar was turned up and his head was down like he was walking into a cold wind, but it was August and windless. I moved into the doorway so I could see him go up the street. He pulled open the camper's passenger door and got in. I couldn't see where Ruah was, at the pay phone or in the camper.

I started to go outside but realized the man might see me in the camper's outside mirror. I moved through the shop to a back door. It was ajar and banged up. Someone had broken in.

I scooted through the door, down a narrow alley to the bigger alley, which led to where the camper was parked. I stayed close to the wall so the man couldn't see me. When I got to the end of the alley, I snuck a peek. The man was sitting in the camper like he owned it. Ruah was getting back in the driver's side. He wasn't afraid of the guy. It was like he knew him. I flattened against the wall so Ruah couldn't see me.

350

"How's it goin', Rue?" the man said. I recognized the gruff voice. It was the guy from Coors Field, Joe Douglas.

I could just hear Ruah. He didn't sound happy. "How did you find me?"

"Been doing some detective work." Whatever he said next was drowned out by a passing car. Then I heard, ". . . a boy named Billy Allbright. It seems you've been traveling with him."

"How did you find me here?" Ruah asked again.

"By doing what I do best, negotiation."

"I bet that set you back a few bucks."

"Chicken feed compared with what we lose every day you miss. By the way, is that real or part of your new look?"

"It's real. It's broken."

"Why are you such a fuckup?"

"Why are you such an asshole?"

I heard Joe's yippy laugh. "If it turns you on to think of me as an asshole, it doesn't bother me."

"What do you want, Joe?"

"The same I always want. You in the closet so you can keep rakin' in the max." He chuckled. "You rub my Brokeback Mountain, I'll rub yours."

"Then why did you plant the bit about me rehabbing at the Y instead of down in Louisville?"

"To smother the truth: you traipsing around the country with fuckin' jailbait. The way I see it, we call a press conference, you deny the gay rumors, and everything goes back to normal."

" 'I'm not gay, I never have been gay,' that kind of thing?"

"I like the sound of it."

There was a pause and then Ruah said, "Will you give me twenty-four hours?"

"Between friends, sure."

I heard a door open. I scooted back down the alley. I didn't know how Joe Douglas knew my name, found us here, or knew about Boot Heel Collectibles. I still had my father's card. The knot in my stomach told me it had something to do with Dumb—me keeping Ruah's cell phone—and Dumber—using it.

I went back in the store through the back. I checked the cash register. It had money in it. It was getting wonkier by the minute. Whoever had broken in had taken the light-bulbs but not the money. I thought about the bad book. Maybe someone else knew about it. Maybe they'd gotten there first and found it. Then a death-cookie thought popped up. What if Joe Douglas knew about it? What if he was the one who'd broken in?

My eye caught a tiny glow of light in the back corner of the store. I moved to it. It came from a small desk crammed behind a display case. The desk was cluttered with paper-work and a phone. Its red message light was on.

I pressed the message button. A voice announced, "Two old messages." I replayed them. "Alright, treasure hunter," a raspy voice said—it was my father's—"listen up, and listen good. Actually," he said with a dry chuckle, "don't listen to me, listen to Walt Whitman. *If you want me again look for me under your boot-soles.*"

I hit the pause button, and repeated the line out loud. "*If*

352

you want me again look for me under your boot-soles." I wondered if the store had a basement.

I played the second message. My father's voice but rushed, urgent. "There's a group, Billy, they want to destroy the bad book. I've hidden it well, but I fear they've learned of your treasure hunt. They may be on to you. Keep a sharp lookout. And please, Billy, hurry." The machine beeped.

My mind ripped. I tried to keep thinking and not get sucked into the panic I heard in his voice. Then I remembered that the machine had said they were old messages. Someone had listened to them already. That's who might've broken into the store: the people who wanted to destroy the bad book. If it was them, and they were ahead of me in the hunt, they might've beat me to it. I stomped my foot. "Shit!"

The sound boomed in my head . . . along with the echo of the first message. *If you want me again look for me under your boot-soles.* It was a clue! Whoever stood near the desk listening to the message was supposed to look under their feet.

I dropped to my knees and looked at the floor in the semidarkness. It was grimy old linoleum. I ran my hand over it. I hit a small tear in the linoleum. I grabbed the tiny flap and pulled it up. It tore like an old rag. I pulled away the part where I'd been standing next to the desk. In the dim light, all I could see were old floorboards. I brushed my hand along them. A splinter stabbed my thumb. I jerked my hand back, then flattened it down where the splinter

353

had jabbed me. There were grooves in the wood. It felt like someone had carved something.

It was too shadowy to see. I thought about running out to the camper to get a flashlight. But there was a quicker way. I found a sheet of paper and a pencil on the desk. I put the paper over the carving in the wood. I swiped the pencil across it, making sure the tip caught all the edges.

I took the impression to the store window. It showed an address: 132 Mars Hill Road. It was the next clue. I let out a breath. The linoleum hadn't been torn up before me. Whoever had listened to the messages first hadn't figured out the next clue. I was the first one to get the address.

I stuffed the paper in my pocket and ran out onto the sidewalk. I panic-stopped.

The camper was gone.

9

Why Ruah took off, I couldn't figure. Maybe it had to do with the part of his conversation with Joe I didn't hear. Maybe it was the twenty-four hours he'd asked for, and he couldn't wait any longer. Whatever, it wasn't like him to leave without saying goodbye. Especially after all the stuff we'd been through. But I didn't have time to worry about it. I had to find the bad book.

I went back in the store and cleaned out the cash register. I told myself I wasn't adding robbery to my heap of

354

sins. I was collecting an allowance from my father for the first time ever.

I found a taxi and asked the driver to take me to 132 Mars Hill Road. "That's way out of town," he said.

I counted the money from the register and what I had left from the last cache. "Is sixty-seven dollars enough?"

"That'll do."

Fifteen minutes later we drove through countryside with a mix of small farms and McMansions. We turned on an unpaved road: Mars Hill Road.

The taxi stopped at a rusty mailbox: 132. "You want me to go down the driveway?" the driver asked.

Weed-choked wheel ruts ran about fifty yards through an overgrown field. At the end, an old farmhouse with faded paint and missing shutters rose from the brown weeds. Behind it, a barn collapsed next to a cement silo.

"You sure you got the right address?" the driver asked.

I'd only looked at the paper a hundred times. "Yeah, this is it. How much?"

I paid him sixty dollars and started walking toward the farmhouse. Getting closer, I saw ragged white curtains in the upper windows. I thought I saw someone move behind a curtain, but it was just a breeze billowing the curtain in the open window. The place looked abandoned. I half expected to see one of those CONDEMNED stickers on the door. Or one of those spray-painted symbols rescue teams leave after a flood, meaning the house has been searched and there are no bodies. There were no signs or symbols, just paint flakes clinging to the siding. For all I knew, there was still a dead body inside.

I knocked on the front door. No one came. I opened the door and stepped inside. I called out, "Anyone here?" No answer.

On one side of the entrance hall was a living room, the kitchen was on the other. I went into the living room. The room was filled with a jumble of furniture, with an old TV in the far corner. The room was a bigger version of my father's store. Bookshelves crammed with Mark Twain junk lined the walls. Boot Heel Collectibles was just the tip of the iceberg when it came to his collecting. It was clear why he called himself a Twainiac. If they made Mark Twain toilet paper, he would've had some. The good news: the shelves weren't disturbed; nobody had ripped through them looking for the bad book. The bad news: my father was more than an idol worshipper, he was a nutcase. And I had a fifty-fifty chance of turning out the same.

I moved through the room, looking for old books, or at least a clue of where to find the bad book. Spotting some books on a shelf in the corner by the TV, I made a beeline for them. The row of leather-bound volumes had different titles, but they were all by Twain.

"Hello there," a voice cracked.

I spun around. Tucked into a bulky chair was an old man all in white: shirt, vest, pants, swept-back hair. His face looked like a dried and cracked patch of alkali flat. But what jutted at me like a pointing finger was his nose—a beak of a thing.

It was my father.

I must've turned as white as him. He rasped, "Looking at a ghost, are you?"

"Ye-ah," I said, my voice cracking.

His face spread in a smile, revealing the only color about him: his deep blue eyes. " '*I hain't come back—I hain't been gone.*' Now, who said that?"

The strange words sounded familiar, but I didn't care who said them first. I only cared who was saying them now. "I dunno."

"Huck says it when Tom thinks he's a ghost come back to haunt him."

"Right." I remembered the line and got why he'd said it. Huck and my father had risen from the *dead* they'd never been.

He lifted a spotty, quavering hand off the chair arm. "I'm your father."

I stepped closer and reached out to shake his hand. It felt like a handful of corn husks. His hand steadied, but holding it made the earthquake inside me shake harder. Two words stumbled out of me. "I'm Billy."

His thin lips disappeared in a smile. "Yes, you are." His hand slid away. "And a sight for old eyes."

"But I thought . . ." My voice trailed off.

"Yes, you thought I was dead."

It suddenly hit me how cruel his trick had been. "Why did you lie to me?"

"It was a bad thing," he answered, still staring up at me. "I hope you'll forgive me." He slowly blinked. "I wanted to ensure your journey was for a long-lost book, not a long-lost father." His eyebrows raised, turning his forehead into an accordion of wrinkles. "Where did you start?"

"Independence, Missouri."

"Good name. How long did it take you?"

"Over a week."

His lips spread, revealing another bit of color: his yellowish teeth. "But the adventure isn't over."

"What do you mean?"

He reached down below the chair cushion and pulled up book pages. "The last chapters of *Huck Finn*. I want you to read them to me."

"What about the group that wants to destroy the bad book? You said they were close."

"Don't worry about them. Even if they find my house, they'll never find the book." He held up the last chapters. "We have the keys that open the treasure. They don't."

It was weird how he'd sounded panicked on the answering machine back at the store, but now was totally calm. Part of me wanted to ask how old the message was, and a bunch of other stuff. But a bigger part of me wanted to do what he asked. It's hard to say no to a father you thought you'd never say yes to.

I pulled up a chair and started reading Chapter 34. Whenever I looked up I caught his lips moving along with mine. He knew it by heart. The chapter was about Huck and Tom planning to break Jim out of the shack he was being held in. When I read what Tom says to Huck, *I should hope we can find a way that's a little more complicated than that,* a phone jangled in the kitchen.

My head jerked up from the page. "Do you want me to get it?"

He shook his head as his answering machine picked up. A woman started leaving a rushed message. She sounded scared. "I'm with the group that's going to burn your book. We just found out where you are. I despise what's in the book, but now they're saying they're not going to stop with the book; they're going to burn everything. They might hurt you. I'm trying to do the right thing and warn you. When we get there I won't be able to help. Please, get away from there before it's too late!" She hung up.

My father's face was tight with worry. I jumped up. "We gotta go. Do you have a car?"

His expression hardened. "No, I have a *book*. And I'm not going anywhere until I put it in your hands." He raised an arm. "Help me up."

"But, Dad!"—as scared as I was, it still felt really weird calling him that—"They're gonna burn the place down, and maybe worse. We gotta go!" I took his arm and helped him up. His arm felt like it would snap like a stick.

He grabbed the cane resting against the chair. "Where we're going, it won't burn."

10

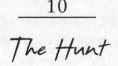

With me holding one arm and him using his cane with the other, my dad and I shuffled to the front hall. "Do you have a car, or not?" I asked.

"No."

"Then where are we going?"

"To free the bad book."

I saw the phone on the kitchen wall. "Maybe I should call nine-one-one."

"No," he snapped. "No police." He tapped the front door with his cane. "Open it."

Outside, we moved at a snail's pace down a path toward the barn. I kept checking the road for vehicles. Vigilantes from Notus came in pickups; I didn't know what kind of wheels book burners went for. I wanted to ask him a thousand questions, but his breath was so short and raspy I didn't want to slow us down.

We reached the silo next to the barn, and he stopped me. I thought he needed a rest. There was a metal door in the cement silo. He banged his cane on it and told me to open it. I did. He waved his cane into the darkness. A light flickered on.

"What's in there?" I asked.

"Our book shelter," he said as he tottered inside.

The silo was empty. The weird part was a sheet-metal ceiling two feet above my head. I had no clue why there was a low ceiling in a silo over thirty feet high. A ladder ran up the wall and disappeared next to a hatchlike door in the ceiling. Even weirder was a gunnysack hanging from the ceiling door.

"Close the door and lock it," he ordered. I pulled the metal door shut and dropped the steel bar, locking us in. The *clang* reverberated off the walls. "Welcome to my *genizah*."

"What?"

He tapped the cement wall with his cane. "*Genizah* is the Hebrew word for 'hiding place.' The Jews never destroy their old scrolls and religious texts when they're worn out. You don't destroy the Word of God, you give it a proper burial in a cave, attic, or even a silo. My *genizah* is a place for something that was, and still may be. That's what the bad book is: a story waiting for resurrection."

I knew he wanted to tell me all sorts of stuff, but I wasn't in the mood for a history lesson. "Can't we just get the book and get outta here? I mean, if they decide to torch the barn we're gonna get cooked in here."

He blinked slowly. He seemed amazingly calm, and oblivious to the danger. As he stared at me, his eyes sparkled like dark raindrops. "Nothing is ever set free without a journey, not even a book." He grinned and lifted his cane. "Now let's begin ours." He poked the cane tip into the gunnysack hanging from the ceiling. It hit something solid. "Take it off."

I reached up, untied the string holding the sack, and pulled it down. Things only got wonkier. Bolted to the ceiling door, upside down, was an old-fashioned typewriter. A sheet of paper hung from the roller. "What's this?"

"A magic typewriter," he answered.

The thing hardly looked magic. It was as paint-chipped and banged up as some of the beater bikes I'd ridden over the years. "What's magic about it?"

"If you rub it the right way it'll open the trapdoor."

"You mean it's a lock?"

"Yes, and only the right combination of keys opens it."

"You know the combination, right?"

"Of course. But what if death had claimed me before you

got here? You would have had to spring the bad book from its prison yourself." He nodded up to the typewriter. "That's why I left you a clue."

For the first time I noticed there were words on the paper rolled into the typewriter.

"Let's see if you've done your homework."

I read the typing on the paper.

```
Bad luck they cannot shake
Once Huck and Jim embrace
The skin of _____.
```

It was another of his rhymes, an easy one.

"Do you know the answer?" he asked.

"Yeah."

"Type it in."

I reached up and hunt-'n'-pecked *r-a*. When I pushed the old keys they just pressed down; they didn't type letters. "They're not working."

"They may not be typing, but they're *working*."

I pushed the rest of the keys: *t-t-l-e-s-n-a-k-e*. After hitting the *e*, something *clicked* inside the trapdoor.

"Very good," he said. "Now open it."

I pushed up on the typewriter. The door it was bolted to hinged open and dropped in the space above with a *crash*. A light came on. I started up the ladder. I didn't get two rungs before something caught my ankle. It was the hook of his cane.

"Where do you think you're going?" he asked.

"To get the book, so we can get outta here."

362

"It's not that easy."

I stared down at him. "What do you mean?"

"Was it easy geocaching two thousand miles to find me?"

"No."

"Then why should the last thirty feet be any less challenging? Come down."

I jumped back to the floor.

He grinned his yellowish smile. "Age before beauty." He leaned his cane against the wall and began to climb. It was more like the crawl of some ancient albino tortoise. I put my hand on his bony back and spotted him all the way.

The chamber above was almost the same as the first except the floor was sheet metal. There was no book, just another typewriter bolted to a trapdoor in the low metal ceiling. He leaned against the wall and caught his breath. I read the words on the paper hanging from the typewriter over our heads.

```
Even though they could have sued,
Grangerfords and Shepherdsons
Much prefer a good ol' ____.
```

So far the clues were no-brainers compared to the geocaching clues he'd given me.

"Know the answer?" he asked.

"Yeah, but I don't get it. Anyone who's read *Huck Finn*, and has half a memory, would know the answers and be able to get through your—what did you call it?"

"*Genizah.*" He pushed off the wall and held my arm.

363

"You see, that's just the point. Anyone who's read *Huck Finn* would never destroy the bad book. They couldn't. They'd be dying to know what happens to Huck and Tom in the sequel."

I thought he was being way optimistic about book burners. I mean, they could've been forced to read *Huck Finn* in school, known the answers, and still wanted to destroy the book. But I didn't want to waste time quibbling.

"Besides," he said, nodding upward, "the very last riddle only you and a couple of others would know."

"What's that?"

"Only climbing will tell."

I pushed the keys for the fill-in-the-blank answer about the Grangerfords and Shepherdsons, and pushed up. The typewriter and the door didn't budge.

"What did you press?" he asked.

"*F-u-e-d*. That's the answer, right? Just like '*sued*.'"

He let out a wheezing cackle. "I thought your mother would have taught you how to spell."

I realized my mistake and pressed the same keys in the right order: *F-e-u-d*. I heard a click and the door pushed up and open. A light came on, illuminating another identical chamber. "How many of these are there?"

He started his slow-motion ladder climb. "Just enough."

11

Genizah

The higher we climbed, the hotter and stuffier it got. Reaching the next chamber, my father's forehead and upper lip were sprinkled with sweat. He'd gone from pale to ash white. "Are you okay?"

"Maybe I need a rest." I helped him to the floor and he leaned against the wall.

"Why don't you wait here," I said. "I'll go the rest of the way."

He sucked in a breath. "You'll need me on the last one."

"I'll shout down if I need help."

He shook his head. "I just need a minute."

I gestured up to the next trapdoor. "At least let me open it so some of the heat escapes."

"Good idea."

I quickly read the clue on the paper in the typewriter.

```
He gives his all, a mighty try,
But Huck can't pray
A simple ___.
```

Another no-brainer. I pressed keys: *l-i-e*. I pushed. The typewriter and the trapdoor opened and banged on the floor above.

As a light strobed on I slid down the wall next to my

father and looked up through the opening. There was another sheet-metal ceiling, but I couldn't see a typewriter. Maybe we'd reached the top. Maybe the bad book was right above us. It took everything not to spring to my feet and fly up the ladder.

My father's voice reined in the urge. "Aren't you wondering how a frail old man could build this thing?"

"Sure," I said. "But you can tell me later."

"There may not be a later."

I looked at him. His sweat had found channels in his skin and his eyes were unfocused. I was no EMT, but I figured I should keep him talking. "So how did you build this thing?"

He took a breath. "Three years ago the doctors told me I had cancer. I got better, but I knew it was coming back. I began building my *genizah*. I built it for the book, and a dream."

"What dream?"

His eyes slid toward me. They were focused again. "The dream of an adventure with you." His eyes were moist. It wasn't sweat.

I didn't know what to say. My tongue felt like a fat tangle. I mean, what do you say to someone who *is* your father but has never *been* your father? It's like being one of those amnesia victims who wakes up to total strangers introducing themselves as your mom, dad, sis, and bro. The best I could do was echo what he said. "We're having an adventure, alright." The crazy book-burning group stormed back in my head. For all I knew they'd shown up and were burning down the house. "Are you ready to keep going?"

He nodded with a faint smile. "I was waiting for you."

366

I helped him to his feet and kept a hand on his belt as he inchwormed up the next ladder.

Soon as my head came through the trapdoor, I saw it. A rusty old safe stood in the middle of the hot room. On top of it was another old typewriter. My father sat on the floor and wiped his brow. I moved to the safe and the typewriter with a page rolled into it.

"What does it say?" he rasped.

```
Father and son
Never in sight.
This is day one
To C. W. Allbright.
```

"It's not a fill-in-the-blank," I said.

"That's right, but it's still a combination. Only you, your mother, and I might know it."

"'Day one/To C. W. Allbright,'" I repeated. "Is it my birthday?"

"Could be. Try it."

I stared at the big old dial on the safe. I was so excited, it was fuzzy and out of focus. I turned it right-left-right using the numbers of my birthday. I pushed down on the handle; it gave; the door *creaked* open.

Resting on a shelf was a thick brown book. My hand shook as I took it out and stared at the cover. A gold Indian shield decorated the cover. Gold letters spelled the title: *Thirty Three Years Among Our Wild Indians*. Except for the gold, it looked as ordinary as a book can be. "This is the bad book?"

He must've heard the disappointment in my voice. "It's not the cover, Billy," he said softly. "It's what's inside."

I guided my father back down the ladders to the bottom of the silo. By the time we got outside, he could barely walk. I told him I was calling the police as soon as we got back in the house.

"No need," he said, clinging to my arm.

I waved the book in my other hand. "But now it's in the open. They'll—"

"Shhh." He cut me off and pulled me to a stop. "Don't you see? I wanted it this way."

Either I was totally confused or he was delirious from climbing up and down inside a silo. "What are you talking about?"

"No one wants to destroy the book."

I stared at the half smile creasing his face. "But the phone messages—"

"All fake, orchestrated, even the break-in at my shop." He tugged at my arm, starting us up again. Confessing his latest trick seemed to revive him. "All part of my last wishes."

"What wishes?"

"To have an adventure, to do it in 'the regular way.'"

"What's the 'regular way'?"

"You'll find out at the end of *Huck Finn*."

12

Negotiation

My father was so spent, he wanted to take a nap. I helped him upstairs to his room.

I recognized the bed's headboard from the DVD. The weird thing was that it wasn't really the headboard; it was the footboard. As I helped him onto the bed he explained how he'd borrowed a page from Mark Twain, who slept in his bed backward so he could admire his fancy carved headboard. My father's headboard had something to look at too. It was decorated with all the illustrations from the original *Huck Finn*. He said they had been his cue cards when he'd memorized the book.

I put the bad book on the bed beside him. Before I left, he asked me to go down to his study behind the kitchen. On his desk was a first edition of *Huckleberry Finn*. He wanted me to read the last ten chapters from that. He also told me I'd find some papers he wanted me to read. When I asked what they were about, he waved me out of the room.

His study was lined with shelves, which held books instead of Mark Twain junk. His desk stood in front of a window overlooking the field behind the house. A thick green book lay on the desk. In black and gold lettering on the cover was *Adventures of Huckleberry Finn (Tom Sawyer's Comrade.) by Mark Twain*. But there were no papers on the desk. I figured he had misremembered and put them somewhere else.

I sat down and started reading where we'd left off in Chapter 34. It was freaky. What my father had put us through to free the bad book was almost as bizarre as the stuff Tom makes Huck do to bust Jim out of jail. Tom's version of "the regular way" meant bolting all sorts of unnecessary action onto the smallest thing. Tom and my father had something in common: they were total *dramas*. I suppose everyone needs a Tom Sawyer in their life to ramp it up. I just never imagined my Tom Sawyer being my dad.

Dusk fell as I started "Chapter the Last." I was barely into it when a loud thump came from the kitchen. I thought my father had come downstairs and fallen. I spun in the swivel chair so fast the book flew out of my lap. I swept it off the floor and was about to straighten up when I saw something in the doorway that froze me—my backpack. It was singed and blackened with soot. Two legs stood behind it. My eyes traced up. Standing in the doorway was a stout man.

Joe Douglas.

I dropped the book again.

He shot me a fake grin. "Some books are like backpacks, you just can't hold on to 'em." His hand pulled out from behind his back. He held up some envelopes. "I bet you lost these, too."

They were probably my father's papers from the desk. I shot to my feet. "Those are mine." Then it hit me: he'd been hiding somewhere for more than an hour, waiting till dark to make his move. It made my skin crawl. "What are you doing here?"

He raised his hands. "Happy to explain. You see, after Nico and Momi Potlatcher called me, I tracked 'em down, which wasn't easy. They needed some help with their hospital bills. I bought 'em a little health care in exchange for some four-one-one. I learned a lot about you, and a little about Ruah. I also picked up a crispy-critter backpack containing some very cool stuff. A DVD with a wonderful old man on it, and a GPS device that directed me to Boot Heel Collectibles—love the name." He gave a chuckle and went on. "After that, it was just a matter of following you and watching you and the old man pull the badass book out of the silo." He gave me another fake smile. "It's like this, Billy. I have a bunch of stuff you want, and you have something I want."

"What?"

He yipped a laugh and kicked the backpack. "It's sure not your dirty laundry"—he waved the letters again—"or your father's last will and testament."

I wanted to whip out my knife, stab him, and see how much he laughed at that. But I didn't. Not then. I had to wait for the right moment.

"I want the bad book."

"It's nothing but a stupid ol' book," I said.

"It may be stupid, but it's worth a lot to me right now. And I know how much it means to you. I'd say it's a fair trade. Your backpack and these letters for an old book with a bunch of Mark Twain scribbles in it."

I dug in my pocket, yanked out my knife and jerked it open. "Get out of my father's house."

He stared at the knife, then nodded. "Okay, you wanna

negotiate, you wanna play hardball. I like that. So how 'bout you let me explain the situation we're in before you cut me up? Can I do that?"

I kept my knife pointed at him.

"Here's the big wrinkle, Billy. Between what the Potlatchers told me about you traveling with Ruah and what I know about Mr. Branch's sexual habits, I've got a story I could sell to the tabloids for twice what this supposedly badass book is worth. I can see the headline now: 'Brokeback Highway: Baseball Star Finds New Ball Boy.'"

I started for him.

He threw up his hands. "Wait-wait-wait! Before you do something we'll both regret, lemme get to my offer."

I stopped, giving him one last chance.

"That's better." He let out a breath. "Here's the contract. You get everything that belongs to you for one thing. You just *loan* me the bad book for a day or two, you know, like collateral."

"What's collateral?"

"I hold the book, you get your stuff, and if everything goes according to plan, you get the book back."

"What plan?"

"I'm gonna show the book to Ruah and give him a choice. He stays in the closet, stays my client, and I keep quiet about the two of you frolicking around the west in an RV. Or, he doesn't accept my terms, I go to the tabloids, and you lose the book. So now you have three choices. One, do you cut me to ribbons, go to jail, and become someone's pretty bitch? Two, do you loan me the book and get everything your dad wanted you to have by helping

Ruah stay in the closet? Or three, do you *not* loan me the book, and be remembered as Ruah's bitch for the rest of your life."

"Nothing happened!"

He shrugged. "I don't care if it did. It's a fag and a boy in an RV. It's what people *think* that matters." He sneered and said, "Including your mother."

I squeezed the knife so hard the handle cut into my skin. I wanted to run at him and plunge the blade in his face. I had to think this through before I added murder to my sins. I had to think what was best for me, and what was best for Ruah.

I remembered how Ruah had told me he wanted to follow the "Don't ask, don't tell" rule. He didn't want to be outed. If that was true, then as much as I hated Joe Douglas, he had a point. If I gave him the book it might help Ruah stay in the closet. But then Ruah would be stuck with him. But that might happen anyway, with or without the book. I tried to think of the worst that could happen. That was easy, the story getting out about me and Ruah traveling together. But there was something just as bad. Not seeing what my father had written in his papers. That's what I wanted most: *his* words, not the words scribbled in a book by a writer who'd been dead for ages. Mark Twain wasn't my father. And *Huck Finn* was just a story.

I was just about to tell Joe Douglas I'd give him the book, when he growled, "Time's up." He reached behind his back and pulled out a pistol. "I'm not a fuckin' *waiter,* I'm a closer. Get the book." He pointed the pistol. "Now."

I dropped my knife. "It's upstairs."

373

He backed into the kitchen. "Let's do it." He waved me into the front hall and stopped me at the bottom of the stairs. "Just to show you how much I trust you, Billy, I'm gonna let you get it yourself. If you try to run, I know who's up there."

So did I, and I wished my father would step out of the shadows at the top of stairs, shotgun in hand, and blow Joe Douglas through the front door. But the only thing coming from the shadows was silence.

I climbed the stairs. My father was still asleep in his room. "Sorry," I mumbled, and took the book off the bed.

When I handed the book to Joe, he dropped the letters on the table in the hall. "Good negotiating with ya, kid. If you're ever interested in becoming an agent, lemme know. You got the chops." He held up the book and waggled it. "I'll let you know if this turns into a loaner or a keeper."

Above the book, through the long window beside the door, I saw a figure coming up the driveway. I recognized the stride: Ruah. If Joe turned and opened the door, Ruah would be caught in the open. Joe started to go. I stopped him with a question. "When will you know, I mean, how soon are you gonna see Ruah?"

"Tomorrow. Don't worry, kid"—he smirked—"when I tell him I have the Allbright family inheritance, he'll come home to papa."

Ruah was still twenty yards from the house. "Mr. Douglas, if I *did* wanna become an agent, what would I do? Do an internship or something?"

"Kid, I was just schmoozing." He laughed. "And that's

your first lesson in agenting: knowing when you're being stroked."

He opened the door and turned into a blur of motion. I heard a crack, and he screamed. The gun clattered to the porch as Joe rolled on his side. He clutched his left knee and bellowed in pain.

Ruah kicked the gun away and stood over him. In his good hand, he held the sawed-off baseball bat.

13

Nothing More to Say

Joe wailed, "You broke my leg!"

"It's just a kneecap," Ruah said.

"Fuck you!"

Ruah picked the book off the floor, looked at it, and handed it to me. "This is it?"

I nodded. "He was gonna use it against you."

Ruah looked down at Joe. "Yeah? Two can play his game."

Joe screamed up at him. "You're so fuckin' outed! Both of you faggots! Your career is over! You hear me? Fuckin' over!"

Ruah never flinched or took his eyes off him. "If it is, it'll be your loss."

Joe stopped squirming. "What the hell does that mean?"

"You're gonna keep being my agent."

I jumped in. "Don't let him!"

Ruah turned to me. "He may be a total scumbag, but he's always been a good agent." He looked back to Joe. "Tell 'im baseball's favorite saying about agents."

Joe scowled and spit, "Born an asshole, died an agent."

"He doesn't deserve it," I protested. "He's worse than a scumbag."

Ruah half smiled. "Don't worry. I've got my own little punishment worked out for him."

He wouldn't say what it was. Instead, he gave Joe two orders: (1) He had to drive himself to the hospital and get his knee worked on. When Joe claimed he couldn't drive, Ruah told him he'd purposely broken his left kneecap so he still could, and (2) Joe had to meet Ruah the next morning in Seattle, where, he said, they'd "finalize their deal." Joe agreed, and Ruah sent me to fetch his car, parked down the road. Giff was parked behind it.

After we helped Joe into his car and he drove off, Ruah and I sat on the porch. I told him everything that had happened with my father and Joe. Then I asked him how he knew to come to the farmhouse. Ruah told me he had gotten suspicious as soon as Joe had shown up at Boot Heel Collectibles. It meant Joe knew too much. Ruah pretended to ditch me to see if Joe would follow me after I left the store. He did, and Ruah tried to follow Joe in a taxi but lost him. Then he went back and turned Boot Heel Collectibles upside down until he found the address carved in the floor. That was how he found the farmhouse.

Ruah rubbed a hand over his head stubble. "Here's what I don't get. Joe got to the Potlatchers in Idaho—he told me that in front of the store—but how? The last time Joe had any kind of bead on us was back in Denver."

For a second I thought about Hucking-up and concocting a story about how it all came about. But there's no way I could lie as good as Huck and Tom. I went inside and got my backpack. I dropped it on the porch and dug out the cell phone.

Ruah stared at it in disbelief. "You had it all the time?"

"I always wanted to give it back," I explained. "I know it's a lame excuse." I handed him the phone.

I watched him connecting the dots. He looked over at me. "It was the call record, wasn't it?"

I nodded.

He chuckled. "I'll be damned."

I couldn't believe he wasn't yelling at me. "Aren't you pissed off?"

"Nah." He shook his head and whacked me on the shoulder. "Once a rattlesnake skin starts a string of bad luck, no one can stop it. You just let it run its course." He stood to go.

"You know, you could spend the night," I said. "My father will be rested up by morning, and it'd be great if you met him."

"I'd love to," he said, "but I gotta be in Seattle tonight."

"Okay, but you can't leave without something." I went into the living room, collected the paperback pages of the last ten chapters of *Huck Finn,* and gave them to Ruah. "It gets pretty wild in the end."

"You finished it?"

"Pretty much. My dad has a fancy copy with pictures."

"So does Huck go to hell?"

I shrugged. "You'll have to wait and see."

As we walked down the driveway, I asked what he meant when he told Joe they'd "finalize the deal" in Seattle.

He grinned. "You'll have to wait and see."

We stopped at the end of the driveway. He chuckled at the awkwardness of the moment. "So, what do you wanna do? Shake? Hug?"—he raised a fist—"Knuckle-bump?"

I laughed nervously.

"Or we could pray."

I shook my head. "Last time we did that I ended up in a fight and got a bloody lip." As he laughed at the recollection, my last word jogged a memory. "Remember when you told me about the Jewish baby? You know, the one who knows the Torah by heart, but then an angel touches him on the upper lip and he spends the rest of his life relearning his religion?"

Ruah nodded. "Yeah."

"That's what I feel like now." I tapped the groove above my lip. "Like my dad touched me here, and I've forgotten everything I ever learned. How to be a Christian, how to talk to my mom, how to live, even how to say goodbye."

He flashed a smile. "I know what you mean." He poked his upper lip. "Reset, reset, reset."

"What do you have to reset?"

"How to play baseball like God wants me to."

"How's that?"

"I found the answer in the Book. Job five, seven."

I waited. "You're not gonna tell me?"

"No. You check it out."

I shrugged. "Okay."

There was nothing more to say.

He wrapped me in a bear hug; I hugged back. It didn't feel strange at all. We were just good buddies saying bye.

As I walked back to the house, lights spilled through the ground-floor windows. The upper floor was dark in the moonlight. I thought I saw something move in my father's bedroom window. I figured it was a curtain again.

I went upstairs to check on him. When I put the bad book back on his bed, his eyes opened. He started telling me about the dream he'd just had. In the dream, he was standing at his bedroom window and looking into the moonlight. He watched two figures walk down the driveway to the road. But they weren't any figures. It was Huck Finn, walking Jim to freedom.

I told him it wasn't a dream. He'd woken up, gone to the window, and seen me walk down the driveway with my friend Ruah.

He gave me a puzzled look, then shook his head. "No, I know what I dreamed; I know what I saw. When you see Huck and Jim, you can't mistake them for anyone else."

I didn't argue. I sat on the edge of the bed until he went back to sleep.

I took the letters off the hall table and into the study. There were two envelopes, both torn open and probably read by Joe Douglas. On the first envelope, my father had scrawled *For Billy, if you came too late*. The other envelope said *To be opened only upon my death*.

I pulled out the first letter and read what he had typed on his store's stationery.

- He apologized for not living long enough to meet me.
- He gave GPS coordinates that would lead me to his *"genizah"* and "the last cache."
- He asked me to read the final chapters of *Huck Finn*.

I left the second envelope on his desk. I took the fancy copy of *Huck Finn* to the living room, lay on a couch, and finished "Chapter the Last."

When I got to the last paragraphs, where Jim tells Huck that his father, Pap, *ain't a-comin' back no mo'*, and Huck realizes that his father is dead, it was too creepy. I had to go check on my own pap.

He was sleeping, breathing steady and quiet.

Back downstairs, I turned out the lights and stretched out on the couch. Slipping into the z-bag never felt so good.

14

Howling Adventures

First thing in the morning I checked on my dad. He was awake but too weak to get out of bed. All the excitement from the day before had wiped him out. I made him breakfast: tea and toast. We turned his bed into a breakfast table for two.

When I told him I'd finished *Huck Finn,* he asked me about the last chapters. I said I was disappointed by the ending. I thought it was weird that Tom's escape plan for Jim was so goofy and far-fetched, and that it felt like Tom and Huck were being cruel to Jim. It also made Huck, who'd begun to treat Jim like a person and not a slave, seem like he'd totally backslid to treating him like a "nigger."

As I told him all that, I had a little revelation. The end of *Huck Finn,* with the bolted-on drama, might've been the first case of an audience getting GLASSED. The first known case of George Lucas Action Sequence and Special Effects Disease.

I explained to my father about that, and he enjoyed hearing a little about the Potlatchers. After that, he told me that lots of people didn't like the ending of *Huck Finn.* "But what they don't get," he said, "is that it's written that way because Twain was setting up a sequel." He dropped his hand on the bad book on the bed. "That's what's so important about this.

"You see," he went on, "at the end of *Huck Finn,* Jim, the slave, is free, but Huck, the boy, is still a captive, a slave to Tom's foolishness. The story of Huck and Jim isn't over until *both* of them are set free." He tapped the bad book. "Twain's sequel is the story of Huck, Tom, and Jim lighting out for Indian Territory and Huck winning *his* freedom."

"From what?" I asked. "From being GLASSED by Tom?"

"Much more than that." He pushed the bad book toward me and told me to open it to page 108. "Read the note Twain has written in the margin. Out loud."

I read the penciled words. *"H becomes converted."* I looked up. "Converted to what?"

"An Indian religion. Huck and Tom abandon Christianity and take up Indian beliefs. Tom eventually returns to 'sivilization,' but Huck doesn't. He wins his freedom from Tom, 'sivilization,' and Christianity."

I stared at him, not quite believing it. "What happens to Jim?"

His wrinkled mouth pushed into a sly grin. "What's the worst thing you can do when talking about a book?"

I shrugged. "I dunno."

"Spoil the ending. But I'll tell you why Twain never wrote his sequel. The story would have caused riots and ruined his reputation. He would have been hanged from the nearest steeple. That's why I call it the bad book. Yet even today, Huck turning his back on Christianity will rub people the wrong way. But in our world, on the brink of a war in which the feuding sides both hold books of mass delusion in one hand and weapons of mass destruction in the other, the story of Huck's escape from the dark side of Christianity is more important than ever."

I didn't get everything he was saying, but one thing was crystal clear. I knew why he didn't send me the book in the mail. Mom would've taken that hatchet off the wall and pulped it.

My father sank back on the pillow and shut his eyes. I thought he was going to catch a nap. I started clearing the breakfast things. He grabbed my hand and held it.

His eyes slowly reopened. He looked up at me with a bittersweet smile. "At the end of *Huck Finn,* the boy doesn't completely escape his past. That's what makes Huck so believable. It's the same for all of us. The past is inescapable. Your mother's no different. Sit down, I want to tell you something."

I sat on the bed.

He gathered his thoughts. "As a child, Tilda was repeatedly beaten by her father. To survive the terror of his beatings, she had two choices. To fight back and probably die, or to submit and live. She submitted. Her surrender was so complete, she ended up bowing down and worshipping her abuser. It forged her compass for living. Life was to be spent trembling at the feet of a higher power."

I was so shocked, at first I didn't believe what he was saying. My brain went into lockdown against it.

He took a difficult breath and went on. "There are two things I'd like you do to for me."

"What?" I heard myself whisper.

He reached out his quavering hand and tapped my hand. "Love your mother for who she is. But don't waste your life trembling before a higher power." His finger tapped my hand again. "Treat God, and all the other gods you meet in your long, happy life, as the most fantastic friends ever invented by humankind."

"I'll try."

"Good." He slid his hand off mine and shut his eyes. "I need to rest now."

I didn't know if he wanted me to stay or go. Even if he'd asked me to go, my legs wouldn't have carried me. My body was paralyzed by what he'd told me. But not my mind. It flooded with a vision.

I was walking in a fog-buried forest. My mother was with me. In the heavy curtains of mist, she was only a shadowy silhouette. She held my hand, keeping me from stepping off the trail and plunging into the swallowing fog. This shadow Mom didn't scare me; she had always looked this way to me. Then light penetrated the forest, and the fog began pulling up through the trees. For the first time, I saw my mother's shadowy silhouette become shape. She looked like one of those hybrid creatures in mythology. She was half woman, half beastly father. Seeing her this way didn't scare me, or even startle me. If anything, it made me sad. It made me want to grip her hand tighter.

Like one of those flying dreams that don't stop, the vision kept playing. I watched the sunlight push the fog higher in the giant trees. Then I spied another creature, high in a tree, on a big branch. It was a little girl with long dark hair, pale skin, bright eyes. She laughed and twittered a song as she danced along the branch. The little girl was Mom too. The little girl I'd never imagined: the free and singing bird she'd once dreamed of becoming, Tilda Hayes before the talons of life swooped down and reshaped her into a Jesus-throated Whac-a-Mole.

A buzzing fly invaded my daydream. I blinked away the vision, and watched the fly land on a half-eaten piece of toast on my father's plate. I gathered the dishes and started out.

"Billy," I heard my father whisper.

I turned back. His eyes were shut. "I'm here," I said.

"Last night, you told me something about a man with a strange name."

384

"Ruah," I reminded him. "His name is Ruah Branch."

"Who is he?"

I thought about all the things I could tell him. But it could wait. "We shared an adventure together."

"After my rest, I want you to tell me the adventure of Billy and Ruah. Promise?"

"I promise."

15

In Plain Sight

I went downstairs and sat in my father's chair. Even though it was only midmorning I felt wasted. I was still trying to sort through everything he'd told me. Especially about Mom. Talk about another reset button getting punched. I mean, given all the things I was going to have to rethink— Mom, Dad, the Bible, gays, even the end of *Huckleberry Finn*—it felt like God had delivered on my big prayer request, put me in high school early, and buried me in *homework*!

And right then, sitting in that chair, I did a face-'n'-brain plant in the biggest danger of changing from a faith-up, born-again Christian, to the doubt-up, learn-again Christian I now was. My colliding chaos of thoughts mooshed into white noise. Okay, since it's the brain, gray noise.

Luckily, the best cure for gray noise was right in front of me. TV.

I turned it on and channel-surfed, looking for some X

Games stuff. Flipping through the sports channels, I heard a reporter say a name: Ruah Branch. Then a sportscaster said they were cutting to a live press conference in Seattle, Washington.

The picture went to a reporter in a crowded room. He said he was at the worldwide headquarters of Pneuma Sports, and that "Ruah Branch, the major leaguer who's been AWOL for over a week, is about to make a statement."

The picture swung to a podium topped with a bristle of microphones. Ruah stepped up on a platform. I almost didn't recognize him. He wore a dark suit and tie; his head and face were freshly shaved. He would've looked like some businessman if it weren't for the gold stud in his ear.

He leaned into the mics. "Good morning. Thanks for coming on short notice. I'm going to make a brief statement and then I'll be happy to answer questions. But first, I'd like the chief executives of Pneuma, and my agent, Joe Douglas, to join me up here. They're gonna help me introduce a slogan for a new campaign we're test-marketing starting today."

Some men and women in suits came up on the platform. They each carried a plastic gun with a short fat barrel. Joe was in the back, on crutches, holding one of the plastic guns. He looked miserable.

Ruah counted off "Three, two, one," and they fired their guns. Balled-up T-shirts flew into the crowd of reporters and camerapeople. Ruah shot one too, as the executives reloaded and fired again. The ESPN reporter unfurled one of the T-shirts. The slogan on it read:

The picture went back to Ruah as he thanked the executives and they left the platform. Joe started to hobble off, but Ruah said, "No, stay here, Joe. You've been such a big part of this, you should be here." Joe looked like he was about to boot.

Ruah turned back to the room. "First, I apologize to my teammates for disappearing in the stretch. Although I noticed without me in the lineup they're still racking up the wins." Some of the reporters laughed. "Second, I want to address the rumors that have been circulating." He scanned the room, then looked into the camera. "To paraphrase the words of a former U.S. senator, I am gay, I always have been gay, and I always will be gay."

The room exploded with shouting and flashing cameras. Ruah didn't flinch. He waited, then raised a hand, asking for quiet. "Now I'll answer your questions."

Everyone shouted at once. Ruah pointed at someone. "Is that why you disappeared for over a week?" a reporter asked.

"Yeah," he said, and rubbed a hand over his head. "And it took me that long to shave my dreads."

There was a burst of laughter and a reporter shouted, "What does Pneuma say about this? Are they on board with a gay spokesman?"

"We had a long meeting last night," Ruah answered. "One of the women execs said it best: 'Gays buy shoes too.'"

Another voice yelled, "What about your teammates? How do you think they'll react?"

"I expect a mixed bag," he said. "Some will shrug and say 'play ball.' Some will say 'I knew it' and collect on a bet."

"What about the ones who don't like homosexuals?"

Ruah shrugged. "I'm hoping they'll say 'He's a fag, but he's *our* fag.'" He waited for the laughter to quiet. "I'm sure there'll be a couple of guys who say I'm an abomination and I'm going to hell. I'm looking forward to a little Bible study with 'em. If they can convince me the fork in the road between Heaven and hell is whether you're straight or gay, I'll promise 'em I won't head for hell till the end of the season."

Another reporter fired questions. "Are you worried about being a target on the field? Do you think you'll be in danger as the first outed player in the majors?"

Ruah nodded. "Yeah, but I'm ready for the heat. The man from Galilee said it best. *The Lord is my helper, and I will not fear what man shall do to me.* If Jesus can be flayed and nailed to the cross, I can endure a few extra knockdowns, beaners, and high spikes."

"What about the fans, Ruah? You think they'll turn on you?"

"If most fans really cared about what we did off the field, they would've turned on players who used steroids. I'm not saying steroids and sexual orientation are the same. I just think the fans love baseball more than they dislike players' lifestyles. I hope they prove me right."

A reporter yelled, "So you wanna be the gay Jackie Robinson: the first active player to break the gay barrier?"

Ruah shook his head. "No. Jackie broke a real barrier:

388

skin color. There's no 'gay barrier.' We're already in the game, hiding in plain sight. If I'm breaking anything, it's the gag order."

A woman asked, "When did you know?"

Ruah spread his hands, playing dumb. "Know what?"

"That you were gay."

He smiled. "About the same time I heard the expression 'You can't control the bounces.' "

"Hey, Branch," another reported called out, "can we drop the gay chatter and talk baseball?"

Ruah laughed. "I thought you'd never ask."

"We heard you have a broken wrist," the guy said.

He raised his left arm and pulled on his jacket sleeve. His cast was gone, replaced by a wrap. "It's a hairline fracture. I should be back in the lineup in two weeks."

"How'd you break it?"

"The closet can be a rough ride." He quickly pointed to another reporter.

"What pushed you over the edge? Why now?"

"You sure you wanna know?"

"No," the man answered, "but it's my job to ask."

Ruah wagged his head. "Okay, but let the record show I gave you an out."

The reporters laughed.

Ruah got a look I'd seen before. He was going to the Book; he was going to preach. But then he didn't. He cracked another smile. "Fielder's choice: you want the long answer or the sound bite of why I'm out."

"Sound bite!" reporters shouted.

"Okay, here's the short. 'Don't ask, don't tell' made me

a slave to silence. Now I'm free." His mouth crooked into a small smile. "If that's not short enough, try this. To quote a friend, 'The Bible made me do it.'"

"But Branch," a reporter yelled, "what if the Bible and God have nuthin to do with it? I mean, where do you think this is gonna end? With you in the Hall of Fame, or the Hall of Shame?"

Ruah's face pinched, then he nodded slowly, staring at the reporter who'd asked the question. "Okay, here's the slider people like you might get some wood on. I'm the new Pete Rose. I'm betting on baseball. I might get tossed out of the game, but that's not gonna stop me from placing my bet. I'm doubling down against 'Don't ask, don't tell.' I'm betting that the fans are ready for a new rule: 'He's gay, so what.'"

He raised his good hand. "Thanks for your questions. I'll look forward to more of 'em in the Reds locker room." He turned and left the platform with Joe hobbling behind him.

16

Ain't A-Comin' Back No Mo'

I flicked off the TV. After getting over the shock of what Ruah had done, I remembered what he'd said the night before about playing baseball like God wanted him to. He said he found the answer in Job 5:7.

I went to the study and dug the Bible out of my backpack. I turned to Job. When my eyes fell on 5:7, I couldn't believe it.

Yet man is born unto trouble, as the sparks fly upward.

He had turned my providence check into his own. I didn't know what to think. It didn't stop me from feeling. My insides were catching major air. I was proud to be his invisible friend, standing beside him. Jerry Silks, his ex-boyfriend, was there too, giving Ruah a shout-out for leading the league in honesty.

I suddenly wanted to go upstairs, wake my father, and tell him all about the adventure of Billy and Ruah.

I took the stairs two at a time.

The bad book was resting on his chest. As I got closer, I noticed the book wasn't moving. I touched his hand.

It was cold.

Maybe I uttered a word or a sound, I don't remember. I just remember lifting the book off his chest, sitting on the bed, and crying till my lungs were as empty as his.

I finally went downstairs and opened the second envelope. The one with *To be opened only upon my death.* Inside was a typed Last Will and Testament.

I, Richard Allbright, leave the following to my only son, Charles William Allbright:

1. A FIRST EDITION OF ADVENTURES OF HUCKLEBERRY FINN

Billy, if you haven't finished reading it, please do. Afterward, feel free to sell it when and if you need the money. It's presently worth $15,000 to $20,000.

2. MY COPY OF THIRTY THREE YEARS AMONG OUR
   WILD INDIANS, by Col. Richard I. Dodge, along
   with the hundreds of notes handwritten in the
   book by Mark Twain.

Billy, a book can liberate the one who reads it, and the
one who writes it. Trapped in the bad book, in Twain's
notes, is the great writer's ghost. You must set him
free. You can do it in two ways. You can become a writer
and finish the story Twain so brilliantly conceived.
Or, you can ensure that the book gets to someone who
will tell the story the world has been waiting to hear
for over 125 years.

3. One Regret
   I regret not learning a vital lesson from Huck
   and Tom. The lesson is this: if you insist on
   wearing God's honest truth hour after hour, day
   after day, the time will come when the truth
   becomes a millstone around your neck. Huck and
   Tom know the importance of "letting-on," of
   lying. They know an occasional falsehood can
   preserve a greater truth.

   Billy, my regret is a particular day I chose truth
   over falsehood. On that day, "letting-on" would
   have made a colossal difference in our lives. If
   only I had let-on to your mother that I still
   walked with Christ, she would not have left me, we

would have been married, and I would have been
your father. I didn't let-on. I brandished the
fiery sword of truth, and you and I were blinded
to each other until—if there is a God—we shared
some time together.

My eyes teared up too much to go on. When I could read
again, the last few paragraphs were about him leaving the
rest of his property, and the contents of his store, to his "re-
liable assistant for many years, Ms. Harriet Martineau."
Her phone number was included. Underneath was his sig-
nature, the date, and the signatures of two witnesses. Below
that, he wrote:

P.S. If I was not afforded the luxury of uttering
some pithy last words on my deathbed, I designate
Huck Finn as my proxy, who pronounced the wisest
last words of all. I reckon I got to light out for the
Territory ahead of the rest. . . .

I read the will three more times before I called Ms. Martineau. I recognized her voice. She was the one who'd left
the panicky voice message pretending to be with the book-
burning group. She was as heartbroken as I was, even
though she had been prepared for my father's death for
months.

She came over to the house and helped me deal with
everything. After the ambulance left, she made some lunch
and we talked all afternoon. She gave me an envelope of

money my father had told her to hold for me. She told me stories about him until after midnight.

When she left I picked up the phone and called Mom. I woke her up, but I figured she wouldn't mind. "Mom," I said, "is it okay if I come home?"

"Praise be—" she said. "Praise be—" She started to cry before she could say anything else.

I told her I'd fly to Kansas City the next day. It was so weird. She didn't ask me where I was calling from, or if I'd found my dad, or anything. She just said she couldn't wait to see me.

As I lay on the couch that night, I thought about what I'd tell her about my adventure. Some things I could never tell her, like the night at Stonehenge. I wasn't telling *anybody* that, ever. But some things weren't so easy. Like what would I say about my father? Would I tell her I'd seen him alive, or should I let-on that he'd died before I got there?

Huh. I just wrote a Huck and Tom word, "let-on." What my father had said about Tom's and Huck's lesson was true. There's no way I could tell her the whole truth and nothing but the truth. I had to let-on about some things.

I decided to tell her I'd seen Richard Allbright alive—true—and for a short time before he died—true. But I wouldn't tell her about his *genizah* and the bad book.

394

17

Homecoming

Harriet drove me to the airport. As the plane took off I watched Portland drop away until we flew through a roof of white clouds. As we rose into bright blue sky, I pulled out the bad book.

It was like my dad had said. Mark Twain had left lots of scribbles in the margins, like a skipping stone flying through the pages. I got the general idea of the *Huck Finn* sequel, and it was good. It was full of "howling adventures," like Tom Sawyer promised. I wondered if I would ever be a good enough writer to fulfill my dad's wish and tell the whole story. I breathed a sigh of relief. I didn't have to answer that yet. I put the book away and leaned back. Going on so little sleep, I z-bagged in seconds.

I had another dream.

- I'm at a desk. I'm writing a note to the Lord and saying what I write out loud. *T.L., if You ever get around to adding more books to the Bible, You might think about this one:*

The Book of Billy
Billy Allbright sat on a wall,
Billy Allbright had a great fall.
All the Lord's horses and all the Lord's men
Couldn't put Billy together again.

But patched up he was and back on his shelf,
Thanks to a fellow known as himself.

- *I know, it's super short,* I say as I write, *but I think more people might read the Bible if there were more short books squeezed between the long ones. Just a thought.*
- I sign the note: *Your big fan, then-now-forevermore, Billy.*

When I woke up, I wrote the dream down in a notebook.

Flying over Kansas City, my stomach folded like a taco. It wasn't air turbulence, it was Mom turbulence. I had no idea how I was going to tell her:

- The New J-Brigade was now an army of one.
- Her Jesus-throated Whac-a-Mole had molted into another bird. A Doubt-up Learn-again Christian.

I got off the plane, walked down the long concourse, and saw her though a glass door. She was standing erect, as always. Her gray eyes looked as bright and shiny as I'd ever seen them. They were more than juiced with the Spirit; they were dancing with light.

Closing the space between us, she clasped her hands together, then threw her arms around me. She squeezed so tight the air went out of me. I hugged back.

She pulled away and gripped my shoulders. "Lemme look at you." Her eyes darted over my face like she was trying to find something, an answer to some question she couldn't put into words. She raised her hand and touched my cheek, like the answer could be felt.

Her warm fingers made me smile and feel jittery all at once. I didn't know when her touch would turn to iron.

"You've changed," she whispered.

I nodded. "Yeah, a little."

"No," she corrected. "When God touches someone, they change *a lot*."

If she believed God had been the one who'd touched me, I was cool with that. "Okay, Mom."

She didn't ask how; that was a shocker. She just said, "He touched me, too."

"What do you mean?"

She shot me a secretive smile. "I have something to show you."

I couldn't believe she wasn't asking about my singed backpack. I mean, it still reeked of smoke. What mom doesn't ask her runaway kid why it looked like he hitch-hiked to hell and back?

As we walked to the car she talked about little stuff: the weather I'd missed, the job she'd taken in Kansas City, how she'd fixed up the house. I kept waiting for her to stop, grab my hand, and say a prayer of thanks. She never did.

When I opened the car door, a great smell billowed out: the smell of grilled meat and onion rings. I got in and noticed the white plastic bags on the back seat. "What's that?"

"A picnic."

18

Picnic

We drove a few minutes in silence. Then she said, "So, tell me something I don't know." She didn't say it like she wanted a confession. Her voice was more like a friendly invitation.

I said the first thing that popped into my head. "I wasn't sure you were gonna be here."

She laughed. "Billy, I would've waited for you until the moon turned to blood."

"That's not what you told me a few days ago."

"You know me," she said, waving a hand. "I'm the mother lion. But that was my last roar."

"You're done roaring?"

She chuckled. "At you, anyway."

She was being so nice and forgiving I had to check and see if I was talking to the right person, and not some demon who'd taken over Mom's body. "You haven't stopped praying, have you?"

"Lord no!" she exclaimed with a laugh. "Why do you ask that?"

"I just thought this was gonna be a three-way reunion. You know, you, me, the Heavenly Father."

"Not today, Billy. I've been talking to God nonstop since you left. It took Him so long to answer my prayers, He and I are overdue for a day of rest."

We drove into Independence and started up the big avenue near our street. She turned early and drove toward William Chrisman High School. She pulled into the school driveway.

"What are we doing here?" I asked.

She pointed at the glove compartment. "Open it."

I did. There was a letter on top of the other stuff. I pulled it out. It was from the school and addressed *To the Parents of Charles William Allbright.*

"I don't want any arguments about it," she said. "You're going to high school."

If I could've seen my face I'm sure I looked like I had most of the time at Burning Man: totally gob-smacked.

"I figured if you survived on the road by yourself," she said, "you can survive this house of sin."

I reached over and hugged her. "Thanks, Mom. Thanks so much."

She eased me away. "Thank the Lord, Billy." She quickly raised a finger. "But not today." She opened her door and got out. "C'mon, time for our picnic."

I carried the food and she carried a blanket. We spread it on the middle of the football field and had a feast. We ate barbecued ribs, scarfed onion rings and french fries, and washed the feast down with buckets of soda. I was mega-hungry, but not just for food. I was starving for answers. It was like *she'd* been the one who had run away and come back a different person.

"What happened, Mom? What changed your mind about school?"

She stopped chewing on a rib. "Your running away was God's way of showing me something."

"What?"

"I prayed for answers to what this was all about, especially in the past few days, when my fears were greatest."

"What were your greatest fears?"

"That I'd never see you again. On earth or in Heaven. Then God showed me something."

"Did you do a providence check?"

"No. I had a dream."

"What was it?"

"The dream's not important, only the message it revealed."

"What?"

She didn't answer right off. She took a long drink of soda, making me wait. "The hardest lesson Christ teaches is this: the greatest love isn't found in what's held, the greatest love is found in what's let go. God showed me that the only way I could have you back was to let you go."

"That's why you're letting me go to high school?"

She nodded. "Yes, but don't start thinking you're free as a bird. There's still a few strings between us. Like living with each other, loving each other, going to church."

I looked in her eyes. They shone bright, with speckles of green reflecting off the grass. I'd seen those eyes before: on a little girl in an imaginary forest. I grinned. "I'm cool with that."

We ate key lime pie and watched swallows swoop and dive for insects as the sun began to set.

Smart neighbors.

When you're homeschooled, you never go "homeschool clothes shopping." In fact, that's probably the first time those words have ever been hung on the same line. Anyway, the next morning, Mom took me shopping for school clothes. We had a few disagreements, but we managed to find stuff she didn't think was hell-wear and I didn't think was weenie-wear.

After that, she went to her data entry job in Kansas City. It gave me the chance to do a job I needed to do: data hiding. I poked around the house looking for a place to hide *Thirty Three Years Among Our Wild Indians*. But the one-pillar doghouse was so small it didn't have room for hiding places. Then, through a window, I saw the birdbath in the backyard.

I scoped it out. It was made of cement. I lifted the big dish off the support column. The column was hollow. I wrapped the bad book in tinfoil and sealed it in a ziplock bag. It just fit inside the column. Then I put the cement dish back on top. It wasn't exactly an old silo, but it was still a *genizah*.

19

Entry the Last

Well, I've written down what happened last summer. So now I have to ask:

- Did I tell the story I promised my dad I would?

Yeah, pretty much. I didn't write *everything*, of course. There's not enough blank journals in the world for that.

- Do I regret any of the "sinful" things I thought and did?

Maybe some of the things I did were a mistake, but I don't *regret* any of them. I learned a lot from them. And a "sin" you can learn from, maybe that's not so bad after all. Huck says, "You can't pray a lie." I say, you can sin a good.

- Will I keep writing?

Not for now; my hand's more twisted up than taffy. Of course, someday I'll pull the bad book out of my *genizah* and honor my dad's wish. I'll release the ghost of Mark Twain, and let him tell the story of Huck, Tom, and Jim lighting out for the Territory.

But right now, I'm one step ahead of them. Last fall, I lit out for the territory of high school. I navigated tenth grade without turning down the hall that ends in the lake of fire.

Some good stuff even happened.

- I made the honor roll, which made Mom proud, and made her homeschool teacher of the year—according to us, anyway.
- Mom found my first edition of *Adventures of Huck Finn* and didn't burn it when she found out how much it was worth.
- I met a girl who was nice enough not to show me the color of her boobs after our first kiss.
- I got my buddy Ben to take up mountain biking, and we're now two of the best rippers on the school MB team. We even invented a race combining biking and geocaching. Maybe someday it'll be on ESPN.
- I finally saw a major league baseball game when the Reds came and played the Royals in an inter-league game. And I had a good time catching up with Ruah.
- My mother broke down and bought a TV, and now I'm big into baseball. But nobody gets why I'm a Cincinnati Reds fan.
- Ruah became a free agent, and Joe Douglas negotiated a megamillions contract for him.
- The real bizarro thing is that Joe became the go-to agent for other pro athletes who wanted to come out of the closet. It earned him a nickname, "the gaygent." The Hilarious Father strikes again.
- Biggest change of all? It looks like we're going to stay in Independence. The one-pillar doghouse isn't base camp for the New J-Brigade, or home to *any* Jesus-

throated Whac-a-Moles. It's just home to me and
Mom.

So, yeah, a lot of changes.

But one thing hasn't changed. I still think *Adventures of
Huckleberry Finn* is a dangerous book. Why? Because it
can change a person. It's like my dad said, "A book can
liberate the one who reads it, and the one who writes it."

Acknowledgments

This book was inspired by a chance encounter with a true-life Twainiac, Robert Slotta, who introduced me to the tome in which Twain outlined his never-written sequel to *Huckleberry Finn*. Bob filled me with his irrepressible passion for all things Twain, which included a few shots of Mark Twain bourbon.

Once begun, the story of Billy Allbright traveled a meandering and hazardous road, and only survived because of many Good Samaritans. Gerri Brioso, Peter Ford, Jen Booth (and Monkey), Lois and Siegmar Muehl, Richard Termine, Matt Evans, Gwen Maynard, Henry Shiowitz, and Cindy Meehl all provided excellent direction and advice and rescued the effort from digressive dead ends and polemical potholes. More than once.

I would be remiss if I didn't also thank five people I know only via their writing and the courage of their convictions. They, along with Twain's Jim, informed and inspired the character of Ruah Branch. While there are many who have broken the bonds of silence, I would especially like to acknowledge this quintet for singing their songs of freedom: Billy Bean, John Amaechi, David Kopay, Patricia Nell Warren, and Mel White, thank you!

A big thanks to designer Trish Parcell for the gift of her cover art. But the greatest gift while shaping this book came from on high. Whether they are a constellation of angels or an array of GPS satellites, my agent and editors—Sara Crowe, Michelle Poploff, and Rebecca Short—are my guiding lights. Without them, *You Don't Know About Me* would have been *You'll Never Know About Me*.